Liz Evans was born in Highgate, went to school in Barnet and now lives in Hertfordshire. She has worked in all sorts of companies from plastic moulding manufacturers to Japanese banks through to film production and BBC Radio, eventually ending up as contracts manager for a computer company. She now writes full time.

Also by Liz Evans

Who Killed Marilyn Monroe?
Don't Mess With Mrs In-Between

JFK is Missing!

Liz Evans

ORION

An Orion paperback
First published in Great Britain in 1998 by Oriel
This paperback edition published in 2000 by
Orion Books Ltd,
Orion House, 5 Upper St Martin's Lane, London WC2H 9EA

Reissued 2001

Copyright © Liz Evans 1998

A CIP catalogue record for this book
is available from the British Library.

Printed and bound in Great Britain by
Clays Ltd, St Ives plc

I should like to dedicate this book
to JOHN and LORRAINE
(because if I don't, they're never going
to speak to me again!)

CHAPTER 1

Henry Summerstone wanted me to find a missing person.

There were a few drawbacks.

He didn't know her name. He had absolutely no idea what she looked like. He didn't know where she lived or worked. In fact, when we got right down to it, he wasn't even certain she was actually missing. A real doddle of a job, in fact.

But to get back to the beginning; I'd sauntered into the office late because (in order of priority) I'd had to wait for a slack period before I could scrounge a free breakfast from my favourite greasy spoon; it was a beautiful late-May morning and I was enjoying the walk along the Seatoun seaside promenade; I'd got nothing to do when I got in anyway.

One of the advantages of being a self-employed investigator is that I can set my own hours. The disadvantage is that at the end of the month when wage slaves receive a salary slip, I get a bill from our distinguished leader – Vetch the Letch – for my share of the office facilities.

The premises of Vetch (International) Associates Inc. are housed in a tall, gloomy ex-boarding house, flanked by rows of similar depressing properties. Once they were all seaside boarding houses. Some still are. Others have been converted into bedsits. And a few, like Vetch's, are offices.

Sauntering up the outside stairs, I stepped into the former hallway. Janice glanced up from her processor screen.

'You've come in then.'

'Amazing, Jan. Why not consider a career move? With powers of detection like that you could be doing my job.'

'A cerebrally challenged turnip could do your job.'

I was thrown. Not by the insult, but by the fact that Janice had managed 'cerebrally'. Her typing tends to suggest she hasn't found the spell-check on the processor program yet.

Before I could recover, Jan jerked her head in the direction of the row of clients' chairs. 'Mr Summerstone wants to see you.'

A figure rose from the gloom behind the receptionist's area. With my eyes still adjusting from the brightness outside, I had only a vague initial impression of tallness coupled with average slimness.

'Hardly, my dear. I have long ago given up any hope of a convenient miracle.'

As he moved nearer, his hand outstretched, the reasoning behind this cryptic remark became clear. Even if he hadn't been carrying a white stick, the characteristic slightly upward tilt of his head would have announced his blindness.

'Oh. Sorry,' Janice said, as the import of what she'd said dawned. 'What I meant was ... Mr Summerstone needs a private investigator. And you're free.'

Her tone implied that they'd scraped the bottom of the barrel. But having come up empty-handed, they'd turned it over and found me lurking underneath.

I was silently furious. It was an unwritten rule in the agency that no matter how inept and/or thick we might privately consider our colleagues to be, in front of the clients we maintained a fiction that we were a bunch of hot-shot dynamos who could solve anything from dognapping to alien takeovers of nuclear power plants.

'Cheers, Jan. Would you like to come up to the office, Mr Summerstone. Stairs are to your right.'

He found the newel post easily and moved upwards with an assured confidence that suggested his blindness was a long-standing state.

When we reached the top floor, I instructed: 'Right-hand door.'

The rubber tip of the stick flicked out and expertly located the base of the wooden door. He'd found the handle before I could reach round him and insert the key.

'Go straight in. Chair's dead ahead about three feet. Sorry about the mess.'

It came out as a reflex action; I spend so much time excusing the state of my housework, my mouth has taken to issuing the apology without any conscious effort on my part.

'Sorry. I didn't mean ...'

Summerstone had located the chair and was settling himself comfortably. Clasping the stick between his knees and folding his hands over the top, he suggested that perhaps it would be best if we both ignored all references with visual connotations.

'Otherwise I fear we shall be here all morning.'

His voice was cultured and well modulated. Slipping behind my desk, I took stock of the rest of the package.

He was getting on; seventies I'd guess. In any event he'd come from a generation that had been brought up to dress correctly regardless of the weather.

Despite the mini heatwave that had suddenly arrived a few days ago, he was wearing a tweed suit, crisp shirt and neatly knotted tie. Shifting my position slightly behind my desk, I confirmed that his brown leather shoes were highly polished.

'You're a local, Mr Summerstone,' I said, making it a statement rather than a question.

'Are we acquainted, Miss Smith?'

Actually I did have a nagging sensation that I'd seen him somewhere before, but I'd been basing my remark on his clothes. He struck me as the sort of person who'd wear tailored slacks and a blazer if he were on holiday.

His eyes were hidden behind oval gold-rimmed glasses tinted a deep bottle green; the rest of the face was sharp-nosed and long-jawed, with a neatly trimmed grey beard. His hair was nearly white but still thick, and worn brushed back in sculptured waves. He had the look of a mischievous satyr.

He agreed that I was correct. 'I do indeed live locally, Miss Smith.'

'Grace,' I offered.

'How do you do.' He rose slightly and offered a formal handshake once more. 'Henry Summerstone. Please feel free to call me Henry if you wish.'

'Fair enough, Henry. So what can I do for you?'

'I should like you to find someone for me. A young woman.'

'Hang on.' Drawing a pad towards me, I started to make notes. 'What's her name?'

'K.'

'K-A-Y?' I spelt it out for him.

3

Henry's thin eyebrows met over the chiselled nose. 'I'm afraid I really don't know. I had gained the impression it was simply the initial K. But you may of course be correct.'

'What about a surname?'

'I'm afraid not. Although I suppose K may have been a reference to her surname rather than her Christian.'

I blew out an impatient cloud of breath. Henry's sharper ears must have caught my irritation.

'Perhaps,' he suggested, 'it would be simpler if I explained in my own words and you ask questions as we go along.'

I agreed that did seem the best option.

'It is,' Henry began, 'my habit to walk along the sea front most mornings.'

'That's it,' I yelled.

Henry jerked back nervously.

'Sorry,' I said, yet again. 'It's just that that's where I've seen you. I used to work out along the beach some mornings.'

Henry inclined his head in acknowledgement of this riveting insight into my personal habits.

'As I said,' he continued, 'I walk. Quite early usually. I have done for years. One gets used to the others who share one's routine: walkers, runners, cyclists and the like.'

'And K was one of these?'

Henry nodded. 'She ran.'

'Er, look.' I didn't know how to put the next question tactfully. But Henry anticipated it for me.

'How do I know she isn't still running straight past me?'

'Yes.'

'Because Beano would have told me.'

'Who's Beano?'

'My dog. He was, is, very taken with K. If she had passed us, I'd have felt the change in him.'

'OK.' I roughed out a couple of headings and asked Henry when he'd actually met K.

'It must have been about six weeks before Christmas. I'd taken shelter in one of those wooden huts along the promenade, under the cliffs. The wind was particularly fierce that day and I was feeling a little breathless. K stopped to adjust her shoe.'

He paused as if re-seeing that moment in his mind. But then I guess that's the way he'd see everything.

'She was wearing one of those recording things.' He looped one index finger from his right ear to his left.

'A personal stereo player?' I suggested.

'I believe that's what they're called. I heard the noise as she sat down. And then stronger as she took the headphones off. I caught a few words ... it was *Little Dorrit*.'

'I don't know them. I tend to go in for middle-of-the-road stuff myself: you know, Alison Moyet, Enya. And a bit of country and western.'

'I was referring to the book. By Charles Dickens.'

'Oh *that Little Dorrit*. Sure. Right. Fine.'

Henry explained he was a great fan of Dickens. 'A writer who embraces all the elements of emotion, don't you find, Grace?'

'Absolutely.' I'd seen *Oliver!* three times on video. But I don't suppose that would count. 'Go on. You said something to this K, did you? About the tape?'

'Yes. I cannot remember my exact words now, but I know we spoke briefly about debtors' prisons and the uselessness of preventing those who owe money from earning any.'

Amongst my jotted notes I added 'pretentious bore' and circled it.

'I daresay you think that makes me sound a bit of a pretentious bore,' Henry remarked.

'Not at all,' I assured him, sliding a blank sheet of paper over the notes. I wondered whether I dared waggle a couple of fingers in front of my nose to test out his supposed blindness. Deciding against it, I told him to go on about K. 'She really didn't give you any other name?'

'No. Call me K, she said. Everyone does.'

'I take it that wasn't the only time you spoke to her?'

'Oh no. After that she'd speak to me whenever we met.'

'About what?'

'Dickens mostly. Occasionally she'd attempt to describe the scene around us for me. She meant it as a kindness, but it was really of little use to me. You see, I have been blind for so long that I no longer relate to the world in a seeing way.'

'How often did these meetings take place? Every day?'

'No. Two, occasionally three times a week.'

'Any particular days? Or were there any days you definitely didn't meet?'

A deep V appeared above the cheese-cutter nose again. 'I hadn't thought about it before, but now you ask, I do not believe I ever met her at the weekend.'

'Fine. Go on. How come you think she's missing? Maybe she just moved out of the area. Or got lazy and started having a lie-in.'

'Possibly. However, there is the question of my tapes.'

'Your what?'

'I have a large collection of audio books and radio plays on tape. Particularly Dickens. I mentioned them to K and she asked to borrow a recording of *David Copperfield*. It's an early version and I don't believe it was ever released commercially. I took it directly from the radio.'

'Isn't that against the copyright laws or something?'

The sardonic smile that tilted the corners of his well-formed lips reinforced his resemblance to a satyr. It occurred to me that as a young man he must have been pretty dishy.

'I doubt if the BBC would wish to be seen to be suing a blind pensioner,' he said dryly.

'I guess not. So you gave K this tape.'

'Tapes. There were ten in all. Twenty half-hour episodes, two per tape.'

'Are they valuable? I mean, they're not collector's items or anything?'

'No.'

'Have you seen … I mean, spoken with K since handing them over?'

'Twice. She was enjoying the recording. In fact she'd practically finished and promised to let me have the tapes back on our next meeting.'

'Which never happened?'

'Precisely.'

I was still inclined to go with my first impression; viz., K had flown the district.

But Henry wasn't having it. 'At first I assumed we just kept missing each other. And then that she was on holiday. Or ill, perhaps.'

'Perhaps she still is.'

'No. I don't think so. It has been too long. Over three weeks. She was an honest young woman. And she knew I was expecting to get the tapes back shortly. Had she been planning a long trip, she'd have returned them before leaving. And if she were taken ill, I believe she would have found some way to get them back to me.'

'Did she know where you lived?'

'No. But it would not have been that difficult to locate me on the promenade. As I said, my habits are fairly regular. I am certain something serious has happened to her, Grace.'

It all seemed rather nebulous to me. I was pretty sure this was going to turn out to be a complete waste of time.

But still, if he was going to pay me to waste it? I checked that he was, and received five days' flat-rate fees in advance, plus a signed contract agreeing to pay reasonable expenses incurred.

I gave him a copy so he could get someone else to read it to him and check everything was above board, and then tried for a clearer picture of the vanished runner.

'You must have picked up some other details, probably without realising. I mean, when she ran, did she sound heavy or out of breath?'

'No. She was very light on her feet. And quite fit, I'd say.'

Probably slim-to-average build, then.

'What about her height?'

Henry stood up abruptly. I thought I'd bored him into flight. I quite often have that effect on men.

'Would you stand up too, Grace.'

Obligingly I disentangled my legs from the desk.

'How tall are you?'

'Five ten.'

He nodded slightly. 'Then K is approximately five feet eight inches, I should say.'

'Great.' We both folded down again. 'What about age? Young, you said. How young? Teens?'

'No. Older than that.'

'Twenties? Thirties?'

'I'm not certain.' He hesitated. 'Under thirty I'd have said.

7

But I don't know why I should say so. I do not recall any mention of her age.'

Henry didn't recall much at all when we got right down to it. He had no recollection of K's mentioning where she lived; who she lived with; where (and if) she worked; her hobbies; her haunts; her friends.

'I'm not being a great deal of help, am I?' he murmured after we'd worked our way (abortively) through an exhaustive list.

'You're doing fine,' I lied, folding his cheque into my inside pocket. 'What about her accent? Was it regional? Or local? Foreign?'

'Definitely not foreign. Or regional that I can recall. It was just ordinary English. Perhaps slightly common. She used a lot of abbreviations and the occasional slang word.'

'OK. Now you say you walk early – how early exactly?'

He shrugged. 'It varies. When I wake, normally. Light means nothing to me, so I don't have to wait for it. However, I'm rarely later than six thirty. Usually earlier.'

I could feel the blood draining from my face. I was going to have to get up at five thirty! I hadn't done that on a regular basis since the end of my inglorious police career.

Looking across the desk at Henry, for a moment I thought he was having sympathy pains. His complexion was a pasty reflection of my own. Then I realised the upward tilt of his head had acquired a list to starboard. He was listening to something beyond the office.

Concentrating against the screaming racket of the herring gulls who were murdering each other on the roof ledge outside the window, I heard it too.

Light footsteps were coming up the stairs.

CHAPTER 2

'You have another client,' Henry said, standing abruptly. 'I would really rather not ...'

His tinted glasses swept in an unseeing arc around the

office as if he was looking for hiding places. Unless he wanted to crawl under the desk or climb out of the window on to the roof parapet, he was out of luck.

Anyway, it wasn't necessary. I'd recognised the feet. And they came attached to my friend and partial namesake, Annie Smith.

'It's OK. It's another investigator. She has the office across the landing.'

Sure enough, the opposite door opened and closed with the silent efficiency of a door that is rented by a woman organised enough to oil its hinges on a regular basis (as opposed to dabbing the full-fat spread from her sandwich over the squeaky bits, which is my usual DIY solution).

Henry sat again. 'I'm so sorry. I just didn't wish … May I have your assurance that this investigation will be completely confidential?'

'Of course.'

'Thank you.' He gave me another small smile. 'The fact is, I suffer from a double handicap. This …' He touched the tinted glasses. 'And *anno Domini*. Old age to you, Grace. People tend to assume you don't have a full set of pistons in the engine. I'd really prefer it if it didn't become common knowledge that I was paying out good money to have you search for a young woman whom I scarcely know and can't describe.'

'Don't worry about it, Henry. You'll just be "the client" when I start asking around.' I rifled through my (empty) diary and informed him I'd be able to fit in a few days this week.

He seemed relieved. 'You'll let me know anything you discover? Anything at all?'

'Sure.' The diary had reminded me of an obvious question. 'You said about three weeks ago, but can you pin down the exact date that you last saw … er, spoke to K?'

The V reappeared over the gold frames. 'It was the beginning of the week, I'm sure of that. Monday or Tuesday.'

'Was it a Bank Holiday?'

His face cleared. 'No. No. It wasn't. I'm certain of that because I recall the appalling crowds coming down for the amusement park the following weekend.'

So K had probably last pounded the promenade in the final week of April. 'Right. Well I'll start asking around.'

'I shall look forward to hearing from you.' He found the door handle without my assistance and then stopped, partially turning as I stood up to show him out.

'There is one thing, Miss Smith ... Grace. I've just recalled that K mentioned a name once. Bernard ... no, Bertram, that was it.'

'In what context?'

'None really. She simply said something like ... "Can't stop, got to ring Bertram before things get hectic" ... or something similar.'

He declined my assistance to get down the stairs. I hung over the banisters watching his light, easy descent.

At the foot of the stairs he leant back into the well, raised his stick and waved a salute. Light glinted off his lenses and for a moment they looked like huge alien eyes. He'd probably heard my breathing as I craned over the stairwell, but it was still an eerie sensation, wondering whether – or how much – he could see behind those glasses.

I invited myself into Annie's office. I find the blue/grey décor picked out with damask pink restful after the chaos of my own pit.

'I rather fancy having my office like this,' I remarked, plumping down on her two-seater sofa and taking care to cross my trainers over the arm rather than on the cushions (she's possessive about upholstery). 'What do you reckon?'

Annie flicked on the kettle switch and delved inside the small cupboard where she kept the crockery and goodies. 'The way I see it, you have two options. One: wait for the interior-decorating fairies to flit in one night Two: get down to the DIY hypermarket and start sanding, painting and sewing like I had to.'

She sounded snappy. I glanced at her curiously.

I had to look at her curiously because the only other bit of her on view was a broad bottom encased in a black skirt – and that wasn't really giving much away. Perhaps that was the problem.

'Em ... have you and computer-what's-his-name got it together again?' I asked.

She'd recently been having a fling with a divorced ex-client until a plump little WPC who looked like butter wouldn't melt had indicated she'd like to take down his particulars.

'His name's Jonathon, as you very well know,' Annie said, straightening up and putting a vicious spin on the lid of a jar of richer roasted coffee granules. 'And no, we haven't, and we won't be. Jonathon is *history*.'

And a particularly nasty period such as the Black Death, judging by the way she was beating the granules to a pulp with a tea spoon. If Jonathon wasn't the problem, something else was definitely jerking her chain. I took another quick look.

Most of her round face was hidden behind a huge pair of prescription sunglasses. All I could really see was a pert nose, thinly compressed lips and a haze of mousy hair which was currently suffering from a slight case of sea-air frizz.

She thrust a china mug of instant at me. I decanted myself from the sofa and rooted inside the corner cupboard. 'You've no milk.'

'No.' Annie shuffled a handful of identical green plastic files over her desk.

I explored further. There was no cubed demerara either. Or chocolate biscuits. Normally Annie considered a good dose of sugar and chocolate as essential for soothing wives and girlfriends whose self-esteem/bank balance/pride had just taken a battering by a cheating spouse/boyfriend/significant other.

'They're locked in Janice's filing cabinet downstairs,' Annie said in answer to my complaint. 'I collect them when I have a client.'

For a moment I took this as a knock about the amount of Colombian roasted and milk-chocolate Hob-Nobs I'd put away recently. Then the light dawned.

'You're on a diet!'

The lips tightened further and the file-shuffling became even more vicious. 'Yes. What of it?'

'Nothing,' I said hastily. Annie's been at least two stone overweight ever since I've known her. It was one of the reasons why she'd resigned from the police force. She's also

11

somewhat over-sensitive on the subject, so I meekly sipped the scalding black liquid and tried to look like I was enjoying the experience.

Evidently I didn't try hard enough.

'Listen, it's bad enough you being bloody anorexic and grazing your way through most of the contents of my office pantry, without having to put up with snide comments on my catering, OK?'

I figured she must have been on this diet for at least seventy-two hours. Ego-boosting was desperately called for.

'I don't know why you bother. I mean, I often wish I could put *on* weight. You look fine as you are. Why follow the rest of the herd?'

'You mean I look like a cow?'

I revised my guess. It must be four days at least since this woman had tasted a Mars bar or a double cheeseburger.

Abruptly Annie whipped the sunglasses off and gave me a piteous look. At least I hope it was a plea for pity. For a moment I had a nasty sensation she was contemplating cannibalism.

'I wouldn't mind being ... you know ... largish,' she said, 'if I could just be miserable about it and have a decent moan.'

'Can't you?' She sounded like she was having a pretty good try to me.

'No. It's not politically acceptable these days, is it? We have to enjoy being ... largish. The flaming media's crammed with fat celebrities telling us "*Big is Beautiful*" and "*Real Women Have Cuddly Curves*" while they try to flog us their latest line in outsize designer wear or feminist best-seller. It's got so you can't read a diet magazine in public without some idiot accosting you and telling you you're letting the sisterhood down.'

It was an interesting thought really. Maybe in a few years would-be dieters would have to meet in secret, exchanging low-cal recipes on coded micro-dots and smuggling cottage cheese across county boundaries in false car bumpers.

I tried to lighten her up a bit. 'You could set up autonomous underground dieting clubs. Each group only sharing foodie information on a need-to-know basis, like spy cells operating in enemy zones. Except you'd be fat cells. Fat cells, get it?'

I choked off the laugh. Annie very obviously wasn't in the mood. Casting around for a safer subject, I indicated the folders. 'New filing system?'

'It's a case. Company relocating to Canary Wharf; bonds and securities. They've done all the standard stuff on the staff: birth certificates, chasing up references, et cetera. Now they want me to do a physical check on selected applicants. You know, drop round the schools they claim to have gone to. Check out old university chums. Ask around old neighbourhoods.'

'Sounds a bit over-the-top. They American?'

'Far East. I think that's the problem. It's difficult to pick up nuances in speech and expressions in another culture. So they want someone to drop in on the lucky candidates' past ... and see whether it really *is* another country.'

'Sounds well paid.'

'Top dollar, as my clients would say. And generous expenses as well.'

'Jammy cow. How'd you land it?'

Annie shrugged. 'Contacts. And they wanted someone based well away from the London area.'

'I'm based as far away as you; how come I don't get jobs like that?'

There was an awkward silence. We both knew the answer. Because ex-coppers who'd left the job under suspicion of taking bribes from pond-life who'd crippled another policeman were not perceived as reliable employees.

'So what are you working on?' Annie asked, a trifle too brightly.

I told her about Henry's missing K. And then slipped in an idea I'd been nursing ever since the reason for Annie's peevishness had occurred to me.

'I'm going for a run tomorrow morning. See if I can pick up a rather better description than Henry's. Why don't you come along? Tone up some of that flab.'

'Do you know, Grace, I think it was probably a wise career move on your part to give the diplomatic service a miss.'

Still, she was a mate. And she proved it by turning out at six the next morning.

At least this late in the year the sun was up and making an attempt to sparkle the sea and warm the sands.

'Imagine doing this in winter,' I called across to Annie. 'In the dark and the rain.'

'So what's the plan?'

'Stop anyone who looks like a regular and ask, I guess.'

'Ask what? If they've seen someone we can't describe?'

'Henry's distinctive enough. And someone must have seen him talking to K. What about this one?'

A walker was speeding towards us. The mahogany shade of his skin beneath the shiny blue singlet and white shorts suggested a healthy outdoor lifestyle and regular work-outs.

We paused. The walker drew nearer. His elbows flashed in time with the rhythm of his knobbly knees. Sunlight glittered from his balding head and danced from the stopwatch bouncing on his concave chest.

'Excuse me ... I wonder if you ...'

'Time ... personal best ... oxygen intake at optimum ...'

Without breaking step he ploughed between me and Annie. By the time we spun round he was already a good ten yards up the promenade. Open-mouthed we watched his small buttocks jiggling beneath the white silk shorts until he was out of sight.

'Like a couple of oranges in a pillowcase,' Annie remarked, resuming her steady pace. 'Let's hope they're not all barmy.'

The trouble was, a lot of them *were*. At that time in the morning we were faced with the fanatical fitness freaks who had no wish to stand around chatting when they could be pumping oxygen, burning calories and racking up the adrenaline.

We changed tactics and tried turning and flanking them, keeping pace as we described Henry and asked if perhaps they'd noticed him – and a young woman he often spoke with.

After three times up and back along the upper part of the promenade, all we'd gained were a few sightings of Henry, but none at all of K.

'Perhaps they didn't exercise along this stretch,' Annie suggested as we paused for a rest.

'Henry must have done,' I panted. 'He lives in St John's Road, so he's got to hit this bit if he walks down to the front. Although,' I admitted, stripping off my tracksuit top and tying it round my waist, 'he did say the first time he spoke to K was in one of the shelters under the cliff. Maybe we should try further along.'

'Thanks. You mean the last half-hour's torture was for nothing?'

Annie knotted her own top round her waist and we set off again. After half a mile the promenade that followed the main road ran out and we dropped down on to the pedestrianised strip that snaked between the cliffs and beaches. And encountered a new hazard.

In theory the tarmacadam walkway was strictly for the use of walkers, runners and anyone else prepared to use two or four feet as a means of propulsion. Cycling was strictly forbidden. It said so on the notices attached to the promenade railings every hundred yards.

The string of bikers hurtling towards us probably couldn't see them since (a) they were hunched over their handlebars with the single-minded determination of a Tour de France finalist, and (b) they were travelling at warp speed.

I leapt up on to the parapet wall whilst Annie dashed for the sea-front railings. I caught a confused blur of plastic safety helmets shaped like rugby balls and wheels spinning so fast they appeared to be solid, and then they were gone.

'Flaming hell,' I complained, rejoining Annie. 'Where are the police when you need them?'

'Working out if they've got sufficient in the budget to pay an officer to walk the length of the high street – by the quickest possible route, naturally.'

'Naturally,' I agreed, as we fell into step again. 'Cutting the budget again, are they?'

'Zeb says it's on the cards,' Annie puffed.

Zeb was her brother. As a detective constable in the local force, he was useful for gleaning those little extra pieces of information that make a private investigator's life just that much simpler.

'Should mean more work in the private sector,' Annie pointed out. 'We could double our turnover.'

Two clients instead of one? Yippee, I cheered silently, straining to keep up. Despite the extra baggage larded under her skin, Annie was making a better job of this than me. I'd obviously got more out of shape than I realised.

Leaning our arms along the top of the iron railings, we stopped a minute to watch the grey breakers shushing against the pebbly ribbon of stones that marked the limits of high tide. Below us the sands still retained the wriggling lines of the council's 'tidy-and-tart' machines which swept rubbish from the beaches in the season and flattened out the efforts of the sandcastle- and hole-digging visitors.

'It did occur to me that if she was running that early she might work as a chambermaid or breakfast waitress or something.'

'Presumably somewhere that's not too bothered about the smell after all that exercise?'

'They might let her shower when she gets there.' We fell into a jog again. 'Of course, she might work in London. If she lives near the front, she'd just about have time to get home, wash, change and make the commuter special if she grabbed a coffee and bacon roll from the station buffet for breakfast.'

A loud rumble from Annie's innards reminded me why she was working out with me. I glanced sideways and met her tight-lipped glare.

'Sorry. Forgot about the diet. What are you having for breakfast at the moment?'

'Unsweetened cereal, low-fat milk and black tea.'

'Yummy,' I murmured as a vision of a fried-egg sandwich swam into my mind.

Annie ignored the lie and asked why I thought early-morning exercise indicated K had a job. 'She might just be a chronic insomniac.'

We both did a quick line-step routine to let a fleet of skateboarders pass. When we came together again, I explained Henry's assertion that he didn't meet her at weekends. 'I think she slept in on Saturday and Sunday. Probably went out later.'

Which – it belatedly occurred to me – made it unlikely she

was a chambermaid, since they usually worked shifts, including some weekends. I said as much to Annie.

Annie stopped dead. 'Oh great! Could I just point out a small flaw in your investigative technique, Sherlock?'

'What?'

'Today is Saturday.'

CHAPTER 3

'Oh shit.'

No wonder nobody remembered K. If she worked out at all at the weekend it was in a completely different time slot to the one we'd been knocking ourselves out in.

'What do you want to do? Call it a day and try again Monday?'

'Dream on,' Annie panted. 'I shall be enjoying a luxury hotel Jacuzzi courtesy of my securities company's expense account come Monday morning.'

It was a low blow. But a girl needs to know how to fight dirty sometimes. 'Pity you won't be able to order anything fattening from room service.'

Mutual bitching out of the way, I suggested we might as well finish here since we were up anyway. 'Race you to the next bay?'

I sped off. Annie overtook me.

We sprinted past the beach café, which wasn't open yet, and the public loos, which were – and towards the wooden chalets lined up at the base of the cliff.

We were going so fast that I nearly missed the fractionally open door.

Annie had spotted it too. By common consent we applied the brakes.

The chalets' doors were normally secured by a clasp and padlock. A few were privately owned, but most were rented out on a weekly basis by the council. You paid your deposit and collected your key from a window by the café. The occupant of this one had by-passed that step in the process, I suspected.

The padlock had been re-attached in a way that made it look to a casual glance as if the chalet was still locked.

'Figgy, hurry up. I'm dying for a pee.'

The door swung open under the pressure of one finger, leaning the padlock hanging by its curved bar from the metal clasp.

'I thought you weren't never … It's me gran's. She lets us use it. Ask 'er if yer don't believe me.'

The speaker had sprung up away from a Calor Gas stove as she blurted out the last three sentences. Baked beans bubbled in the saucepan balanced on top of it. A quick glance notched up a rolled sleeping bag in one corner. Wire baskets from the local supermarket that were being used for the storage of folded clothing, crockery and food. There was also a scruffy soft-canvas bag and a pair of tom-toms stacked in another corner.

She'd made some attempt to brighten the place up, sticking pictures torn from magazines on the walls and a vase of artificial flowers on the drop-down flap at the rear of the hut.

'We're not from the council. How long have you been squatting here?'

'If you're not council, it's none of your business.'

The words were aggressive but her voice shook slightly over them. At the first sign of opposition, she'd crumble. She moved forward slightly into the light. It showed up a thin face framed by long, straggling mousy hair.

'Needs a wash,' she said unexpectedly, pushing it behind her ears. 'It's a mess.'

'It's fine,' we both lied in unison. And took the opportunity of girlish closeness to introduce ourselves.

'I'm Mickey.' She gave us a cautious smile. 'You really not council?'

'Honest. We're just looking for someone.' Once again I went into the Henry and his girlfriend routine.

She moved a little nearer the door; showing up the patches of red and peeling sunburn on her cheekbones and nose. 'I 'ave seen the man. Couple of times. He's got a big black dog.

We had a dog like that when I was little but my mum's bloke had him put down. I've never seen a girl, though.'

Venturing right out, she shielded her eyes against the increasing glare from the sea. 'Looks like it's gonna be all right. Be able to sit on the beach *all day*. Brilliant.'

She was like a kid looking forward to a treat.

'How long have you been …?' I nodded towards the chalet.

'Since Easter. It's just temporary. Till we find a place to stop for real.'

We'd all been looking out at the ocean, so we failed to see the bloke until he slid into the scene.

It was like watching one of those old-fashioned slide projectors. One minute the frame was filled with grey spray, creamy rollers, ochre sand, gulls still buff in their juvenile feathers, and blue-painted iron railings, then suddenly a black apparition appeared stage right.

It took a second to register that the fluid movement was due to the canary-yellow roller-blades. The rest of him was funereal black: jeans; short-sleeved T-shirt; studded belt; sunglasses; spiky hair. He braked suddenly in front of us; close enough for it to start to feel like intimidation.

'What'ya know, Mickey?'

'They're asking about the blind bloke with the dog, Figgy. You ain't seen a girl with him, have you?'

'No. Why?'

He was sliding back and forth on the blades as he spoke, the movement setting up a sloshing in the kettle he was holding. I guessed they probably used the public loos for washing and water supplies.

'Because I'm trying to find her,' I informed him. 'But if you can't help, we'll be off. Bye.'

'Byeeeee …' He gave us a mock bow.

Life on the promenade was hotting up. The dog walkers were out in force now, trying to beat the eight a.m. ban on exercising them on the sands. Once again we clocked up several recognitions of Henry and zilch on K.

'Looks like you're in for a solitary work-out come Monday,' Annie said as we rounded the final bend and the snack bar and beach of West Bay came into sight.

I opened my mouth to broach the subject of food and got trumped by a loud 'Yo! What'ya know, girls!' from behind.

Figgy arrived at full tilt and circled us like an Apache warrior on speed who'd just found the wagon train. We both pointedly ignored him and kept on jogging.

'Heh, do I detect hostility here? Don't you want to know about the bird with the blind wrinkly?'

'Thought you didn't know anything about her?'

'Knowing is relative, ain't it …?' He swung in front and skated backwards. 'Thing is, couldn't say anything in front of Mickey. See, she was kind of a babe, that bird. And Mickey gets wound up if I talk up other birds.' He stopped back-pedalling and leant his elbows on the promenade railings. 'Information's worth money, ain't it?'

'Is it?'

'I reckon. I mean, I got it. You want it. Basic economics. Cost you fifty.'

'Dream on, Figgy.'

Annie and I moved off. He skated in front of us and drooped himself over the railings again. 'So give us a figure.'

'Two quid.'

We finally settled on ten. 'Give us a sample of what we're buying. For good faith. How tall was she? About my height?'

'Tall?' The question seemed to surprise him. He looked me up and down. 'No, tad shorter, I'd say.'

At least it looked like we were discussing the right woman. 'What about her age?'

'What about my cash?'

I indicated my sweatshirt and pants. 'I don't carry money in this outfit, Figgy. I'll owe you.'

'Now *you're* in dreamland.'

Simultaneously we both looked at Annie. With a heavy sigh she balanced her trainer on the railings, unlaced it and pulled out a ten-pound note.

Figgy held out eager fingers. I dangled the note just out of reach. 'The girl. When did you see her?'

'About a week after Mickey and I came here. She and the wrinkly were on one of them bench seats under the cliffs. Just past our place.'

'And she was a babe?'

'Yeah!' A reminiscent smile played round his mouth. 'She had these little pink shorts on. Legs went on up to her throat. Don't know about the ...' He cupped his hands over his chest. 'Had a baggy jumper on.'

'Was she wearing anything else?'

'Trainers.'

'And?' I twitched the note further out of reach.

'You mean the cassette player?'

It sounded like we'd got the right girl all right. I asked him how old she was.

'Mid-twenties, I guess.'

'Dark, fair, redhead?'

'Dark. About down to here ...' He touched his shoulder blades. 'She had it pulled back. You birds shouldn't do that ... it's more of a turn-on all kind of loose, like.'

He looked pointedly at my own blonde hair which I wore short and in a through-a-hedge-backwards style which I'd evolved with the help of a pair of nail scissors.

Rolling forward, he twitched the note from my fingers. 'Interview over, girls.'

He glided back the way he'd come. Ten feet away, he spun round and shouted: 'Yo, girls. Want her address?'

'Slip you her telephone number too, did she, Figgy?' I mocked.

'Didn't ask. Saw her coming out of a place once, though. Cost you twenty.'

'Don't look at me,' Annie said in response to my pleading look. 'I'm strictly a one-shoe girl.'

'I'll get back to you.'

'Looking forward to it.'

Figgy wheeled and glided away with easy strokes.

'Do you think he's for real? Does he really have an address?' I said doubtfully as we followed him at a slow amble.

'*An* address, yes. The address ... who knows? Can you get the twenty?'

I was off-guard. I admitted to having a cache of readies at the office.

'Great. See to it you put my tenner under my door.'

'Aren't you coming back?'

21

'No point. I've got the files I need at home. I've a bit of washing and pressing to do before I pack. And then I'll drive up tomorrow. Miss the Monday-morning traffic.'

'Where you heading?'

'Bradford first, then Leeds. Then Leicester. After that I'll touch base here and head out for a couple of candidates with West Country addresses.'

We'd reached the chalets again. A couple more were open now; legitimately this time, judging by the deckchairs outside.

Figgy and Mickey's navy-blue home was closed and (ostensibly) padlocked, but we glimpsed the tops of their heads leaning back against the promenade wall on the beach below. The smell of hot baked beans drifted up to mingle with the sharp tang of newly exposed seaweed left by the now-retreating tide.

Annie's stomach growled again.

'Fancy cheating and having a fry-up?' I suggested.

'No thank you. If I'm going to do something I like to do it properly.'

This was true. Resolute could be Annie's middle name. In fact, for all I knew, it *was* her middle name – given her parents' penchant for saddling their children with odd Christian names in order to add a smidgen of originality to their boring surname. Annie's full name was Anchoret and her brother Zeb had been blessed with Zebedee.

We parted at the foot of the steps beyond the beach café. Annie's flat lay over the other side of town, but I could cut through the side streets from here to the office.

I half expected to find someone else in, since none of us worked what you might call regular hours; but the front door was double-locked. I'd tied my keys to the lacing in my trouser band. The knot had become entangled, so I ended up standing on tiptoe and flattening myself against the wood in order to unlock the door. Disabling the bleeping alarm, I ambled upstairs, opened my filing cabinet and retrieved the plastic package of bank notes I'd stuck to the back of one of the sliding drawers.

I put Annie's tenner under the door in an envelope (well, it was going on expenses anyway). After that I'd intended to get myself some breakfast then track down Figgy, but an angry crash and cough from the radiator on the landing caught my attention.

I felt the painted metal. It was red-hot. Brilliant! Vetch the Letch had forgotten to turn off the automatic timing on the boiler for the weekend. Which meant that the tank was currently full of hot water. It seemed a pity to waste it. Taking a towel and shower gel from my locker, I entered the third room on the top landing.

When Vetch had enherited this former boarding house from his gran, he'd had most of the rooms converted for office use, but this bathroom had survived the decorators for some reason. It still bore the ancient linoleum, free-standing tub, copper piping and green algae from the days when Granny had driven weekly boarders out to huddle on freezing beaches until she let them back in at six o'clock *prompt* for high tea.

Filling the tub to the top, I lazily relaxed and read the ancient notice left behind by Granny Vetch, informing me:

Baths are to be taken between four and six o'clock on Tuesdays and Thursdays only.
An additional Is. 6d. to be paid in advance for each bath taken.

'And a bargain at half the price, Vetch,' I informed my absent boss. Lathering gel into my hair, I used my coffee mug to bail rinsing water over it and then snuggled back down again to twiddle taps with my toes, practise tightening my stomach muscles, blow ripples across the sudsy water and generally hang out my meeting with Figgy until I figured he'd be sweating on whether he was going to get my twenty pounds or not.

Eventually I got bored and heaved myself out. Dragging my fingers through my hair, which was already more or less dry, I pulled my tracksuit on again, gathered up my bits and pieces, sauntered back to my office – and stopped dead.

A total stranger was rifling through my desk drawers.

CHAPTER 4

'How the hell did you get in?'

'Through the door, natch,' my visitor said, swinging her boots off the desk. 'How do you think?'

'I mean how did you get into the building?'

'So do I. I opened the front door and walked in. It's not difficult, I've been able to do it ever since I was three years old.'

For about thirteen years then, I guessed, putting her at sixteen going on twenty-five.

I recalled my dance with the door key and the laces to my jogging pants trying to get the door open. I couldn't remember facing up the front-door panels on the inside. I'd forgotten to lock up behind me, hadn't I?

'You a detective?' She sounded doubtful.

'Yes. Why? Don't I look like one?'

'Not really. I sort of thought you'd be in leather jeans and jacket, with this real mean attitude. And maybe a gun.'

At least she hadn't said I *thought you'd be a man*. I started to like her, despite her desk-rifling activities.

'I thought perhaps you were the cleaner.'

I went right off her again. 'Do you mind if I get to my seat? Snoopers usually take the other chair.'

She didn't seem at all abashed. Sliding the drawers shut, she stood up. 'I wasn't snooping. I just got bored waiting for you. You ought to have magazines for customers to read. Like the dentist.'

'How'd you know this was my office?' I asked, reclaiming my place.

'Other doors were all locked, natch.'

Thank heavens for that, I breathed silently.

'I heard you splashing around in there. I didn't knock 'cos it really pisses me off when they interrupt me in the bath.'

It did me too. I started to like her again.

'So what can I do for you ... er ... We haven't done names, have we?'

24

'You're G. Smith. It's painted on the door. What's the G for?'

'Grace.'

She'd had to fetch the client's chair from the other side of the office. It gave me a chance for a quick stock-taking.

About five three. Bright-orange Lycra top over a bust-line I'd have killed for; short blue denim skirt, denim jacket and bright-blue Doc Martens in a crocodile-skin pattern.

Her face was round and would probably sag in later life, but at present it was all peachy skin, red lips and big brown eyes with long curling lashes beneath a liberal coating of make-up. She wore her chestnut hair as short as mine, but it lay in shiny wisps which said 'ridiculously expensive stylist' rather than 'blunt nail scissors'.

And somehow I had the feeling that the over-large gold hoop earrings had genuine hallmarks and the *flash trash* watch probably hadn't cost less than three figures.

'So what do I call you?' I asked.

'Bone.'

'What?'

'Bone. You know, like T-bone, jaw-bone ...'

'Funny bone?'

'Yes. That's it.'

'I can't call you that.'

'Why not? Everyone else does. What should I call you? Smithie?'

For years I'd been trying to persuade people to call me Smithie, and they'd all persisted in addressing me as Grace. Now I'd finally got a client who was going to play ball, it suddenly sounded incredibly childish.

'Let's stick to Grace. So what can I do for you, er ... Bone?'

'I want you to find my boyfriend.'

Two missing persons in two days! Maybe the budget cuts in the police service were beginning to bite already.

A nasty thought occurred to me.

'Of course I know what he looks like!' Bone snapped in answer to my enquiry. 'What do you think we did – got it together in a dark room?'

She dragged her shoulder bag round on to her midriff and unzipped an inner compartment. 'There! That's him.'

It was a strip from a photo booth. Nobody ever looks like the smiling models displayed on the outside of those machines. This bloke was startled in the first shot; grinning inanely in the second; and attempting to eyeball the camera with a macho sneer in three and four.

'Well bad, eh?'

I nearly took this as a comment on his behaviour. He had a Romany darkness which in past times had tended to be associated with deflowered virgins and naked romps on the moors. Then I saw Bone's besotted face and realised this translated as: *I fancy his looks something rotten.*

I pulled a pad from the drawer. 'OK. What's his name?'

'Tom Skerries.'

'Address?'

'I don't know. Anyway, he's probably moved.'

'Why?'

'He was going to leave his wife. He said she was becoming a real drag.'

I looked at her. She was sitting with her knees pressed together, her lower legs splayed and the boots turned in at a ninety-degree angle. Her face was calm and untroubled.

'Didn't it bother you? That he was married?'

'No. Why should it? He wasn't married to me, was he?'

That was rather my point, but it was plainly not one that Bone even recognised, let alone entertained.

'So how long have you and Tom been an item?'

She frowned and delved into her bag again. I wondered if she needed a diary to remind her when she and Mr Wonderful had first connected. Instead a packet and disposable lighter appeared.

'Smoke?'

'No thanks.'

She lit one and leant back, blowing a stream of smoke into the air, and frowning slightly. I think I was supposed to understand that she had so many fanciable blokes beating a path to her door that it was hard for her to remember when Tom had first joined the crowd.

I wasn't fooled. I'd have bet money that she could remember the exact instant she'd first laid eyes – and whatever else – on Mrs Skerries' husband.

'When was the big gale? That tanker nearly got blown into the beach,' Bone finally said.

'Beginning of February.'

'It would be about two weeks after that, I guess. See, the King Charles Oak blew down, took most of the wall with it.'

I didn't really see the connection, but I asked her if this was at home.

'No.' She expelled another cloud of smoke. 'School. St Aggie's.'

Well, I'd been right about there being money in the family. St Agatha's was an exclusive (and expensive) school that took little 'gels' from the Pony Club when they were seven and regurgitated them as fully paid-up Sloane Rangers with the telephone number of Harvey Nichols engraved on their souls at eighteen.

'So what's this wall got to do with Tom?'

'He came to put it back. Not the original one, natch. It was ancient. Queen Elizabeth the First slept on top of it or something. The school's been trying to get rid of it for aeons but it had some preservation order on it.'

'So it was a lucky break when the tree fell on it?'

The slightly bored been-there-done-that expression vanished for a fraction of an instant. She giggled and suddenly looked a lot prettier. 'I'll say. Goldie was practically dancing around the grounds.'

'Goldie?'

'Ms Goldfinch. The headmistress. Anyway, the next week she's got the Health and Safety people round to say that section's dangerous and could fall on someone so they have to pull it down. And once they get started, well – totally amazing – the shockwaves somehow loosened all the other bricks, so the whole wall has to come down and a nice new one goes up.' The smile lit her face again. 'Natch it's three feet higher than the old one. As if that's going to stop us bunking out at night.'

'As if. You're a boarder then?'

'Weekly. I come home weekends. Most weekends,' she amended, the bored look resettling over the peachy skin.

'And Tom built this new wall, is that it?'

'Not all by himself, natch. But he was the creamiest. You can see.'

She indicated the strip photos that were still on my desk. 'All the girls fancied him. But he wanted me. Couldn't get enough of me, in fact.' The silent, unspoken *natch* hung between us.

'Did Ms Goldfinch know about this ... er ... did she know you and Tom were dating?'

'Of course she didn't. She'd have told my parents. And then *natch* they'd have got really heavy and boring about it.'

She'd come to the end of her cigarette. I could see her looking for somewhere to stub it out. A lot of visitors wouldn't hesitate to grind it into the floor. But Bone squeezed it out between fingertips varnished electric blue and flipped it into the waste bin. Street attitude versus Ms Goldfinch's lessons in good manners; strike one to Ms Goldie.

'So how did you get together?' I asked. 'Weekends?'

'Later. First of all it was in the boiler room at school. See, it kept pissing down the next couple of weeks after the gale.'

'I remember. Basement area outside my flat flooded.'

'So did our patio. At home, I mean.'

'So they couldn't build the wall.'

Bone nodded vigorously. 'They had to dig out new foundations, but they kept filling up. And they couldn't pour the concrete either.'

I got the picture. At every opportunity the workmen had dived down the warm boiler room for a smoke, a read and a chance to flex their pecs at a bunch of bored teenagers.

'How many workmen were there?'

'Two full time. Jez and Enos. Jez wasn't bad, I suppose. Enos was ancient.'

'So Tom just helped out on a casual basis, did he?'

I was scribbling notes officiously, but I had every intention of binning most of them, since I'd already decided the most likely scenario was good old Tom had got bored with his bit of posh and moved on to the next conquest.

'Yes. That's right. He came round odd days. And then towards the end Mr Payne joined in as well.' The attractive smile flitted across her face again. 'Goldie really laid into him;

told him if he didn't get the job finished by the end of the week he could whistle for his money.'

'Mr Payne owns the builder's, does he?'

Bone nodded.

'Do you know his first name?'

'Larry.'

'Have you asked him about Tom?'

'No.'

'Why not? Wouldn't that have been easiest?'

The sulky look descended again. 'He's really thick with Goldie. Anyway, that's what I'm paying you to do, isn't it? Ask.'

'When did you last see Tom?'

'Nineteenth of April,' she said promptly. 'We went to TED's.'

TED's was our local nightclub, The Electric Daffodil. It generally catered for a slightly older clientele than the teenage scene. Squinting at Tom's passport photo, I asked Bone how old he was.

'Twenty-three. I know TED's is a bit ... you know ... for *old* people ... but I think he wanted to take me somewhere special. And there's not much around here, is there? It's such a *dump*.'

'Where did he take you other times?'

'Pubs mostly.' She listed four.

I did a few mental calculations. She'd gone out with him for a couple of months at most. Probably bunked off school a few times and otherwise it was weekends when she was home and Mummy and Daddy weren't paying too much attention to who she was with.

Boredom on Tom's part seemed more and more likely as a possible explanation for his suddenly dropping out of Bone's life. I tried to let her down gently. Perhaps, I suggested, Tom had got a temporary job out of the district? Building walls in Worksop or something.

'Doesn't stop him phoning me, does it?' she snapped, her eyes flashing. 'Now you find out why he hasn't.'

'Look, this sort of thing ... it costs quite a bit, you know. I mean, there's my fees ... and expenses on top.'

With a weary sigh, she dragged the bag on to her midriff

again and extracted a wallet (designer-monogrammed). Rifling through the stacks of notes, she started to count out twenties. When there were fifteen of them piled on my desk, she stopped.

'Will that do for now? You can bill me the rest when you find him.'

I've always been a great believer in the redistribution of wealth; particularly in my direction. If she was that determined, I figured the kindest thing to do would be to find Tom and then persuade him to phone her and invent some face-saving excuse to let her down gently.

Scooping the notes up, I produced a blank contract form and filled out the details of our agreement.

'I'll need your full name and address.'

'What for? I don't want you to find *me*, do I?'

'In case I need to get in touch.'

'Give me a ring on my mobile.' Casually she reached over and scribbled the number on my pad. 'OK?'

'Well … I suppose …'

She stood up, pulling down the skirt and wriggling the Lycra into a smooth plain over the bust. 'There's just one thing. I want him found before the twenty-first of June.'

'Any special reason?'

'My friend Claudia's parents organise an annual midsummer ball for charity.' She raised her chin. 'I know that sounds pretty gross, but it's not too bad. They have champagne, a band, auction – you know, all the usual boring performance. Claudia's invited all the girls from our year. With partners, natch.'

The languid tone wasn't fooling me. She couldn't suppress the glint of excitement beneath the sweep of curling lashes.

'And you want Tom to take you.'

'I've *told* everyone Tom's taking me. They're *green*.'

'I see.'

The full red lips compressed. 'Good. Then you make sure you round him up before the party. Because it's my fucking credibility that's at stake here.'

I looked into the face that was an odd mixture of sophistication and childish innocence. And I understood. It wasn't Bone's heart that had been touched – it was her pride.

Here was a girl who was used to getting anything she wanted. At the moment she wanted Tom on her arm at that party. And she intended to have him – whatever it cost.

'OK,' I agreed. 'I'll be in touch. Soon.'

'Fine,' she said in a tone that implied she'd expected nothing less. 'I'll see you then.'

Once she'd gone, I put the notes in a plastic bag, taped it to my stomach, pinned Figgy's twenty into the pocket of my jogging pants, reset the alarm and relocked the door.

I figured I'd let him sweat for long enough. I didn't want him going walkabout – or skateabout – before I got the lovely K's address out of him.

CHAPTER 5

Life on the beaches was hotting up. The promise of fair weather was holding and the sands were already liberally sprinkled with striped deckchairs and windbreaks.

The town's heyday had been in the first half of the century. From the sixties onwards holidaymakers had started deserting it for Alicante, Palma and Corfu, preferring to get drunk for two weeks on a sun-soaked beach rather than sip warm beer and play bingo whilst the rain lashed the promenade. We still got some die-hards who preferred to spend their fortnight by a bracing North Sea, but most of the visitors these days were day-trippers or weekenders at best.

Mickey was where I'd last seen her breakfasting on baked beans.

She'd removed her sweatshirt and jeans and was leaning against the base of the sun-warmed promenade wall in a shirt and bikini bottom. As my shadow fell across her, she linked both hands over her eyebrows and squinted upwards.

I dropped down beside her and pulled my own top off. 'Hi. Figgy around?'

'He's gone up the town.' She wriggled her shoulders into the warmed stone. 'Said we needed some shopping.'

'What do you do for money? If you don't mind my asking.'

'We work. We're self-employed.'

A shrill whistle from above made us both jump.

'Catch!'

Mickey reached up and fielded the brown plastic bottle hurtling towards her head.

Grinning, Figgy flicked something bright yellow at her. 'Got this as well. Don't want you getting sunstroke or something.'

He leant his arms along the top railing and balanced a roller-blade on the lower one as he watched her examining the peaked cap and high-factor sunscreen with pleasure. It was a decent brand. Together they must have cost him most of my tenner.

'So? Got my twenty?'

'Got my address?'

'Up here.' He pushed himself away from the railings and skated to the top of the wooden steps.

A couple of small kids with brightly coloured shrimping nets were admiring his wheelie techniques when I got there.

'So,' he said, speeding at me and swerving off at the last second. 'Money?'

I unpinned the twenty, but kept a tight grip on it. 'House?'

'Flat,' he corrected.

'Where?'

The yellow blades scissored, keeping him balanced, as he started to describe the route from here to K's flat.

'Hang on ...' I interrupted as we went down the tenth Whatchamacallit Street and round the umpteenth Whatsit Corner. 'Doesn't this place have an address?'

'Bound to.'

'Then you can take me there,' I said firmly, pinning the note back in my pocket.

'Fair enough. Hang on.' He rolled to a position above Mickey and shouted down the plan. 'And you make sure you stick plenty of that stuff on, I don't want you burning.'

He freewheeled easily back to me. 'Got a motor?'

'Yes thanks. But not with me.' And if, as looked likely, the place was going to be crammed with day-trippers, I wanted to hang on to my parking space outside my flat.

From the directions I'd disentangled, it sounded to me like

32

K's flat was over in the North Bay area. Which was a bit of a hike, but walkable. Or, in Figgy's case, skateable.

We took the promenade wherever we could. It was far busier now and he had to weave round trippers, leaning and dipping in complicated figures of eight, skating backwards at high speed then spinning right just as it looked as if he was going to crash into the rubbish bins that had been concreted into the pavement to prevent some of our residents playing 'first one to hit the beach tent' with them after the pubs closed.

I jogged at a steady pace behind him, trying to appear at the peak of physical fitness. Evidently appearances didn't deceive.

'Wanna rest?' Figgy grinned, swooping down on a return loop.

'No thanks,' I smiled, through gritted teeth and the beginnings of a stitch. 'I just like to pace myself.'

'Yeah?' He slowed to come alongside. I hoped the electronic pings, whistles and bells from the amusement arcades that lined the opposite side of the road were hiding the noisy thumping of my heart.

Plainly they weren't.

'That fat babe was in much better shape than you.'

'Thanks.'

'Where's she got to then?'

'She's packing. For an important business trip,' I added, because that *fat babe* had got up my nose. I wanted him to understand Annie was an intelligent and interesting woman – albeit an overweight one.

'Yeah?' He came to a halt beside the kiosk selling postcards, plastic buckets and spades, shrimping nets, bunches of flags, beach skittles and several dozen other items designed to part money and Daddy.

'What does she do then?'

'She's a private detective. We both are. Did you think nosiness was our hobby?'

'Never thought.' He examined a pair of cheap sunglasses with bright-yellow frames. 'Think these would suit Mickey?'

'I daresay. But they say you should buy decent lenses. Cheap ones can give you eye-ache.'

'Better wait for me twenty then, hadn't I? Onwards.'

He skated swiftly away, leaving me to sprint to catch up.

'You and the fat bird an item? You know ...' He crossed his middle finger over his forefinger.

'No. We're not. And her name is Annie.'

'What's yours?'

'Grace Smith.'

He thrust his hands into his jeans pockets and was sashaying beside me with smooth easy strokes. 'It's not far now. We got to cut in right somewhere along the front road, near as I can remember.'

'From what you said, it's on the Downs Estate. Be easier to go through here.'

I started to make my way along identical rows of small roads lined with two-storey semis. Every other one had a black-and-white board propped in the front window announcing 'Vacancies'.

Figgy seemed happy enough for me to do the leading. 'Live around here then, do you, your Graciness?'

'No. I've got a place near yours.'

'With the fat bird?'

'No. *Annie* has a flat by the park.'

'Swishy.' I guessed he was looking sideways at me, although it was hard to tell behind those damn sunglasses. 'She ain't really a detective, is she? That was just a wind-up, wasn't it?'

I stopped dead and faced him. 'Listen, sunshine, she's a bloody good detective. In fact she's probably the best one the agency has ever had.' I jabbed him in the chest and sent him rolling back a few inches. 'So don't go judging by appearances! Understand!'

'Hey, do I detect unresolved hostility here?'

'Oh, cut the amateur psychology crap, Figgy, and get moving.'

'Chill out. We're here.'

He jerked a thumb at something over my shoulder.

It was as I'd thought. K's (supposed) place was on the Downs council estate. As it happened it was about the first building in that particular sixties ghetto and stood just beyond the last of the private boarding semis, so it had a slightly more exclusive look to it than the rows of terraced houses that stretched away beyond it.

'How about me twenty note then?'

'How do I know this is the place?'

'You're just gonna have to trust me.'

'When did you see her coming out of there? Recently?'

'Easter Sunday. Mickey felt queer. I was looking for an open chemist to get her something.'

It made reasonable sense as to why he was wandering around up here. With reluctance I said goodbye to my nice crisp note.

'Cheers!' With another grin he spun round and flashed away.

I had a nasty feeling I'd just been taken for a mug.

CHAPTER 6

It was called Beamish Court. A smallish, square, brick-built block with a communal back garden laid out with grass, flowerbeds and washing carousels.

There were four entrance bells lined up by the security door. None of them were named. I leant on each in turn and got no response.

Stepping back I scanned the windows and tried to look like a committed atheist in case the residents were lurking behind the nets worried I wanted to discuss the true meaning of life.

Nothing seemed to be moving. I played another scale on the bells just in case.

'I think she's taken the baby out, darlin'.'

Looking round, I found myself being watched by a short(ish), plump(ish) woman clutching plastic bags from the local supermarket in both hands.

I guessed that she was probably in her mid-sixties, but it was hard to tell under the make-up, which of was of the deep pancake, pencilled eyebrows and raspberry jam lipstick variety that was in fashion forty years ago. But the *pièce de résistance* was her hair; it was the colour of a tropical sunset and piled up on top of her head like an enormous walnut whip.

'She's out, darlin',' she repeated, lifting one bag awkwardly and waving it in the general direction of the bottom right-hand flat. Presumably number 2, since that was the bell I was leaning on.

'Oh, right. Thanks.' I leant off. 'Actually I'm not sure I've got the right flat. I'm looking for a young woman, about mid-twenties, long dark hair, quite pretty.'

'You mean Kristen?'

Quite possibly I did.

She beamed, raising the other bulging carrier and pointing to a dark-blue Fiesta standing by the kerb. 'That's her car.'

'Oh? Great.' This looked liked being an easy fee.

I was already working out which expenses I could get away with charging to Henry's account when my new acquaintance added: 'She sold it to me when she left. Lovely little motor, darlin', and only eight hundred pounds. My son, now, he paid fifteen thousand for his motor, and it don't run nearly as sweet.'

Whilst she was talking, she'd dumped the carriers on the step with a grunt of relief and unlocked the front door.

'You don't happen to know where Kristen went, do you, Mrs ...?'

'Simonawitz Rachel Simonawitz.'

'Grace Smith. Pleased to meet you.'

'You too. Come in, come in.'

I picked up one of the bags and carried it to the door of the left-hand ground-floor, flat. Rachel muttered with irritation as she fought with several keys and security locks before finally pushing the door open. A blast of central heating and a large white Persian cat rushed out to greet us.

'Oh, get in, Balthazar. Mama's got you some lovely smoked salmon.'

She nudged the cat under its belly with a gold shoe. It deigned to return to the hall whilst Rachel bolted and relocked from the inside. 'My son puts all these on. A good boy, he worries about his mama.'

I wondered aloud whether he'd mentioned it wasn't such a

good idea to invite complete strangers into her flat without checking their credentials first. 'I could be a deranged axe-murderer.'

'If you were, darlin', you wouldn't tell me before I take the locks off,' she said with irrefutable logic. 'Besides, life's too short to be worrying about when you're going to die. We all got to go some time. This way.'

She led the way to the kitchen on the left of the hall corridor. It was small, but beautifully fitted out with oven, washing machine, dishwasher and fridge in the fanciest brand names I couldn't afford.

Rachel flicked open a wall cupboard and started taking down assorted crockery. 'I'll make us a little snack, then we can talk.'

'Thanks.'

'You want to make yourself comfortable in the lounge? Straight across the hall.'

There was plenty of evidence that Rachel wasn't short of a bob or two. The sideboard held a dozen china crinolined ladies that cost a hundred apiece, I reckoned. The concealed lighting in the glass-fronted cabinet was glittering in the facets of two dozen collectable crystal pieces. A bow-fronted Regency-style cabinet held a state-of-the-art television and video. The matching chest of drawers proved to be another fake. The drawer fronts swung out together as one piece to reveal a hi-tech music system. And every surface was crammed with heavy silver frames, mostly of the son, I guessed; plus a woman who looked enough like Rachel to be her daughter, their respective partners and a tribe of grand-children.

Even with the best camera angles and lighting, I reckoned Rachel's kids were in their fifties, so I mentally added another ten years or so on to my estimate of her age.

Finishing my snooping, I sank back into a chair. Balthazar strolled in and fixed his blue eyes on me. I stared back. He arched his back and sprang into my lap, kneaded my legs and dug his claws straight through the soft fabric of my trousers.

With a suppressed scream I leapt up and slung him off. He landed neatly, sauntered back with his nose stuck in the air –

and leapt straight into the warm, squashed cushion I'd just vacated.

Rachel nudged open the door with her elbow. 'Well, here we are then. Are you two making friends?'

'Bosom buddies,' I assured her, staring into the unwinking blue slits and vowing to come back as a Rottweiler in my next reincarnation.

'Good.' She put two plates – one piled with filled rolls, the other holding a large sliced chocolate cake – on the inlaid coffee table. 'I'll just fetch the rest.'

Rest?

She trotted back with a large bowl of baby cherry tomatoes; another of crisps and a platter of pickled cucumbers. The final trip added a cafetière of fresh coffee, cream jug, demerara sugar and a box of after-dinner mints. This was my kind of snack!

'Now you just tuck in darlin', don't be shy. I'll just put the news on.' She flicked the remote at the television.

We chomped in companionable silence for a while, until the news programme moved on to the next stage in the saga of Abercrombie Electronics Inc.

'Ugh … boring darlin'. You want this?'

I shook my head. The story had been running since Christmas. Abercrombie's had tried to defraud the Government, got caught, and now the investigation was running through their subsidiaries like death watch beetle. There wasn't a week when some new director wasn't facing prosecution, a Select Committee, or confiscation of his Executive Washroom electronic swipe card.

It was all being done in the name of outraged public. The public were frankly bored silly by the whole performance. We zapped the sound.

'Nice place you've got here, Mrs Simonawitz.'

'Rachel, please, darlin'.' She waved a plump hand, setting several gold bracelets jangling. 'All paid for by my son. He's a diamond, my Saul.' She swallowed a morsel and chuckled. 'A real diamond: a dozen faces and you can see clear through all of them.'

She poured us both coffee. 'Every time I mention how

they've got a spare bedroom, he buys me something nice, to make the flat more comfortable.' She gave another rich chuckle. 'Thing is, I wouldn't live with my daughter-in-law if we were at the North Pole and there was only one igloo to be had. But they don't know that.'

I grinned and helped myself to a pickled cucumber. 'Did he pay for the car too?'

'Naturally. Mind, I had to be a bit cunning there. There's no way they're going to want me to have a car so I can drive over whenever I feel like it. So I dropped a few hints about a coach tour to New England that's a real bargain at a thousand pounds. And then I ask if maybe they're going to Florida this year, because this is also a place I always wanted to see.'

She laughed and slapped my knee so hard I nearly sent the coffee over the carpet. 'I had a cheque for a thousand pounds the very next day. Chocolate cake?'

'Please.' I let myself be helped to a wedge that must have weighed half a pound and asked her when exactly she'd bought the car.

'End of April. The thirtieth,' she said promptly, pushing brown crumbs into one corner of her mouth.

'But you must have known Kristen was leaving before that? To get the money, I mean.'

'She asked me if I wanted to buy the previous week. Saul's cheque just cleared in time. She wanted cash. It was always cash with Kristen.'

'Did she say where she was going?'

'No, darlin'. I asked her, but she just ...' She jangled the bracelets in a vague waving motion. 'If she didn't want to tell you something ... she could be ...'

'Evasive?'

'Slippery. So why do you want to find her?'

I produced my business card. Rachel was thrilled enough to find she'd met a real-life private detective to offer seconds on the gâteau.

'My client is worried about Kristen. She just seems to have dropped out of sight.' It was an unfortunate choice of words given Henry's handicap. 'He thought something might have happened to her. Something unpleasant. But you're positive she left here of her own accord?'

'Sure. She said she was going. And then she went. No mystery, darlin'.'

Evidently not. But I pressed Rachel for more information. Kristen, it seemed, had moved in last October.

'What was she like?' I asked. 'Shy? Friendly?'

'Not shy,' Rachel said, refilling our cups. 'Friendly? Yes, sometimes. Few times I invited her down to eat, and she's good company. We have a bottle of wine and chat; but only about the television programmes, or the films maybe. Or something in the papers. If I try to talk about her family, or where she come from, then suddenly I find we're talking about the TV again and don't know how we got back there.'

'Where did she work, do you know?'

Rachel shook her head. 'I asked her, several times. But it was one of the questions she, you know ...'

'Slid out from under?'

'Yes.'

'What about friends? Boyfriends?'

There was a fractional pause before she said: 'No. Not that I saw.'

'What about the other two flats? Might she have told them where she was going?'

'I shouldn't think so, darlin'. Ada ...' she stabbed a finger at her chandelier light fitting, 'over me, she's been in hospital since Christmas. I visit her three times a week, poor darlin'. And the Colemans next door had their first baby last year.' She patted the air with both hands like she was thumping an invisible keyboard. 'You never saw such crowds. Her mother; his mother; her sisters; his cousins ... you got to put your name down a year in advance if you want to baby-sit there.'

She sounded regretful. But I took her point. If Kristen was that reticent about her life with the effusively hospitable Rachel, it was unlikely she'd battled her way through hordes of Coleman relatives to confide in the new mum.

'I assume Kristen was renting the flat over the Colemans?'

'Number four,' Rachel agreed, popping in a mint.

'Is there anyone in it now?' Maybe they'd got a forwarding address for the mail.

'No. The place is empty. Kristen said someone was coming, but I suppose they changed their minds.'

'Are these places private? Or council?'

'Oh, private, darlin'. We all bought them. There's only me and Ada left from the originals now.'

'So who owns number four?'

'Guy Stevens. A nice boy. Inherited it from his grandfather. But he don't live there. He works on those cruise liners. Sends me lovely postcards from all over the world.'

'So the flat's rented out ... how?'

'Well, the agency does it, darlin'. This young man comes round sometimes, counts the sheets and knives and forks.'

'Inventory.'

'*Gesundheit.*'

Rachel chuckled. It was evidently an old joke.

'Which agency?'

'Weekes.'

I knew it. It was a small independent estate agent quite near my flat. Perhaps they could help. 'What's Kristen's surname?'

'Keats. Like the poet.'

A double K; it more or less confirmed I'd got the right woman.

'Tell me, Rachel, did Kristen ever mention someone called Bertram?'

'No. Why? Who is he?'

I hadn't the faintest idea. But since it was the only name Henry had been able to come up with, it seemed worth checking out. Reluctantly I drained my fourth cup of coffee and said I'd better be going. 'Thanks for lunch.'

'This? It's nothing. All I do is heat the coffee. You come back for dinner and I show you what a good cook I am. You promise?'

'It's a deal. I'll give you a ring.'

She beamed and scribbled her number on a scrap of paper before showing me to the hall.

Something occurred to me as I looked up the short flight of stairs to the top floor. 'If Kristen had sold you her car, how did she move her stuff?'

'There wasn't that much. Just a couple of suitcases. A car picked her up.'

'A mini cab?' I asked hopefully.

'I thought so at the time. It was a big car like they have. Four doors.'

'But now you don't think so?'

Rachel scooped up Balthazar, who was twisting around our legs in a pathetic display of imminent starvation. 'I don't know, darlin'. See, I think he came back to look for her.'

'When?'

'A few days after she left. In the morning. I don't bother to get up early no more. What's the point? There's always more than enough day left when I do. So anyway, Balthazar and I are lying in bed, listening to the radio, when I hear this noise upstairs. Like someone's knocking at the flat.'

'How'd they get through the front door?' I asked, recalling the security system on the block entrance.

Rachel patted the air again. 'The Coleman boy. He goes out to work early. He never closes the front door behind him properly. My Saul told him off about it more than once.'

'So did you see the dawn knocker?'

'No. Not really, darlin'. I got up to tell them there was nobody in up there. But he'd gone.'

'Then how do you know it was the same bloke? It could have been anyone.'

Rachel shrugged. 'When I look out the front, there's this big car going down the road again.'

'Did you get a look at the driver?'

'No. First time, when he picks Kristen up, it's rainy and dark and he doesn't get out of the car. She puts the cases in the boot and gets in beside him. And the second time, I just saw the car driving away.'

'Are you certain the driver was a man?'

'Now you come to mention it, no. I guess I'm just old-fashioned. If it's a big car, I assume it belongs to a man. A dick substitute, isn't that what they call it?'

Maybe *they* did. But I was a bit surprised Rachel did.

She chuckled and tapped my arm. 'I got that one from Kristen. She could be fun, you know. Once she brought down this video – men dancing. At least that's what the label said. They never danced like that in my day – more's the pity.'

The car had been a dark colour, but she had no idea what make.

Maybe the estate agent would be more help.

CHAPTER 7

Perhaps I'd win the lottery or wake up and find my fairy godmother had granted me a perfect 36C bust. Either was more likely than this estate agent being helpful.

I wondered if I could do him under the Trades Description Act. After all, their advertising assured me: *'Seven days to a sale equals a Weeke. Try us. We are here to help.'*

The estate agency was sandwiched between a launderette and a general grocery store opposite the Dog and Duck public house. Lingering on the pavement, I'd read the neon-coloured cardboard stickers advertising bargains in baked beans and soap powder for a few moments whilst I tried to see between the display boards in next door's window.

There seemed to be two figures moving around in there. Edging a little closer whilst scanning the 'des res' and 'to let' notices, I made out a man sitting at the front desk, apparently speaking to someone who was out of my sight at the rear of the office.

She'd appeared after a few seconds, shrugging a coat on, and dropping a bunch of keys into the bloke's front desk drawer. Clipping out of the door and across to a yellow convertible parked at the kerb, she shouted back: 'One hour max, Jason. They're time-wasters, I'd bet my bonus on it.'

I'd let her drive away and then gone in myself. Jason sprang up, pushing a floppy blond fringe from his eyes and flashing a perfect set of white teeth. He looked about twelve.

'Hi. Jason Weekes. Really great to meet you. We're glad you've chosen Weekes. Whatever it is – selling, buying, renting – we can do it for you. And we can do it a hundred per cent better than the rest. In the next five years we'll be the biggest estate agent in the south. Ten years the whole country.'

I'd asked him how many branches he had at the moment.

'Well, just this one, actually. But I only took over at Christmas. My dad ran things just like his father did. You've got to move with the times. Duck, dive, weave, turn problems to your advantage. So what's it to be? Penthouse? Country cottage?'

I'd been tempted to say 'penthouse' just to test my theory that he hadn't got any on his books. Instead I'd made a fatal mistake. I'd told him the truth.

Working on the 'all professionals together' routine, I'd flashed my business card and explained I needed information on a former tenant of number 4 Beamish Court.

The effusive charm vanished. He still looked twelve. But the sort of twelve that promises he and a few mates will be sorting you out in an alley after school unless you hand over your dinner money.

'Our files are totally confidential. Now, if that's all you want, darling ...'

I wanted him to promise he'd never call me 'darling' again. But I kept my own smile in place, and added a dash of pleading. 'My client is very worried. He's afraid something may have happened to Miss Keats. Couldn't you at least check if she left a forwarding address?'

'No.'

'No she didn't leave one? Or no you can't check?'

'Both. So if you're not interested in moving ...'

'Well, I had been thinking about it actually ... My flat's a bit cramped ...'

The twelve-year-old choirboy reappeared. 'Ah right, now you're cooking. Buy or rent?'

'Well ... renting, I guess ... One or two bedrooms ... lounge ... fitted kitchen ...'

Jason was nodding and tapping in details on his computer screen as I spoke. 'If I could take an address? And phone number?'

I gave him the office's.

'Great, great ...' He filled in the final box and sent me

44

whirling on to the hard disk. The cursor responded by spitting back lines of numbers.

Leaning across, he flicked up sheets from assorted files in the nearest cabinet. 'Here you are ... can I call you Grace?'

'Why not? After all we're already on terms of endearment ... *darling*.'

At least he blushed whilst handing over the details of about a dozen flats. 'They're all local. But if you were thinking of moving out a bit ...'

'No. This will do fine for now.'

'Great. Take a look through. Let me know which ones you want to view and I'll fix you up pronto.'

I fanned the sheets and scanned them quickly. Beamish Court wasn't there, which suggested Rachel had been right about it already being re-let.

'What about that one?' I pointed to a board of photographed properties beyond the woman's desk at the back of the shop.

Jason moved across to take a look. 'Which?'

'Next board ...' I directed. 'Up the top. Is that flats?'

'No. Sorry. Detached house. Five bedrooms. Three-quarters of an acre. Lovely property.'

'Bit out of my price range. I'll get back to you.'

He held the door open to let me out. It had a Yale lock. The back door probably didn't, since there was only one Yale key on the ring I'd just taken from his top desk drawer whilst he was negotiating the pictures in the display board at the rear of the shop.

I can pick basic-type locks, but it's a hellishly fiddly business that takes ten times longer than you'd allowed. And as for sliding a credit card into the gap like they do on the TV – forget it. What you'll end up with is a busted plastic oblong. And if you're really lucky, one end will have broken off and jammed in the lock so that the police have something nice and clear to go on when they start trying to trace you.

There was a shoe repair and instant key-cutting booth up in North Bay. I used the back roads since from the odd glimpses I caught of the front, the main promenade route was now well and truly gridlocked with day-trippers' cars.

By my reckoning I had forty minutes until Jason's assistant

got back, and even then I had to pray that none of the filing cabinets were locked and he didn't need to use the keys.

Apparently he didn't, since he looked pleased to see me when I abandoned the car once again and shot back into the estate agency.

'Hi! So decided already? Which viewings can I fix up for you?'

'Actually, no. There was one thing I forgot to ask. Are there any restrictions on pets?'

'Hey, no problemo, I'm sure.' Jason thrust the fringe from his eyes again and gave me a we-can-work-this-out wink. 'I mean, like, if we're talking tropical fish or a budgie here?'

'Not exactly.'

'Cat? Dog?'

'Vietnamese pot-bellied pigs.'

'You what?'

'They were so sweet when I got them. But I must admit they have been putting on weight a bit recently. In fact they're becoming quite ... porky ... although I wouldn't say so in front of them. They're very sensitive, you know.'

'Is this a wind-up?'

'Certainly not!'

'Oh, right ... er ... well ...'

He wasn't quite sure. I kept a straight face.

'Well ... maybe you should go for a cottage? We've got a couple of ...'

'Absolutely not. I want a flat. It's OK. Andy and Fergie are house-trained.'

'Yes ... er ... look, I don't think ...' Jason squared his shoulders. You didn't get to be the biggest estate agent in the south by falling at the first hurdle. 'Look, Grace, leave it with me, OK? I'll get back to you.'

I gave him my widest smile and put an arm round his shoulders. His head came up to my chin. 'No problemo, Jason. I know we're going to crack this one together.'

'Yeah ... sure ... absolutely ...'

He wriggled out from my arm and held the door open for me.

'See ya then, Jason! I'll tell Andy and Fergie you're rooting for them!'

I gave him a matey wink and sauntered out, satisfied that I'd managed to get the keys back in his jacket pocket without him noticing.

(Yes, all right, I know they were in the drawer originally, but would you risk a thousand-pound bet on the exact location of your keys at this moment?)

According to the sign on the door, the estate agency closed at five thirty, but unfortunately the grocery store and the launderette both stayed open until late.

I checked out the back of the shops and found the small yards were only divided by wire-link fencing which gave a clear view all along the parade. As I was hanging around wondering whether I dared risk it, a woman came to the back door of the laundry and lit up a cigarette. Standing on the back step, she blew smoke rings whilst having a shouted conversation with someone in the shop.

The grocer's door opened and an arm threw out several old cardboard boxes to join the pile already in the yard.

Plainly this was a busy little ol' yard.

In the end I left it until gone eleven before slipping back. I hadn't noticed any alarms when I was in the shop, but nonetheless I held my breath as I inserted the door key, twisted and pushed gently.

It was silent enough for the car horns, shouting and all-pervasive 'shush' of the ocean to float over the rooftops from the beach front. I stepped inside, relocking the door behind me and keeping a shaded torch pointed downwards.

This back room was obviously used as a combined rest room, storage area and general office. There was a small sink, and a cupboard with a kettle on top and mugs, coffee, sugar, biscuits, etc. inside. A few boxes stacked against one wall contained printed sheets of details of properties for sale and rent, and a two-drawer cabinet held office stationery and cartridges for the fax. The rest of the furniture consisted of a couple of ancient plastic chairs and a battered desk which held the combined fax/copy machine. Unlike the front offices, which looked like they'd recently been redecorated and recarpeted, this room was still the tattered and stained pale primrose that had probably been chosen by Jason's dad.

There was a door in the right-hand wall and I opened it just to check it didn't lead to a top flat. I didn't want the tenant tripping down while I was in the middle of breaking into Jason's files.

It was just a tiny loo and washroom with a small extractor fan providing the ventilation.

The only thing worth investigating seemed to be a padlocked cabinet affixed to the back office wall. Locating the correct key from my new collection, I opened it.

Six wooden battens were screwed along the back of the cabinet, with a dozen hooks to each. About half had keys hanging from them. I flicked the labels over and found Beamish Court on the top row. Four keys: two for the front door of the block and two for the flat, at a guess.

I found myself hoping none of Jason's clients had left anything valuable at home. This place was a burglar's goldmine.

The front of the shop was trickier to move about in. With no blinds, any torch, even a shaded one, was going to be seen from the pavement. Trying to keep myself between the windows and the light, I investigated the cabinet Jason had used first.

The files seemed to run alphabetically by the property address. By rights Beamish Court should have been between Appletree Yard and Bream's Road. It wasn't.

I flicked further back, hoping it had been misfiled. It hadn't.

Frustrated, I slammed the drawer back none too gently. And for the first time noticed the neat lettering under the 'A–F' marker. It said 'Active'.

Either these were athletically motivated files or this was Jason's shorthand for 'Unsold and Unlet'. I flashed the torch over the next cabinet and found this lot were 'Sorted'.

Relocking the first cabinet, I explored this one and found the file for Beamish Court in the top drawer. I carried it into the back room where I could use the torch more freely, settled myself at the desk, opened the cardboard cover and worked backwards through the filed documents.

The first sheet was a brief formal letter from Jason dated four days ago:

Mr D. Green,
9 Buckingham Road
Dover
Kent

Dear Mr Green,

RE: 4 BEAMISH COURT

Whilst I am very sorry to hear of your marital difficulties I must remind you of the terms of our above agreement and point out that if we do not receive a full month's rent by the end of May then we must consider your rental of this property at an end and make the necessary arrangements to return your deposit and relet to another tenant.

Yours sincerely,

Jason Weekes

Managing Director

I turned to the sheet underneath and found a closely written three-page letter from Mr Green. 'Marital difficulties' seemed an understatement in the circumstances; as far as I could judge, Mr Green was in a state of full-blown warfare with the soon-to-be-ex Mrs Green (a.k.a. *the money-grabbing, duplicitous, unnatural slag*). At present Mr Green seemed to be in the family home fighting a rearguard action to prevent Mrs Green stripping up the garden lawn, pond, ornamental birdbath and entire contents of the garden shed/workroom.

It was gripping stuff; I bet their neighbours never needed to watch *EastEnders*.

Reluctantly I turned over again and found two references, one from Barclays Bank and the other from a car dealership, both vouching for D. Green's suitability as a tenant. Under that was the rental agreement he'd signed, which showed that he should have taken up the tenancy on 1 May.

I turned that and found a photocopy of a handwritten note from Jason addressed to K. Keats.

20th April

Dear Kristen,

Re our telecon – sorry, I've checked and my colleague has

already signed up next tenant from 1 May onwards, so 'fraid can't let you hang on until Friday. Must ask you to vacate on Thursday 30th as arranged; please drop keys off at office by close of business Thurs. and I'll have your deposit refund ready (cash as agreed).

(However, I have a spare bed if that would help you out – perhaps we could discuss over a drink? I'll ring you later.)

Jason

Had she given him a ring, perhaps? I made a mental note to check whether Jason drove a four-doored, dark-coloured car and read on.

The next letter was a brief formal notice from Kristen dated 29 March giving a month's notice on her tenancy.

It was beginning to look more and more like I was wasting Henry's money. She'd plainly known for weeks that she intended to leave. Perhaps he'd built up their relationship to be far more than it really was. No doubt she'd get around to posting his audio tapes back to him one day.

I ploughed on. Receipts showed Kristen had paid her rent on the first of each month by cash. There were two references. One was from a letting agency in Leicester and confirmed that Miss Kristen Keats had proved a satisfactory tenant on two occasions; on the first she'd been a joint tenant of a house in Earl Shilton approximately five years ago; on the second she'd rented a one-bedroomed flat in Leicester for six months some two years ago.

The other reference was from a local company. It was dated the end of the previous September, signed by S. Ayres, and informed Mr Weekes that Miss Kristen Keats was employed by them as a test engineer.

I'd been reading backwards, letting my eyes slide up from the bottom and coming to the heading on the notepaper last. The company logo was something of a surprise. I'd half expected some one-man-and-his-dog outfit, turning out lumps of metal in a grotty prefab-type industrial shed. But Wexton Engineering was a decent middle-sized business, occupying a fair-sized factory on the outskirts of the town.

I was aware of a few preconceptions diving face-first into the dust. Somehow, what with Figgy's description of 'a babe' and Rachel's assertion that Kristen had been reluctant to discuss her job, I'd been unconsciously building up a picture of something a bit more salacious, such as an exotic dancer, and – OK let's admit it – someone not too bright, even if she was into Charles Dickens in a big way.

Now it looked like Kristen was the sort of girl you hated in school – beauty and brains combined.

I flipped back in the file and confirmed that – apart from her tenancy agreement – there was nothing else relating to Kristen. All the other papers were connected to earlier tenancies, plus the odd bit of correspondence from the flat-owner complaining about delays in forwarding the rent.

Shutting the file, I stood up ready to take it back to the front of the shop – and nearly dropped the lot from shock.

The combination of moonlight and torch-beam outside was just enough to let me make out the outline of the WPC's helmet moving quietly down the yard towards the back door.

I'd underestimated Jason. The sneaky little devil must have a silent alarm installed in here somewhere.

CHAPTER 8

I got my own torch off and dropped to the floor without any conscious effort on my part.

The first thing I knew about it I was sitting crushed into the corner with my legs drawn up into my chest, whilst the white beam of light stabbed downwards through the back window – sending thick ink-black reflections of the security bars across the scuffed floor.

The light moved back to the door. The handle rattled and shook, then the circle of illumination disappeared abruptly as the torch was turned off. Perhaps it was just a random check by the beat officer rather than a response to an alarm call.

Nothing much seemed to be happening, except my heart was getting an aerobic work-out here. I strained to hear footsteps moving back to the gate and was frustrated by the roar of a late-night express train suddenly howling past on the tracks that ran behind the shops.

Keeping myself pressed against the wall, I stood cautiously, and shuffled sideways until I could glance through the toughened glass panel in the top section of the door.

The WPC's hat was no more than six inches from my nose. Thankfully she was turned away, her shoulders hunched in a manner that suggested she was talking into the radio fixed to her top pocket.

Dropping to a crouch, I crossed the floor while she still had her back to me and got to the entrance to the shop. The street lighting and picture windows in the front would have given me a nice clear view of the police car parked outside, even if it hadn't been attracting attention by sending blue beams scything across the carpet in regular sweeps.

Another car was pulling up behind it. At least that answered one question. Jason drove a (very old) Porsche; which probably eliminated him as the caller Rachel had seen driving away from Kristen's flat.

From my half-huddled position on the floor by the open door, I watched Jason having an argument with the officer. I couldn't make out the words, but the waving hands and tossed fringe were pretty graphic. I almost expected him to stamp his foot.

Instead he suddenly produced a bunch of keys, thrust one into the door and pushed, letting in a breeze that made loose sheets of paper rear up in the filing trays.

His voice filled the silence, making me realise that the front windows of the shop must be double-, if not triple-glazed, to cut out the sound. Which was probably why I hadn't heard the police car approaching.

'... you can see for yourself the place is locked up. I don't see why you have to drag me away from a party to do your job ...'

'You're the key-holder. You're on the list. Sir.'

I'd have known the voice, even if the square-shouldered, square-headed outline hadn't been familiar. Not only Jason, but my favourite copper as well: Terry Rosco – chauvinist porcine *extraordinaire*.

'Didn't it strike you as the teeniest bit unlikely that a

bloody burglar would lock up after himself? Look, see for yourself … computers intact …'

There was a loud slap as Jason's palm came into contact with the VDU.

'Cabinets secure …'

I could hear him dragging at the drawers I'd recently relocked. Crouched against the wall, I was keeping one eye on the back and praying the WPC would move round to the unlocked front door and join Terry. But the girl had obviously remembered her training. She was sticking to that back entrance in case the intruders were flushed out. Damn her.

'Petty cash intact …'

Metal jingled against tin in the front office.

'Now if you could use a bit of intelligence in future and stop calling me out every time a train goes over the damn points and sets the effing alarm off …'

'I'd do something about that if I were you, sir …'

'Really? And what do you suggest? Ask Railtrack to reroute the south-coast lines?'

'Get another alarm. Before we start charging you for wasting our time, mate.'

'You can't do that …'

I pay my taxes … I finished silently for him.

'I pay my taxes …' Jason snapped.

'So do all the poor sods we can't get to because we have to keep coming round here every time the eleven twenty puts his foot down.'

I was almost prepared to put my prejudices on hold and like Terry for a good three seconds there, until he added: 'What about the back?'

'What about it?'

'Best have a look now we're here.'

Oh, thanks a bunch, Terry!

There was nowhere to hide. Even the central section of the old desk was a straight-through design, rather than closed off at the front by a nice old-fashioned modesty board.

There was nothing for it but to bluff it out. I straightened up and was conscious of the file crackling against my stomach. I must have stuffed it down the front of my jogging pants when I dived for the corner.

Taking it out, I slipped it into the nearest open box of property details. The keys went into another box.

Jason had actually set one foot in the back room when Terry's radio crackled into life.

'Hang on …'

Terry retreated towards the front door, muttering into his transmitter as he went. Jason took a few steps back as well.

In the darkness they hadn't spotted me standing silently against one wall behind the door. On a sudden impulse, I darted into the tiny washroom as Terry called back down the shop.

'We've got another shout. Bunch of toe rags causing bother up the arcade, so if you're sure everything's OK back here … Sir?'

'Isn't that what I've been telling you for the past ten minutes? Do you want me to count the effing digestive biscuits as well, or can I get back to my party now?'

'Soon as you like, mate.'

I let out my breath in a sigh of thankfulness and promised to give generously to the poor in future.

'Mind if I take a slash before we go?'

To hell with the poor, I groaned.

The door was thrust open, trapping me behind it. Terry didn't bother to put the light on. Holding my breath, I listened to the zipper parting company and Terry tinkling against the porcelain.

The temptation to scream 'Boo!' at the top of my lungs was almost irresistible. But I resisted – just.

Thankfully Terry was a natural slob. Readjusting his trousers with a satisfied grunt, he crashed down the flush and left without using the washbasin behind him.

Putting the seat down, I sank on to it, letting my tensed muscles relax, and stayed there for twenty minutes before retrieving the keys, replacing the file and slipping out the way I'd come.

I went straight home and celebrated Saturday night with a bag of chips in bed. Frankly, it was all the excitement I could take.

Sunday's weather looked to be even better than Saturday's. Judging by the small section of sky visible from my front basement window, there wasn't a cloud in the eggshell-blue dome that was arcing over the ex-boarding houses opposite.

This front section of the flat was one huge room which served as a living/sleeping/eating area. Originally it was the kitchens of the boarding house, but someone had started to convert the building at some time in the past, so that the internal staircase to the ground floor was now blocked off and a separate gas and electricity meter had been installed for each floor. As well as this room, I had two smaller ones at the back of the house. One was the bathroom and the other was a narrow, windowless area which I'd designated 'the guest bedroom' since I kept a spare fold-up bed in there.

I hadn't bothered to set the alarm clock, since there was very little I could do on either of the cases today – apart from contacting Henry and telling him I thought his particular problem was a non-starter.

After a fairly leisurely breakfast (cornflakes and Ribena, I'd forgotten the milk again), I pulled on a T-shirt and sarong skirt prior to hitting the town.

Just before I left, I checked the telephone directory, made a note of the number for Wexton Engineering and found that there was no builder listed under the name of 'Laurence Payne' (or any other 'Payne' if it came to that), nor did Tom Skerries – Bone's missing boyfriend – seem to be on the telephone at home.

It was pretty much a rerun of Saturday along the front – only more so. All the locals who'd been busy hitting the supermarkets and hoovering the bedrooms yesterday were now staking their claims on the beach; spreading towels, setting up deckchairs and banging in windbreaks to define their patch of sand. Within an hour or so the first arrivals from the M25 would be filling up the gaps until the whole of the yellow-grey areas were heaving with oiled flesh.

'Just my luck to be heading north the first decent weekend we get,' Annie remarked, clicking down the locks on her suitcase and adding it to the overnighter already standing on her lounge floor.

'You can always go to Blackpool,' I suggested.

I'd cut round via the park in order to wish her good hunting and run my theories re the probably-not-missing Kristen Keats past her. 'I'll miss you.'

'Yeah. No one to scrounge biscuits and coffee from at work,' she snorted, disappearing into the kitchen.

'Cynic,' I grinned, finishing off the ones I'd just helped myself to.

'Realist.'

Her voice echoed from the depths of the fridge. She briskly dropped partially used cheese, milk carton and vegetables into a plastic carrier and pushed it at me. 'Here, throw these in the bin on your way out. They won't keep.'

'How long you expecting to be gone?'

'Depends what I find. Couple of weeks maybe.'

She locked up the flat and we made our way down to the ground floor and across to where her car was waiting by the park railings.

'Want me to water the plants or anything?'

'No, you're OK. Zeb's going to keep an eye on the place. Bye.'

Having waved her off, I couldn't put off the moment any longer. I headed northwards, ready to face one of the tasks I disliked most in the world.

CHAPTER 9

'Left?'

'Scarpered, checked out, moved on to pastures new,' I elaborated, since Henry seemed to be having difficulty with 'left'. I'd already repeated it three times.

I'd come up here with the intention of refunding some of his advance. It's always a wrench for me to give back money after it's made itself at home in my heart, but in the circumstances not doing so would have seemed like stealing money from a blind man's pocket.

'She – Kristen – gave a month's notice on her flat. And she told her neighbour she was going. It's pretty water-tight,

Henry. She intended to go – and she went. QED, as they say. I'm sure she'll get the tapes back to you. Probably planning to pop back for a visit once she's settled wherever.'

Henry didn't look convinced. At least as far as I could tell behind the bottle-green-tinged glasses he didn't. Even on a bright, sunny May morning, this room had a gloomy shadiness to it.

It was principally due to the large clump of rhododendron bushes that were tightly packed along the front garden wall, blocking out most of the light. At present they were decorated with feathery pom-poms of magenta, scarlet and apricot. But most of the time they must have been a solid wall of glossy green vegetation. I nearly asked Henry why he didn't have them trimmed back; but I stopped myself just in time.

St John's had been a classy address once. It was a continuation of one of the main shopping streets, and at the time most of the small double-fronted detached villas had been built, in the 1920s, they'd been intended for prosperous middle-class families.

Nowadays the sort of people who could pay for that amount of space bought it in one of the country villages, rather than in an area that was likely to be disturbed by the lager swiggers and candyfloss crunchers at weekends.

In the meantime the gardens in St John's had been mostly concreted or gravelled over to make small car parks, and the rooms were either bedsits, dentist's/doctor's surgeries or some kind of council-financed help group.

The house before Henry's was being used as a drug advice centre, and the one beyond it had the windows boarded up, but there was a notice announcing plans to turn it into a council playgroup.

'It was bad enough having the damn druggies moving in,' Henry had grumbled when he'd answered the door to me ten minutes previously. 'Most of them are muggers or house-breakers. But screaming brats one side and unwashed addicts the other – it really doesn't bear thinking about. Would you buy a property in that situation?'

'I guess not. Are you moving then?'

'Thinking about it,' he'd admitted, showing me into the

sitting room. 'Mind, I've been thinking about it for the past twenty years. If only I'd matched deed to thought, I shouldn't be venting my spleen on you now. Take a seat. Throw the dog off if he's in your way. He thinks I don't know he slips on the furniture when I'm not looking. Don't you, Beano old boy?'

He gave a sharp bark of laughter, as if this was a private little joke between them.

A black, shaggy-coated retriever cross who was lying across a deep armchair raised his head briefly from a tangle of front legs and waved a desultory tail.

'Been a bit off-colour. Reason I didn't bring him along the other day.'

Taking the matching chair across the fireplace, I asked if he managed to get around all right without the dog.

'Oh, yes. He's not a regular guide dog. Not trained, I mean. He just knows my little ways. Been flying solo for years. Do it with my eyes closed, you might say. Cup of coffee before you make your report, m'dear?'

He declined my offer of help in the kitchen, giving me time to take a quick look round the room. Beano's suspicious eyes swivelled with me as I prowled, taking in the dark, heavy, old-fashioned furniture. The curtains and carpets were from the same period. Expensive when bought forty-odd years ago, but now showing distinct signs of coming to the end of their rot-by date.

It took a second to realise what was odd about the room: there were no ornaments, pictures or mirrors. The television set and video recorder were also anachronisms. I could see the point of the hi-fi, but what was he going to do with a video?

I checked the banks of audio tapes in a glass-fronted cabinet and discovered that about a third were book readings and dramatised plays, and another third were classical music and dance-band stuff. The remainder were hard to classify because they were proprietary brands of tapes which I assumed Henry had used to make his own recordings. All the boxes had coloured plastic strips with raised dots taped to their spines. Braille, I guessed. I'd never actually seen it before.

Opening the bottom section of the cabinet, I found a well-stocked drinks cupboard. And judging by the labels, Henry didn't believe in buying cheap when expensive would do.

'Would you prefer a stronger snifter?'

His Moroccan leather slippers had let Henry slide up on me. He was staring straight ahead over the coffee tray, but I daresay he knew the sounds of his own cupboard doors.

'Sorry. Penalty of the job. Terminal nosiness.'

'I see.'

He moved with confidence across the room, lowered the tray on to the coffee table and poured two cups, using his thumb to judge the level.

'Could you help yourself to milk and sugar?' He leant forward, the cup waving slightly as he waited for me to intercept.

As I accepted it, he over-balanced and tilted forward, putting out his free hand to stop the fall. My sarong skirt had fallen open as I sat down, but I hadn't bothered to adjust it since the dog hadn't seemed upset by a view of my knickers. Now Henry's questing hand landed smack on my thigh and sent a chill across the bare flesh.

'Good lord, m'dear, are you wearing any clothes?'

'Er ... yeah.' Trying to balance the jiggling cup, I hastily dragged the sarong edges together and tucked them between my legs whilst knowing it was a stupid gesture. He was hardly in a position to notice if I was sitting here stark naked. Was he? Once again I'd had a terrible urge to snatch off those featureless glasses and waggle my fingers in front of his face.

I'd covered over the moment by giving him a quick run-down of the progress on his case. Which had taken all of two minutes and left him repeating blankly: 'Left? *Left?*'

'I thought I'd best come round and tell you straight off. I'll knock some kind of bill up and drop it in during the week with what's left of your advance, OK?'

'You mean you're bailing out on me?'

'Well ...'

'Just because Kristen has moved doesn't mean she's left town, does it? Might just have found new digs.'

'I guess so.'

Personally I didn't think so. Why make such a mystery of it in that case? And why sell her car? My money would be on her finding a new job, complete with company car, well out of this district.

'You could give Wexton Engineering a ring tomorrow,' I suggested. 'I expect they've a forwarding address for her.'

'I'd rather you did that, m'dear. If you have no objections to continuing our partnership?'

I hadn't any at all. After all, I was getting paid for it. But I felt obliged to point out it was an expensive way of placing phone calls.

'I don't mind the money. What else do I have to spend it on, apart from Beano?'

The dog waved a lazy tail in response to its name.

'Are you still on the furniture, you rascal? Come on.' Henry clicked his fingers sharply.

With a yawn, Beano ambled over, sniffed me delicately – and poked his nose in a very personal place.

'Do you mind, you cheeky mutt, I hardly know you.' I struggled to dislodge the enthusiastically sniffing nostrils. Beano seemed to take it as encouragement to push harder.

'What's he up to?' Henry followed the dog's backbone up over his head, down the muzzle and around the moist nose. 'Come out of there.'

Cupping the muzzle, he managed to get the slobbering beast out of my crutch. I hastily rearranged the sarong and reclamped my legs together.

'I'm so sorry about that. If it's acceptable to you, Grace, I'd prefer it if you did the initial recce at Wexton's. I don't wish to look … foolish.'

'Fair enough. I'll get back to you soon as I have a line on Kristen. OK?'

'A–OK,' Henry beamed.

The front was well and truly buzzing by now. Crowds were wandering up and down along the seaside promenade and milling around the entrance to the games arcades, rock shops and souvenir booths.

The children's play area was doing brisk business on the

swing boats, roundabout and trampolines, and a light wind was teasing at the striped canvas fringes of the Punch-and-Judy booth which had already set up for business.

Further away, on the cusp between the powdered dry sand and the wet flats left by the retreating tide, a string of donkeys plodded placidly up and down with small children clamped to their high-sided saddles and a medium-sized figure in dark trousers, rolled-up shirtsleeves and a battered straw trilby following at the end of the string.

All in all, I decided, it wasn't a bad old place to live at times.

The sun was burning down on the back of my neck and arms, reminding me I ought to buy some suntan oil. Fortunately I don't burn easily. The blonde hair is out of a packet and my skin type has more in common with my brown eyes than Scandinavian-type fairness.

I wandered along to the kiosk where I'd stopped with Figgy the other day, and asked for the cheapest bottle they stocked.

'That'll be six pounds eight pee, love.'

'You what! They charge less for the stuff they pump out of the ground!'

'Well, love, if you want to rub raw petroleum over yerself, be my guest. You want this, it's six pounds eight pee.'

Once I'd greased myself up like a chip destined for the fryer, I flicked off my sandals, carried them over the sands and helped myself to a seat on the upturned bucket that served the donkeys' owner as a chair.

'Afternoon, December.'

December Drysdale nodded his hellos before taking off the trilby and running the back of his forearm over his head and a pair of eyebrows the texture of scouring pads. 'Aft'noon, lass. Who's next then?'

The first child in the queue for rides pushed forward and pointed: 'I wanna ride that one.'

December folded his arms and glared down at her. 'And what's the magic word?'

Blue eyes widened. 'Dunno.'

'*Please*. I want to ride that one, *please*.'

A larger boy behind her swaggered forward. 'Don' yer tell

our Chantal to say no fucking please. We're paying, ain't we? You gotta do what we say, Grandad.'

'I'm not your grandad, son. Some other poor devil's got that problem. And anyone who wants to ride my donkeys says *please*. Got it?'

'Stuff it then. C'mon, Chantal, we'll go on the trampolines 'stead.'

As a piece of business acumen, telling your customers to get lost might not strike you as too bright. But what most people didn't know about December was that running the donkey string was more or less a hobby as far as he was concerned. He did it because he loved them.

He actually lived on the income from being part-owner of one of the busiest nightclubs along this stretch of coast, plus assorted bingo halls, cinemas and a considerable collection of shrewd business investments that he'd been building up for the past forty-odd years. Which – apart from the fact that he'd become a friend during my last case – was one of the reasons I wanted to talk to him.

I waited until he'd finished the next trip before joining him at the head of the queue and helping to lift the next lot of paying customers into position. Several of the donkeys came across and nuzzled at me, whickering moist breath into my hair. They remembered me. I felt absurdly privileged.

Once they made tracks along the beach again, I fell into step beside December at the rear and we followed the hypnotically swaying tail of a donkey who went under the name of Errol Flynn.

'Where are you stabling them now?' I asked.

During my last case, December's donkey stables had ended up partially burnt to the ground and I'd been lucky not to go up with them.

'Farm where I winter them. I brought them in in the horsebox this morning. It's a bit of a bother, but I didn't want to disappoint the kiddies. And it'll only be for the week. This weather'll break by the weekend.'

'How do you know?' I scanned the sky, expecting some bit of countryman's lore relating to early-nesting gulls or fur-covered crabs.

'Bank holiday, isn't it? And half-term. Stands to reason.'

We'd reached the furthest point of the donkeys' route. They wheeled on an invisible roundabout, Lana (Turner), the big lead grey, taking them round in an arc before the leisurely trek back.

'So what can I do for you, lass?'

'What makes you think this isn't a social visit?'

'Is it?'

'No.'

'Well then?'

'I was hoping you might be able to fill me in on a couple of companies. Wexton Engineering for starters.'

'One of our few local manufacturing industries.'

'Yeah, I know that.' Even I'd recognised the name. They cropped up occasionally in the local papers doing their civic duty for the area by sponsoring flowerbeds and carnival floats, or donating computer software to the local primary school. I said as much to December. My natural suspicion of businesses who want to kid you they exist purely to serve the community must have tinged my tone.

'Nothing wrong with doing a bit for those less fortunate. Maybe if you tried it, people would like you better.'

I'd forgotten December's ability to go straight to the heart of the problem without feeling any necessity to travel via tact or diplomacy.

Maybe, I informed him tartly, if people liked me better, I'd be more inclined to do things for them.

'Maybe,' he agreed placidly. We'd reached the end of the ride and he loaded the next contingent of riders before asking me what I wanted to know about Wexton's.

'I was rather hoping you might have an "in". You know, own shares in the company or something.'

He shook his head. 'It's not a public company. The family still own it, far as I know.'

'The Wexton family?'

'I imagine so. Although I don't think there's been any Wextons on the board for years. Old Jack Wexton started it back before the last war. He did very well in that particular piece of unpleasantness. Made a fortune turning out machinery parts for the fighting forces, by all accounts. Trouble was, Jack never lived to enjoy it. Dropped dead a few years after the war ended. Bloke who runs it now is called Bridgeman. Stephen Bridgeman. Married to Jack's grand-daughter, I think.'

The breeze had strengthened slightly, sending a cooling draught to ruffle my sarong and tease my hair. Lifting up my face, I enjoyed the sensation, whilst my bare toes gripped the ribbed sands and squeezed the soft worm casts left on the surface.

December's gravelly tones broke into my thoughts. 'There were rumours they were in trouble a few years back.'

'What kind of trouble?'

'Financial. Same as most companies in the recession. Especially those who'd been relying on military contracts.'

We wheeled again. The deckchairs were encroaching on to the wet flats now, where there was more room for childish civil engineers to construct castles, ditches and complicated drainage channels. It would be hours before the sea rushed back to fill in their efforts. The tide here was a big one and the waves retreated for miles over flat sands. At the furthest point of low tide, the ocean would be no more than a silver ribbon on the horizon.

'Why those companies relying on military work especially?' I asked, returning to the subject of Wexton Engineering.

'Competition. Value for money. Free markets. And them other right-sounding phrases the government suddenly started throwing at the voters. See, before it was like a sort of exclusive club. You got on the list for government work, and after that they just kept putting in the repeat orders. Well, didn't have much choice really, did they? If they wanted more of your gizmos, they had to buy them from you. And since no one in their right mind ever made a gizmo that could be replaced by a rival manufacturer's gizmo, it was as good as printing your own money.'

'What do the government do now, then? Go on a gizmo diet?'

'Got a bit cannier, by all accounts. Nowadays, if they pay for the gizmo design, they make sure they've got the right to have anyone they choose build it. And if that happens to be the bloke who owns a shed under the bypass and can do them a good price because he hasn't got a massive great wages bill – well, that's got to be good for the tax-payers, hasn't it?'

'And this is what happened at Wexton's? They've been losing out to electronic sweatshops?'

'Partly. Mind, I don't say they're in a bigger hole than anyone else. There's lots of companies done a lot worse than them.'

Heaving a four-year-old off Errol's back and delivering the warm, sticky body back to its mum, I called across to December, 'Did you have money in these losers?'

He tapped the side of his nose. I knew him well enough by now to guess he'd got out in time.

December was momentarily distracted by the rearrival of Chantal. Presenting a clutched handful of silver, she pointed at a small brown donkey whose headband carried the gold lettering 'Bette' (as in 'Davis').

'I want to ride that one. *Please.*'

'Fair enough, lass. Up you come. Where's your brother then?'

'Up the first aid. I bit him.'

Once we were in motion again, December asked me why I was interested in Wexton's.

I gave him a brief run-down on the elusive Miss Kristen Keats. 'I reckon she's probably just moved on. But the chances are a new company would have asked for a reference … so if I can just get Wexton's to cough it up … case solved.'

'It sounds easy.'

I flicked a sideways glance at him. His expression was blandly noncommittal. '*Too* easy is what you mean, isn't it?'

'Did I say that?'

'No. But you have some pretty eloquent silences.'

His lips twitched. 'Well, let's face it, lass, you've a rare talent for turning the simple into a right can of worms. What was the other company you wanted to ask about?'

'Other?'

'A couple of companies, that's what you said at the start.'

'Oh? Yeah.' I'd nearly forgotten Bone's missing boyfriend. 'I'm trying to trace someone who works for a builder called

Laurence Payne. Only there's no builder of that name in the telephone directory. I wondered if you'd heard of him?'

December laughed, a deep bray that drew a sympathetic roar from Errol.

'Oh yes, lass. I know Larry Payne all right!'

CHAPTER 10

Apparently Laurence Payne had been on the doorstep clutching a quote for rebuilding December's stables almost before the firemen had finished damping down. December reckoned he had a contact in the fire service.

'Got others in the gas and water companies by all accounts,' December explained, decanting the latest lot of riders and propping up a handwritten notice which stated: *The Donkeys are Having a Rest for Five Minutes*. 'He pays a fee for every address where a bit of structural work might be called for.'

He'd taken the bucket, so I squatted down on the sands by him and drew my legs into my chest. 'Did you give him the job?'

'No.'

'Any particular reason?'

'I don't like what I've heard about his business methods.'

A burst of squawking from a flock of gulls who were squabbling over a discarded roll distracted me for a moment. Lifting, hovering and stabbing with vicious beaks, they ripped the stale bread to bits.

It reminded me I was hungry. I also discovered I was still lugging Annie's rubbish around with me. Delving inside the plastic carrier, I found a half-used carton of milk, a lump of cheese and assorted shrivelled vegetables.

Taking a swig from the carton, I nibbled the cheddar and offered a twisted carrot to Humphrey Bogart.

'Don't feed them on the beach, lass, you'll have all the kiddies round wanting to give them rock and candyfloss and heaven knows what.'

'Sorry.'

I put the carrot into the bag and left it lying on its side with a wink in Humphrey's direction.

With an expression of wide-eyed innocence, he lowered his head and started wandering casually across the sand, each shuffle of his hooves bringing the swinging muzzle a fraction closer to the discarded bag.

'Laurence Payne,' I prompted. 'You've heard rumours about him.'

'A lot of people have heard rumours about Larry Payne. Including the police, I'd have thought. I'm surprised you didn't when you were in the force.'

It was nice of him to put it that way; rather than *before you got kicked out*.

'He must have got past me. What's his claim to fame?'

'Divine intervention.'

'Sorry?'

'Acts of God tended to strike his rivals' work.'

'Oh.' I began to get the picture. 'Employ anyone other than Larry to put your windows in and you were up to your neck in broken glass next morning?'

'Something like that. Mind, it's been a while since there's been anything like that. Gone quite respectable these days, has our Larry. Got himself on a few committees. He wants to give something back to the community.'

'Why?'

'Because he fancies being Sir Larry.'

Humphrey had made it to the bag. With soft lips he mumbled the carrot out and swung his rump towards December.

'Where can I find his sir-ship?'

'His yard's along the coast in Winstanton. It's right behind the old oyster sheds. You can't really miss it. There's a big blue arch over the entrance. It trades as Swaylings.'

'I thought that place was a boat-builder's.'

'It was years back, when folks wanted fishing boats. I think it was Larry's dad who went in for the land rather than the sea. Another case of diversifying to suit your markets.'

'I don't suppose they work Sundays.'

'I'd say Larry would have them working any time he thought he could make a profit.'

I thought about my options. I could get up off this beach, wash off the oil, extract the car from its parking space, drive along to Winstanton, hope there was someone working at Payne's whom I could persuade to give me Tom Skerries' address, and then go round and try to talk him into letting Bone down gently.

Alternatively I could lie here for the rest of the afternoon and go through the above rigmarole tomorrow.

Peeling off the T-shirt, I handed December the sun oil. 'Can you do my back?'

December left at five o'clock. I helped him walk the string back up the slipway and load them into his friend's horsebox that would take them back to their temporary home on the farm.

We both stood for a moment looking back across the beach. The scent of warm suntan lotion rose in a thick miasma that was so dense you could almost touch it. Then I asked the question I'd been dying to ask all afternoon.

'How's Kevin?'

'He's very well. He'll be at the club later. Might drive in myself, after I've got the lads settled. I like to keep an eye on the books. You could drop in for a drink if you like.'

'Yeah ... well ... you know ... I'll see ... I might be busy later.'

'I don't expect you to pay for it.'

I guess I deserved that. If you dedicate your life to spending as little of your own money as possible, you have to develop a pretty tough skin. But for once damage to my wallet hadn't been on my mind.

Kevin was December's son. He managed The Electronic Daffodil, their jointly owned nightclub. I'd become involved with him during my last case – rather more heavily involved than I'd planned.

If I renewed our relationship now, Kevin would have reason to expect a full-frontal, no-holds-barred twosome from Day One. After all, I'd practically ripped his clothes off on our first meeting.

And to be blunt, I just wasn't sure I wanted to get that involved. Since my last real relationship had broken up soon after my ignominious departure from the police force, I'd been wary of getting seriously entangled. On the other hand, I couldn't see him wanting to go back a few weeks and revert to a *casual-drink-and-a-chat-if-you're-free*-type evening.

'I'm a bit tied up tonight,' I said.

I went back to the sands after he'd driven off, but they felt lonely now.

Lying on my back, I watched the sun sliding down behind the huge Beach Rock Hotel that stood guard over the western edge of the main beach. When the coloured lights started to come on along the promenade, I shook the grains from my clothes, dusted down the sticky coating that was clinging to my oil-covered skin, and wandered back on to the pavement.

The beach's loss was the prom's gain. The open arcades and bingo halls were packed. Over the back of the buildings a steady thump of music and rumble of heavy machinery was punctuated by loud squeals and laughter as the amusement park swung into full gear.

Even the beachward side of the main street was crowded with groups three and four deep as they grazed their way through cardboard cartons of chips, chicken nuggets, pizzas and cheeseburgers.

Everyone was making the day last as long as possible before they made the drive back to home and Monday-morning blues.

I was half tempted to join them, but for once I didn't feel very hungry. In the end I rescued the car and drove out to Wexton's Engineering, parked on a patch of scrubland fifty yards from the gate, and walked back to take a look at the place.

It was an L-shaped two storey-building protected by high fencing that looked fairly new and displayed snarling pictures of rabid dogs warning that the premises were guarded by security services.

The building itself didn't look like it dated from pre-war. So presumably the original company had moved premises – probably in the sixties or early seventies, I guessed, judging by the front entrance of the factory.

This section formed the shorter bar of the L and looked to be built of brick. The longer bar was more modern – glass and concrete. The section joining them was constructed of a far paler pink brick with whiter mortar, and looked to be a very recent addition to the uninspiring architecture.

The lights were on but I couldn't see any sign of movement inside, and the entrance gates were padlocked shut.

I returned to the car, put the car radio on and listened to the newscaster telling me Manchester had recorded their second hottest May temperature since records started. Motorways, needless to say, had been choked solid, queues had stretched for over twenty-five miles at one point, there had been several incidents of road-rage assaults and a bridge had collapsed due to metal expansion.

The good news, however, was that a low pressure area was swinging in from the west and temperatures were due to plunge by the end of the week.

On this happy note, I flicked the radio off and heard the approaching engine.

I expected it to go past, but instead a small, light-coloured van drew into the entrance to the factory. The driver got out, opened the gates, and swung them wide. A light came on beyond him, illuminating the car park area in front of the building and showing that the visitor was wearing the distinctive mustard-coloured uniform of Mackenzie's – a private security company.

I watched him drive a few feet inside, and walk back to the gates. Before he could close them fully, a motor-scooter came flying along the road at speed, flashing its headlight and sounding the horn.

My first thought – joyriders – was squashed when it turned into the entrance and stopped. The passenger pulled off her helmet and shook out a ponytail of red hair streaked with pink.

I couldn't hear the words but the pair seemed to be having some kind of argument with the guard. They won.

With a shrug of his shoulders, he opened the gate wide and motioned them in. The bike glided to a parking space by the main door whilst he locked up again. He didn't bother to move the van. Instead he flicked open the back doors and shouted a command.

Two large German Shepherds jumped to the ground, tails wagging eagerly. In response to more arm-waving and commands they sped off round the side of the building.

The bikers went inside with the guard. A few minutes later, the one with two-toned hair appeared in an upstairs office. I watched her emptying the waste-paper baskets into a large plastic sack.

Below her on the ground floor, another girl, her black hair cropped in a skinhead style, was spraying and dusting along windowsills.

I don't find housework all that riveting; either doing or watching. Restarting my engine, I cruised away and completed my tour of outstanding cases by visiting Payne's builders yard.

I parked at the back of the town by the Winstanton railway station and wandered down to the front on foot through the little streets of whitewashed fishermen's cottages.

It was all done for effect, of course. I doubt if the original oyster-catchers cared passionately whether their paintwork was up to scratch or their flower tubs kept up the tone of the area. But so what? I'm a sucker for a bit of olde-worlde window-dressing.

So I did the tourist bit – peering at unlikely curios in the antique shops; wandering along the harbour and silently marvelling at the guts of anyone actually buying and swallowing raw oysters from the snack bars along the harbour quay.

I made my way along the road to the gate whose white Roman lettering on a faded blue background arch announced it was 'Swayling's – Building Contractors'. Below in smaller letters was printed '(L. Payne and Son)'. The 'Son' had a large black cross painted over it.

The yard was dark and deserted. Standing by the locked gates, I peered through the bars and watched phosphorus playing over the ocean as it sucked and slooshed greedily over the shingle beach and teased at the old slipway.

The building in the centre of the yard looked like it might have belonged to the original boat-maker's. Probably a storage shed of some kind, I figured, making out the stone ground floor and the wooden upper storey with its outside staircase leading up to a single door.

Somehow I'd been expecting something a bit grander from a bloke who had his sights set on a knighthood. But perhaps Larry Payne reckoned there was more mileage in donating profits to party funds rather than sinking them back in the business.

Anyway there was no sense hanging around here. Tomorrow I'd make a quick call on Mr Payne, get Tom Skerries' address and sort out Bone's love life.

Had I been listening a little harder at this point, I'd probably have caught the Fates' ironic laughter beyond the crashing of the surf.

CHAPTER 11

'Off and bog – arrange into a well-known phrase.'

It was an interesting challenge.

I'd decided to phone Payne's yard first before I concentrated on the more elusive Kristen Keats. Sure enough, it was listed under 'Swayling's' in the local phone book.

The woman who answered was friendly enough at first, until I mentioned Tom Skerries' name.

'Tom? No, I'm sorry. I'm afraid we don't have anyone of that name working here, Mrs ... em ...?'

'Smith.'

'*Smith*?'

You could almost hear the *Oh yeah, pull the other one* flowing down the earpiece. I don't know why people imagine it's invented. If I was going to use a fake name, I'd pick something a bit more unusual than the most common surname in the country. Anyway, why did she think I needed to invent a pseudonym to speak to Mr Skerries?

'But you did have,' I persisted. 'He was working on a new wall at St Agatha's Girls' School a few months back.'

I caught a murmur of a deeper voice in the background.

The line became muffled for a moment, as if something had been placed over the receiver, and then she was back on, insisting they didn't know anyone called Skerries.

'Dark-eyed, dark-haired, a dead ringer for Heathcliff after a night out with the lads ...' I prompted. 'He was working on St Aggie's wall with a couple of other blokes called ...'

I hadn't taken my notes from the cabinet before I rang, and now I found I couldn't for the life of me remember what Bone had called the other two workmen.

'And are you from St Agatha's, dear?'

'No. I'm not. I left school years ago. But thanks for asking.'

The blanking of sound on the line announced that this information was being passed on. She came back to ask if I wanted a quote for building work.

'Er ... no thanks. I just need to speak to Tom Skerries. I couldn't find him in the phone book – so if you could give me a number, or an address?'

'I told you. We don't employ Tom Skerries.'

'Look, where's the big deal? You could have got the number in the time we've spent arguing.'

'I'm not arguing ... I ...'

She was cut off abruptly and a man's voice asked if it was about a job. 'Conservatory? Patio? Something like that, is it, love?'

'No. Is that Mr Payne?' I guessed.

'Yes. It is.'

'Well, it's like I was explaining to your secretary, Mr Payne, I just need to get in touch with Tom Skerries. He used to work for you ...'

'No he didn't. Now you listen to me. We don't know Tom Skerries. We have no number, address, date of birth or star sign for Tom Skerries. If you want some building work done then we should be happy to send one of our representatives round to give you a quote. Otherwise ... off and bog – arrange into a well-known phrase.'

His voice had been rising in volume. By the time he'd reached his final suggestion I had to hold the receiver away from my ear to avoid a punctured eardrum.

'Well, thank you very much, Mr Payne, for taking part in our magazine's telephone poll to find the most helpful builder in the county. We'll let you know when the results are to be published.'

I hung up while he was still spluttering.

Whatever Tom Skerries had done to upset the future Sir Larry, he'd obviously made a pretty good job of it. I put Bone's problem aside for a moment, and got down to tracking Kristen.

My first call, to Wexton's, produced the predictable information that Miss Keats didn't work there any more.

'Oh hell, you mean we've missed each other again.'

'I'm afraid so. Krissy went a few weeks back.'

'Blast. We're always doing this. We used to share a house up in Earl Shilton, near Leicester, you know?'

Unfortunately she *did* know. Apparently she'd lived up that way herself and she and Krissy had actually used the same local pub!

'Not at the same time, of course, because it's at least fifteen years since my husband and I moved down here ... but still, it's *amazing*, isn't it, coming all this way and then finding someone who actually knows the *very* bar ...'

Since the only contact I'd ever had with Leicestershire was driving through it, I pushed the conversation on quickly.

'Krissy and I ran into each other a couple of months ago. And we absolutely swore we'd get together this time ... I've been meaning to phone her for weeks ... but you know how it is ...'

She did. She sympathised with the way time just *flew* by. But she couldn't help me. 'I've just no idea where Krissy went. She was quite *mysterious* about it. Although she did promise to stay in touch. In fact, I was only saying to Suzie last week ...'

'That would be Suzie Ayres, would it ...?' I hazarded, glancing over the information I'd gleaned from the estate agent's files. A Ms S. Ayres had provided one of Kristen's references for the flat.

'Yes. That's right. Mr Bridgeman's personal assistant.'

'Perhaps she's got a forwarding address for Krissy?'

'Oh, I don't think so. In fact I'm sure she hasn't ... because I was saying to her in the staff kitchen ...'

I finally managed to stem the tide of words long enough to

extract the information that I couldn't speak to Ms Ayres just at present because she'd gone to the dentist and wasn't due in until later.

Which suited me quite nicely. I established that the office staff generally finished at 5.30 p.m., although Suzie usually left about 5.45 unless she was doing overtime.

Promising to try again later, I hung up on her and dialled the local tax office. The girl there was sympathetic to my problem and agreed it was very difficult when your job meant you had to move around every few months.

'Would you be knowing where your file is now, Miss Keen?'

'Well, I'm not entirely sure. It's several moves behind me, you see. If you could just keep an eye out for it and check everything's up to date?'

'Sure, that'll be no problem at all. If you want to give me your reference number?'

Unfortunately I was the sort of muddled tax-payer who just couldn't lay their hands on that sort of detail. I did provide her with a (fictitious) date of birth, address and telephone number, however. 'Are you the one who'll be handling my file?'

'That's right. Surnames G to M, that's me.'

'Great. If I could take your name then?'

'Shona Donovan.'

The tax office also shut at 5.30 p.m.

After I'd thanked her, I spent another hour dialling the local banks. It wasn't a route I had much faith in, but I gave it a go anyway.

Posing as a previously stranded motorist who Krissy had loaned money to at a service station, I was devastated to have lost her address. Luckily I'd remembered the town and I was certain I'd seen her using a cheque book from their bank – so if they could just confirm it would be OK to post the money for her account?

All four branches in town regretted they had no customer of that name.

I did the same routine with the building societies, substituting pass book for cheque book. Same result.

Well, it had been a bit of a long shot. These days, with

electronic banking, there was really no need to drag your account around with you. If Kristen had one, it could be anywhere in the country.

There were people who could hack into the system and provide you with that sort of information, but they charged a fortune, and anyway I had my pride. It was my job, so I'd do the work.

The chances were that Wexton's would have the information, since they almost certainly paid by the BACS system.

Anyway, I'd had enough of desk work. Rummaging in a filing cabinet drawer, I extracted a heavy black wig, a pair of glasses with thick black plastic rims and a brightly coloured scarf. Unearthing a battered briefcase I'd picked up in a jumble sale, I carried the lot down to the car and drove back to the flat.

The clothes I wanted were on the floor of the old pantry cupboard which now served as my wardrobe. Below-the-knee tweed skirts and pie-frill blouses aren't my usual choice, but this lot had come in a pot-luck bag from another jumble sale.

The difference in the sea front was almost painful. It was as if a plague had hit the town. There were still odd gulags of chairs and windbreaks scattered over the sands, but unlike yesterday, when you'd have been hard put to find a spare patch for a one-storey sandcastle, now you could have sculpted a full-sized Taj Mahal out there. The only sign of a crowd was grouped around something in the middle of the promenade.

Pulling into one of the empty parking bays, I went to see what the attraction was.

The taut boom-boom of inexpertly played drums filtered between the watching figures. Peering over two shoulders, I found myself watching another display of Figgy's skating skills. Whilst Mickey beat out a rhythm on the tom-toms clasped between her knees, he pirouetted, jumped, swooped, spun and twisted in a dizzying performance.

The gasps and spontaneous clapping at each new movement confirmed my own impression that he was a cut above most street buskers. The music built to a climax. Suddenly – without warning – Figgy stopped dead. Gathering himself, he skated a few steps and hurled himself into the air, drawing his knees into his chest and executing a back somersault before landing perfectly and swooping low in a deep bow to the audience.

There was a collective sigh of appreciation before the applause started. With a happy smile, Mickey bounded up and started to circulate with a plastic cup extended.

It was my cue to leave.

Returning to the car, I pulled the wig and glasses on and arranged the scarf around the neck of my T-shirt.

Crossing the road, I went into a small arcade. Amongst the flashing games consoles and slot machines, they had one of those 'Print Your Own Business Card' machines.

There were addicts even at this time of day, feeding coins into the slots, dragging down on handles and watching luridly coloured fruits whirling round. Concentrating against the ker-clunk of the handles and the occasional thin tinkle of descending change, I followed the instructions on screen; selecting my typefaces, layout and colours.

Whilst I obeyed the 'Please Wait', I whiled away the time wondering what the kid operating the two metal grabs was going to do with a neon-coloured troll even if he succeeded in picking one up.

Just as the machine spat out my card, he got a turquoise beastie that seemed to have been constructed from cheap polyester carpet, and answered my question by unlocking the back of the glass cabinet and throwing the toy back in.

'Gotta keep your hand in,' he grinned at me.

'Quite ...'

He was wearing a plastic identity tag with his picture and name on it. Most of the arcade staff along the front had them now; it prevented any problems with 'walk-ins' offering to get change and disappearing into the night with the slot-players' ten-pound notes. It also established who was entitled to throw you out when you started kicking the machines and shouting 'Fix!'

This one was called Enrico. He was probably a student from the foreign-language college.

'So tell me, Enrico, do you make those badges here on the premises?'

77

His English wasn't quite as good as that *Gotta keep your hand in* had suggested. But I got through eventually and he agreed that, yes, they made him a picture here. 'We have a camera. In the back. It takes a little picture and then the machine, she ...'

Seals it in a plastic coating was definitely beyond his vocabulary. But we managed with a lot of arm-waving and slapping together of palms.

'Yeah, right. Listen, Enrico ... do you think you could do me a favour?'

His mouth pulled down at the corners, and he flicked an uneasy glance back into the dark depths of the arcade as if hoping for rescue. I was a bit piqued for a moment, until I remembered the wig and glasses. OK, even I didn't think I looked worth pulling in that get-up. But he didn't have to make it so damn obvious!

'See, the thing is,' I said, grabbing his arm before he could make a bolt for it and quickly reassuring him it wasn't his body I was after, 'my mum's coming down to visit me.'

'Your mamma?' Under my grip, I felt his forearm muscles relax beneath the olive skin.

'That's right, my mamma. I told her I'd got a really good job. With the government, you know? Big salary, big pension?'

Enrico nodded. Yes, he understood that bit.

'Only the thing is – I lied. I haven't got a job.'

'That is sad.'

'Isn't it just. But I can't tell Mum the truth now; she'd be really upset.'

'So you lie?'

'That's the idea, Enrico. She'll only be here for a few hours. She's on her way to catch the ferry,' I improvised freely. 'So I'm going to keep pretending. And I thought if I had something on me that sort of proved where I worked ...'

I produced the newly printed card. 'But it would look better with my picture on ... and in a ...' I slapped my palms together.

'Pleestic jacket?' Enrico said.

'Absolutely. Can you use the camera, Enrico?'

78

'Sure. But the boss ...' He looked behind him. 'He comes back soon ...'

'It'll only take a few minutes.' I produced a folded fiver from my jeans pocket.

Enrico's grasp of British finance was better than his grasp of the language. We finally settled on ten pounds, and fifteen minutes later I had my nice new identity tag, complete with picture, signature and *pleestic* jacket. He even threw in a clip to attach it to my blouse.

Not that I intended to at present. Wexton's was later. I threw the wig and glasses back in the boot and set off to sort out the Larry Payne Academy of Charm and Brick-laying.

CHAPTER 12

I parked by the yard gates, next to the notice that read: '*Entrance in Constant Use. Do Not Obstruct.*'

The yard was carrying a lot of building materials of one sort or another. Which suggested that business was good if Payne could afford to have that much money tied up in stock. The dark-green four-door Saab, with a current number plate, parked at the foot of the office stairs was a pretty good indicator too.

I'd hoped that by leaving it this late Laurence Payne would be out supervising one of his chain gangs somewhere. But I was out of luck.

The first floor over the old storage shed had been divided into two offices. The door from the outside staircase led directly into the outer one, which I bounced into after a perfunctory knock.

Two pairs of eyes met mine. I had a brief impression the woman was glad of the interruption. The man bending over her shoulder to read something on the computer screen just managed to hide the flash of impatience as she asked: 'Yes? May I help you?'

She probably could have done if her boss hadn't been there.

I had no doubt this was the future Sir Larry. Everything about him, from the feet planted four-square on the polished plank flooring to the forward thrust of his broad shoulders, exuded a mixture of self-assurance and arrogance.

He wasn't tall, five six at the most, but the stout body under the brown suit looked well muscled and his square hands were rough and blunt-nailed. This was a man more used to working outside than messing around in an office with computers, and the expression on his broad face as he glared at the screen suggested he wished he was taking a pickaxe to hard-core right at this moment.

The light from the VDU flicked over his tanned skin, catching on the ruddier patches on his cheeks and nose where the weekend's heatwave had caught them. His hair was a mass of tight grey curls – thinning into a pronounced widow's peak which had already receded a third of the way along his skull. His eyes were small, light brown, sandy-lashed and assessing me with increasing impatience.

He wanted me to state my business and go. So I did.

'Skerries! Bloody Skerries. Are you bloody females thick or what? How many more times do we have to tell you there's no one called Skerries works here. Never has been. Do you want to check the sodding wages slips?'

I wouldn't have minded, actually, but he was out from behind that desk before I could take up his kind invitation, and thrusting his face into mine. The advantage of being five ten was that he had to look up to make eye-contact, although I've got to say he didn't look like he felt at a psychological disadvantage.

I surreptitiously moved my feet and balanced my weight in case he decided to get physical. The disadvantage of the height difference was that it wasn't going to be as easy to aim a knee where it would do the most damage.

The secretary preserved Sir Larry's chances of future fatherhood by calling across: 'I've moved the heading over The Seascape now. What do you think?'

Payne leant his palms flat on the desk and twisted around so that he could see the screen. 'Well how do I know? I can't tell on that thing. Print off a copy, for heaven's sake!'

Her hands flashed over the keyboard and a laser printer whirled into action, spewing out sheets of paper. It seemed to be one of those artist's impressions of a housing estate.

Payne snatched it up. 'It's rubbish. The proportions are all wrong. If I built a house that leant like that the bloody roof would be in the garden first strong wind we got. What's the point of spending a fortune on this fancy software when you turn out stuff looks like it was drawn by a three-year-old?'

'You should have paid for the training course as well.'

'What for? Learn on the job, that's my motto. No substitute for experience. Are you still here?'

I smiled. 'Yes thanks.'

He started his aggressive strut towards me again. I caught a pleading look from the secretary. She didn't want blood splattering on her crisp new artwork.

Since he was so set against Tom Skerries, I decided on a half-truth. Whipping out one of my genuine business cards, I held it in front of his nose.

'Private investigator! One of them's set a bloody private dick on us now!'

One of who? I wondered. 'Nobody's set me on you, Mr Payne. I told you. I want Tom Skerries. He owes money.'

I could see that it was an idea that appealed to him. He relaxed slightly. 'Who's he owe?'

'My clients prefer to keep their business dealings private. They're the shy sort.'

'They must be the soft-in-the-head sort if they're lending cash to the likes of Skerries.' A flicker of sadistic pleasure twinkled over the ruddy face. 'Got himself in hock to the loan sharks, has he? Serves him right.'

'An interesting comment on a bloke you claim not to know.'

'I said he didn't work here. And he doesn't. Never has done. So go tell your bosses to look elsewhere for the little scroat.'

He ripped the door open. I left. And he stood at the top of the steps to make sure I did. Behind him I could hear the secretary asking something about the print-out.

Payne snapped back: 'No. There's no time. Get me a

presentation fixed up for that committee do tonight. I'll pass a few folders out. See who takes the bait.'

Her lighter voice, the words indistinguishable, floated across the yard and was followed by an impatient instruction to 'Get a bloody sandwich then. I have to work through lunch, don't I?'

I pulled the car away and tooted loudly before taking it a few streets and parking up again.

One of the fishermen's cottages had been converted to a café. *Tastee fresh-cut sandwiches, local crab salads, delicious cream teas*, the blackboard announced.

I bought two tastee sandwiches to go, and wandered back to the front. Leaning in the doorway of a craft shoppe, I watched Payne's yard.

Ten minutes later, the Saab pulled out. I gave it another five and then strolled across the yard and back up the stairs.

She was muttering over the screen again, multicoloured icons flickering in her glasses.

'Chicken salad or cheese salad?' I asked, holding out the two paper bags before she could tell me to get lost.

'Is this a bribe?'

'If you're susceptible. Otherwise it's lunch. They abolished slavery in 1833, you know.'

'Yes, I did. But I don't think anyone's told Larry.' I half expected her to refuse, but she did more things with the computer, then stood up and walked over to the kettle. 'Tea or coffee?'

'Whatever.'

She made two mugs of tea and then indicated the door. 'Let's eat outside.'

I followed her downstairs. Beneath the short-sleeved white blouse and beige trousers, she looked like she'd kept herself in shape.

We perched on a large lump of pre-formed stone casing, facing the sea. A few holiday-makers were doing the same, sitting on towels spread over the shallow strip of pebbles between the yard and the shore.

'Nice location.'

'It's too small really. We have to rent another yard a few miles away for storing materials and most of the vehicles.'

'Don't you get flooded?' I asked. The edge of this yard was only about two feet higher than the breakwater.

'No. Never. It's something to do with the angle of the sea floor and the direction of the tides. Were you really sent by a loan shark?'

'No.'

I gave her a brief run-down on Bone's case without mentioning any names.

'Poor kid,' she said, holding the chicken sandwich two-handed and biting in with evident relish.

'Mmm ...' Sipping my tea, I glanced sideways at her. Seen from this angle, and in sunlight, I suddenly had the feeling of having met her before. Except I couldn't quite pin down where and when.

A slight sea breeze teased at her hair. It was more or less the same style and colour as the wig I'd left in the car. Only hers was natural, I'd say, with perhaps a bit of help to hide a few grey stragglers, since I put her age at around the same as her boss's – fiftyish.

Retrieving a slice of tomato that had just fallen on to her beige trousers, she dropped it into her mouth and asked me what I intended to do if I found Skerries.

'Get him to ring my client and let her down gently. If he's capable of being that subtle.'

'Oh yes. Tom can be quite charming when he puts his mind to it.'

'And when's that?'

'Mostly when he comes into contact with any female who's attractive and willing. I don't think he likes the thrill of the chase much.'

She caught my speculative look and laughed. 'No, definitely not me. I didn't qualify on either count.'

'So who did?'

'Well, several of our female customers, judging by the calls we've been getting over the past few weeks. Some of them even ring up using half a dozen different names just to see if we'll put them through to him.'

Which explained the scepticism when I'd announced myself as 'Smith' earlier on.

'Is that why the slave-driver is claiming amnesia over Skerries' employment?'

'No. And he wasn't lying. You wouldn't find Tom on our files. You see, Swayling's has never turned down work. Which sometimes leads to us having half a dozen jobs on the go at once.'

'Don't tell me. Do just enough to make sure it's not practical for the customer to go elsewhere – and then disappear for days while you set up the next job.'

She laughed again. And once more there was that niggling sensation that I knew her from somewhere.

'Something like that. Anyway, we have some casual labourers that we can call on when things get too crazy. Tom was one of those. He'd do odd days for us. St Agatha's wall was the longest on-going job he worked on. Larry always keeps the private schools sweet. He gets a lot of work from that quarter.'

'So how did Skerries manage to get up Payne's nose?'

'He was poaching our customers. Only in a small way: garage drives, new gate posts, brick-built barbecues, that sort of thing. But Larry's very territorial; if it's a Payne's job, he won't stand for anyone else on the turf, as he used to say – before he got an attack of the pretensions.'

She flicked a crust at a few hopefully lurking pigeons. A gull descended immediately and snatched it from their beaks. Screwing up the paper bag, she finished her tea. 'Larry thinks Tom was using our materials.'

'Nicking them, you mean?'

'Yes. Our stock control isn't all it might be. Particularly when things get a bit hectic. Larry went out to check on some patio work Tom had done on the sly. There was some Italian stone in it that's not generally available in this country. We'd just imported a consignment for a special job. It looks like Tom must have had a spare set of keys cut for the yard gates. And naturally it's all my fault for leaving them around.'

She said it without rancour, as if she'd worked here long enough to be immune to Payne's tantrums. 'But the worst thing is – Tom isn't even a particularly good builder.'

'Is that bad? I'd have thought Payne's would have been

pleased. Teach 'em to stick with the pros and avoid the cons in future.'

'Well, yes, but ... I think Tom gave the impression he was working for Payne's – on a sort of unofficial, cash-in-hand basis. At least that's what the customers are claiming now.'

'You mean they want you to fix the botches?'

'Yes. Which is bad enough. But one man got quite badly hurt. A garage door fell off on him. He's threatening to sue for injuries sustained. And then there's the implication that we were trying to avoid VAT by taking in cash in hand. It's not the sort of publicity Larry wants. Especially not at the moment.'

'Now he's hoping for an earldom or something?'

The lenses of her glasses were photochromatic; they'd darkened in the sun to two expressionless black orbs. Nonetheless I saw her laughing muscles twitch. 'I think a few letters to put after his name will probably do for starters.'

'So you're denying all knowledge of Tom Skerries.'

'Who?'

'Right.'

There was something I simply had to ask. Nodding to the yard sign with its obliterated 'Son' after 'L. Payne and', I asked: 'What's the story there?'

'Son is trained to carry on family empire. At sixteen son announces he isn't interested and wants to take up hobby as full-time career. Father declares job is only fit for a bloody poofter. Son calls father sad, boring little money-grabber. Father tells son to grow up or push off and see how far he gets on his own. Son packs rucksack and pushes off the very next day.'

She stood up, brushing crumbs off her lap. 'Well, I must get back to the salt mines.'

She'd had all of ten minutes for lunch. I asked if that was normal.

'No. It's my Monday treat. Normally I get five.'

'His sir-ship really expects his pound of flesh, doesn't he? How long have you worked for him?'

'About thirty years.'

She didn't look like a masochist. 'Why didn't you dump the dickhead?'

'It's not that easy. We never did names, did we? I'm Marina Payne.'

She slid the glasses down until they perched on the tip of her nose, and grinned at me.

'I'm Mrs Dickhead.'

CHAPTER 13

I could only assume that Tom Skerries had slipped into the gene pool when the life guard wasn't looking. Evidently, however, his two brain cells had finally made contact for long enough to work out that they were living in a receptacle that was due for demolition unless Tom kept his head down for a while.

I could simply fill Bone in on the situation to date and suggest Tom would be in touch once things cooled down a bit – some time around the next Ice Age I should think, judging by Payne's mood this morning. But somehow that felt like short-changing her. It would be better if I could locate the testosterone-loaded loser and get him to give her a ring.

I wrestled with the problem whilst I wandered along the front, and bought myself a 99 as dessert.

The tide was well out now, leaving huge stretches of sand exposed and the sunlight glinting off tidal shallows and scrunchy drifts of tiny pearl-white shells. Rolling up my jeans and dumping my shoes in the car boot, I strolled down to the edge of the ocean and watched oil tankers sliding over the horizon.

When I ran out of beach and vanilla whip, I towel-dried my feet on the wig and pointed the car towards North Bay.

After I'd finished apologising for slagging off her husband, and Marina Payne had laughed and told me if I thought *that* was rude I'd plainly led a very sheltered life, she'd wished me luck with locating Skerries.

'How do *you* locate him?' I'd asked. 'If you had a job for him, I mean. As far as I could see, he's not on the phone at home.'

She'd left a message at the local social club. 'It always seemed to be open. There's a lot of unemployment on the Downs Estate. I think some of them spend every waking hour in there.'

It was actually debatable whether the few men grouped around the plastic tables inside *were* awake. They seemed to be drinking and watching horse-racing on the large wall-mounted colour television whilst in some kind of catatonic trance. Only the one propped against the outer side of the bar counter paid any attention to me.

Flicking a disinterested glance as I walked through the front door, he called: 'Members only, love. Application forms on your right. Committee meets end of month.'

'I don't want to join. I'm looking for someone. Tom Skerries.'

This at least got me a bit more attention. Two dirty laughs from the TV watchers and a speculative once-over from the barman that made me wonder if I'd remembered to put my knickers on.

He switched the leer off as a woman bustled through from the back carrying a crate of mixers. She thumped it on the bar. 'Who's this?'

'Looking for Tom Skerries, she reckons.'

'Then tell her. Let him sort his own mess out, he's not hiding behind my skirts.'

The man showed no inclination to take any notice of this order, so she crashed the bar flap open and waddled through. Grabbing hold of my forearm, she marched me back to the door and pointed: 'See there?'

There were two low-rise blocks of flats at right angles to each other opposite us, with a trodden patch of grass held between them. The social club formed the third side of the square, with fencing along the main road finishing off the fourth.

Her flabby, brown-spotted arm was pointing to the right-hand block. 'Second floor, second from the far end. That's the Skerries' flat.'

'Cheers.'

I could see the flat door opening as I moved across the

87

grass. A woman was backing out, manoeuvring a pushchair over the step and on to the walkway.

By slackening my pace, I managed to be at the top of the stair flight just as she reached it. 'Want a hand?'

'Yeah.'

Taking the base of the chair, I backed down whilst she kept the handlebars high off the steps. The baby regarded me wide-eyed over a dribble-splashed pink jumpsuit decorated with yellow teddy bears.

'What's her name?'

'Shannon.'

'Are you Mrs Skerries?'

'How'd you mean?'

I wouldn't have thought there were many ways of being Mrs Skerries, but a wary look had come into her hazel eyes. She wasn't bad looking; at least she wouldn't have been if she'd tidied up the straggling brown hair, taken a few pounds off the thighs and changed into something a bit more flattering than the shapeless grey tracksuit and well-worn trainers.

'I was looking for Tom Skerries.'

'Why?'

If I hadn't had hold of the other end of her daughter's pushchair, I was sure she'd have bolted at that point.

So he can ring one of his girlfriends and let her down gently wasn't going to win me any prizes for tact. Or any co-operation either.

'It's sort of personal,' I said vaguely. 'Is your husband in?'

'No.'

We'd reached the bottom of the stairwell. She wrenched the chair from my hands and set off at a determined pace towards a footpath that led down the side of the social club. A couple of mums had come out of the other block and were bumping prams diagonally over the green in the same direction.

I tried to fall into step beside Tom's other half. She increased her pace.

'Look, can I just talk to you for a sec?'

'I 'ave to get Liam from playgroup.'

'I'll give you a lift.'

'And Pierce from school.'

'It's a big car.'

'I'm going round me mate's after.'

'I'm very sociable.'

'I don't wanna talk to yer.'

'Well, that's fine ... er, I don't know your name.'

'Donna.'

'OK, Donna, if you just tell me where to find Tom ...'

'I can't ... and why the hell should I anyway?'

Good question really. I mean, normally people answer questions because they've been asked. If they start to analyse *why* they're doing it, I'm in trouble.

Donna stopped dead abruptly. 'I can't talk to yer now. Come round the flat later.'

'Sevenish?'

'No. Make it nine.'

She charged away, hurrying to join up with a group of other mums and prevent any more questioning.

I glanced at my watch. It was just gone three o'clock; another two and a half hours to waste. In the end I was parked up at the edge of town, next to an unvandalised telephone box, by five o'clock. At five thirty-three I dialled the tax office, and got an automated message informing me the office was closed until eight thirty the following morning. So far, so good.

I'd changed into the tweed skirt and frilly blouse in the ladies' loo of the local cinema before driving up here. Now I used the rear-view mirror to slap on foundation and an orange lipstick that made me look like a badly developed colour snap. The wig was still gritty after I'd used it as a foot towel, but banging it vigorously against the car side sorted out most of the problem. The winged glasses completed the get-up.

'What is the female equivalent of "dork"?' I murmured at my reflection in the mirror as I locked up.

Most of Wexton's staff were already driving and cycling out when I walked in at five forty. The reception desk was deserted, but a woman came out from the back office, pulling on her coat as I approached.

'Good afternoon. Shona Donovan, from the tax inspector-ate. Could I see whoever handles your personnel matters? I believe we've dealt with a Ms Ayres in the past?'

'Suzie. Yes, that's right. But it is rather *late*. She may have already left, I'm afraid.'

Checking my watch, I looked surprised. 'Good heavens, is that the time now? I've been on the road all day. You lose track.'

Hastily she jabbed out a number on her phone. 'Suzie? There's a Miss ...?'

'Donovan.'

'Donovan down here to see you. Something about tax ... She'll be down in a moment,' she informed me with obvious relief. Her duty done, she set a switch on the phones and hurried outside.

I was watching her climb into a waiting car when a voice behind me said: 'Ms Donovan?'

I apologised for arriving so late and without an appoint-ment. But not too profusely; after all, I was *tax*. It gave me a great feeling of power.

Ms Ayres walked me back up to her first-floor office explaining that she had to get away to see to the dogs.

'And Mother,' she added as an afterthought. She scarcely glanced at the identity badge that had cost me a tenner in Enrico's arcade. And she showed no inclination to telephone the tax office and check my identity.

Her office exhibited all the signs of someone packing up for the day: plastic cover over computer; roller blinds drawn down over file cabinets; handbag open on the desk.

Everything to plan. Until the boss appeared.

The door behind Ms Ayres opened suddenly just as I was coming to the end of my opening speech on the terrible problems we were experiencing with Ms Kristen Keats's tax returns.

The man who stepped through was absorbed in flicking over the stapled sheets he was holding, so I had the opportunity to get a quick impression before he noticed me.

Fifty-something, tall, angular, brown hair tinged with grey, thin face. Certainly no Sean Connery, although he plainly made Ms Ayres' heart beat a little faster, judging by the sparkle that lit her grey eyes.

'Suzie, I've marked up some changes for the post-mortem … oh, sorry, I didn't realise you had someone with you.'

Ms Ayres' introduction and explanation managed to convey the message that whatever was wrong with Kristen's tax returns, it certainly wasn't down to *her*.

I rushed to lay all the blame on the tax office. 'Bottlenecks, I'm afraid. It's nobody's fault. Just one of those things.'

'I'll leave you to it then, Suzie. And book a table at the White Hart for lunch, will you. Good night.'

I was included in his general smile as he retreated back behind the door marked: *S. Bridgeman – Managing Director*.

'Did someone die?'

Ms Ayres looked blank. 'I beg your pardon?'

'The post-mortem?'

'Oh, I see.' She gave the superior laugh of one who understands the jargon. 'A *contract* post-mortem. We've just finished a rather important contract for the MoD. Now, Kristen …'

Efficient wrist flicks whisked out her desk drawer, extracted keys from the file indexer and opened a cabinet.

I responded with an equally efficient performance with my briefcase. We both consulted files.

I opened the batting: 'I've tried to contact Miss Keats at her last known address, but she appears to have moved. And I understand that she no longer works here?'

'Not since the end of April.'

'This is so frustrating. If I could have the name of her new employer?'

'We don't have it.'

'Did they not ask for references?'

'No. Possibly they will do so later, but to date …' Ms Ayres ruffled paper.

I duly grimaced, clucked and blew out exasperated breaths.

'We have details of her previous employers,' Suzie offered. 'But you'll have those already.'

'If I could just check … her last employer was?'

'That would be the voluntary agency: Third World Initiative Teams.' Ms Ayres ruffled again. 'I don't seem to have their full address. But they'd hardly have been relevant to her work at Wexton's.'

'And before that there was ...' I ran my finger down an imaginary list on the file I kept tilted from her sight. Dragging up what I recalled from the estate agent's file, I remembered a six-month tenancy with the Leicester letting agency and hazarded, 'the Leicestershire company ...'

'Okranshaw Electronics,' she agreed readily. 'And before that AD Aerospace in Manchester.'

'Mmmm ...' I snapped my fingers. An idea had just occurred. 'What about her bank? Now wouldn't she have notified a change of address to them? Perhaps they'd be prepared to pass a message on.'

Ms Ayres ruffled with great willingness. 'I'm afraid we don't appear to have that information. Kristen was paid by personal cheque.'

'Unusual these days.'

'Yes, isn't it.' She was ruffling at dizzying speed now. A French-manicured finger stabbed down triumphantly. 'But I do have a note that she asked to be paid that way while she was moving banks. I daresay she just forgot to tell us. Why not try the local branches?'

Because I'd already gone down that route, Suzie. I smiled my thanks at her helpful suggestion and wondered whether perhaps one of Kristen's friends might know where she'd gone?

'Kristen didn't have any close friends. She was scarcely here long enough to make them.'

The file was shut and replaced. My interview was at an end; Mother and the mutts called.

'Well, thanks for your time.'

'Not at all.' She was by the door, plainly expecting me to join her. I let myself be ushered back downstairs again with promises that she'd ring the tax office if Kristen got in touch.

The reception area was manned by a guard from Mackenzie's. Whilst he unlocked the glass doors for us, I casually asked Suzie how Kristen had got the job.

'She applied on spec. Read the newspaper reports. Slightly gruesome. But I suppose jobs are hard to obtain these days. Why do you ask?'

I invented an unemployed cousin.

'I'm afraid there's a moratorium on recruitment at present.'

Suzie slid into a Mini parked in a *Reserved* space and was backing out before I could follow up on the reference to 'gruesome'.

She braked and wound down the window, calling across to ask if I wanted a lift.

'That's very kind. But my car's just ...' I waved vaguely at the boundary fence.

'It's not yet six o'clock,' Suzie shouted angrily.

Was the woman a part-time traffic warden as well?

I was composing excuses for sloppy parking when it dawned on me she wasn't speaking to me. The cleaners were dismounting from their motor-scooter by the front entrance.

'The agency knows you aren't supposed to start until six thirty.'

Both women had kept their crash helmets on. The driver raised her shoulders.

It is very difficult to argue with a blank, featureless visor. It's a bit like having a conversation with a microwave oven. Suzie contented herself with vague threats to contact the agency, plus an instruction not to disturb Mr Bridgeman.

Sitting in my own car, I waited until her tail-lights were just two glowing red dots weaving up amongst the country lane that led away from the town, and then quickly got rid of the wig and glasses.

Since I had a few more hours to waste, I changed out of Dolly the Dork's outfit back in the office and made free with Vetch's hot water again.

There was no one else in the building. Whilst in theory there were six agents working out of the agency, only Annie, Vetch and I seemed to be here on anything like a permanent basis.

I checked my desk to see if there were any messages. Neither of my clients had called for a progress report apparently. The only note was a scrawled sticker from Janice:

Annie rang – 3.15 p.m. Says it was just for a chat. She's at Leeds Holiday Inn.

Janice.

No other messages all day.

P.S. There never are. Don't have many clients, do you?

I rang Annie but there was no answer from her room, so I wandered down to the front intending to visit my favourite greasy spoon, and then remembered they closed on Mondays.

In the end I settled for a double cheeseburger with extra onions eaten in a shelter, watching the waves, before driving back up to keep my appointment with Donna Skerries.

She seemed even more nervous than earlier. For a moment I thought I wasn't even going to get inside the flat. But eventually she shuffled back and allowed me inside the hall. Through a left-hand door I caught a glimpse of a living room strewn with toys.

'Where are the kids?'

'Me mate's got 'em.'

I'd turned towards the living room. She blocked my way, banging the door shut quickly. 'We gotta talk in the kitchen.'

She led the way to the end of the hall. The grey tracksuit had been replaced by a sleeveless fuchsia top which showed the outline of her bra, and blue jeans that clung to her bottom with the tenacity of a non-stick coating.

'In here.'

The kitchen blinds were drawn, leaving the room in semi-darkness. I just had time to register this fact when something hit me hard and fast in the stomach. With a gasp I doubled over and saw the knee heading straight for my nose.

CHAPTER 14

I fell sideways. The power behind the upthrust had to go somewhere. And since it couldn't go into my face, it reacted against her, sending her swaying backwards.

Taking advantage of the fact she was off-balance, I locked both my hands round the heel of her static leg and heaved hard.

She went over, landing heavily on her back. A kitchen chair

caught by her flailing hand went with her. I managed to stand, using the table as a lever, but the trainer she'd planted in my stomach had had one hell of a leg behind it.

Whilst my bowel muscles were still protesting, she'd got to her feet and drawn back her right arm. I fended the fist on my forearm and lashed out with my own trainers, aiming for the kneecap.

With a muttered 'Bitch!' ground out through gritted teeth, she swayed and came back at me again. This time both fists were jabbing with short boxer's punches.

I retreated. The only thing to hand was the flip-top rubbish bin. I scooped it up two-handed and held it out, elbows slightly bent and ready to absorb the force.

Her right jab put a dent in the side. But at least the pain disrupted her rhythm for a second. Taking advantage of it, I hurled myself forward with the bin still held at shoulder height and jammed it into her face.

Surprised, she stepped back, tripped over the upturned chair and sprawled back again. Several mugs jumped off their hooks and rolled across the Formica before smashing on the floor.

I grabbed the chair and forced the legs down across her black T-shirt. It was a tight fit; she was a well-developed girl. But at least she wasn't too athletic. Whilst I was straddling her and keeping her top half pinned down, the short, thick legs under the black leggings couldn't get a big enough swing to kick me in the kidneys.

Donna finally decided to join in the fun.

'Let her up!'

She rushed over and pitter-patted open-handed blows against my nearest shoulder. After the last round, it was about as painful as being assaulted by a flock of rabid butterflies.

'Pack it in, Donna, or I'll have to demonstrate my famous right elbow in the gob technique. And put the blind up, for heaven's sake.'

At least she stopped slapping. 'Let 'er up. Nola, Nola, you OK?'

'Course I'm not. This tart's suffocating me.'

I could feel the effort her chest was making to expand. The words were wheezing out.

'OK, I'll let you up. But try anything like that again and I'll stick it across your throat, understand? And will you *please* put the blind up, Donna.'

She turned the light on instead.

Nola struggled up to a sitting position, glaring at me from a round face framed by black hair cropped to within a millimetre of its life. I was reminded of a drawing of a fat hedgehog in a picture book I'd had as a child. The thought made me smile.

'You needn't think you've won, tart. You won't be laughing once I've kicked yer teeth in.'

'Stop it, Nola, just shut up, will yer ... Look what you've done to me kitchen, you stupid cow!' Donna made an attempt to clear up the shattered mugs, winced and stuck a bleeding finger in her mouth.

Nola levered herself against the sink cupboard. 'If you're just gonna slag me off for trying to help, I'm going.'

'Well go then! I never asked yer to interfere, did I? I can handle it. I already told 'em I don't know where Tom is, ain't I? And they can see I ain't got no nicked bricks or nothing here.'

'Is it possible,' I asked, 'you're under the impression I'm Larry Payne's messenger service? Because if so, not guilty.'

The stomach muscles were beginning to recover from the protective numbness they'd entered after Nola's foot arrived in their midst, and they were now starting to hurt like hell. I straddled the chair, keeping the back between me and Nola, and massaged my lower bowel area cautiously.

'So what you want then? If you ain't from that builder?'

'I'm a detective.'

'See what you've done. You've gone and hit a copper now, Nola. She never meant nothing by it, honest.'

'She meant to knock my teeth in,' I pointed out. 'However, I'm a private detective now. I've left the police. But I still know plenty of people in the force.'

And most of them crossed the road rather than share pavement with me. But there was no need for this pair to know that.

'So what you want?' Nola demanded.

She'd stayed on the floor, leaning against the cupboard, her legs bent and hugged to her chest with those short, muscular arms. I had the same feeling of *déjà vu* I'd had when watching Marina Payne. This was another face who reminded me of someone else, but once again I couldn't for the life of me think who.

'I've been hired to find Tom. By one of his fans. She's just a kid. I was hoping to persuade him to spin her some story. Let her down gently, you know?'

'And you come here to ask Donna for help. You've got a flaming cheek!'

'Actually I came here to find Tom. But I gather I'm out of luck. Keeping out of Payne's way, is he?'

Donna shrugged. She was still sucking the cut finger and it made her look about ten. 'Might be.'

I looked to Nola, who said: 'He's just scarpered again, ain't he. He always takes off when he gets fed up playing daddy. Took off for three months after Liam was born.'

'He says all that screaming does his head in,' Donna said, still defending her man.

'I suppose the rest of us just love it, do we?' Nola levered herself up and cautiously placed her weight on the knee I'd kicked.

I was pleased to see it seemed to be hurting her as much as my stomach was paining me.

Hobbling to a cupboard, she unearthed a plastic brush and dustpan and started sweeping up the shattered crockery.

After an ineffectual attempt to help with the toe of her trainer, Donna stood watching. 'You broke Liam's Thomas the Tank Engine mug, he'll be ever so upset. He won't drink his chocolate milk from nothing else.'

'Then don't give him none.' Nola shot the dustpan contents into the bin and dragged the liner out, twisting the top into a knot.

'He's gotta have his milk. It's good for him. You don't understand. You ain't got kids.'

'Ally-bloody-luyah …' Nola said with feeling. She was interrupted by a shriek from outside.

'That's my Liam!' Donna pushed me aside and rushed down the hall.

Nola followed her out on to the walkway at a slower pace. Two little boys of around three and six, with their dad's gypsy looks, were rushing round with a little red-haired girl on the central green. Directly below us, Shannon's pushchair was being wheeled back and forth by her minder.

As soon as I saw the candy-striped hair, a memory clicked into place. I knew who Nola reminded me of. To paraphrase an old joke, she reminded me of her.

'You're the cleaner from Wexton's Engineering.'

'Yeah. What of it?'

'I saw you up there Sunday night. Arguing with the bloke from Mackenzie's.'

'Yeah. Normally we do it Friday night, or Saturdays. That's why the guard was giving us hassle, he ain't used to letting us in Sundays. But Bonnie couldn't do it till Sunday.'

I took a few deep breaths and found it wasn't too painful. 'Fancy a drink?'

'Yer what?'

'A drink. Lager, draught bitter, orange juice ...'

'Rum and Coke.'

It would be. Still, at least it was going on Henry Summerstone's expenses.

Donna had to be persuaded. 'I oughta get the kids to bed.'

'They can stay up a bit late. It's summer, ain't it. You gotta get out,' Nola scolded. 'Just 'cos he's gone off, ain't no reason for you to mope in the flat. Now go fix yourself up.'

'Does she really not know where her husband is?' I asked as soon as Donna disappeared back into the flat.

'Hasn't a clue. He'll come back. Next week, next month, when he's ready. Just does as he likes. I told her she oughta stick up for herself more. Get some respect. But it's always me has had to fight the battles for her, ever since we was the same ages as Pierce and Liam.'

'You sisters?'

'Yeah. Don't look it, do we? She was always the pretty one, got all the blokes. Still, least I was spared being put up the stick by Tosser Tom.'

There was something about her tone made me wonder if

perhaps she hadn't had hopes in that direction once, but I never found out because Donna reappeared.

Fixing herself up had consisted of putting a brush through her hair and adding fuchsia lipstick and a gold-coloured necklace and hoop earrings.

Getting out consisted of walking twenty yards across the green to the club building.

'Visitor,' Nola bawled in the general direction of the bar. The woman I'd met earlier in the day thrust a book across.

'It's fifty pee.'

Once I'd been signed in, Nola announced they'd get a table. 'Donna has lager and lime.'

They pushed a way through the smoky, packed hall. The television was showing American basketball now, via a satellite channel.

I'd just ordered their drinks, and my orange juice, when the older kids charged in followed by Candy-stripe with the pushchair. After a quick conference at the table, Donna's oldest kid came running over.

'Auntie Bonnie wants a gin and tonic. And please can Liam and me and Hannah have cherryades and cheese'n'onion crisps?'

'You'll get fat.'

'I don't mind.' Dragging up his Batman T-shirt he peered at his round white stomach whilst I gave the order.

'Pierce Skerries,' his mother scolded half-heartedly when she saw the load. 'Did you ask this lady to buy yer things? Now what have I told you about that?'

''Member to say thank you,' her son said, wide-eyed and innocent, as he quickly took one of the pre-filled plastic beakers and put his thumb through the silver-foil top before he could be told to take it back.

'Yeah, well ...' Outmanoeuvred, Donna took charge of her daughter. 'Come on, we'll go in the children's room. Say thanks, you two.'

Bonnie's little girl mumbled her thanks. Liam, however, insisted that I bend down so he could give me an enormous hug and an enthusiastic kissing.

'Thank you ever so much!' he beamed, fixing me with

melting brown eyes framed by mile-long lashes beneath curls that were just crying out to be ruffled.

Oh yes, I could definitely see how his dad had a string of panting girlfriends all beating a path to his cement mixer.

Donna took them off to another room beyond the bar. I glimpsed brightly painted walls, a climbing frame and another telly playing cartoons before the door shut again.

'Wouldn't they prefer the beach?'

'They go there weekends and holidays. Ain't that right, Bonnie?'

Candy-stripe nodded. She seemed a woman of few words. And none of those stretched beyond two syllables.

'Thought it were better Bonnie stayed if you wanna ask about Wexton's. You do, don't yer?'

Despite looking like a hedgehog who was into heavy metal, Nola seemed to be the shrewdest of the trio. I agreed my interest was in Wexton's.

'Thought it was. Bonnie's worked there longer than me. 'Ow long is it? Four years?'

'Five.'

'She's a detective. You never said your name.'

'Grace Smith.'

'Like Hannah,' Bonnie said.

'She nearly called her Hannah Grace,' Nola translated.

'Fascinating. So you've worked for Wexton's for five years, have you, Bonnie?'

'No.'

Nola interpreted again. 'We don't work for Wexton's. We work for the cleaning company.'

'Are any of the regular staff there when you clean?'

'Sometimes. If they're on overtime, the production lot stay on. Work weekends too.'

'Did you ever come across a woman called Kristen Keats? She was a test engineer.'

I was about to describe Kristen, but the laugh Nola and Bonnie exchanged told me I didn't need to.

'Boss's perk,' Nola said succinctly.

'Stephen Bridgeman, you mean?'

'Yeah.'

'He and Kristen were at it?'

'Well, we never caught 'em ... you know ... did we, Bonnie?'

'No.'

'Then why do you think they'd become a hot item?'

'Well ...' Nola drew her stool nearer to the round table. Heaven knows why; most of the other tables were having to shout to make themselves heard above the TV game.

'They're always working overtime together the past few months.'

'Didn't Bridgeman work it before?'

'Yeah, he did. But that was when the girls on production did it as well. He'd go round out there, checking up on them, talking to the blokes in test. Or he'd be in his office – on his tod. Last few months it's been him and her, all huddled up round the computer screen. Never cosied up to Rob like that, did he?'

They both laughed again.

'Who's Rob?'

'Rob Wingett. He used to do her job. Before he got killed. He was nice, Rob was, weren't he, Bonnie?'

'Yeah, Rob was great.'

'Always joking and larking with us, Rob. Some of them don't say nothing to you if you're the cleaner. But Rob was nice.'

'What happened to him?'

'Motorbike smash. He'd got that diabetics,' Nola elaborated. 'They reckon he passed out. Broke his neck.'

At least that cleared up Ms Ayres' odd remark about Kristen's application being 'gruesome'.

'Why'd yer wanna know about Kristen?' Nola demanded.

'I've just been hired to find her. My client's worried about her.'

'Ain't she still working at Wexton's, then?'

'No. Left a few weeks back.'

Bonnie tossed her striped ponytail and lifted her empty glass. "Nuther?'

To my surprise, Nola took up the tray. 'My round.'

When she fought her way back through the smoke fug again, I asked if she could get me into Wexton's.

'Well, I dunno. Why'd you wanna get in there?'

'Fishing for straws,' I admitted honestly. I just couldn't get to grips with Kristen at all. Perhaps there was something in her personal file or her workdesk (assuming she'd had one) that might give me a new lead.

'Can you let me in the back way?'

Nola shook her head. 'No chance. The doors have all got alarms on them. Anyhow, the security blokes are always prowling around, they'd see yer.'

'Could cover,' Bonnie contributed.

'You could cover for one of our shifts,' Nola translated. 'We ain't really supposed to, but our supervisor never comes round anyhow. Bonnie's mum covers for her sometimes.'

'Tomorrow?'

But neither of them was keen on that idea. They both preferred Thursday, when the regular guard had a night off and was replaced by assorted stand-ins.

'They won't know if you're a new cleaner or not,' Nola explained. 'It'll be OK if yer with me. They got a bit keen a couple of years back, after the break-in. But they ain't too bothered again now.'

Bonnie lit up a filter-tip. 'Me wages.'

'What? Oh yeah. Bonnie keeps her money for the shift, all right?'

I agreed that was fair enough.

'And a tenner,' Bonnie added.

We arranged that I'd meet Nola by the social club at six thirty. She'd pressed for earlier but I wanted to give Ms Ayres and Stephen Bridgeman time to get out of the building. As it was, if either of them was working late, I was going to have to do the Jif Shift again later.

Since I'd nothing else to do, I stayed on for another round and watched a dire American quiz show on satellite TV before driving back to the flat.

The one parked car in the street was sitting opposite my house. I found out why when I went to walk down the steps to my basement door.

My first thought – that the figure hunched on the staircase was looking for somewhere to sleep off a few early six-packs – evaporated when he raised a pale face topped with a thatch of light-brown hair and I recognised D.C. Smith, Annie's brother (the one blessed by his parents with 'Zebedee', if you were paying attention to an earlier chapter).

'Hi, Zeb. Coming in?'

'Thanks.'

He accepted coffee (black, I still hadn't cracked the milk shortage) and slumped on the bed, cradling the hot mug to a chest that plainly contained an aching heart.

I hoped he wasn't going to start confiding in me about his love life. I'm no good at that kind of empathy stuff. I have enough trouble making sense of my own emotions.

'What's up?'

'Annie's flat.'

'What about it?'

'It's got squatters.'

CHAPTER 15

'You can't stay in there!'

'Don't see why not.' Lounging in the small gap left once the safety chain was on, Figgy folded his arms across his chest and grinned.

Despite the fact he was inside – inside my best friend's flat, to be exact – he was still wearing his sunglasses, so I could see my own tight-lipped face reflected in the convex glossy blackness.

'Because it's not your flaming flat, Figgy, that's why not.'

'Lots of people live in flats that ain't their own. Bet you do yourself.'

'Yes, but they pay this thing called rent.'

(OK, I didn't. But I wasn't getting into that right here.)

'I don't mind paying rent. You tell your mate to get a contract drawn up and me and Mickey'll sign it.'

'Annie doesn't want rent. She wants her flat back.'

'Told yer that, did she?'

'Yes,' I lied firmly.

Annie hadn't actually instructed me to regain possession, for the simple reason that she didn't know she'd been dispossessed. Zeb hadn't got around to telephoning her with the good news yet.

'Why not?' I'd demanded, as he'd sat on my bed sharing my coffee and his troubles.

'Well ... you know ... no sense worrying her if we don't have to. They might have gone before she gets back.'

'You mean you hope they will. And what's with this *we*? She left you to mind the flat. Probably thought she could trust a policeman.'

He raised pleading eyes. 'What am I going to do, Grace? She'll go spare if she finds out.'

'I don't know. What about getting a warrant for criminal damage and arresting the pair of them? They must have broken in.'

'Aaah!'

'Aaah *what*?'

'I went round to see if the place was OK. And ... well ... when I was cutting back across the park, the bloke ran into me and knocked me over. He was on roller-blades.'

'He always is.'

'He was very apologetic. Even offered to pay for dry-cleaning me jacket. I told him to forget it ... I was on duty, see ... and, well ...'

I could see what was coming. 'When did you notice Annie's keys were missing?'

'Later. Well, quite a bit later,' he admitted sheepishly. 'That's why I went back to the park. To look for them. And then I saw the lights were on in Annie's flat.'

'Prat.'

Zeb looked even more guilty. He really is very easy to intimidate. Annie says it comes from having four big sisters.

'Do you think I should phone Annie?'

'No. Not yet. I mean, they may only stay a few days. Could be gone by the time she gets back.'

Zeb clutched this straw with visible relief. 'They could, couldn't they? I don't know why they had to pick on Annie's in the first place.'

I'd been thinking about that. And I had a nasty feeling I could just have had a hand in it. Figgy's sneering remarks about Annie as he'd skated up the promenade with me the other day came back. What had I said? Something about her having a flat by the park? And packing to go on a business trip? But I'd never mentioned her surname, had I?

On the other hand, he had needled me into telling him she was a private investigator. And Vetch's was the only PI business in town.

I'd checked with Janice the next morning. 'Has anyone been in asking for Annie recently?'

'Several people. *She* has clients.'

'You've definitely got to sue that correspondence course, Jan.'

'What correspondence course?'

'Charm by Post. Ten easy lessons on how to get on with people. I reckon they left out Lessons Two to Eight.'

'Ha-bloody-ha!'

She glowered at me. And unlike most of the females I came across, she could do it eye to eye. In fact, I think she had an inch on me.

I told her she'd have liked the bloke I was asking about. 'Black's his favourite colour too,' I explained. 'He's midnight from hair to calf. With bright-yellow roller-blades. Looks like a puppet from *Sesame Street*.'

Running complacent hands over her own black outfit of tights, shorts and sleeveless waistcoat, Jan had denied ever having seen Figgy. But she did finally admit that someone had phoned describing Annie and asking what surname to put on the credit check report they were sending her.

Great. The local directory listed twenty-five A. Smiths. But only one had an address bordering the local park. Figgy must have thought it was a sign from heaven when Zeb turned up with the keys.

I glared at him now and asked: 'Can I come in?'

Figgy shook the black spikes. 'Nope.'

'Oh come on, Figgy. I can hardly throw you out single-handed, can I? I just want to see the flat's OK.'

He shut the door in my face. I thought that was it. But to my surprise, it opened a second later – minus the safety chain.

'Come in, your Graciness. Mickey, we've got a guest.'

Mickey came out of the bedroom. She looked shy and

uneasy, both hands restlessly twisting the mousy hair over one shoulder whilst she nibbled at her split ends.

'Coffee?' Figgy offered.

'Thanks. It's in the green and gold canister. I know because this is my friend's flat.'

Mickey looked even more worried. Figgy simply grinned. I was relieved to see he'd taken the roller-blades off. At least we wouldn't have to worry about getting the floorboards repolished.

Mickey made the coffee, handling each item with almost reverential care.

'What happened to the beach hut?'

'Couldn't stop there no longer, could we, Mickey? Need a bit of TLC, don't you, baby?'

Mickey flushed. She ducked her head, but I could see a tide of pink rising up the back of her neck.

She put the crockery and cafetière on a tray. Figgy took it from her. 'I can manage, Figgy.'

'Go sit down. I'll be Mum today.'

Mickey blushed again. And the penny dropped. The baby who needed the TLC wasn't Mickey.

'Congratulations. When's it due?'

'N'vember.'

She wriggled back on Annie's sofa, one hand laid lightly over her stomach as if she couldn't quite believe what was in there.

'You still can't stop here. Go down the DSS, they'll have to give you something if Mickey's expecting.'

'They wanted to put us in a bed and breakfast. But that ain't what Mickey needs. A proper home, not a load of moody from some landlord about what time you get in your room. And some grotty bathroom covered in everyone else's crud.'

Mickey was holding her coffee cup as if she was afraid it was going to explode. She plainly wasn't comfortable here, so I decided to put the pressure on her.

'Annie will be able to get back in easily, you know. I mean, this is her home. No court is going to expect her to sleep on the beach so you can scrounge a free ride.'

Tears filled Mickey's eyes. I felt a real cow.

'Oi!' Figgy showed he was really serious by resettling his glasses and pushing them close to my face. 'Listen, let's get it straight, Miss Detective. We're not scroungers. We can't get a flat because we haven't got a deposit or references. And we ain't got the deposit because I can't get a job, because we haven't got an address to put on the application form ...'

'Yes. OK, I've got the message. Life's tough. That's no reason to expect Annie to bail you out.'

'I don't. I just need to borrow her flat for a bit. We'll keep it clean. And soon as I get a bit of cash together, she can give us a reference and we'll move on.'

'A reference! For what?'

'Being great tenants ...'

'Don't push your luck, Figgy.'

'You know, you want to take up meditation. Deal with that internalised stress.' He gave me a big grin. 'Don't want to rush you, your Graciness, but we've got to get a bit of shopping in.'

I guess the hope showed on my face.

'I'll be stopping at home while she goes up the shops, if you were thinking of calling round with another set of keys. Byeeee ...'

Annie rang me that afternoon from Leeds. She was a bit stressed out trying to track down the background of a candidate of Asian descent.

'I wish I'd learnt a bit of Urdu, or something. Everyone seems to be related to everyone else. And all the kids are named after grandfathers, or uncles or whatever, so you get four or five generations all with the same name.'

I made soothing noises and rubbed the auricle of my ear, which was sore after a long session on the phone dialling every bank in the Manchester and Leicester areas doing the stranded-motorist-rescued-by-Kristen-Keats routine. None of them had an account in that name.

'So what are you going to do next?' Annie asked.

I explained about my new career as an office cleaner.

'Are you sure you can remember how to operate a duster? Only there's never been any sign of a talent in that direction in your office or flat.'

'There's no need to get sarky. I'm a great believer in the Quentin Crisp theory of housewifery.'

'What's that?'

'After four years the dust doesn't accumulate any further.'

'You've proved that one twice over, I reckon. Anyway, I mustn't keep you any longer. My phone bill must be into three figures by now.'

'What makes you think I'm on your phone?'

'Vast experience. Well, I think I'll just have a quick dip in the pool before I hit the trail again. Is my flat OK, by the way?'

I assured her Zeb had checked it out twice. And I'd swung past that way myself only that morning.

'Great. Have fun with the polishing then. And get off my phone.'

Resetting the lock-out code which I'd managed to bypass (she'd used Zeb's birthday), I shut up Annie's office and informed Janice I'd be at home tomorrow since I'd be expending kinetic energy in domestic lavation.

'Going to muck out at last, are you?' she called, not taking her eyes from the word processor.

She'd definitely been memorising the thesaurus. I'd have to find out what all this self-improvement was about some time. In the meantime, there was the flat to be tackled. I drove up to the supermarket and picked up their own-brand super-economy bleach, washing powder, scouring cream and polish.

I don't believe in piecemeal laundry. Everything at once should last me until September, I reckoned.

I lugged the curtains, blankets and duvet round to the launderette first thing and then divided everything else into same-shade heaps. The washing machine only seemed to work at one temperature anyway, so I've never found there was any point in worrying whether it was wool, silk or woven yak's hair.

Once the first lot was sloshing away in its biological solution, I filled a bucket with water and started on the flat.

After the first half-hour, the clothes I was working in were soaked and filthy. Stripping them off, I dropped them on the 'whitey-yellow-greyish' washing pile and made myself a nifty little mini-dress from a black plastic rubbish sack.

We all had washing lines strung across the back yard, and by using the other tenants' and adding a couple more of my own, I had every scrap of fabric in the flat flapping around out there by the evening. Virtue oozed out of my every pore – along with a fair amount of sweat because the plastic was acting as a sauna.

There was just one more chore left to do. I'd noticed brown water-staining on the ceiling in one corner of the main room a few weeks ago and had scrounged a part-used tin of white paint from the upstair tenant for a touch of remedial DIY. As there were no dry scarves left for head protection, I used a plastic shower cap I'd once filched from a hotel somewhere.

By standing on tiptoe on a chair, I dabbed out the stains quite effectively. I'd just jumped to the ground to admire my efforts when the doorbell rang.

Assuming it was Zeb with another update on the squatter problem, I ripped the door open. My mouth fell open. I knew it was hanging on my chest, but somehow my jaw muscles seemed to have become paralysed. Along with just about everything else.

Kevin Drysdale's brown eyes travelled up the bare feet and paint-streaked rubbish sack and stopped at the elastic band of the shower cap that was cutting into my eyebrows.

'Hi, sexy.'

CHAPTER 16

'Pasta, steak?'

'Absolutely.'

'Which?'

'Both.'

'Something's given you an appetite.'

Kevin smiled. The light from the candle in the middle of our table flickered, deepening the crevices in his face and smoothing out the rest of the blemishes in an even golden glow.

Once I'd overcome paralysis and an irresistible desire to slam the door in his face, I'd gone for the cool hey-what's-the-big-deal approach to my grunge outfit.

'I was wondering whether you might fancy dinner?' Kevin had said, lounging on my doorstep all blue silk shirt, chinos, sports jacket and seriously gorgeous smile.

'Tonight?'

'Unless it's inconvenient.'

'Why would it be?' I asked, feeling the sweat running down under the rubbish sack dress. 'Give me half an hour.'

I pushed him out to amuse himself for thirty minutes whilst I dumped the bag-lady ensemble, and swore revenge on the malicious spirit that had done this to me.

The bathwater was cold after my marathon laundry session. And I'd washed all the towels.

Haring around the back yard, I dragged the least damp towel from the line and added anything that felt dry, dumping the muddled pile on the stripped mattress before jumping in the bath and splashing like a demented seal.

Thank heavens for a drip-dry hairstyle. I disentangled underwear and a slip-style dress from the jumble on the bed, added jewellery, strappy sandals and a (dryish) shawl and I was ready for anywhere.

Which turned out to be an Italian restaurant in the middle of Canterbury.

'I'll have the spaghetti marinara,' I told the hovering waiter. 'The full-size portion.'

He scribbled on his pad. 'And for a starter, signora?'

'That is for starters. For the main course I'd like a fillet steak – well done. Assorted vegetables and extra onion rings. And can you bring some more bread sticks, please.'

We had a litre of the house red. There was a framed newspaper cutting of a famous wine column on the wall by the table rhapsodising about its rich blackcurrant flavours and hints of vanilla with a smoky finish. It tasted just like red wine to me.

After a few large swallows I felt myself starting to relax and enjoy the atmosphere. It was a genuinely old building of rough stone walls, uneven floors and beams blackened by open fires.

I put my elbows on the table and linked my fingers, intending to rest my chin on them. It always looks good when the heroine does it on the TV. Presumably her hands never stink of bleach. I hastily unlinked before I was gassed.

'How's your dad? I didn't see the donkeys on the beach.'

'He's been taking them down. Shorter hours, though. You must have missed him.'

'Mmm ...' I gulped more wine. The blackcurrant and vanilla were definitely eluding me.

Kevin topped me up. 'I'm driving. I hope you can finish this.'

'I'll give it my best shot. Cheers!'

The smoke from the guttering candle was stinging my eyes. Kevin moved it to one side, leaving only a basket of bread as a barrier between us.

Did I want a barrier? I wasn't too sure. In fact, I wasn't too sure why he'd suddenly turned up again. So I asked him.

'I was rather hoping you might phone me, Grace.'

'Why?' It came out more abruptly than I'd intended.

'Because I like you. And you seemed to like me. And it is considered acceptable for the woman to make the first move these days. Isn't it?'

'I can't remember,' I admitted. 'I mean, it's been a while since I've moved in either direction, forward or backwards, if you see what I mean. How about you?'

'I've been rather static since I married Minnie.'

'When was that?'

'Nine years ago.'

'How long have you been separated?'

'Six months.'

'Why did you marry her?'

'Because she was pregnant. Do you always conduct conversations like they were police interrogations?'

'Sorry.' I felt myself blushing, something I hadn't done in years. Thank heavens for lighting designed to create an intimate ambience and hide the menu prices. 'I told you I wasn't very good at this.'

Thankfully the spaghetti arrived at that point. I concentrated on ploughing through it, suddenly bolshily determined that he could take up the chit-chat from here.

He did. He asked me *why* I hadn't phoned him. 'Last time, at the club, we seemed to get on pretty well ... and I thought ... you know ...'

I emerged from the plate, conscious of the ends of spaghetti hanging from my mouth. Taking a deep breath, I sucked and swallowed.

'Last time is the problem. Look ...' I collected my thoughts, trying to explain to him something that I still hadn't fully explained to myself. 'After what happened at TED's, I wouldn't blame you for thinking I make a habit of ripping my clothes off and going for it ten minutes after the first hello. But ... you see ...' I refilled my glass and took a large gulp. 'You see ... I don't. In fact, I haven't, not since I bust up with my live-in after I left the police. Or got invited to leave, if you want to be pedantic.'

'Why was that?'

'Why did I leave the police?' I'd already told him about that misunderstanding which had resulted in a vicious villain walking away from a serious assault charge and yours truly inexplicably several thousand pounds richer.

'Why did you leave the boyfriend? Or did he leave you?'

'I don't know. After it happened – getting the boot, I mean – I took it all out on him. Maybe I was hoping he'd leave. I don't know now. Anyway, he did. And he rented out his flat, changed the locks, left my belongings in the garage and flew off to Singapore – just in case I didn't get the message. Why did you and Minnie split up?'

'Because we had almost nothing in common apart from the kids. And after eight-odd years we finally decided to stop pretending we had.'

The starter plates were whisked away and the chequered tablecloth swept clean preparatory to the arrival of the main course.

Kevin had ordered sole. 'Aren't you worried about mad cow disease?' he asked as I heaped veggies around my fillet steak.

'There's whole herds of Friesians out there reckon they caught it from me,' I grinned.

He smiled back. But the tension was still there.

'So is that it? You didn't call because you thought I'd be expecting a ten-minute quickie?'

'Sort of.' I was still struggling to put it into words. 'I do like you, Kevin. And I fancy you too. But I can't just … I want friendship first … and a relationship … a developing relationship … Oh hell, am I making any sort of sense over that side of the table?'

'Just about. You're an old-fashioned girl at heart who wants to be courted rather than jumped.'

'I don't know about courted. I mean, I'm not expecting you to do anything corny – like turn up with a bunch of red roses and two tickets to Venice. No, scrub that … I quite fancy Venice … but I want … I'd like us to go back to Day One … if you're planning to see me again. If you just want quick sex … well, I'm not your girl.'

'Fair enough.'

Fair enough *what*? I wondered. Well, the next move was down to him. At least I'd got a great dinner out of it.

'Dessert, signora. Or perhaps just some coffee?'

The waiter's tone indicated only a real pig could manage anything more than a small black coffee. Well, oink oink to him.

I had tiramisù with a side order of fresh strawberries. Followed by three cappuccinos and a plate of chocolate mints.

'Brandy?'

'If you're having one.'

'Let's have them in the bar. I've a present for you.'

For a ghastly moment I thought he was going to pull a jeweller's box from his jacket pocket. I had fleeting visions of one of those a-girl-like-you-should-wear-gold/diamonds conversations.

The roll of fax paper came as a bit of a surprise.

'Company report on Wexton's Engineering. Dad said you were asking. What's the interest?'

I gave him a brief rundown on Kristen Keats. 'To be honest, I think she's just got fed up or had a better offer. But I've got to give the client something for his … or her … money,' I corrected myself, recalling Henry's insistence on confidentiality.

I scanned through chunks of incomprehensible figures listed under headings like Assets, Liabilities, Capital Reserves, Provisions, etc. 'What on earth does this lot mean?'

Kevin took it from me and ran a professional eye down it.

'Basically it means Wexton's are solvent. But not as profitable as they ought to be. They've got a lot of assets but their turnover hasn't increased much in the past ten years. And they've got a fairly hefty loan or loans they're paying off, by the looks of it. They probably increased their capital assets in anticipation of orders to come – and then the orders didn't oblige. Mind you, this stuff is generally about two years out of date; they could have put on a bit of pace by now.'

About the only bit of the faxed report I could understand was the summary of company directors.

The business had started trading in 1936 and the directors then were shown as Jack Arnold Wexton and Alfred Carnegie.

That situation continued until 1948, when the directors changed to Alfred Carnegie, Joan Barbara Reiss and Blanche Ann Wexton.

'Is that when Wexton died? Nineteen forty-eight?'

'I would assume so.' Kevin slid slightly closer on the bench seat we were sharing so that he could read over my shoulder. It also had the effect of pressing his thigh tighter to mine. 'Joan Reiss is the old man's daughter. She's in her seventies now. Minnie was on a charity fund-raising committee with her.'

'What about this Blanche Wexton?'

'Another relative, I suppose. Can't say I've ever come across her. Anyway, she's off the scene by 1950.'

He pointed to the relevant line of fuzzy print. For the next thirty-seven years the three directors of Wexton's Engineering were shown as Derek Patrick Reiss, Joan Barbara Reiss and the ubiquitous Alfred Carnegie.

Then, ten years ago, Derek dropped out of the picture and was replaced by Stephen Bridgeman.

'Stephen's married to Joan Reiss's daughter, Amelia,' Kevin explained.

'December said. Derek, I assume, was Joan's husband? Is he dead or retired?'

'Both.'

'And he left his share of Wexton's to his son-in-law rather than his daughter? Bit chauvinistic, isn't it?'

'It may have been practical. Stephen was heading up their technical side anyway. Giving him a share in the company would have sharpened up his commercial instincts. Made him go out there and hassle for the contracts. Engineers can get a bit wrapped up in the technical answers and forget there's a financial pay-off at the end – either for or against. And Stephen couldn't have kept Amelia in the style to which she's determined to stay accustomed if the company folded.'

I swirled the brandy, watching the thin layer of pale gold adhering to the balloon's side. 'Is it my imagination, Kevin, or do you know Stephen Bridgeman rather better than a few lines on a faxed report?'

'Same golf club.'

'Aah.'

'Minnie made me join.'

'Poor baby.'

'Is this evening about to end in a childish squabble?'

'No. Sorry. You dad's always telling me off about my mouth. Does Stephen play away? And I'm not talking about the fairways here, Kevin.'

'I gathered.' He finished his own brandy and thought a moment. 'Nothing serious that I've heard of. Well, he'd be a fool to try it, wouldn't he ... with his mother-in-law owning part of his company. I'm not sure what the actual share-out is ... but I suspect if Joan and this Alfred Carnegie voted against him, his hands would be pretty well tied.'

'Who is Carnegie? He must be about a hundred and one by now if he was a mate of Jack Wexton's.'

'Old, certainly. But he may have been younger than Wexton. Whoever he is, he's another one I've never met. Are you working on the theory that Wexton's – or Stephen – is somehow connected to this Kristen person's disappearance?'

'I haven't got a theory. I'm just casting around in the dark, hoping something will pop up. Preferably Kristen.'

Kevin made a scribbling motion on his palm at a passing waiter. I took the hint and finished my drink.

There was nothing so gaudy as multicoloured necklaces

strung along the buildings here. Nor the intrusive electronic *pow-whee* of the games arcades and the rumbling music clash of the amusement arcades. Just the huge bulk of the ancient cathedral looming over lowly buildings and bathed in the slightly harsh light of the *son et lumière*.

We walked back to the car via the pedestrianised shopping streets. Rather than going directly to the BMW, Kevin wandered through the old city gate and along the river path.

'What now?' he asked.

For a moment I thought he was talking about us, then I realised he was probably harking back to our last conversation about the case.

Even if Bridgeman was just a putting partner, I didn't think it was too smart to tell Kevin I was planning to snoop round his factory tomorrow night. You never really know where people's loyalties lie, do you?

I made vague noises about something turning up.

'Mr Micawber was relying on that too.'

'Well, in his case it came true, didn't it?'

I shivered slightly, The temperature had dropped quite a bit since this afternoon. Kevin put an arm round my shoulders, drawing me in to him.

A couple of ghost swans glided silently past us on flat black waters.

I leant against Kevin. The suspense was getting to me. 'So am I going to see you again?'

'Sure. Mind, it might be a bit difficult in the near future ...'

'I prefer people to call a spade a bloody shovel, thanks, Kevin. If you mean get lost, don't say it's *a bit difficult.*'

I knew it was my own fault. I'd laid out the rules and he didn't want to play. Fair enough. But I still couldn't help feeling rejected.

'Hey ... woah back ... I mean *a bit difficult.* It's half-term. Minnie and I will be playing happy families. We agreed when we split that it wouldn't affect the kids. But we won't be playing mummies and daddies. OK?'

I shrugged. 'Sure.'

I could hear myself sounding like a teenage kid in a sulk. I felt awful, but I couldn't stop myself. Luckily I was saved from further self-embarrassment by the appearance of four genuine teenagers flying out of the darkness from the direction of the city gate.

Half running, half stumbling, they rushed along the river path. One, a blonde whose hair looked white in this light, appeared to be having trouble, and another girl was supporting her as they wobbled along in high heels and tight skirts.

'Hurry up, Claudia. We'll get expelled.'

'I can't help it. Livia's pissed. Anyway, who cares? I'm always getting expelled. School's a drag.'

They were nearly opposite us. I called across to the first girl, 'Evening, Bone.'

There was a collective gasp of fright. Even the laid-back Claudia looked worried for a moment.

Bone waved them on. 'It's OK. She's nothing to do with St Aggie's. She's a private investigator. She's on a case for me.'

They hurried past in the direction of St Aggie's back wall. I caught a brief glimpse of Bone's face. She'd really enjoyed saying that!

'Who the hell were they?' Kevin asked, once they'd disappeared round the bend in the river path.

'Just examples of the finest that private education can buy.'

CHAPTER 17

Nola was already waiting for me when I arrived at the Downs Estate on Thursday evening.

Leaning against the scooter, she was chatting to the barmaid whilst the woman scrubbed graffiti from the front door of the social club. There was a low buzz of voices and the higher rumble of the TV sports presenter's commentary from inside.

'Thought you'd changed yer mind. Got Bonnie's tenner?'

I handed it over. She tucked it inside her bum bag and passed me an identity badge. It had Bonnie's picture on it. A pre-striped Bonnie when her hair had been a mousy brown. By no stretch of the imagination did it look anything like me (I hoped!).

Nola wasn't bothered. 'Don't matter. Stick yer thumb over it. Let's go then.'

She handed me a crash helmet. I hesitated. Nola was wide; I was tall; the scooter was very small. I wasn't sure this was a viable combination.

'We can use my car.'

'Best not. Guard's used to me scooter. He won't think nothing of it if you come with me. Don't want him suddenly taking notice, do we?'

I suppose it made sense. Nola knocked up the kick rests and started the scooter. Her bottom, in off-white jogging pants, overhung the seat like proving dough.

The ocean, once again, was out. The only glimpse of it we had was the oblong of salt water trapped by the low walls of the paddling pool as the tide retreated.

The beach was practically deserted despite the long, light evenings now. A few dog-walkers were striding along far out on the water's edge. I wasn't certain, but something about the upright posture of one made me think it might be Henry Summerstone. Behind him the clumping, graphite-grey clouds of the approaching squall were already boiling up on the horizon.

Nola swung the bike left, cutting off my view of the coast. Inland the sky was still blue and cloudless, the dying sunshine casting heavy shadows across the boarding-house gardens and newly planted council beds of fledgeling geraniums, begonias and petunias.

Somebody had been brightening up the front of Wexton's too. There were a couple of narrow beds under the front windows and a deeper one away to one side, bordering the far edge of the car park. It looked like the gardener had miscalculated the number of plants needed, since a stretch of white busy Lizzies ran out just before the end of the car-park bed.

The guard let us in without comment when Nola waved her identity badge at him. He didn't even bother to look at mine.

'Anyone working?' Nola said casually.

'No, love, you've got the place to yourselves tonight.'

This was good news. If I'd found the upstairs offices

occupied, I'd have had to come back another day. And three days of housework was bordering on the obsessional as far as I was concerned.

Nola banged between sets of internal doors. Through other doors to the left I could see open rooms with metal benches set crossways, a bit like old-fashioned school desks. Their back sections were lined with child-size plastic baskets in primary colours; some holding tiny components and others with what looked like those mini green boards that you find inside transistor radios if you're careless enough to drop them on hard surfaces. Most of the bench tops were clear, although a few had half-assembled component boards on them and a selection of miscellaneous technical gadgets that I couldn't identify.

'Is this where Kristen worked?'

'Further down ... in 'ere.'

Nola opened another set of doors and flipped on the strip lighting to show a room lined with floor-to-ceiling metal racking. Most of them seemed to contain computer VDUs attached to a Spaghetti Junction of cables.

'Don't touch nothing,' Nola warned.

'Why? Is it dangerous?'

'Don't think so. But it has to stay on. I pulled a plug out once and they went ballistic. Reckoned I'd cost them hundreds of pounds. So now we don't move nothing, OK?'

'OK.'

She emerged from the dark, claustrophobic canyons of equipment racks to an open area at the back of the room. There were a couple of metal desks back here, but with file storage rather than plastic baskets.

The left-hand one held two half-dismantled computers. Nola indicated the right-hand one. 'That's Rob's desk.'

'Rob's?' It took a second to register. She was still thinking of it as belonging to Kristen's predecessor, Rob Wingett.

It was no more than a bench really, with two narrow drawers underneath. Neither was locked. I rummaged around amongst sheets of paper filled with incomprehensible diagrams, mathematical symbols and extracts from technical reports. None were sequential and most seemed to be photocopies. Scrap paper, I guessed.

There wasn't much else: pens, pencils, erasers, rubber bands and paper clips tangled in cluttered confusion. A tin for barley-sugar lumps which turned out to be empty.

'That was Rob's,' Nola said. She'd been standing watching me, arms folded to support her drooping bosom. She sighed. 'He was great, Rob.'

'You said. Did he stay late a lot?'

'Fair time, yeah. He just sorta got lost in the job, if yer know what I mean. We used to joke about his wife thinking him and me was carrying on. Not that we were. I don't mess around with other women's blokes.'

I didn't suppose they messed around with Nola much; she wasn't exactly snog-of-the-month material.

'Was he working on something special?'

'He worked on everything. He was dead proud of that. Everything came through his department at the end.'

'And Kristen? Was she down here a lot, out of hours?'

I had no idea where this line of questioning was leading, but with no definite path to go down, I just had to take a few steps down each turning and hope I'd pick up Kristen's trail.

'Sometimes. But not so much. They ain't had the work recently.'

I continued to delve in the desk. If Kristen had left anything behind it certainly wasn't here. Every non-work item I came up with, from the out-of-date calendars to the fluffy stick-on trolls with advertising slogans, packet of bendy straws and tarnished cutlery, Nola promptly said: 'That's Rob's.'

I stared round in frustration. 'Did Kristen work anywhere else?'

'Through there.'

The next room held three metal chambers, with assorted dials, switches and gauges below a glass box that looked like a microwave oven. Each one had a large notice screwed on to it stating: '*To be operated by authorised personnel only. Annual re-calibration essential.*'

'They leave things in there. For days sometimes.'

Unless they'd left Kristen in there, this room was of even less interest to me.

'Hurry, will yer,' Nola demanded. 'I want to get finished.

They're taking names for the Sunday-night karaoke up the club tonight.'

'I'm done down here.' In the absence of a handy over-looked letter or whatever giving a few clues to Kristen's destination, I was going to have to trawl through her past. Via the personnel files. There was always Bertram, of course.

'Nope. Never 'eard of no Bertram here. Dunno all of the blokes, of course, but I ain't never heard anyone called that,' Nola said in answer to my question.

She unlocked a cupboard in the corridor and dragged out two vacuum cleaners, black sacks, buckets and two dinky baskets full of cleaning materials, whilst she issued a stream of instructions.

'Make dead certain you empty *all* the waste-paper bins. They always notice the bins. Put them well inside the sack before you tip, that way you don't get nothing stuck on the carpets. Make sure the bogs are clean and give the basins a good scrub. Stick a mop over the floor if you've time, otherwise it's just if someone's spilt something. Dust and hoover everywhere in that cow Ayres' office and Mr Bridgeman's, but don't move no papers, we ain't allowed. We ain't got time to do more. They want to pay crap rates, they can have a crap job.'

I put all the lights on on the top floor and did a quick check to confirm there wasn't anyone beavering away in a quiet corner.

Ms Ayres' desk was simple. Two seconds with a skeleton key and I'd confirmed the bunch of keys I'd seen her drop in the file indexer the other night was there.

I decided to do a bit of cleaning before I got down to the serious business. I had no way of knowing the guard's routine and it seemed prudent to establish myself as a bona fide cleaner.

There was no production work up here. It was all offices, computer suites and a boardroom. And those winking VDU screens watching me at every turn. If there were name-plates or diaries lying around, I checked for the elusive Bertram.

He remained stubbornly elusive. There wasn't even a hint of him; not one Christian name began with 'B'.

The guard passed me as I was lugging my full sack back to the head of the stairs. 'All right, love?'

'Terrific, thanks. You?'

'Can't complain. Don't do you no good if you do, does it?'

On this cheery thought he marched on. Ten minutes later, whilst I had my rubber gloves in the urinals, he appeared again.

'Do you want to …'

'No thanks, love. Just doing me rounds. Back in half an hour.'

It was nice of him to be so precise. I whizzed through the ladies' loo in ten minutes flat. All that training yesterday had plainly paid off.

When I got back to the managing director's area, I sprayed pine polish lavishly and flicked a duster over desks, bookcases, files and equipment. There wasn't much variance between Ms Ayres' office and Stephen Bridgeman's; it was furnishing by committee – air-force-blue carpet, pale wood furniture and framed prints of impressionist seascapes.

I located Kristen's file amongst the 'Past Employees' section of Ms Ayres' filing system. There was no photograph. As I discovered this I realised that I'd been half hoping for one. It would have made Kristen more substantial.

Ms Ayres was a filing fanatic – thank heavens. She'd squirrelled everything away. The first note on Kristen's file was dated 18 July and stated:

Miss Kristen Keats telephoned enquiring if vacancy exists for test engineer. She saw report on Robert Wingett's accident in paper. Mr Bridgeman has authorised me to send application form.

And there was an address in Bayswater! Hallelujah!

I flipped on. Kristen's formal application contained the same home address in Bayswater, plus a telephone number.

I scanned the rest of the document quickly. She'd gone to school in Bath and university in Leicester, which would explain the earlier rented properly in that city. After that she'd worked in Manchester for eight months as an assistant design technician at AD Aerospace. Her reason for leaving was 'company restructuring'. Which probably translated as 'redundant'.

She didn't have any better luck with her second job. Okranshaw Electronics in Leicester had closed down six months after Kristen joined them as 'deputy acquisitions executive'.

After that it had been seven months with the Third World voluntary agency, 'assisting in teaching and basic engineering projects amongst undeveloped communities'.

That seemed to have come to an end last July, a couple of weeks or so before she'd contacted Wexton's. It all made logical sense.

'And why shouldn't it …?' I asked myself as the photocopier spewed out sheets of paper. Tucking Kristen's details down the front of my jogging pants for further study, I read on.

There was a reference from AD Aerospace which merely confirmed the basic details of Kristen's employment with them. And one from a former director of Okranshaw who now appeared to be running a craft shop in Cornwall. It was vaguely complimentary about Kristen's time with the company, without going overboard.

There wasn't much else. A formal contract of employment. A brief handwritten internal note from Kristen giving a month's notice. Another form listing her final payment and holiday entitlements and countersigned by Kristen.

I stuffed everything back inside the plastic holder and tried to replace it in its slot. It was one of those hanging filing systems and the edge kept snagging. Irritated, I pushed harder. The file shot straight through the back and fell to the floor, showering papers over the base of the filing cabinet.

'Blast.'

Getting down on my knees, I started shuffling papers. I'd just got the lot in order when I heard voices in the corridor. Stretching up, I pushed the file in and pulled the shutter down to close off the cabinet, but didn't have time to replace the base padlock before the office door swung open.

'Thank you for the lift, Stephen. I'm sorry I had to drag you down to the garden centre again.'

'No problem, Joan. Least I can do in the circumstances.'

I'd assumed it was the security guard and Nola, but instead I found myself kneeling on the floor staring up at Stephen Bridgeman. There was an older woman behind him, half hidden by his body as they both looked down at me crouched by the filing cabinet.

I caught my breath, wondering if Stephen would recognise me. Hopefully there was no reason that he should. Last time, I'd been Shona, scourge of the tax-payer, in a brunette wig left over from the last production of *Cleopatra*. And now I was in coffee-stained joggers peering up through lank strands of blonde hair.

Dropping my eyes, I mumbled: 'Sorry. Guard said no one was working up here. Shall I go?'

'No need. We shan't be a moment. You're new, aren't you?'

'Covering …' I muttered. 'Regular girl's sick.'

I sought round for a plausible reason why I'd be sitting down here. The cleaning basket was by the cabinet where I'd left it. Squeezing a blob of scouring cream on a rag, I scrubbed at a double plastic socket in the wainscoting. Originally it had been white; now it was the colour of sealskin.

From the corner of my eye, I could see their feet hadn't moved. Cautiously I glanced sideways. Had they noticed that the padlock hadn't been replaced?

They were both staring at me. 'Sorry …' I shuffed back on my knees. 'Did you want to get here?'

It was the woman who answered, telling me to 'Carry on, dear. I've been wanting someone to clean those sockets for months. What a pleasure to meet someone who believes in doing a decent job for a change. I'm sorry, did you tell us your name …?'

I tossed up with inventing another false one. But what was the point? I'd probably never see her again. 'Grace.'

'Well, keep up the good work, Grace.'

She inclined her head. I had the feeling if I'd knuckled my forehead and murmured, 'Yes, ma'am, very good, ma'am,' she wouldn't have found it inappropriate. Instead I compromised with a half-bow from the kneeling position and stuck my nose to the wainscoting.

They went into Bridgeman's office, but unfortunately left the door partially open.

By shuffling along to the next socket on my knees, I managed to click the padlock back into place, but I still needed to get the keys back in Ms Ayres' desk and relock it.

I had a better view of the inner office from here. Stephen was scrolling through a document on the computer screen.

'It all looks pretty clear next week. Although frankly, Joan, I'm not sure this is such a good idea.'

'Why ever not? Amelia will expect some kind of celebration.'

'But perhaps not a big party? She might prefer a quiet family do.'

'Rubbish. She's fifty. Why wouldn't she want a party?'

'*Because* she's fifty.'

I caught the ironical note in his voice. But either the woman didn't or she was so used to getting her own way she ignored it as unimportant. The latter probably. She looked the type who was supremely confident it was everyone else who was out of step.

He'd called her Joan, so presumably this was his mum-in-law: mother of the soon-to-be-embarrassed Amelia and a major shareholder in Wexton's Engineering.

From my viewpoint by the next socket, I watched her watching the screen over Stephen's shoulder.

I guessed she must be in her early seventies at least. But the sort of seventy who still had a good number of hours left on her time-clock. There was nothing frail about Joan Reiss. Her figure was slim rather than thin, her movements still brisk and easy. The skin on the oval face looked soft and well nourished and the light-grey hair was swept back in a short, expensive cut to show off a still firm jaw-line.

Leaning over the desk, she was now tapping on the computer keys, causing other files to flash up on the screen. Judging by Stephen's face, he'd rather she went back to discussing the birthday party.

'The six-monthly position hasn't improved a great deal, Stephen.'

'We're having the post-mortem on Sumata next week. The MoD are very impressed, we know that.'

'And we also know they have no obligation to place the production order with Wexton's. It was a mistake for you to devote so much time to that contract. The price hardly justifies it.'

'Quarter of a million isn't to be sneezed at.'

'No. But when you consider the hours you put in …'

'I enjoyed it. Getting back to design, development …'

'It wasn't the best utilisation of man-power in my opinion. You should have stuck to your original plan to pass it over to the design team as soon as they were clear of the medical contract … Your time would have been more productively spent widening our customer base.'

'Thank you, Joan. But I think you can leave the day-to-day running of the company to me, don't you?'

Or, to put it another way, *Mind your own business, you bossy old bat*, I thought, silently snuffling round the wainscot in search of my next socket.

'Obviously. Or I shouldn't have supported your appointment as managing director when Derek died. However, as a major shareholder in the company, I think I must be allowed my contribution. And I feel we must look for new customers.

'And I am, Joan. I am. Now, since it's late … and since we both want to get home …'

'I'll stop interfering. However, I shall bring this up at the next board meeting. Perhaps Bertram knew best after all.'

At the mention of Bertram, I gave up any pretence of cleaning and strained to hear Joan's next words. Which, regrettably, were: 'Are you ready to leave?'

'No. Can you give me ten minutes, Joan? There's something I've remembered. Do you mind?'

'Not at all. I'll get those last dozen busy Lizzies in. May I have the car keys?'

Stephen dropped a bunch into her hand. 'You don't have to do this, you know. We could get in a contractor.'

'Rubbish. I enjoy my little bit of gardening. It's the only patch I've got since I moved into the flat.'

She swept out, bestowing another approving smile in my direction. I simpered.

As soon as she'd gone, I switched on the vacuum cleaner and howled around by Stephen's door. He glanced up from his computer screen. I gestured closing the door and received a nodding agreement and a smile of gratitude.

I did a noisy circuit of the office. From the side window I could see the security guard heaving a bag of compost from the boot of a silver Mercedes. Joan Reiss was kneeling by the flowerbed, using a trowel handle to knock the busy Lizzies from their foam boxes. The two German Shepherds were sitting close, watching her with tongues hanging out. Perhaps it was the patch where they buried trespassers.

Pushing the hoover with one foot to keep the engine noise at 'moving' rather than 'stationary', I slipped the keys back into the indexer in Ms Ayres' desk and relocked it. On an impulse I flipped open the heavy leather desk diary, and checked the entries for the week Kristen had disappeared. It all looked pretty routine.

There had been a progress meeting on Monday afternoon and two staff reviews on Tuesday. Wednesday was empty from Stephen's point of view; I assumed the cryptic notes in pencil were Ms Ayres' reminders to herself. '*Ensure all papers ready for K.K.*' obviously referred to Kristen's leaving documents. '*Check A.B.'s hotel res. tomorrow*' was anyone's guess. On Thursday they'd had '*K.K.'s leaving presentation at three o'clock*' just before '*Medsec tech mtg*' at 4 p.m. On Friday there was a note of a meeting with the MoD at 10.30 a.m., with a further ringed note: '*See over 7 May*'.

I took another circle of the desk with the hoover, whilst I flipped the pages to the following week and read upside down:

> *10.30: Sumata Progress Mtg:*
> *Wg Cmdr. G. Daley*
> *Mjr A. Rolands*
> *Mr D. Simmonds*
> *Mr R. Reeves (Qual.)*
> *Mr W. Oliver*
> *Mr A.B. Grant*
> (Lunch bkd 1 p.m. White Hart)

The list had been crossed through and annotated: '*Moved*'. Reading backwards I found the rest of Stephen's week had been as boring as the previous one. Another staff review, more meetings, a telephone conference on Wednesday, an accounts review on Thursday. There were no social engagements; presumably he kept those on the computer diary he'd been reading through with his mum-in-law. Nor were there any handy little entries on the lines of '*brick up test engineer in cellar – 4 p.m.*' Whichever way you read it, the two weeks surrounding Kristen's last days at Wexton's had been routine.

Switching off, I rewound the hoover flex and headed back to base. As far as I was concerned, Wexton's was clean enough.

'Hey, you! Hang on!'

I looked back. Stephen Bridgeman was striding towards me holding a sheet of paper. The photocopied papers from Kristen Keats' file crackled against my stomach. Had I left one in the copier? Or perhaps one had dropped out of my trouser leg during my crawl round the skirting board?

I took a deep breath and prepared to lie like hell.

'Are you looking for more hours?'

'What?'

'My wife's looking for a cleaner. If you're interested.'

'Well ... I, er ...'

'She pays a good rate. Better than you get from the cleaning company, I would imagine. Shall I get her to give you a ring ... discuss it ... you can always say No if it doesn't suit you.'

'I ... I don't have a phone.'

'OK.' He folded the paper he was holding, and scribbled a number on it. 'Here. That's my home number. Amelia's there most days. I'll tell her to expect you ... Grace, you said? Is there a surname to go with it?'

'Smith. Thanks.'

I pushed the number in my pocket and heard the photocopies stuffed down my knickers crackle. Bridgeman didn't seem to notice. Or maybe he just assumed I was into bizarre underwear.

It didn't matter anyway. I didn't expect to see him again. With all the information I had on Kristen now, tracking her down should be a breeze.

By Friday night icy fingertips were beginning to do some really serious tap-dancing down my spine. Henry was right. There *was* something odd about Kristen's disappearance. Things weren't adding up.

I'd got Nola to drop me off near the office after our cleaning stint on Thursday evening. I wanted to phone the Bayswater number on Kristen's file.

The lilt of the Indian subcontinent sang down the wire, accompanied by the heavy beat of a bass amplifier in the distance.

'Night porter's lodge. Ravi speaking.'

The address on Kristen's application form had just given a street name and number. I'd been assuming it was a private house.

'Is that fourteen Endlecombe Street, Bayswater?'

'So they say, ma'am. Although I am inclined to believe this might more accurately be described as Notting Hill.'

'What are you? A hotel?'

'That is indeed what it says on the sign. The Endlecombe Hotel.'

When I haven't had time to prepare a cover story, I tend to fall back on the truth.

'I'm a private detective. My name's Grace Smith.'

'Indeed? How extremely exciting. I myself am studying for a degree in psychology.'

'So this is just a night job to top up the grant?'

'Yes, indeed. Regrettably my parents are unable to provide the assistance they would wish to.'

We had a brief chat about the shortfalls in the government's funding for higher education, plus Ravi's ambitions to go into marketing eventually. All the time the persistent thump of the bass amplifier got louder, until it was joined by several voices running through a collection of Anglo-Saxon swear-words and what sounded like someone being thrown down the stairs. And then total silence.

'Is that something you should go sort out?'

'Not at all. My duties are to open the front door for residents and to report any deficiencies in the plumbing so that the management may ignore them.'

'Right. And how long have you been doing this, Ravi?'

'Since my course commenced at the beginning of last September.'

So he could have been there during the end of Kristen's tenancy. I explained to Ravi that I'd traced her to this address prior to her more to Seatoun.

'I really need to get in touch with her. Don't you have some sort of booking-in system?'

'People come to the desk and ask for a room. We give them a key if they have the price.'

'That's it? You don't get them to fill out a form?'

'We have a register.'

'Great, well, Kristen would probably have checked in early last summer, I think ... I wonder if you could just ...?'

He could. He did. She wasn't there.

'But she must be. If everyone signs the book.'

'Oh yes indeed. In fact, flipping through these pages I find that even Miss Sharon Stone, Mrs Margaret Thatcher and Mr Wyatt Earp were required to leave their signatures.'

'So Kristen might have been incognito?'

'I'm sure Miss Cognito would have been quite acceptable.'

Kristen, however, had received at least one letter from Wexton's whilst she was staying there.

Ravi explained that mail was left on a board in the front lobby until it was collected or withered with age and dropped to the floor.

'What about credit-card receipts. Perhaps she paid by one.'

'I consider that unlikely. Most of our guests pay by cash. A credit transaction would require a degree of trust that is sadly lacking in this establishment.'

I got the message. The hotel management were as dodgy as the guests. I thanked Ravi for his help and wished him good luck with the degree.

'And to you too, Ma'am. I trust your search meets with success.'

I told him I was sure it would. Thereby inviting the fates to kick me in the teeth. Which they promptly proceeded to do for most of Friday.

I worked backwards; most recent contacts first.

The Central Register of Charities had no address for Third World Initiative Teams. The woman explained that it was possible the agency wasn't registered in Britain, but she'd see what she could find.

I left a number and moved back a step in Kristen's life to the now defunct Okranshaw Electronics, whose ex-managing director was currently running a craft shop in St Ives.

'Hardly remember the girl, to tell you the truth. Quiet little thing. Took her on as a favour to Tony, far as I can remember. Went to college together, I think.'

'Tony?'

'Tony Brown. My chief acquisitions executive. Buyer to you and me. Gave them all fancy titles instead of raises.'

'Do you know where he is now?'

'Africa, or South America. Somewhere like that. Went off to get in touch with himself. I don't know why he bothered. I had to get in touch with him most days, and believe me, it generally wasn't worth the effort.'

'I don't suppose you have a home address for him?'

'Haven't got a home address for any of them. Burnt all the files when the business went belly-up.'

'Is that legal?'

'Who cares? If someone wants to sue me they're welcome to try.'

'But you must remember *something* about Kristen. You wrote her a reference.'

'Write the same reference for anyone who asks. Now if that's all, I've got a delivery of pixie pottery due to arrive any second.'

AD Aerospace at least had Kristen's details on computer. Posing as an old university friend, I asked if perhaps someone up there was still in touch with her.

The girl in human resources thought it was unlikely. 'That whole division was downsized.'

'You mean they were made redundant?'

'The *jobs* were redundant, not the people,' she reproved gently.

'But it was the people who got kicked out?'

'Well ... yes.'

The administration offices at Leicester University were even less forthcoming. They didn't give out any information on students over the telephone. If I wanted to put a request in writing, they'd consider it.

Her high school in Bath had amalgamated with another the year that Kristen had left and both sets of records had been placed on microfiche and sent to the county archives. The school secretary was equally happy to pass the buck and suggest I put my request in writing.

As a last resort, I stuck a handkerchief over my nose and mouth and through a barrage of simulated sneezing and sniffing asked the receptionist at Wexton's if she could put me through to Bertram.

'I'm so sorry. You'll have to speak up.'

'Bertram ... I want to speak to Bertram ...'

'Bertram *who*, would that be?'

'He said ... achooo ... said he worked at Wexton's ... atishoo ... Bertie ...'

In italic letters she denied they had *anyone* working at Wexton's with that name. And she really thought I *must* have the wrong company.

I was inclined to think she was right. Hanging up, I looked at my watch with disbelief. It was lunchtime. A whole morning and nothing to show for it but a sore ear. Was I losing my touch?

'Never had one, did you?'

I hadn't realised I'd spoken aloud. Taking my trainers off the desk and uprighting the chair, I twisted round to find Janice, the receptionist from hell, standing in the doorway in her usual vampire array of black and silver. Today it was long cheesecloth dress, lace-up boots and ansate-shaped ear-rings that brushed her shoulders.

'I been trying to buzz you for ages.'

'I had a lot of calls to make. Business.'

'Yeah, well I didn't think you had that many friends.'

'Did you just pop up to flex your bitching muscle, Jan? Or is there a reason for this visit?'

She extended a slip of paper. 'You got a message. On the phone.'

I got a lot of messages on the phone. But if Janice intercepted them, I generally didn't find out until days later. I read:

Jason thinks he's on to a place locally that will suit Andrew and Fergie. Be in touch soonest.

For a moment I suspected it was a wind-up from Janice. Looking up, ready to trade a few more well-chosen insults, I surprised an odd expression on her face. It took a second to recognise it: friendliness. It was bizarre.

I glanced back at the incomprehensible message. And the light went on. Jason, the twelve-year-old estate agent, was still searching for a flat to house my Vietnamese pot-bellied pigs!

I looked back at Janice. She ground a Doc Marten into my floorboards. 'It's not really, is it ... you know ... the real ones?'

'Is it likely I'd be looking for a flat for royalty, Jan?'

'No. Well ... I didn't really think it was. Just ... you know ... they have hideaways, don't they?'

'On Highland estates and Caribbean islands, Jan. Clapped-out seaside towns is taking the drive to give the plebs value for their taxes just too far. Why the interest? You a royalty groupie?'

'No, I'm not. It's just that ... I want to be famous.'

'Doing what?'

'How'd you mean?'

'What are you planning to do? Sing? Dance? Act? Nude sword-juggling?'

'No. Nothing like that. I just want to be famous. Like Paula Yates.'

'So appearing at a few royal premières as "mysterious brunette companion" would be a good leg-up. Well, I'm afraid Andy and Fergie are pigs; the trotter and bacon chop variety ...'

'Oh. Yeah ... well ... didn't think it was really them, did I?'

Her usual expression reasserted itself. A subtle blend of

boredom and contempt. Swinging away, she shouted back from the landing: 'That blind bloke rang too. Summer ... something ... wanted to know how you were doing.'

Henry accepted my lack of progress philosophically.

'Can't be helped, m'dear. Forward planning only as good as intelligence received, eh?'

'I'm really sorry. Normally, given the amount of background I've got on the subject, I'd have expected to be able to bring you something ... but Kristen seems to have a lot of past but no visible future.'

I winced as I realised what I'd just said. Beano, who'd padded over to rest his jaw on my legs, jumped in sympathy.

Henry, who seemed to have superhuman powers of hearing, suggested we not start that again.

'I'm blind. Not visually challenged or whatever other mealy-mouthed rubbish they've cooked up these days. A spade's a spade, so let's not pussy-foot round the damn subject.'

He sounded bitterer than I remembered from our previous encounters. Perhaps it went like that: some days acceptance; others an unreasoning anger at what the Fates had dished out.

Abruptly I said: 'Are you totally blind, or is there some vision? Light and dark, for instance?'

In response he put down the coffee pot, and whipped off his glasses. I stifled a gasp. His left socket was empty; the lid shrivelled above the useless hole. The right eye was still there, but an old scar ran diagonally across it, the keloid skin raised and puckered where it had healed.

He held his face full on mine for a moment and then replaced the glasses without comment.

'Sorry' seemed inadequate. So I simply asked him what he wanted me to do about Kristen, since it seemed fairly clear she'd left the area of her own accord.

'Find her, of course.'

'Are you sure? I mean, I've spent a lot of time on this already ...'

'You say she was having an affair with this Bridgeman fellow ...?'

'I wouldn't put it that strongly ... I mean, it's just cleaners' gossip. There doesn't seem to have been anything definite, except the fact they both worked late together.'

'Nonetheless, it would seem worth a recce.' He'd risen whilst he was talking and made his way across to the sideboard. Opening a drawer, he took out a leather wallet and extracted a fold of notes. 'There's another five hundred there, count it if you like. If it proves insufficient, please tell me. But I want you to find Kristen. Do we have a deal?'

'Deal, Henry.'

Next stop was the public library. I photocopied the numbers of all the Keats in the Bath area telephone directory. Since there were only three, I got all the Keates with an 'e' thrown in for my ten pence. In total there were fifteen numbers.

Seven answered. And none of them had a relative called Kristen; or even the more mundane Christine, Christina or any similar-sounding name.

I figured the rest were probably at work and decided to get back to them that evening. Which left me with several hours to kill.

I hit the town. Well, somebody should.

An early hint that the gloomy weather forecast might be wrong had melted away like butter on hot toast. The flat, sealskin-grey clouds that had been massing out on the horizon the previous evening had multiplied and boiled inland, carrying with them the promise of showers and a chilling north wind that had driven everyone off the beaches and into the amusement arcades, cafés and gift shops.

I headed for the side street that contained Pepi's, my all-time favourite café.

The red Formica tables were packed, but I managed to bag one of the high stools in front of the serving counter, where I could inhale the delicious aromas of frying grease and onions.

Shane – the owner – acknowledged my appearance with a quick burst of 'Hard Headed Woman' before bawling into the hatch: 'Egg and chips twice and one scrounger's special.'

I didn't mind. Freeloaders can't afford to be oversensitive.

Years ago Shane had been a rock singer. There were black-and-white publicity stills pinned over the café walls to prove it. A mean and moody Shane glowered from under an Elvis Presley greased hairstyle, whilst he posed aggressively in jeans and white T-shirt. The hair had long gone, but he still had the wardrobe. It was just six sizes larger now.

A loaded plate with fried food overhanging the edges was banged down in front of me and napkin-folded cutlery slid within reach.

'Shane. I love you, let's elope.'

I added salt, vinegar and a generous dollop of glutinous red sauce from the huge red plastic tomato, and dived into cholesterol heaven.

Behind me the level of noise was rising to ear-aching level. A lot of the customers were kids who were half-term happy and yelling across to their mates at other tables.

A slightly more upmarket screech caught my attention. Its owner was reading out the plot on the back of a video. Twisting round, I located the four girls at one of the window tables. The voice I'd recognised belonged to the girl who'd been helping her drunken friend back to school the other night.

The mate was there too; her wavy hair now blonde rather than white in the café lighting. And squeezed in beside her, sipping at a can of Coke, was Bone. She saw me at the same time as I recognised her.

'Hey, Smithie … over here!' She didn't exactly click her fingers, but the implication was there.

I deliberately sauntered over very slowly; acting like a bolshie kid could be infectious.

Bone used her hip to shift up the blonde and make room for me on the seat.

'You were supposed to phone me on the mobile.' She tapped the phone, which was resting on the table.

'It's a tricky report. I thought it best to talk face to face.'

'Oh? OK, I understand.'

The blonde leant forward beyond Bone. 'Are you really a private detective?'

Bone jumped in before I could answer. 'I told you she was, didn't I, Livia? And you needn't start fishing, you nosy cow; this is well private, got it?'

'You broken up for half-term now?' I asked quickly, since I didn't fancy refereeing a teenage cat fight.

'This morning. Are we going to watch this video or not, Claudia?' Bone demanded.

The redhead who'd been précising the plot shrugged. 'Molly doesn't fancy going back to your uncle's place. She says he feels her up.'

The fourth girl flushed and ducked her head.

'Well, she's got to go back, we've dumped all our stuff there. Unless you're planning to go to France without your luggage, Moll?'

Molly shook her head. Claudia kindly informed me that her parents had a converted *gîte* in Brittany. 'We have to drag over every holiday and make like we really adore playing tennis and swimming in the pool and all those draggy things. It's such a *bore.*'

'Must be,' I sympathised. 'Er ... Bone, could I have a quick word? In private?'

'Sure.'

Locking us both in the one-cubicle ladies' loo, I filled Bone in on the situation with Tom Skerries and told her it was unlikely he'd be around for Claudia's party.

'What's his address?'

'Why?'

'I've paid you, haven't I? I'm entitled to any information you've found out.'

'No you're not. You're entitled to what you paid for: Tom Skerries' location. And at present that's in hiding somewhere until people stop wanting to kick his head in.'

In the wash-basin mirror, I saw the muscles of Bone's jaw tighten. 'I still want to know where he lives.'

I tried reason. 'Look, Bone, his wife's got enough problems. She's on her own with three kids and a bloke who takes off whenever he gets a bit bored with rusks and disposable nappies. Give her a break, eh?'

'I paid you. I *want* him. He promised he'd come to the party.'

To hell with reason; I got tough.

'Listen, he's not there but his sister-in-law *is*. And she's got a nasty temper and a fast right hook. You aren't going to look too great at the party with busted teeth and a broken nose.'

At least that made her think. I could see the indecision flitting through her eyes whilst she gnawed her bottom lip. But she was a stubborn girl.

'He *has* to come. I've *told* everyone he's taking me.'

Everyone being Claudia and Livia, I guessed.

'I've hired a dinner jacket for him and everything.' She gave me a pleading look and repeated: 'I've *told* everyone. I'm going to look well cretinous if he doesn't come now. Here.' She pushed more banknotes at me.

Refusing money goes against my principles. 'If I don't flush him out before the party, I'll refund this, OK?'

Back at the office, five more Keates with an 'e' answered my calls and disclaimed Kristen. I stuck the other three numbers on my jumper to remind me to try again and then decided I might as well check Janice's answerphone before I went home.

It's located under her desk downstairs. She normally switches it on if there's no-one in the building when she leaves, and writes up the messages the next day. The winking green light showed three calls had been picked up. Sorting out a pencil and pad I listened to a solicitor needing a court order served (I bagged that one); an anxious breeder who'd lost a pedigree bitch (a natural for Vetch, I decided, slipping the details under his door); and the woman from the Charity Commissioners apologising for the fact she could find no trace of the Third World Initiative Teams.

So another day down the line and still Kristen refused to give up any part of herself. It was definitely odd. If I hadn't had an eye-witness description of her from her neighbour, I'd almost have been inclined to believe she didn't exist.

I re-set the machine and was just punching the security code into the building alarm when the phone buzzed. After the recorded message had ground through its usual invitation, Annie's voice filled the hall.

'Just letting you all know I'm still alive since I've got time to kill before my dinner date turns up ...'

Grabbing the receiver, I told her to spit out all the details.

'Hi, Grace. Don't get excited; I was just trying to dispel the office rumour that I have a sad social life. The date's with my sister. She's flying up to Leeds for the night. Perks of working for an airline. And speaking of siblings, have you seen Zeb recently? I keep trying to ring him, but I'm beginning to get the feeling he's avoiding me. Any idea why?'

Probably because he knew damn well he'd blurt out he'd let two squatters into her flat. He's a rotten liar; I can't think how he got past the police entrance exam.

Luckily I'm not, and I think Annie believed me when I said he'd mentioned a big job a few nights ago. At any rate, she moved on to the subject of my life instead.

I gave her a brief description of the non-event that was currently the Kristen Keats investigation, an even briefer run-down on Bone's boyfriend, and a no-detail-spared picture of my evening with Kevin.

'So you've got a bloke who's more-or-less unattached; charming and good-looking; and as fanciable as double-choc ice-cream with hot fudge sauce. And you told him you just wanted to be friends?'

'Yes.' I doodled a fudge sundae on the message pad.

'You know what your trouble is, don't you?' Annie said.

'What?' I surrounded the sundae with a necklace of daisies.

'You're suffering from a chronic inferiority complex. Because this is a date to die for, you've convinced yourself you don't deserve him.'

'Thank you, Claire Rayner.'

'You're welcome.'

'So when are you coming back? I miss our girlie dissection of life and all the loathsome things therein.'

'You mean you have to buy your own pizza and bottle of wine.'

'That's too.'

'I've got a couple of days here and then I'm moving down to Leicester. Should be back middle to end of next week.'

'Couldn't do me a favour in Leicester, could you?' I explained about the university's refusal to give out information over the phone. 'But there's probably some kind of old students' association or something. See if you can sweet-talk her old home address out of them, would you?'

'If it doesn't cost me anything, but no promises. I'd have

thought this charity lot were your best lead. She's bound to have made some friends there. Particularly if they've had her roughing it in some Third World hole. All that using the same bucket for a loo makes for significant emotional bonding, from what I can remember of the family camping trips.'

'No ...' I said slowly, filling in doodles on my pad. 'I don't think that lead is going to go anywhere.'

Looking down at what I'd just written, I suddenly knew that wherever Kristen had been in the time between leaving Okranshaw's and joining Wexton's Engineering, she definitely hadn't been working for that Third World charity.

CHAPTER 19

The doodle read: Third World Initiative TeamS.

Not exactly the sort of catchy acronym a bona fide charity would choose.

I mentally saluted Kristen for sticking a blatant lie right under their noses – and getting away with it. She obviously had guts. Or chutzpah, as Rachel Simonawitz put it.

I'd been feeling a bit guilty about not taking up her invitation to dinner, so I'd wandered round to the flats mid-morning Saturday and indicated I was free this evening.

'Darlin',' she apologised, jangling enough gold to restock the Klondike as she balanced a huge black hat on top of the walnut-whip hairstyle. 'My Saul is coming to pick me up any minute.'

'My fault ... I should have rung first.'

Rachel patted the air dismissively. 'Surprise visits are best. What about tomorrow?'

'Tomorrow is good for me.'

'Wonderful, darlin'. Come about twelve, and we eat early. That way we got time for a little snooze maybe before supper.'

Definitely my sort of hostess.

Saturday, I have to report, was a dead loss. For everyone except the owners of the arcades, cinemas, shops and cafés.

The rain fell steadily all day. Not vicious squalls like Friday, but a light, unrelenting downpour that descended in straight rods, gurgling along the gutters, running down the drains and dripping off the canvas awnings over the rock and novelties shops.

The sea was flat and grey, the overcast oyster sky merging into the pewter waves that heaved and swelled sullenly but didn't seem able to work up enough energy to create a white-topped wave to break the monotonous view.

I sat in a wooden shelter for a while with a group of pensioners, watching the water pooling on the thick canvas coverings of the deckchair stacks. When the excitement became unbearable, I went back to the office and re-tried my three Bath Keates I hadn't been able to contact yesterday.

Two still weren't answering. The third didn't have any relatives called Kristen, but he was in touch with an extended family on the planet Zakov who communicated with him via waves beamed into his television set.

I told him he needed a special licence for that now they'd put in satellite TV and went home to flop out in front of my own television, which just *looked* like it received transmission via a distant galaxy.

For want of something more constructive to do on the case I summarised what I'd got so far on Kristen:

1. Mid to late twenties. Approx. 5 feet 8 inches tall. Long dark hair. Possibly a 'babe'. Intelligent.
2. Secretive about her past. Why?
3. Got job at Wexton's after reading notice of previous test engineer's death. (NB Check this out.)
4. Despite being a 'babe' only socialising seems to have been with Rachel Simonawitz – why?
5. Why did she get paid by personal cheque from Wexton's? How did she cash them?
6. Why didn't she open a bank/building society account locally?
7. Who was the driver of the dark car Rachel saw at the flats?
8. Who is Bertram?

It all added up to precious little. There was only one query that I could do something about immediately. I dialled a local number and was answered by a voice that sounded like pure sex dipped in honey. It belonged to a pensioner who spent most days in the public library to save on the heating bills and was happy to ferret out any information you cared to name for a flat fee of four pounds an hour.

With an effort I dredged up what details I could recall of Wexton's previous test engineer. 'It would have been early last summer, I'd guess. His name was Wingett. Rob. Short for Robert. Crashed his motorbike. Check the daily papers as well as the locals, can you, Ruby? See if the reports went national? Say six hours' limit?'

'Will do, my lovely. The money will come in very handy for my little trip to the seaside.'

'You *live* at the seaside, Ruby.'

'I know. But you like to see a different few gallons of salt water sometimes, don't you? Take care now.'

By Sunday the rain had become intermittent again, but the wind had increased, ruffling the sea into cream frills. Wandering up to Rachel's, I was passed by several cars, loaded to the window tops with kids and luggage, whose drivers had already decided they could spend the rest of the weekend in cheaper misery at home.

'Such a pity for the parents. Children, they can be happy anywhere,' Rachel lamented, taking my damp jacket whilst I tried to brush off the thick scum mark of white hairs that Balthazar had left round my black jeans.

The flat smelt deliciously of simmering herbs and home-baked rolls. I demolished several as an appetiser, ripping open the thick crusts to get to the still steaming bread.

'You shouldn't have gone to all this trouble,' I mumbled half-heartedly.

'No trouble, darlin'. I like to cook. And now Ada is in hospital – may the Lord spare her – I don't get no one to cook for; except sometimes maybe when Guy comes home.'

'Guy?'

She pointed upwards with her index finger. 'Upstairs, old Mr Stevens' boy.'

I remembered now. Kristen's flat had been owned by someone's grandson. 'Any sign of a new tenant?'

'No. Such a shame, darlin'. It's a nice clean little place. Guy painted it all up after his grandfather – God rest him – died. That reminds me ... stir this for me ... if I don't do it now it will go clean out of my head. Such a memory I have these days.'

Handing me a wooden spoon, she disappeared into the bedroom. Balthazar took the opportunity to stroll in and give his impression of feline starvation.

'Forget it, puss. If God had wanted cats to eat before me, he'd have taught them how to use can-openers.'

Rachel returned with a large brown envelope and a roll of sticky tape. The cat went into yowling overdrive.

'Hush, baby. Mama will give you your dinner soon as she wraps up Uncle Guy's mail.'

Opening a unit drawer, she extracted a bundle of letters and started pushing them into the larger envelope. The implication hit me.

'Does the postman drop them off here, or have you got a key to the upstairs flat?'

'Oh no. He won't give them to me. He puts them through the slot upstairs and then I go get them. When Kristen was here she brought them down for me.'

'And since she's left? Do you take her mail as well?'

'Of course, darlin', no sense it sitting up there.'

'Can I take a look at it?'

She shrugged and extracted more envelopes from under the tea towels. 'It's junk. I was thinking maybe I should put it in the bin. She's not coming back, is she?'

'Doesn't look like it. In fact she appears to have dropped off the planet.'

Rachel was right; it was just junk. Apart from a letter from the estate agent formally confirming the end of the tenancy, which had been posted – I checked the postmark – at least a week after she'd left, she'd got a catalogue selling useless gadgets, a brochure from a holiday company giving escorted tours to the Far East and a personalised standard letter from a bucket shop offering free travel guides, maps and mosquito repellent to the first fifty customers to book a long-haul flight.

Dumping the lot in the bin, I asked if I could take a look round Kristen's flat.

'Sure. But there's nothing there.'

The layout was the reverse of Rachel's, with the kitchen and main bedroom overlooking the front and the living room and bathroom the back garden. What I'd assumed to be an airing cupboard in the downstairs flat proved to be a small second bedroom. Despite crawling over everything, I didn't find so much as an old shopping receipt.

I tried the phone. It had already been cut off but the back-up battery was still in place. Taking it from the socket, I trotted downstairs again and borrowed Rachel's line. It was a waste of time. There were no numbers pre-programmed in the memory and the redial button connected me to a local pizza takeaway.

I replaced the phone upstairs and followed my nose back to lunch.

The main course was some kind of spicy lamb casserole with chick-pea dumplings. We shared a bottle of claret with it and moved on to muscatel for the puddings.

'Grand Marnier oranges, darlin'? Or treacle and pecan pie?'

'A little of each, perhaps?'

Rachel waited until the coffee before asking me how far I'd got in tracing Kristen.

I hesitated. I'd promised Henry to keep the investigation confidential. On the other hand, it was his *involvement* he didn't wanted bandied about. And there was always the possibility that something I'd uncovered so far might jog a memory in Rachel.

Not that I'd uncovered much. Practically all my results were negative. No school records; no college records; no workmates; no home address; and definitely no voluntary worker.

Rachel roared with laughter when I got to the bit about the Third World Initiative Teams.

'Twits! Twits! Oh yes, that is my Kristen. She had chutzpah, you know.'

The sunset-coloured walnut-whip hairstyle shook in time with her chest. For the first time, I realised it was a wig.

'So what you going to do now, darlin'?'

'Pursue the Bridgeman connection, I suppose.'

'You think maybe she was carrying on with this man?'

I sipped my coffee and nibbled a marzipan. 'I think it's unlikely. If you were married and your girlfriend had a cosy little bachelor flat, where would you spend the evenings?'

'But she never brought nobody home.'

'Exactly. Maybe she just wasn't interested. She could even have taken off rather than go through the hassle of a sexual harassment case. Are you quite sure you never heard her mention anyone called Bertram?'

'Sure I'm sure. Pretty girl like that ought to have a romance. Believe me, if she'd have mentioned a man, I'd have got him round here to look him over.'

'I believe you, Rachel.'

I thought about Kristen whilst I lay on Rachel's sofa, flicking through the TV channels and digesting lunch. Employing someone with access to the confidential computer files of somewhere like the Insurance Contributions Agency or the Central Banks Clearing Houses might be productive. But as I said, they charged serious money. And in some obscure way, it had always seemed like cheating to me.

Which really only left one possible connection still unprobed. If Kristen had taken herself off because of something Bridgeman did – or didn't – do, perhaps he knew about it. It might not be something he wanted to share with the devoted Ms Ayres and her personnel files.

It was a tenuous chance, but I had nowhere else to go for the present. Balthazar watched through suspicious green eyes as I lifted Rachel's phone, dialled the number Bridgeman had given me and asked for Mrs Amelia Bridgeman.

'Speaking. But if you're going to try to sell me fitted kitchens or double-glazing ...'

'I'm a cleaner. I do up the factory sometimes. Your husband said you were looking for one.'

'Stephen?' Her voice was light, with an almost girlish inflexion. 'Stephen found me a cleaner? How terrific. When can you come? I'm absolutely desperate for someone to deal with this mess, so if you could make it soon ...'

'Tomorrow?'

'Terrific. I'll see you then. Ciao.'

I had to shout to stop her hanging up before I'd got a time and house directions and given her my name.

'Smith. Even I should be able to remember that. Ciao again then.'

Rachel emerged bleary-eyed and wigless as I replaced the receiver. A net plastered near-white hair to her head. 'Was that for me, darlin'?'

'No, me,' I said truthfully.

'You've not got to go? I got little picks in for supper.'

'It'll keep.'

Rachel beamed, stretched, went to adjust her wig – and found it wasn't there. My stomach muscles had unconsciously tightened, preparing to share her embarrassment.

With a roar of laughter, she told me her Saul was always saying she'd forget her head one day. 'And now I started with my hair ... oh dear, oh dear ...' Still chuckling, she trotted back to the bedroom and returned pulling it on like a tea-cosy.

'Now, is there something nice on the television tonight? Or we can go get a video if you like.' She plumped down beside me and told me it was so nice to have company. 'The Colemans, next door you know, they go round her mother's Sunday evenings. And the flats are so quiet ... it's like being in your grave.'

'Doesn't Saul invite you over?'

'Every other Saturday. I don't like to push.'

'What about your daughter?'

'My Berenice? She lives in Geneva. Her husband's a scientist. Very clever. Nothing but the best for my Berenice.'

She sighed heavily. I squeezed her hand. With a grateful smile, she patted mine and told me not to mind her. 'You visit your parents a lot, darlin'?'

'When I can,' I lied.

The truth of the matter was, I wouldn't have been welcome if I had. My dad is an ex-policeman who was left in a wheelchair after an attack whilst on duty. Everyone knew who'd done it – he used to stand outside our house and taunt my dad sometimes – but nobody could prove anything. The low-lifes he hung around with gave him an unbreakable alibi.

But despite their inability to charge anyone for his injuries, Dad remained loyal to the force. So when yours truly got invited to leave, he chose to believe the evidence that I'd taken a bribe to alibi a local villain, rather than my story that I'd been set up.

The familiar waves of depression started to wash over me as I ran through that night – and its consequences – in my mind.

Giving myself a quick mental shake, I said: 'Fancy going to a karaoke night?'

I wasn't sure we'd get into the Downs Estate social club. But a message sent into the smoky, noisy atmosphere brought Nola to the door to sign us both in. She didn't seem to find it odd that I'd invited myself round for the evening. And Rachel's offer to pay for the next round made her instantly acceptable. We squeezed on to a table with Nola, Donna and Bonnie.

An anorexic kid with acne like raspberry porridge was on stage wriggling his bottom and asking if we thought he was sexy.

'No!' we roared in unison.

'Ta, Howie, you're off, mate ...'

The bloke who been propping up the front of the bar on my first visit led the applause while he edged the pupative Rod Stewart off the stage.

'Now we've got Brian ... you're on, mate ...'

Gary Glitter strutted forward to a synchronised hand-clap. Evidently he was one of the star turns.

Donna sat silently, picking at the hem of her mini-dress. Under cover of the noise, I leant across and asked if she was managing OK without Tom.

'Sure. Nola helps out. And I got money from the Social.'

'You've not heard from him?'

She shook her head. Tonight her hair was hitched up in two unlikely bunches that swung back and forth in alternate swishes. 'No.'

'Good riddance,' Nola said, gulping down half a pint of the rum and blackcurrant Rachel had paid for. 'You're better off without that waste of skin. Money don't stay in his pockets long enough to shake hands with the fluff.'

'That ain't true!'

'It bloody well is!'

Unexpectedly Bonnie interrupted: 'No it ain't. He had a whole wedge up the post office.'

'When?' Nola demanded.

'I dunno. Weeks ago. He was getting a tax disc for the van.'

'Oh yeah ... all right, if it's something for *him*,' Nola conceded.

Donna's indignant protest that he'd got the kids new trainers was cut off by a geriatric and overweight Tina Turner taking the stage and assuring us she would survive. Our eardrums mercifully hung in there with her until she finished to a round of relieved applause.

The compère leapt on stage again. 'Right, ladies and gen-tel-men ... now the moment you've all been waiting for ... In the red corner ... our very own ... Miss Nola Baldwin ...'

Nola sprang to her feet and raised her fists, twisting from the waist to all four corners of the room.

'And in the blue corner ... from the Springhill Working Men's Club ...'

I missed the name of the skinny blonde with pecs who rose from her seat to a storm of cheers and boos. With an arrogant sweep of a two-foot mane of peroxided glory, she eyeballed Nola, then sauntered to the stage.

Squaring her shoulders, Nola slouched forward.

'It's a grudge match,' Bonnie explained.

'I thought it was karaoke.'

'It is ...'

It was 'Do You Wanna Dance' with attitude. A two-minute bout each and enough aggressive body language to intimidate a horde of Mongols.

Donna wriggled her way past our knees. 'I'm going to pee.' She looked directly at me. 'It's out back if you want it.'

I could take a hint. I hooked my bag and followed her between the ecstatic crowds who were urging Nola on.

The loos were cleaner than the rest of the club would have led me to expect, but tiled in an incongruous shade of turquoise and decorated with dolphins.

'Nice, ain't it?' Donna said, touching a fin. 'Tom done it. He's ever so good with his hands.'

'Looks like a swimming pool.'

The words left my mouth before it occurred to me that that was probably exactly what the tiles had been intended for ... before Tom Skerries diverted them.

The heat in the bar had raised a pink flush on Donna's cheeks. Now it deepened to a hot chilli. 'He does it for me ... and the kids ... to get us out of this place. He ain't bad ... honest. He's going to get us a bar ... abroad ... somewhere warm. We're gonna run it together ...' She broke off as the outer door was pushed open.

Bonnie shot past us and rushed into a cubicle. 'I'm bursting.'

Donna fixed pleading eyes on me. 'He loves me and the kids really. He likes to think he can pull any girl he wants. But it's just talk. Nola thinks I'm daft to put up with it, but she don't understand ... she's never had a proper boyfriend ... not one who loved her ... and Tom *does* love me ...'

'Sure.'

She'd seized the swinging bunches and was now twisting them round and round her hands in a nervous frenzy, until she'd formed two coils on the top of her head. 'This girl, the one wants you to find Tom ...'

She fixed pleading eyes on me. I told her what she wanted to hear. Just a kid with a crush. And was rewarded by a brilliant smile.

'That's what I thought. He's always got kids hanging round him when he works on the estate.'

'This one's got more money than sense. Don't get phased by it, Donna. I don't think she even fancies your Tom, to tell you the truth ... it's just a case of showing off to her mates. Girls like to do the pulling these days, you know.'

Donna's smile became even wider. 'Always did, didn't they?' Pulling her bag across her stomach, she delved inside. 'I was wondering ...' She took out a purse. 'How much do you charge? To find people, I mean?'

'People being Tom?'

The bunch twisting restarted. 'Yes. I mean, I know he's

gonna come back soon … but he don't usually stop away this long. Not without ringing me up to let me know he's OK.'

'How long's he been missing?'

'Nearly a month.'

'He didn't say anything? Tell you he was blowing?'

'No. He just never come home. First off I thought maybe he'd got a job away. He does that sometimes, see? Works late and then sleeps over in the van. But he's never done it for more than a week before.'

'Had you had a row?'

'No. We've been getting on dead good lately, honest. He was really working hard to get some money together so we could have our own business.'

'Did he take anything from the flat?'

'Like what?'

'Clothes, money, passport, CD collection?'

'He keeps that sort of stuff in the van. Case he works away. Not the CDs, course … he don't have …'

I interrupted quickly. 'OK, I get the picture … he just drove off into the sunset one day and never came back … drove where, do you know?'

'No. I took Liam and Pierce up the school and then I went up the shops with Shannon. He'd gone when I come back. I'd got him shepherd's pie for his tea, too. What do you think I should do?'

'Stick it in the freezer.'

'No … I never meant …' Enlightenment that it was a joke chased across her face. She smiled uncertainly and extended the purse in an unspoken question.

'Forget it, Donna. I'm already being paid to find your husband. If I get any joy, I'll let you know same time as my client. OK?'

'OK. Thanks.'

'You really can't think of anyone he might have gone to see?'

She couldn't. She'd rung family, friends and acquaintances and there was no sign of her wandering boy.

The crash of the cistern reminded us both that Bonnie was still in the end cubicle. She emerged and trotted to the basins, rubbing her stomach. 'Curry.'

Donna backed towards the door. 'I'd best get back. I gotta support Nola.'

I'd have followed her out if I hadn't felt the gentlest pull on the back of my jeans; as if a finger had been hooked in the waistband. I turned a tap and put my hands under the stream, massaging liquid soap in until I heard the outer door close.

'Yes?'

'Balls,' Bonnie said, ripping down a slightly less grubby section of the roller towel.

'Could you elaborate a bit here, Bonnie?'

'Tom. That van. Shag city.'

'Did you and he ...?'

'No way. Tried, though.'

'And you think that's where he's at now?'

Bonnie nodded. Peering into the mirror, she spat on her finger and smoothed it over her eyebrows. 'Never said. Donna's a mate. But I saw her ...'

'Who?'

'Dunno.'

'God, this is like pulling hen's teeth, Bonnie. Could you take a deep breath and go for a sentence of more than four words? *Who* did you see and where?'

She faced me, hands planted firmly on hips plastered in blue leather skirt. 'I dunno. I took my Hannah up the square to get some balloons for 'er birthday party. We was watching the street 'tainers ... some of them are dead brilliant ... and I saw Tom up there.'

'In the post office getting his tax disc, yes?'

'Yeah. But first off I saw his van. And *she* was in it. Squashed down the passenger seat, she were, like she didn't wanna be seen.'

'Could have been someone he was giving a lift.'

'Nah. I don't reckon. I saw him, didn't I? He was dead pleased with himself ... reckoned he was on to a good thing, it was all over his face. Never said to Donna, she's a good mate ... but he's off with her.'

'Did you tell Nola?'

'Nah. Tell Donna, wouldn't she? Always rubbing her face in it what a loser Tom is. It's 'cos he never fancied her.'

'I'd worked that out, thanks, Bonnie. What date's your Hannah's birthday?'

'First of May.'

The day after Kristen disappeared. It was a stupid idea, but I asked Bonnie what this woman had looked like. 'Dark-haired? Pretty?'

'Dunno. She had a cap on, Tom's I think, so I never saw her hair. And she had her hand up to her cheek. Sort of leaning on it, hiding her face. Why? You know her?'

'How can I tell? We'd best be getting back, hadn't we? The match must be on round ten by now. We wouldn't want to miss the knockout.'

I thought I was joking. Until we opened the doors back into the bar. A riot-control squad would have felt at home.

They'd squared off. On the far side of the room were the home supporters, judging by the chant of 'Nolaaa ... Nolaaaa ... Nolaaaaa ...'

Those nearest were punching the air to an unintelligible chorus.

Somewhere in the middle I could see the barman mouthing something which was probably along the lines of 'The police are on their way.'

But I never got to find out. As our side of the room surged forward, we got carried with them. I saw someone throw a punch at Rachel and stagger back as she seized a drinks tray and dented it on his head. The wig slipped over her eyes. Worried that she was going to get seriously hurt, I used my weight to force a path through the scrum in front of me.

Monday morning I woke up in Rachel's spare bedroom with Balthazar asleep on my stomach and a soaking wet tea towel lying over my nose.

Sitting up, I found that the bed was one of a pair of bunks, by the simple expedient of banging my head on the top one. Rachel appeared in the door as I cursed, rubbed my head and struggled to take off a pale-blue nylon nightdress that was clutching at me from all directions.

'Darlin', how do you feel?'

'Bloody lousy,' I admitted. My voice sounded a bit strange, but I put it down to the nightie which was coming over my head at the time. 'What habbened?'

'You got hit. But you wouldn't let me take you to the hospital, so those nice girls from the club helped me bring you home.'

'Sorry. I suppose I should have guessed ib might get violent. Are *you* OK?'

'I'm fine, darlin'. I haven't had so much fun in years. You want a nice cooked breakfast?'

'Ib you're offering.' My voice still sounded nasal. And my nose seemed blocked. I went to pinch it and sniff in order to clear it. A violent shaft of pain shot up my sinuses.

'Don't do that. You'll make it bleed again.'

The warning was too late. Large spots of blood were materialising on the nightdress. 'Have you got a mirror?'

'In the hall.'

Not really wanting to know, I padded barefoot down the corridor in my knickers and stared into the wall mirror.

A gargoyle stared back at me. The swelling blob in the centre of my face that had once been my nose was flanked by red bruising which was turning to purple under my eyes. From the holes a steady drip of blood fell and splashed on to my breasts.

Rachel peered over my shoulder. 'I put ice cubes in the tea towel to stop the swelling, but it don't look like they worked too good. Maybe you should have a little lie-down. I'll bring you breakfast in bed.'

'Thanks, Rachel. Bud I can't. I god a job interview.'

CHAPTER 20

'Dorry I'm a bid late.'

'Are you? Gosh, I hadn't really noticed. This place is such a madhouse when the sproglets are on holiday.'

The section of house I could see behind Amelia Bridgeman appeared relatively sane to me. It was a low, long building that looked like it had originally been built as a farmhouse. A left-hand wing had been added more recently, but the spreading Virginia creeper had already obliterated most of the joins. The double garage to the right wasn't quite as easy to disguise, but the builders had done their best, even to the extent of roofing it with the same weathered and mossy roof tiles as the original house.

Once it must have been a comfortable ten-minute horse-trot into the village for the farmer, and half an hour in the opposite direction if he wanted to sample that new-fangled sea-bathing from the town beach.

But over the past fifty years the town had crept outwards over the farm fields until the village was no more than a back suburb of Seatoun. The Bridgeman's house was the oldest in an exclusive stretch of detached properties linking the town housing estates with the cluster of old village cottages.

I was late getting there because there had been a two-hour wait in the casualty department. After prodding and squinting at my nose, the doctor had delivered his opinion that it was badly bruised but probably not broken. I finally left with gauze padding taped across the swelling lump and the darkest pair of sunglasses I could find perched on top of the dressing.

Driving up to the Bridgemans' house, I'd been rehearsing plausible explanations for my appearance. I needn't have worried. The woman who swung the heavy metal-studded door open was sporting the fading evidence of bruising below her eyes.

'Mrs Bridgeman? I'mb Grace Smith ... I phoned ... about the job ...'

Her lips, frosted in pink, dropped open, revealing a set of the finest teeth private dental insurance can buy.

'Hi! Did you have an auto accident as well? Isn't that an *amazing* coincidence?'

Once again my famous powers of deduction were dropped on from a great height. Had I been asked to guess at a description for Amelia, I'd have gone for a younger version of her mother: Jaeger suit; Gucci-style loafers; gold and pearl jewellery sufficiently discreet to announce it was the real stuff; hair and make-up by Blend Into the Well-Heeled Crowd Inc.

In real life Amelia's size-ten rear was poured into blue jeans. Her size 34A breasts were bouncing under a silky white top that showed off her light-golden tan. Several slim silver chains round her neck were outshone by a heavily chased silver bangle studded with turquoise clasped around her left arm. Her blonde shoulder-length hair was expensively tousled and her make-up was of the frosted-bimbette variety.

Aware that I'd been staring, but forgetting I'd got the sunglasses on so she couldn't see anyway, I said quickly: 'Great nail varnish.'

Another giggle was accompanied by a tossing of the locks. 'Isn't it fabulous? Everyone's wearing it on the coast.'

'Really?'

'Not this coast.' Amelia spread her hand and wriggled the fingers. 'The West Coast. I've been out in LA for weeks. Have you ever been there? It's just fabulous. The lifestyle's so different.'

'It's one I missed.'

'You *must* go. I got the jewellery there too. It's hand-crafted Indian work. What do you think?'

She waved the bracelet.

'Fabulous,' I murmured.

'Isn't it?' she gurgled, oblivious to the send-up.

I discovered that if I took a deep breath and spoke slowly, I didn't sound like I was talking into a bucket. 'How long were you there?'

'Oh, *weeks*. I was visiting my daughter. You know how kids are. Just step on a plane and land up in some other continent. I only got back a couple of days ago.' She squinted at a tanned arm and asked me if I thought it was fading already. Before I could answer, she tossed the mane again. 'Well, I guess you'll want to see round. Grace, wasn't it? Call me Amelia. So, where shall we start …?'

She opened the door to the left of the front entrance. 'Sort of television room.'

The door was closed before I had more than a quick glimpse of a casually furnished, low-ceilinged lounge with an open fireplace and a cabineted TV and video in one corner.

The next room was designated 'the library'. Unsurprisingly it had bookshelves around three walls and a desk thrust up under the window. The door opposite led to a rambling kitchen floored with expensive Italian terracotta tiles and furnished with an Aga, several Welsh dressers holding assorted china services and gleaming copper pans, a small pine table and a butcher's block on wheels. The storage racks were full of those odd-shaped bottles of vinegars and oils with suspended herbs and veg floating in them like laboratory specimens. The sort of last-minute present you buy for the amateur cook who's got everything, when someone else beat you to the latest Delia Smith. I gave one to my sister only last Christmas.

Amelia trotted round with me on her heels. She waved a hand into an archway, so that I could see that what had probably been the original larders now housed a washing machine, drier and freezer with enough controls to run the Starship *Enterprise*.

'This is the kitchen,' Amelia announced.

I couldn't resist it. 'Gosh, really?'

She took it well. 'Yeah, OK. That was pretty silly. Look, I've got a great idea: how about I just lead the way, and you ask questions if you want to?'

She didn't wait for an answer, but swung away with a wiggle of that flat little bottom. Annie would have killed for it.

The back of the house had been knocked through into one long, narrow room. The far section held a couple of sofas and easy chairs. This nearer end had the dining table, presumably because it had the best view through the french windows to the patio and back garden.

'This is great,' I said. And I meant it.

'It is, isn't it? We usually spend our time in here. When my husband isn't *lost* in his study, that is.'

Bridgeman's study turned out to be in the far end of the newer wing. The room before it was another sitting room, but larger and more expensively furnished than the one behind the front door.

'Stephen's study is a real no-no,' Amelia said in that breathless, dippy-little-me tone. 'But I guess it's the same at the factory. Is that Ayres woman still guarding him like a piranha?'

I mumbled something about only being temporary at the factory. Amelia was already running up a staircase at the far end of the wing. The main bedroom was in this building, together with the *en suite* bathroom and a separate loo. No expense had been spared to make them look like a set for *Hollywood Wives*, right down to the sunken bath with the gold taps shaped like seahorses.

The top of the original house held three more bedrooms and a couple more bathrooms. I got the tour at dizzying speed, while Amelia giggled and wiggled her way back to the top of the main staircase and down to the front hall.

I had to admit she looked pretty good for fifty. If I hadn't known it was her half-century this week, I'd have put her age at fifteen years younger.

The doorbell rang as we reached the hall.

'Oh gee, he's here already. Is that the *time*?'

Amelia's blue eyes narrowed assessingly as she squinted into a compact she'd taken from a small shoulder bag hanging over the staircase newel. 'What do you think? More foundation?'

Her bruising had a head start on mine. It had lost its puffiness and faded to dirty yellow. Dabbing a sponge, she quickly pressed some all-in-one cover over the worst of the damage, flicked the hair forward and thrust on a pair of designer sunglasses.

The ringer had retreated by the time she got the door open again. He was adjusting the driving seat in a white Mercedes convertible. Amelia jumped, wiggled and waved at the same time, shouting that she'd be right there.

'Don't you just love soft-tops? I hired one in LA. That drive along the Pacific Highway ...'

'Fabulous?'

'Heavenly.' Amelia skipped towards the waiting car. 'Don't know how long I'll be. Help yourself to coffee or wine or whatever. Ciao.'

The last I saw of her was the sun glinting off the bracelet as she waved with one hand and accelerated from 0 to 60 in three seconds.

Bemused, I went back inside and shut the door. The woman seemed to be a total flake. She'd just left a complete stranger alone in a house full of valuables.

Deciding I'd better look the part while I snooped, I opened

the cupboard under the stairs in the hope of finding a vacuum cleaner. I actually found the cellar Amelia had missed out on the whistle-stop tour.

Flicking on the light switch, I trotted down. The room had been hewn from the chalk. It was at least as old as the original farmhouse, perhaps even older; although a few modern refinements such as electricity and a new floor had been added.

The Bridgemans used it as a storage area. For form's sake, I poked amongst the kids' bikes, discarded furniture, sports equipment and old toys. There was enough dust to tell me no one had disturbed this lot for years. Except for one small area. A couple of old deckchairs and a picnic basket were jumbled together. However, there was a cleaner rim of floor along one edge; as if they'd been moved recently and not quite realigned with their previous position. Dragging them clear, I felt along the wooden block floor. One section responded to pressure and opened to reveal a recessed handle. Pulling it swung up a section about eighteen inches square. I'd found the Bridgeman family safe. It was set in concrete inside the original stone cavern floor and – I tried it – securely locked.

Rearranging things as near as I'd found them, I dusted myself down, went back to the cellar stairs – and found another door under them. It was a bit like being inside one of those Chinese puzzle boxes. By a quick mental walk around the upstairs rooms, I figured that the room I'd been exploring must be under the TV room and library, whilst the one under the cellar stairs must be beneath the kitchen.

Oddly enough, it had a solid metal door with a security keypad instead of a conventional locking mechanism. Needless to say, it was also shut tight.

'Curiouser and curiouser,' I muttered in my best Alice voice, trotting back to ground level.

I located the vacuum in a narrow cupboard in the utility section of the kitchen. Polishes, dusters and sprays were on the top shelf. Gathering up an armful, I stowed them in the pouch pocket of a striped apron, tied it on and plugged the vacuum in, strewing flex down the hall. Once the scene was set, I helped myself to a glass of red wine from a half-full bottle in the kitchen and made another round of the house at a slower pace, vaguely swishing the duster and squirting sprays at odd intervals.

It didn't yield much. There was the usual assortment of magazines, books, discarded letters, bills and accumulated junk of life in the drawers and cupboards. Oddly enough, most of the photographs that spilled from folders and leapt from overstuffed drawer seemed to be of Amelia and Stephen or Joan and an older man who was probably the long-departed Derek Reiss.

Perhaps the kids had grown up to be so spectacularly odd that not even their mother could love them. From the framed photos scattered around the house, I guessed the Bridgemans must have four – two of each – but none of them seemed to have faced the camera after the toddler stage.

My best shot at finding some trace of Kristen's trail was going to be in Stephen Bridgeman's study. If it was a no-no, for Amelia, then it was almost certainly a yes-yes for anything her husband didn't want her to find. Such as a handy contract for a new flat elsewhere. Or perhaps a few credit-card receipts for dinner *à deux* somewhere local. You never know, maybe Kristen ran off with an Italian waiter.

The door to the study was locked. Returning to the kitchen, I started rummaging in the dresser drawers. I hit pay-dirt in the third one. A plastic container full of assorted keys. Don't ask me why, but people always seem to keep their spare keys in the kitchen.

Stephen's study had been furnished by Conventionally Boring R Us. The bookcases mostly contained scientific magazines and books on such fascinating subjects as cellular data technology, protocol analysers and virus sentinels for the twenty-first century. I decided I'd wait for the films and turned my attention to the desks. He had two. They were almost excessively tidy. Pens, papers, floppy disks, personal files, all neatly lined up and stored in their correct places, but sadly no notes on the lines of *'That b***** Mario at La Traviata has been chatting up Kristen again.'*

Since he hadn't even bothered to lock it, I doubted there was going to be much of interest in there, but I flicked through the filing cabinet anyway. Insurance, taxes, pension plans, bank statements, credit-card statements, school fees. It was all boringly predictable. A routine life documented by metres of paper. Most people couldn't disappear no matter how hard they tried. The electronic trail they leave behind is too thickly layered. So why on earth was Kristen Keats proving so elusive?

More in hope than expectation, I glanced down the last credit-card statement. There was a hotel – the Heathrow Sheridan – shown as a charge on 30 April. More promising. Maybe they'd had a final fling before Kristen slipped away.

I'd been so absorbed that I'd filtered out all external sounds. Now I became aware of a car engine approaching.

One side of the study windows overlooked the front drive. Glancing through, I saw Stephen's silver Mercedes slowing in front of the double garage. The electronically operated doorway tilted and opened to swallow it.

Thrusting things back into place, I relocked the door, sprinted to the kitchen, replaced the keys and seized the vacuum cleaner, which was still plugged into the hall socket. I was just about to hit the 'on' button when I realised there was already a faint humming sound coming from the front sitting room.

Cautiously I slid the door ajar. The kid lying on his stomach flicking through the television channels gave me an incurious look and returned to the remote control. He'd muted the sound so cartoon characters fought, screamed and snarled to a background electronic hum.

'Hi.'

'Hello,' he said, never taking his eyes from the screen.

'So who are you?'

'Patrick.'

'I'm Grace. I'm the new cleaner,' I added, in case he was scared at finding himself alone with a total stranger. If he was, I have to admit he was hiding it well. 'When did you get here?'

'I've been here all the time.'

He deigned to look at me for a moment. He was a good-looking kid; dark-haired and dark-eyed. About eight or nine years old.

'You were looking in my daddy's study. That's not allowed.'

'Isn't it? Well, your mum didn't really explain where I was supposed to clean before she left. Listen, Patrick ...' I dropped down beside him. 'Do me a favour and don't tell anyone. I might lose my job.'

He shrugged, bending and flicking one leg back and forth. 'OK.'

I breathed a silent thanks as the curtains ruffled in the breeze created by the opening front door.

It wasn't Stephen. It was Joan Reiss, carrying a bag of groceries in her arms. Today it was navy silk palazzo pants and matching tunic with gold chains.

'Good afternoon, Grace. Stephen mentioned you might ... Good heavens, my dear, whatever's happened?'

'She had a car accident, like Mummy,' Patrick said from the carpet. The kid must have been listening ever since I arrived at the house.

'I see. How unfortunate. Where is your mother, Patrick?'

'She's testing another car.'

'And have you been out in the fresh air today?'

'No.' Patrick switched the sound back on and flopped his chin on his hands.

His grandmother gave me a tight 'children – whatever would you do with them?' smile.

She moved across to the kitchen and started unloading her shopping. 'Has my daughter arranged hours and such with you, Grace?'

'Well, not really ... I mean, the car came and ...'

'Really, that's so typical.' Straightening up, Joan folded her brown paper sack with crisp snaps and slaps into eight symmetrical squares. 'The last girl did two mornings, usually Monday and Thursday, although that could be altered if it doesn't suit. The pay is five fifty an hour. Do you iron?'

I did. Extremely badly. But since I'd no intention of making a career of this, I gave a smile that could have been interpreted as *Just point me at the steam button and let me loose on them shirts, lady*.

'Good. It's just a question of keeping the dust down, really.

It doesn't get too dirty. The children are at school during the week. Do you have commitments, Grace?'

It took me a moment to work out she was asking if I had a family waiting at home. 'No.' I trotted out the cover story I'd been working on: dead-end job, redundancy, going back to college to get qualifications. 'This is just for some extra cash.'

'I see. Well, that's very commendable. So you wouldn't object to some additional hours? I'm giving a party for my daughter on Wednesday. We'll use outside caterers, of course, but there's bound to be extra work. Waitressing, washing-up.'

'Sure.' I started thrusting the vacuum and sprays back into their cupboards.

'Good. Patrick, have you had your lunch?'

'No.' The kid slouched in and cuddled up to his gran.

'Well, how about I make you a nice cheese salad? Would you like that?'

'No.'

'No, I didn't think you would. Pizza?'

'If you like.'

Patrick kept his head lowered and kicked at the table leg. He wanted it understood he was upset about something. On the other hand, he wanted to be fed.

His grandmother unwrapped a frozen pepperoni pizza and slid it into the oven with brisk, efficient movements. 'Set the table for me, please, Patrick. Three places.'

'Is *she* having some too then?'

'The lady's name is Grace,' Joan reproved gently. 'And no, she isn't. Your sister is around somewhere. Ah, there you are, we're just fixing lunch,' she added to someone in the hall. 'This is my granddaughter Eleanora, Grace.'

I turned with a pleased-to-meet-you smile; and froze.

It was Bone.

CHAPTER 21

At least she didn't go for 'What the hell are *you* doing here?' Instead I got a casual 'Hi' before she wandered across to the fridge and took out a can of Coke.

The sound of a car drawing up outside, followed by slamming doors and Amelia's light 'Ciao', provided a welcome distraction.

'It's Mummy.' Patrick shot across to the window. 'You won't forget, will you, Gran? You'll ask her. You *promised*.'

Joan was briskly dealing out place-mats on the kitchen table. 'Yes, all right, Patrick. I hadn't forgotten. But you must let me choose the right moment.'

'She won't say yes anyway,' Bone said, tilting the can to her lips.

'Yes she *will*.'

'Won't.'

'She will. She *will*.' Red-faced, Patrick rushed out.

Joan told her not to tease her brother. 'And use a glass, please, dear.'

Bone raised her eyebrows at this attempt to enforce ladylike manners on her. But I noticed she also poured the Coke into a tumbler. Evidently Joan ruled the roost around here and the chicks stayed in line.

Amelia arrived a second later in a breathless whirl of tossing blonde locks, giggles and jangling jewellery. 'That car is just unbelievable. I told the salesman – his name's Raoul, isn't that great – that I just had to have it by my birthday. He says there may be a premium for early delivery, but Stephen won't mind. He's such a generous sweetie.'

Joan remarked that he needn't have been quite so generous if they'd have had Amelia's previous car to trade in.

'But I was just so bored with it. You know how it is.'

She'd heaved herself on to a work surface and was swinging her legs backwards and forwards. I half expected Joan to tell her to 'sit up properly, dear' but instead she asked me if I'd finished cleaning. She dragged her fingertips over the top of the fridge as she asked, and frowned at the dusty digits.

'Em ... well ... you know ... you didn't exactly say what you wanted ...' I mumbled, edging towards the door. 'Maybe if you made a list or something ...'

'If you think that's really necessary ...'

'Yeah ... right ... great ... I gotta go now ...' I'd reached the hall, but Bone was following me out. Now her back was to her family, she started jerking her eyebrows up and down and mouthing instructions to meet her out back.

I was half tempted to make a run for it, but I didn't want her blurting out anything to her nearest and dearest in case I had to nose around Wexton's again, so I dutifully sauntered casually out of the front and round the side of the house.

Bone grabbed my wrist as soon as I appeared at the back. 'This way.' She dragged me along the path bordering the terraced patio, and down a winding route that wove between clumps of bushes and flowerbeds towards what looked like the barn of the original farmhouse.

As soon as she opened the door I knew it had been converted. The mixture of moist air and chlorine was unmistakable. I had a client who had their very own swimming pool! Was I going up in the world or what!

Bone flicked on a switch, activating the underwater illuminations in the turquoise pool and picking out the swirl of dolphin mosaics endlessly following each other's tails on the bottom.

There were several assorted exercise machines ranged down this end, and a row of wooden cubicles opposite which I assumed were changing rooms until Bone instructed me to 'hang on' and marched across to bang one of the doors open.

I caught a glimpse of a sun-bed before she marched to the next and threw it back to reveal the slatted wooden seats of a sauna. 'You know you're not allowed in here by yourself. Get lost.'

'Won't.' Patrick hunched his knees into his chest and pouted.

'Gran wants you. Your lunch is getting cold. She says if you don't go eat it right now, she's not asking Mummy.'

'She didn't? Did she, Bone?' Patrick's huge eyes widened even further. The poor kid looked really scared. 'Honest?'

'Honest.'

Disentangling himself, Patrick fled.

'What's up with him?' I asked.

'He hates school. He wants to go and live with Gran so he can be a day pupil instead of boarding.'

'Will your mum let him?'

'No, of course she won't. Make it bloody obvious she didn't want us here, wouldn't it? She could easily run us into school each morning. Or we could get a taxi. Loads of kids do. But she only wants us around at weekends when Daddy's home. No sense us being here in the week when he's at work all the time. So she makes out boarding school is good for us. Builds self-reliance and all that psycho-babble rubbish.'

I asked her if she hated school too.

'Me? No. I quite like it.' Abruptly she remembered it wasn't cool to like St Aggie's, so she added a bored shrug. 'I mean, it's OK, you know. Better than hanging around this dump.'

'Some dump.'

Bone threw a bored look around the expensively converted room. 'Claudia's folks have a flat in Knightsbridge and another overlooking Central Park. As well as the country house, of course. She says it's brill. You can just walk straight out the front door and go clubbing. Daddy said we could get a flat in London, but maybe I'll talk him into an apartment in New York instead. Claudia says the club scene's dead brill in the States.'

Kicking off her shoes, Bone sat on the edge of the pool, flicking waves over the glinting surface with her toes. She was dressed in slightly over-large jeans and loose chequered shirt today. Combined with a lack of make-up it made her look a lot younger than she had previously. I had a sudden nasty thought and asked her how old she was.

'Fourteen, why?'

'I thought you were sixteen or seventeen.'

'Everyone does. Brill, isn't it?'

I wondered if Tom Skerries had known her age. If he hadn't, finding out might have been another powerful reason to drop out of sight.

'Course he did,' Bone said in answer to my question. 'What's the big deal anyway?'

'You're under-age. He could have been arrested. That might have been a pretty big deal for him, Bone!'

The toes became even more agitated, sending a mini tidal-wave slopping over the opposite edge. 'I never said we *did* it, did I?' She threw me another pout over her shoulder and asked if I'd found him yet.

'No. I'm still on it. But it's not going to be easy. Maybe you should line up an understudy for Claudia's party. Aren't there any other blokes available?'

'Sure. Dozens. But I want Tom. I said he was taking me.' She stopped kicking, drew her legs up, and started picking at the soft skin around one of her big toes. Without looking at me she asked: 'Did she do that? The sister?'

It dawned on me that she thought my face was the result of a punch-up with Nola whilst chasing Tom on her behalf. She didn't even seem to find it odd that I'd come to report when she'd never given me her home address. No doubt she put it down to my hotshot powers of deduction. I mumbled vaguely about the problems of the job.

Bone abandoned her toes. 'I've been thinking, what if I paid his wife? I could give her fifty pounds for him to take me out. I mean, it would be just like hiring a car or something for the evening, wouldn't it?'

'I've told you, Bone. She doesn't know where he is.'

'She might. If you offered her the cash. Will you?'

It seemed simplest to agree. At least it would stop her from nosing around trying to find Donna's address and causing more trouble. In the mean time, Bone wanted me to go on looking for Tom. She didn't ask; she ordered. There was a lot of her grandmother in Bone.

As we made our way outside, I asked her where the odd nickname had come from.

'My brother Theo. He used to call me Eleanora-bone when I was little. Ellie-gnaw-a-bone, see?'

I saw.

We were threading our way back along the winding paths between the shrubbery. It was a couple of hundred yards to the house, but even from this distance the sound of two voices, one shrill, the other calm, drifted from the open upstairs windows. Most of the words were indistinguishable, until Amelia's angry instruction to 'Leave me alone and stop interfering!' rang clearly over the rhododendrons. 'I don't want a damn party. How dare you make plans without telling me!'

'Don't be silly. Of course you want some kind of celebration. I've already sent out the invitations.'

'Then you can just damn well unsend them. You're always doing this. When are you going to stop running my life for me, for God's sake!'

They passed beyond the open window, their voices blending again into an amalgam of calm reason and shrill accusations.

'Wonder what that's about,' Bone remarked.

I told about the birthday party her gran had just arranged for Amelia's fiftieth.

Bone gave a shriek of laughter. 'God, that's brill! She'll hate it!'

Amelia had struck me as a party animal. I said as much to her daughter, who nodded. 'Oh, sure. Normally. But not with that face. Serves her right!'

'Why? Was she responsible for the crash?'

Bone swung round, walking backwards in front of me. 'Don't tell me you fell for that stupid car-crash story?' She took her hands from her pockets and seized the skin on either side of her forehead, drawing it back to give her eyes an Oriental slant. 'She's had a face-lift, hasn't she.'

'Has she?'

'Of course she has. She had to. She's menopausal.'

'I don't think it's obligatory.'

'It is for her. She's always pretending to be younger than she really is. Did she tell you she'd gone out to California to see my sister Charlotte?'

'She mentioned it.'

'Bet she gave you the impression Char was just a kid.'

I *had* rather got the idea Char was a student or something. Apparently not.

'She's twenty-eight,' Bone informed me scornfully. 'She's just had her third kid. That's *supposedly* why Mummy went out there. But since Char wasn't due until last week there was no need for Mummy to fly out on the first, was there?'

'Some babies come early.'

'Char's don't. And anyway Mummy came home two days after the latest sprog arrived. Hardly the doting grandmother. She had a face-lift because of Daddy. She's dead predictable. I mean, Char's twenty-eight, Theo's twenty-one and I'm fourteen.'

She paused. Plainly I was supposed to deduce something from this. I failed her. With an exasperated sigh, she pointed out that there was seven years between each of them. 'She landed him by getting pregnant with Char, and then popped out another one of us whenever she thought he might be getting the seven-year itch. She thinks he's like Harrison Ford or someone and all these other women have the hots for him.'

'And do they?' I asked. If Amelia's suspicions were correct, it would seem to reinforce the cleaners' theories *vis-à-vis* Kristen Keats and Stephen Bridgeman.

'No. I mean, I expect he may have fancied a few other women. Married blokes do fancy playing away sometimes, don't they?' she said with a knowing sigh. Then rather spoilt the woman-of-the-world act by adding that her dad wouldn't actually, you know, *do* anything. 'It's all in Mummy's mind.'

I pointed out that there was a flaw in her seven-year theory, since Patrick didn't look seven to me.

'He's nine. But that was the year Grandad Reiss died and left his share in the company to Daddy. I daresay Mummy thought he would take off now he was the one with the money. So she popped out Patrick to keep him in line.'

'Sounds like dodgy planning to me. A screaming baby is more or less guaranteed to drive some blokes out.' They certainly seemed to have that effect on her erstwhile boyfriend Tom. But not Stephen Bridgeman, apparently.

'Daddy likes us,' Bone said with supreme confidence. 'We're the most important people in his life. And now she can't get herself pregnant again, she's starting having lumps of flesh chopped off instead. I think it's pathetic. I'd never do anything as gross as that.'

We were nearly at my car. I'd been tossing up whether to risk asking about Kristen Keats or not. I decided to chance it.

'Listen, Bone, I'm on another case at the moment, chasing up a missing person. You might know her.'

I gave her a rapid description of Kristen, not really expecting any recognition. But surprisingly enough, Bone nodded. 'I saw her at the factory. She had this really neat pink suede mini-skirt. I wanted one, but she'd got it from one of those retroshops in London, sold genuine sixties stuff.'

'When was this? That you saw her, I mean?'

'Last Christmas holidays. Gran took us into Dover because Patrick wanted to watch the boats. God, he's such a pain. I mean, like, we had hours and hours watching these grossly boring ferries and freezing our butts off.'

'Why go then?'

She shrugged. 'Nothing else to do. And anyway Daddy gave me some money so I got some new boots in the sales. On the way back Gran wanted to go into the factory to get something and she was there, with Daddy.'

'Doing what?'

'I don't know. Working on one of those boring computer programs. Who's looking for her?'

'Just a friend. She seems to have gone missing.'

'Honestly?'

'Well, probably not. It's more likely she's just got bored and moved on.'

That was something Bone could relate to. I could sense she was already losing interest in a big way in Kristen. In fact, anything that didn't directly relate to her own entertainment was pretty boring as far as Bone was concerned. Before we lost the thread altogether, I asked if she'd ever seen Kristen here.

'Here? No, why should she come here? It's not like she was a friend or anything. She just worked for us.'

'Right.' We'd reached my car by now. I'd parked it slightly to one side of the house because I didn't want the double garages giving it an inferiority complex. I'd got the key in the driver's door before Bone asked the question I'd rather been hoping she wouldn't. Why was I working here as a cleaner?

'Undercover. Can't discuss it now,' I snapped briskly. 'OK?' I gave her a straight we're-all-women-together look.

Luckily she was still young enough to be intimidated. 'Er … yeah … you'll be in touch then?'

'Sure. We've a contract, right?'

'Right. Well, er …' Hands thrust once more into jeans pockets, Bone said she'd see me and slouched back to the house.

Relieved to have got out of that one so easily, I returned to coaxing the car door open.

'She tells lies.'

The voice was so close to my ear that I felt my stomach bounce off the back of my throat while my heart boogied against my ribs. 'Bloody hell,' I gasped at Patrick. 'How much do you charge to haunt a house?'

'What?'

He was two inches from me, arms hugging a suspiciously lumpy chest, and a sulky pout letting me know he wasn't happy with the world. I asked him who told lies.

'Her. Bone. Gran didn't say I had to come in *at all*.'

'Yeah, well, that's sisters for you, Patrick. We can be real bitches sometimes.'

'*And* she lied about that Kristen lady. She did come here. She was a friend of Daddy's. I heard them talking.'

CHAPTER 22

I took his hand in a gesture of encouragement. And to make sure the pesky little eavesdropper didn't run off before he spilt the beans on his dad.

'Are you making this up, Patrick?'

'No!'

'You sure?'

'Yes. I *heard* then.'

'Heard them where?'

The lashes fluttered downward. He ground his toes into the drive, hugged the lump beneath the jumper tighter, and muttered he didn't know.

'I knew you were making it up.'

'Am *not*.' The eyes flashed up again. 'She was talking to Daddy in his study, I *heard* them.'

'When was this?'

'Long time ago. Before Christmas.' The drive got the toe-grinding routine again.

I took a guess. 'Bunked off school, had you?'

He nodded, eyes still on the ground. 'It was double rugby. We always have games Friday morning. I hate games. I'm no good at it. They all laugh at me.'

I felt a twinge of sympathy for the kid. He was a very young nine, not like the streetwise kids on the Downs Estate. And those almost girlish features didn't help.

'So you came home. How'd you get here?'

'Bus.'

'And your dad was here? With Kristen?'

'Yes. He wasn't supposed to be. I didn't think anyone would be here. Mummy used to go to her health-club place on Fridays.'

'Did they see you? Daddy and Kristen, I mean.'

'No. I just heard them. Daddy was cross. He said he was working at home that morning because he wanted a bit of peace and quiet and she shouldn't have come bothering him. And then she said she had to because he wouldn't listen at work. And Daddy said she'd still have to go but he'd speak to her tomorrow morning. And then when it *was* tomorrow, he went to play golf. And he only goes to play golf with his friends, so that Kristen lady must be his friend, mustn't she?'

'You could be right, Patrick, but I think it might be best if you kept that a secret.'

'Why?'

'Because sometimes people like to have secret friends.'

'Oh?' He considered this, swaying as he cradled the woolly lump to his heart. The pressure squeezed it out of the V top of his sweater. It was a mobile phone.

'Is that yours?'

'No. It's Bone's. I took it. I'm going to hide it where she'll never find it.'

'I couldn't borrow it first, could I?'

He demonstrated how to feed in Bone's security number. I phoned the office on the off-chance something had happened during my housework shift. For once it had: Jason thought he'd found me a flat that would suit Andy and Fergie.

'He wants you to ring him so he can fix up a trot-around. His cruddy joke, not mine,' Janice informed me. 'And Annie rang. She wants you to call her back.'

'Did she say why?'

'Said she'd got that address you wanted.'

'What address?'

'I dunno, do I? Some girl's. Can't remember the name.'

My brain finally clicked into gear. 'Kristen! Did she say Kristen?'

'Dunno. Might have been.'

'Tell me, Janice, does being totally apathetic come naturally to you? Or do you have to work at it?'

'I couldn't be bothered.'

Patrick watched with interest as I punched in the number for directory enquiries and then realised I didn't know which hotel Annie was staying at in Leicester. Janice didn't know either when I called her back again. Or if she did, she wasn't telling me.

In desperation I dialled the local police station and asked for Detective Constable Zebedee Smith. A voice so thickly steeped in Glaswegian dialect even Billy Connolly would have needed sub-titles to crack it, asked how it could be of assistance?

'Zeb?'

'Oh it's you.' The home counties accent replaced the Celtic brogue. 'I thought it might be Annie.'

'Well if it was, she's not going to be fooled by the lousy disguise Zeb. I take it the squatters are still in residence?'

'Yes. The girl reckons she's pregnant. You think she's feeding me a line?'

'I doubt it. She told me too. And she's not squatting in *my* sister's flat.'

'Oh god. You have to be so careful these days. You know how funny the public can get about police brutality ... maybe I *should* just leave it to Annie.'

'Good thinking Zeb. After she's finished chucking them out, she can come round and knock your teeth out for letting them in the first place. And speaking of Annie, have you got the number of her hotel in Leicester?'

'Why? You're not going to phone her!'

'Don't panic Zeb. It's strictly work. Now cough it up.'

I wrote the number in the dirt on the car bodywork. Twisting his head sideways, Patrick chanted it aloud as I dialled the Holiday Inn.

Miss A Smith wasn't in her room, nor answering the hotel tannoy system. Leaving an urgent message for her to contact me, I clicked the phone shut and threw it on the passenger seat.

'Are you going to steal Bone's phone?'

'What? Oh no, sorry.'

'I don't mind. I was going to bury it.'

'You little rat, I knew it was you. Give it *back*.'

Bone burst out of the back door. Grabbing the phone from my hands, Patrick sprinted away with his sister in pursuit and screaming insults.

I dropped back to the flat first and got rid of the stink of disinfectant by changing into my second-best outfit of seventies flared jeans with natty material inlets and a fluffy orange and pink jumper. The hotel confirmed that Annie hadn't returned, so I figured I'd earned a meal break.

The fridge, I discovered with regret, still hadn't learnt to breed food (bugs in an odd shade of green – yes; food – no.) It was a toss-up between hitting the supermarket again or dropping into Pepi's. Pepi's won by about ten lengths.

The depressing weather was lifting slightly in response to the last few hours of the Bank Holiday. One of the deckchair stacks had been de-sheathed from its tarpaulins and the kids' roundabout was circling to sounds of thinking organ music. Out on the wet strand, December's donkeys were picking their sure-footed way amongst heaps of olive-coloured seaweed.

I walked the length of the promenade, mooched down the main shopping street, mingling with those weekenders who'd stuck it out to the bitter end, and approached Pepi's via the back streets.

It wasn't that I liked the scenery, but I wanted to confirm what I'd suspected ever since I left the flat. I was being followed.

I was nearly at the café's front door before I remembered that it was shut on Mondays. Only it wasn't. The telltale steam over the windows was definite evidence of habitation. I pushed my way through the lovely greasy fug to the counter where Shane was wondering at the top of his lungs why he had to be a teenager in love whilst he dusted powdered chocolate over mugs of cappuccino.

'Afternoon, Shane. How come you're open?'

'The customers are a right picky bunch. Don't like eating on the pavement.'

'Lucky you became a singer. You'd never have made it as a comedian.'

'Those who are hoping to scrounge freebies should not mock.'

'Thanks for offering. Can I have one of those cappuccinos?'

'Best ask the bloke who paid for them. Back in a tick.'

The jukebox switched tunes. 'Ain't true love a wonderful thing ...' Shane sang, sashaying between the crowded tables with his tray of coffees.

I watched his jeans-clad rear bouncing around like a couple of sacks of gravel. The coffee customers were at a table by the window. As Shane reached them I took my eyes off his bum for a second and flicked a quick glance through the condensation covered glass. My tail was just sauntering past.

'So why are you open?' I asked when Shane jigged his way back.

'Always open Bank Holidays. And the missus's teeth always play her up. Family ritual, you might say. She went home half-hour since. So if you want feeding, Smithie, get yourself the other side of this counter.'

'I'm not a waitress.'

'I know. But I can't afford to be fussy. Here y'are. And d'ya mind sticking the shades back on, there's people trying to eat in here.'

I'd forgotten the damage to my nose. Tentatively I touched the bruising. It seemed slightly less tender than a few hours ago. But I was going to have to take care. My nose had only just recovered from a previous assault on my last case, and if it kept getting mushed like this, my little lecture to Bone on the subject of permanent disfigurement could come horribly true.

Shane lifted the counter flap. I stepped through. Why not? I had time to waste until I could get hold of Annie, and the deal included free food and phone.

Disappearing into the back kitchen, Shane left me to call the orders through the hatch, dish out the drinks and fry up on the front burners when we got busy. I phoned Annie every twenty minutes, leaving the café's number, until the hotel switchboard operator and I were on first-name terms.

The temperature started to creep up. A heavy woolly wasn't the best clobber for a fast-food chef. I could feel the sweat trickling down my back and was just wondering whether I was desperate enough to whip the thing off and borrow Shane's vest when I spotted a familiar green coat approaching the door.

My first thought was that Annie had finished in Leicester and driven down this afternoon. This was swiftly followed by – not unless she's discovered a diet that shifts about four stone of blubber in two weeks.

I stuck my head in the glass display case, rearranging the few cakes we had left, until she'd hitched herself on to a counter stool.

'Hello, Mickey. I thought I recognised the coat.'

'Oh! I … er …' She flushed bright pink and clutched Annie's coat around her thin frame.

'I'd take it off if I were you. It's boiling in here.'

'What? Oh yes, all right.'

She carefully folded the coat inside out and laid it with exaggerated care over the next stool. 'I took ever such good care of it, honest. And I'm gonna wash the other things.' Her fingers fiddled nervously with the collar of a blouse Annie had bought in a sale last summer.

'Figgy not with you?'

'He's at the flat. Cleaning. We're keeping it really nice, honest.'

'I'll mention that to Annie. The owner, remember?'

'Yes.' She looked even more miserable. Basically Mickey was not a natural-born scrounger. 'We *will* go soon. Soon as Figgy gets a job.'

'As a matter of interest, what does Figgy do for a living?'

'He's an ice-skater.'

'Well, that should narrow down the choices at the job centre.'

'He doesn't expect to get a job skating. But if he could get

175

something that let him have time off to practise ... He's ever so good ...'

'I know. I caught your performance the other day. I was impressed.'

Mickey flushed with pleasure. 'Were you? Honest? I'll tell Figgy. He nearly got a part in *Starlight Express* once, you know. But he had to say no, on account of his ankles. Busting them. Because of the ice-skating, see?'

I didn't really. Wheelies on rock-hard pavement struck me as rather more dangerous than roller-skating on a professional stage.

Retrieving a couple of cream and jam jumbo doughnuts from the showcase in response to a shouted order, I asked Mickey if they were still performing, in view of her condition.

'Figgy is. He's got regular spots: mornings outside the post office – when people are doing their shopping, see? Then afternoons on the prom; that's for the beach babies, he says. And then two evening sessions outside the amusement park six o'clock and ten thirty.'

'What's he doing for music?'

'He takes the radio cassette now.'

'Annie's radio, you mean?'

'Well ... yes ... but ...'

'I know ... you're taking ever such good care of it.'

Mickey looked guilty. Then the pinched look changed to wide-eyed alarm. She slapped a hand over her mouth.

'Loos are in the back.'

With a moan, Mickey fled.

I checked out the café. My shadow had taken the opportunity to slip into one of the spare seats by the window whilst I was chatting with Mickey and was now lurking behind a newspaper held at face height. I was tempted to go over, knock it down and shout 'Gotcha!' – but I figured we'd go on playing the game for a while longer.

Mickey reappeared looking several shades paler.

'Better?'

She nodded.

'Don't you think you should be outside? Some of Shane's cooking makes *me* want to chuck up. And I'm not several months gone.'

'The doctor said I should try weak black tea, 'cos I didn't want to take tablets in case it hurts the baby.'

'Right.' I thrust a mug under the spout and released hot water in a cloud of steam.

Mickey delved into her – or rather Annie's – pockets and counted out a collection of small coins.

'On the house,' I said, ever generous with Shane's profits.

She sipped the scalding liquid like I'd just offered champagne. 'That's where I've been. Up the doctor's. Signing on. That's why I took the clothes. If you look like you're sleeping rough, they say the lists are full.'

'The health authority would make someone take you on, Mickey.'

'Crap doctors, Figgy says. The ones no one else wants to go to. You've got to have a good address to get on the list at a decent surgery, Figgy says.'

'Right little know-it-all, isn't he, your Figgy?'

Some colour came back to her face. 'He takes care of me.'

'Lucky you. I wish someone would take care of me.'

'Do you?'

She seemed surprised. That made two of us. I didn't know where that had come from. Before I could do any in-depth analysis, the phone rang.

It was Annie. She'd spent the day tracking down a cookie who'd lied his way through his entire application for the bonds and securities company and she was anxious to tell me just how smart she'd been.

I, on the other hand, wanted Kristen Keats' home address. Shane wanted to exercise his vocal cords by running through his rock-and-roll repertoire.

'So would you believe there are eight men in this family – all called Amin?'

'Lack of imagination is obviously hereditary. Have you really got Kristen Keats' address?'

'Sure. I found this computer buff who hacked into the files on former students for me. You owe me the price of a couple of drinks in the students' union bar, by the way. Anyway, this Amin, the one I was tracking …'

'Have I the right …?' Shane bawled, drumming spoons against the saucepan lids.

I dug my finger harder into my spare ear, cradled the receiver against my shoulder and fished for a pencil. 'What's the address?'

'Most of them were living in the same house. That was part of the problem. I mean, the address checked out. And there's four cousins around the same age ...'

'Da-do-run-run-run ...'

'Not that address, Kristen's address. You can tell me the rest when you get back ...'

'So anyway ... you'll never guess how I tripped him in the end ...'

'I gotta a girl called ...'

'SHUT UP!'

Well, it worked. The only sound in the café was the hiss of frying fat. I looked out over a room of surprised faces and the top of one head whose owner had apparently dropped something under the table.

'Sorry ... er ... carry on ... Annie, you still there?'

'Yes. But one of my eardrums isn't. You can do your own leg-work in the future, you ungrateful ratbag.'

'Deepest grovels and I'll even buy the pizza next time. Brownie's honour. Just give me Kristen's address.'

'You were never a brownie. Got a pen ...?'

I pinned an order pad to the wall with my elbow and scribbled. 'Is that R-O-C-H-E-L-L-E? As in western France?'

'No. It's R-O-Z-E-L. It's not in France. It's in Jersey. There's a phone number too.'

Out of the corner of my eye I'd seen the plates were piling up on the serving counter as Shane whisked cooked orders through to the rhythm of 'Hot Dog Buddy Buddy.' I'd also sensed the natives were getting restless. Being well-bred, reserved British types, most of them had kept their moans to themselves. One table finally cracked.

'Oi, Blondie ... our chips are getting cold.'

'Well come get them, then ... you glued to the seat or what?'

I punched in the Jersey number. Now I was this close, there was no way I was being diverted.

'Isobel Keats speaking.'

I nearly did a cartwheel. At last I'd got a hook on the

elusive Kristen. 'Hello, we've not met, but I'm trying to trace a Kristen Keats.'

'This is Kristen's mother speaking.'

Jackpot!

I checked. The Kristen I wanted had worked for AD Aerospace and Okranshaw Electronics.

'Yes, that's correct. My daughter worked for both those companies. Before she joined the voluntary agency. May I ask what your interest is, Miss ... Mrs ...?'

'Grace Smith. I've been hired to find Kristen by ... a friend who's worried about her. Kristen hasn't been in touch for the past few weeks ... and before that they'd been in pretty regular contact since Christmas, so ...'

'I'm sorry, Miss Smith, there seems to have been some sort of mistake.'

'Why?'

'Because our Kristen died over a year ago.'

CHAPTER 23

'It might have been better if Kristen had never been born.'

Isobel Keats' hand shook slightly as she poured a thin stream of pale-biscuit-coloured tea into a translucent china cup. The set-up suited her. Everything about her, from her porcelain skin to her pale-blue eyes and white hair, had a transparent air. She made me think of an insect husk after the juice had been sucked from its occupant.

But there was plainly still a spark of life burning inside somewhere. When I'd explained on the phone about 'Kristen' working at Wexton's and living in Seatoun until a few weeks ago, she'd been initially suspicious – and then some other emotion had cut in. Part anger, but part something else I couldn't quite identify – then.

She'd asked if I'd be prepared to come to Jersey. 'We should like to meet you face to face, Miss Smith, but I'm afraid my husband is unable to travel far.'

'Well ... I ...'

I *could* come, of course. But I wasn't entirely sure Henry was going to cough up for the fare. Isobel must have read my mind.

'We shall be pleased to cover your expenses. We should be most grateful. Kristen is ... was ... very precious to us. If someone is using her name ... well, we should like the matter resolved.'

'Fair enough. If you can fix up a flight, I'll come out.'

She'd rung back half an hour later with instructions to collect the ticket from the British Airways desk at Heathrow. I took down the flight details to the rhythm of Shane begging us not to step on his blue suede shoes, and bawled them back to her whilst he bemoaned that damn hound dog.

I have a theory that when calculating times for any journey that involves negotiating the M25, it's best to double the number you first thought of – and then add in today's date for good luck. By this method, I just managed to dump the car in the long-stay car-park at Heathrow the following morning and hitch a lift to the terminal as the information screens were flashing the final boarding call for my flight.

By the time I'd sprinted to the relevant gate and been welcomed aboard by a set of gleaming teeth and immaculate make-up, the rest of the passengers were already seated.

Taking my seat at the back of the plane, I passed the thirty-five-minute flight nibbling on the courtesy packets of roasted peanuts, sipping ginger ale and watching the cabin staff going for the Olympic record for distributing and collecting plastic glasses. They just managed to hurl the last cup into the trash sack as the 'fasten seat belts' sign flashed on and the tannoy thanked me for flying British Airways and hoped to see me again.

I have to say that Jersey was seriously gorgeous. No high-rise buildings or wide, featureless fields; instead, the taxi wove through narrow roads bordered by stone walls and thick hedgerows all sprinkled with nodding clusters of wild flowers enclosing tiny patchwork fields.

I guess I'd been subconsciously expecting Rozel Bay to be a sort of toy-town version of Seatoun. Mini arcades and tacky shops selling even tackier souvenirs and greasy burgers dripping fried onion. This, however, was the seaside for those with taste. A small beach and harbour fringed by a few tiny streets of old cottages. The commercial section was discreet: upmarket antiques and outfits in the shops; cream teas and seafood salads served in patio gardens beneath fringed umbrellas.

The Keats' cottage was in a row of six, all built of the warm pinkish-tinged blocks I'd noticed in a lot of the older houses on the taxi journey.

'It used to be the traditional building material of the island,' Isobel explained when I commented on it. 'Did you notice the marriage stone over the front door?'

She drew me back into the narrow street to point out the carved initials: 'I & C 1721 AD'.

'We took the initials as a good omen, Isobel and Charles. It was as if the house had been waiting for us. Somewhere warm and safe to grow old and welcome our grandchildren. Now we just ... grow old.'

'I'm sorry. Look, I didn't mean to cause you any further upset.'

'I rather doubt you could, Miss Smith.'

'Grace, please.'

'As you wish. Would you excuse me a moment while I settle Charles.'

She'd carried a tray out into the slightly overgrown tangle of back garden. Her husband was sitting by a small folding table. Through the leaded window, I saw him say something to her and shake his head violently.

We'd been introduced briefly when I first arrived. Flesh pared to the bone, a tall frame permanently stooped and dull brown eyes were my first impressions. My second was that while the engine was running, some of the spark plugs had given up a while ago.

Isobel had more or less confirmed this by excusing her husband. 'He doesn't wish to talk about Kristen. There are some days he prefers to act as if she hadn't existed. In some ways it might have been better if Kristen had never been born.'

We both looked out of the window to the figure seated in the garden, his head turned stubbornly away from the window.

'How did Kristen die, Mrs Keats? If you don't mind my asking.'

'I doubt it would make any difference to you if I did.' The colourless lips suddenly tilted in a fraction of a smile. 'I'm sorry, that was unpleasant. Please forgive me. It's not your fault. It's simply ... you look around for someone to blame. To hit out at. Do you understand?'

I nodded. 'Kristen?' I prompted.

'Kristen.' The name came out like a long sigh. 'She wasn't wanted. I suppose when we married we both thought there *would* be children, but when none came ... well, we had a good life. We were content with each other. Then, on our silver wedding anniversary, I discovered I was expecting.'

I didn't want to know any of this. But I sensed Isobel needed to talk. And until she'd gone through this mental flagellation, we couldn't reach the answers that I needed.

'I considered an abortion. We both felt we were too old for children.' Moisture gathered along the inner rims of her eyelids and spilled over. 'I don't know when she became the centre of our existence. One, two weeks after we brought her home?'

'Bath was home then?'

'Yes. Charles's dental practice was in the city. Although we are both from Jersey originally. We returned here when Kristen went to university. A relative left us this cottage. It seemed so providential. Somewhere that our grandchildren could come – would want to come for their holidays. Now we just sit here and wait.'

'Wait for what?'

She turned surprised eyes, glinting through a film of tears, on me. 'To die, Grace. What else is there left to wait for now?'

I knew I ought to say something comforting, but frankly I couldn't think of a damn thing.

Isobel smiled bleakly. 'It's all right. There *is* nothing to say.'

'You didn't have any more children? After Kristen?'

'No. There was only Kristen. If she hadn't been born, Charles and I would probably have grown into a contented old age together. But once we'd had her ...'

She gave herself a shake. I almost expected to see flakes of dried skin rise in a cloud around her and drift out into the shaft of sunlight streaming through the window to dapple the floor in diamond patterns.

'Charles adored her. He was so determined not to let his age become a handicap to her. He didn't want to be an old-fashioned father, the sort of man who saw girls as only fit for marriage. So he pushed her in the opposite direction. He insisted she take scientific studies at school: maths, computer studies, physics. Poor Kristen ... she tried so hard to please him, but the truth is, her heart wasn't in it. It's ironic really. When there were so many girls fighting for success in male professions, Kristen would, I suspect, have been quite happy to sit at home practising embroidery and playing the piano. She was born a hundred years too late, my poor love.'

'She took engineering at Leicester, though?'

'Yes. She had considered dentistry like her father, but her grades weren't sufficiently high. She managed to scrape through with a two-two degree, but she hated every job she had afterwards. Until she joined the voluntary agency.'

'She really worked for the Third World Initiative Team?'

'No. She was with a small agency called Childscope. They sent her to Central America. Initially it was to provide assistance with a water purification scheme, but they were desperate for someone to teach basic maths at the local school. The original volunteer had changed her mind at the last minute ...'

'So Kristen stepped in?'

'It was the first time she'd been really happy for ages. It just shone out of her letters. She enjoyed the children so much. She was even talking of training as a teacher when she returned to England.'

'I take it she never did?' I said gently.

'No.'

Isobel sat silently staring ahead for a moment. I could feel the effort going on inside her as she tried to gather together enough strength to talk.

'Her appendix burst. They think she'd been in pain for several days and hadn't said anything. They operated, but peritonitis had set in. It was all so fast ...' The tears spilt now in huge drops on to her lap. 'We didn't even get to say goodbye ...'

I took her hand. There didn't seem anything else to do.

'We scattered her ashes out there. The children helped us. When you rang ... when you said ... I knew it was quite absurd ... we saw the body ...'

I finally identified that other note I'd caught in Isobel's voice whilst we bawled at each other over Shane's rock repertoire on the café phone. It had been hope. For a brief second, I'd raised the prospect that Kristen might still be alive.

In a few minutes I'd stripped away the healing of fourteen months and laid the wound raw. Now that pain and disbelief and anger had to be worked through all over again.

'Oh God, I'm so sorry, Mrs Keats ... I didn't think ... I mean, I'd no way of knowing ...'

'It's all right.' She sat up straighter and fixed her trembling lips in a thin line. 'This person, this woman who claims to be Kristen, are you certain it is not merely a coincidence? Someone with a similar name, perhaps?'

'With exactly the same schooling and employment record?'

'No. I suppose not.'

'It's more common than you think. Get hold of a few documents and you can have a whole new identity. Half a dozen if you like. Can I ask what happened to Kristen's papers? Birth certificate? Driving licence? Passport?'

'They're upstairs. In her bedroom.'

'Did you register her death? In Britain, I mean?'

'No. We were advised it wasn't necessary.'

It must have been a real bonus to Kristen's *doppelgänger*. A whole new life and no corresponding death if anyone chose to cross-check.

Isobel rose abruptly and excused herself for a moment. Through the window, I watched her fit an old panama hat on her husband's head. It bobbed and shook slightly under her attentions before sinking even further on to his chest.

'He sleeps a great deal now,' she explained, resettling herself in the back parlour, but leaving the door to the garden open.

'You must get lonely.'

'Yes.' The single word was a dismissal of the entire subject.

I was getting to the crux of my visit. Sitting forward, I rested my forearms along my knees and said: 'Isobel, if I describe someone to you, could you tell me if it rings any bells?'

'Very well.'

I mentally gathered together what I knew of the fake Kristen. 'Mid to late twenties. About five feet eight inches tall. Dark hair to the shoulders. Pretty. In great physical shape. Likes Charles Dickens. Can be good company when she chooses, but equally capable of playing things close to her chest. Sufficient engineering knowledge to pass as a test engineer in an electronics company. And ...' I added, recalling the receptionist at Wexton's Engineering who'd discussed Leicester public houses with 'Kristen', 'she's probably spent some time living in the Leicester area.'

'That's Julie Francis,' Isobel said promptly. 'She always insisted on the full double-barrelled pronunciation of her Christian names.'

So not Julie Francis, but Julie-Frances.

'What's her surname?'

'Keble. Julie-Frances Keble. That's how she and Kristen met. They shared a room in the halls of residence their first year at Leicester. The rooms were allocated on an alphabetical basis; Keats – Keble.'

'And after the first year?'

'One of those shared student houses in a place called Earl Shilton.'

'So they got on OK?'

'Oh yes. They got on.'

There was something about her tone that invited me to probe further. So I probed. Isobel agreed she hadn't much cared for her daughter's friend.

'It's hard to say why. Kristen brought her here to stay one holiday. As you say, she could be good company. But there was *something* ... perhaps it's just the benefit of hindsight, after what happened ... but she went out with one of our neighbours one evening. Philippe Martin. He's in his sixties.'

'Some girls go for the mature type.'

'Yes. I wasn't being judgemental. Philippe is a widower and

his private life is his own business. It's just that ... she made him pay. One hundred pounds.'

'He told you?'

'No. She did. She was quite open about it. Said she needed some books for her course. She said it was all very well for nice middle-class girls like Kristen who had parents to bail them out when the grant ran out, but she had to hustle cash where she could.'

'Didn't she have any family?'

'Her parents died when she was very young. She was raised by an elderly aunt who died the summer before Julie-Frances started university.'

'What about other friends?'

'I don't believe so. I daresay there were other students she mixed with ... but I gained the impression that Kristen was her only close friend.'

'Did either of them, Kristen or Julie-Frances, ever mention a Bertram?'

'I don't think so. Who is he?'

'I wish I knew. Was Julie-Frances reading engineering as well?'

'Yes. She was, I believe, considered exceptionally talented by her tutors. She would undoubtedly have obtained a first-class degree. Unfortunately she never graduated.'

'How come?'

'She was arrested.'

CHAPTER 24

Apparently, at the beginning of her final year, Julie-Frances had taken a weekend trip to the continent. It was supposed to last three days. In Julie-F's case it turned into free board and lodging at Her Majesty's expense for a couple of years.

'There was cocaine in the car. The man she was with claimed to know nothing about it. He said Julie-Frances had smuggled it in without his knowledge. She said it belonged to him. The jury didn't believe her.'

'Did you?'

'Kristen did.'

'And you?'

'I'm not certain. The man was older ... a businessman from the Midlands. He'd never been in trouble with the police before. Whereas Julie-Frances ... she was short of money ... and if someone had paid her ...?'

'He could have taken her along as cover. Somewhere to dump the blame if he got stopped at Customs.'

'Yes. That was her defence.'

'What happened to the bloke?'

'He was cleared of the charge. But as things turned out, it did him little good. He died of a massive heart attack two days after Julie-Frances was sentenced.'

'Did Kristen keep in touch with her? After the sentencing?'

'They wrote.'

'Would she have known about Kristen's ...' I hesitated.

'Death, Grace. I have no patience with euphemisms. Kristen has not passed over or gone to eternal rest. She has died. To answer your question – yes, there was a letter waiting when we came back from ... from seeing to Kristen. Julie-Frances had just been given the date for her release. She came to see us. I was quite touched. She was the only one of Kristen's friends who'd bothered.'

'When was this?'

'Last August. The week after the flower festival.'

Her eyes turned to where her husband was nodding amongst the early flowers. He looked so still he could be dead. One day I guess he would be.

'Can I see Kristen's papers?'

'Come with me. I'll show you.'

They'd been pushed into an old concertina-type cardboard file on Kristen's wardrobe shelf. A few clothes still swung on dusty hangers; they were all conventional outfits, nothing too revealing, too bright or too outrageous. This wasn't a girl who'd ever worn a pink suede mini-skirt.

'She slept in here,' Isobel said softly. 'In Kristen's room. I stood in the door and watched her. For a moment, with her hair spreading out over the pillow ... it was as if Kristen had never left.'

'They were alike then – physically?'

In answer, Isobel reached across and dipped into an end pocket of the file. She emerged with a clutch of photographs and selected one.

They were sitting on a low stone wall in front of a three-storey building. The fuzzy groups of youngsters in the background suggested it had probably been taken somewhere on the university campus.

I didn't need to ask which was which. The girl to the front sat with her fingers linked over a long flowered dress that touched her lace-up boots. Crinkly brown hair framed a smiling face that had Charles Keats' eyes. The girl behind was leaning back on one hand, her long legs stretched out to show the expanse of tanned skin between the shorts and the trainers. Only the hair was wrong. The ragged cut hung to her earlobes.

'Did she grow her hair?'

'Yes. It was far longer last summer.'

The resemblance between the two women was superficial, but close enough. It was odd to be looking at a picture of 'my' Kristen. I'd been chasing a ghost for weeks and now suddenly she'd become flesh. I strained at the glossy print, trying to make some contact with the two-dimensional image.

Isobel had been continuing to investigate the file. 'I can't find Kristen's passport. Or her driving licence. And her degree certificate has gone too.'

'Birth certificate?'

'It wasn't in here. It's in my papers.' Isobel made to stand up.

I pulled her down. 'I shouldn't bother. It's easy enough to get a copy. What about a cheque book? Or pass book?'

'I have those too. There was a problem. The bank and building society were converting or merging or something. And with Kristen dying abroad, there was quite a bit of confusion.'

Which may have been why Julie-F hadn't risked opening an account in Kristen's name yet. Best to let the dust settle first in case anyone recognised the name.

'Why has she taken them, Grace?' She fanned other prints

over the bed, touching her daughter's face in each. 'Is she about to commit another crime?'

I pointed out that Julie-Frances' reasons might be completely the opposite. 'Not everyone's anxious to employ an ex-con. Especially once the word "drugs" is mentioned. A lot land up back inside because in the end the only people who'll give them a break are the low-lifes who put them inside in the first place. Maybe Julie-Frances needed a clean background so that she *could* go straight.'

'Then why are you investigating her?'

'Not investigating. Tracing. She's missing.'

'Isobel? Isobel, where are you? I can't find the shed. Who's taken the shed, Isobel?' The querulous voice drifted through the partially open sash window.

'I'm sorry. He thinks he's back in Bath. I'm coming, Charles.'

I followed her downstairs slowly. By the time I reached the garden she'd resettled him into the high-backed deckchair

'Can I help?'

'No thank you. I can manage. I was just about to fix some lunch, if you'd care to …?'

'Who's she?'

'This is Miss Smith, Charles. Remember, you met her earlier?'

'What does she want? Is it an emergency? I don't do extractions on Saturday.'

'I'm sorry. It's a bad day. It's because we were talking about Kristen earlier.'

'I'll go. Thanks for the help.'

'Will you let me know if you find Julie-Frances?'

'Sure.'

She saw me out of the back gate. It was let into a low stone wall that bordered a narrow, pavement-less road. The weather was kinder than on the mainland. The sun was beating down in a steady flow that sparkled off the windows and made the stones warm to the touch. A couple of tourists wandered past, licking ice-creams and studying a book entitled *Walking the Channel Islands*. They were forced to swerve apart to avoid another wanderer in blue chinos who had his head buried in a large open map.

189

Isobel shook hands formally and thanked me for coming. 'Are you sure you won't stay? Your return flight isn't for some hours.'

'No. Thanks. I'll do a bit of sightseeing. I could use the exercise. There is just one thing ... you don't remember the name of the man who was caught with Julie-Frances, do you?'

'William Carr. I believe his businesses had got into financial trouble. Julie-Frances' counsel tried to convince the jury that the drugs were supposed to clear his debts. Unsuccessfully, as it turned out. I don't think the people he owed money to were ... very pleasant.'

'You haven't got any names, I suppose?'

'No ... at least ... would you excuse me a moment?'

She disappeared into the cottage. I watched the blue chinos turn down a short street that led to the tiny quay. A breeze had caught the map and it was wrapping itself round his head and shoulders. He was still twisting and pirouetting as he disappeared from my sight and Isobel re-emerged.

'Here you are ... it's the only one ... I found it tucked in a book.'

Isobel held out a thin envelope addressed to Miss K. Keats. The postmark was four years ago. 'I meant to throw it away. I keep meaning to get rid of so many things, but somehow ... what's the point ... they'll clear it all out some day soon.'

I thrust it in my jeans pocket, promising to send it back. Isobel told me not to bother. 'Goodbye, Miss Smith. And good luck.'

'Bye. And thanks again.' She was standing at the gate when I reached the end of the road. Raising my hand, I shouted back: 'I'll ring you as soon as I find her, Mrs Keats.'

There was a signpost saying 'Cliff Walk' and pointing up the road. It was only a light gradient, but I felt the pull on the backs of my calves. I was definitely going to have to do something about getting back in shape.

From up here you could see down on to the tiny harbour with its toy-town boats bobbing and jostling on their mooring line, and the beach with a few sunbathers already spread out like raspberry-pink starfish.

I climbed a little further and looked down on to the zig-zag road below. The two walkers had finished their ice-creams and were now following my footsteps with the grim determination of dedicated masochists. Beyond them, the blue chinos was ambling along at a leisurely pace, adjusting the angles on a natty white cotton hat that still had its price tag dangling from the brim.

The path scouted the edge of a tiny field raised into earthen ridges that sprouted rows of greenery. My veg comes from frozen food cabinets (since I subscribe to the theory that it was a total waste of time to scrape a carrot when there are others so willing to do it for you); however, I dredged up a vague memory of visiting allotments with my dad and decided these could be potatoes.

Pleased to have cracked the back-to-Mother-Nature bit, I approached the sea path with swinging shoulders and head held high. The beaten track plunged along between overgrown hedgerows. Behind me the walkers' voices were carrying clearly on the still air, chattering loudly as they plodded towards me.

There wasn't going to be room to pass on the narrow path, so I moved ahead at a faster pace. The dark-green bramble-bounded path was liberally sprinkled with the ever-present wild flowers. I hadn't a clue what they were, but judging by the snatches of voices drifting along the path, my fellow walkers were amateur botanists. Every clump was greeted with loud exclamations and a Latin name that was three times longer than the plant.

I glanced back. Their matching bright-red jerseys and green breeches were bobbing and bowing to each bank as they discovered new delights. In front of me the hedgerows gave way to an open path that curved along the edge of the cliff.

Towards the seaward side the land fell away in clumps of golden gorse to a sheer drop; on the left-hand side it climbed to the cliff top in a bank of newly green ferns, their frothy leaves waving and dipping gently in the whispers of fresh sea breezes.

I took my sunglasses off for a moment to squint into the light glittering from the waves. The bridge knocked a healing bruise, reminding me it was still there. It occurred to me that the Keats had been the first people I'd met since the fight at the club who hadn't commented on my injuries. Perhaps it was just good manners, or maybe, as Isobel had said, they were untouched by much of life now.

Finding myself a large rock amongst the ferns, I sat down and pulled out Julie-Frances' letter. It seemed to have been written whilst she was being held on remand.

Dear Krissy,

How's life in the free world? This place stinks. I can't believe they wouldn't give me bail. I just keep finding more disadvantages to being an orphan. I bet if I'd been able to produce a nice respectable mummy and daddy (retired professional, no less!) they'd have let me go.

Not that I can imagine Aunt Florrie welcoming a jailbird into her sanctuary. The old bat would probably have been saying Hail Marys on the court steps and sprinkling me with holy water as they locked me in the prison van.

My solicitor says it will be at least six months before the case comes to trial, if I'm lucky (lucky! Six months is fast-track service, would you believe). Ask one of the law lot if I can sue for being stuck in here for half a year, would you?

I've got a new room-mate. Supposedly sliced up a bloke with a razor. But she loves him really. I write her love letters for her. Very descriptive, it's certainly given me a few ideas for when I get out!

It's a pity Bill can't read them. It would probably turn the boring old fart on. Nothing much else did. You should have seen him acting the hard man in Paris: 'Heh, garçon – champagne and don't bring me any domestic rubbish.'

Where does he think champagne comes from, for heaven's sake - Peru?

You remember all those hints he'd been dropping about owing money to 'heavy people'. Well, we met one. He was on the ferry dock at Dover checking out the cars. Honestly, Krissy, he was about as intimidating as a munchkin. All muscles and dialogue courtesy of Bob Hoskins playing a small-time gangster.

'Don' think you can bottle out on me, Carr ... I got friends who got friends. Don' matter where you run, we'll find you.'

(The whole speech to be delivered with clenched fists, clenched teeth and clenched bum.)

If Bill had had any sense he'd have got out and given the silly little twerp an ache to go with his name. Instead of which he's matching him clench for clench and telling him not to worry, he'd got it 'sorted'. It was all I could do to keep a straight face. I nearly told him to forget it there and then. I would have done if I wasn't two months behind with my bloody rent.

My solicitor says Carr is going to instruct some top-drawer barrister. He's broke but he can afford to pay fancy fees, unlike Cinderella here who's stuck with legal aid.

If you really mean it about visiting me, can you bring me some shampoo and conditioner? And some cigarettes (decent brand) – they're useful in this place.

Anyway it looks like I'll miss Christmas in Jersey. What do they do for New Year?

Best of luck with the job-hunting.

Julie-Frances.

I made a note of the only really useful point in the letter and then lay back in the ferns watching the clouds scud across the eggshell-blue sky. A hawk or some-such was hovering above the headland. It hung nearly motionless, with just the slightest adjustment in its wing angle to maintain its position.

The botanists tramped by, still loudly pointing out assorted flora to each other. The bird seemed undisturbed by their passage.

I lay still, listening to another set of footsteps approaching.

The bird suddenly closed its wings and dropped.

The feet were opposite me on the path. Raising my head fractionally, I glimpsed blue chinos through the angle of my feet.

The hawk rose into the sky again. Something squealed and struggled in its claws.

I sat up quickly. 'Hello, Mr Bridgeman.'

Under the stupid white cotton hat, Stephen Bridgeman turned a startled face in my direction.

CHAPTER 25

'Oh, there you are, Miss Smith — or are you someone else today?'

'Should I be?'

'I've no idea. But you do seem to be a versatile girl: tax official, cleaner, waitress. Is there any limit to your talents?'

'If there is, I've never found it. Mind you, there are those who reckon there's no beginning to them.'

I grinned and stood up. Dusting down the seat of my jeans, I suggested we continue the conversation in a more conducive atmosphere.

'Conducive to what?'

'Conducive to lunch. I hope you brought plenty of cash; you're paying.'

'Why should I wish to do that?'

'Because you've been following me around since I left your house after my cleaning stint yesterday, so I figure you're keener on my company than I am on yours.' I indicated the cliff path. 'Back to Rozel or forward to wherever?'

Wherever turned out to be Bouley Bay. We sat at the beachside café munching through a large plate of mixed sandwiches, double apple pie and cream and two strawberry milkshakes (Stephen had mineral water and a cheese toastie).

Once my stomach had stopped rumbling, I asked: 'Did you really spot me as a phoney when I was playing Shona, terror of the tax office?'

'Not then, no,' Stephen admitted. He stretched out his legs and crossed his ankles. 'It was when you reappeared as an office cleaner and Joan and I found you near the cabinet with the personnel files. Even then I wasn't certain, but I thought I'd better find some way to keep you in view, so to speak, until I could check you out.'

'So you offer me a home-based stint with the lav cleaner. Very neat, but why not just follow me that night?'

'It would have been difficult to explain to Joan why I suddenly had to take her car again.'

'The silver Merc is your mother-in-law's? I thought it was yours.'

'No. Mine was off the road that day.'

'What do you drive?'

'The same.'

'Same colour?'

'No. It's dark blue. Could we get back to you, Miss Smith? And why you're interested in Kristen Keats.'

'Why are *you*?'

'I asked first.'

'True, but I'm the one with the answers and you're the one who wants them, remember?'

We eyeballed each other over the white metal table. I wasn't being entirely honest. I was deeply interested in why the managing director of Wexton's Engineering should be interested enough in a former employee to follow me all the way to Jersey. But I figured I'd done my bit when it came to sharing information; I'd practically wrenched out my vocal cords bawling out those flight details over Shane's Elvis impression so that Stephen could take them down under the café table.

There had always been the slight possibility his interest was personal; maybe he had a fetish for skinny blondes in rubber gloves. But it looked like my first guess was correct – it was my attempts to trace Kristen that were of interest to Bridgeman. If so, why?

He evaded the question again. 'Were those her parents? She never said she came from Jersey.'

Probably because 'his' Kristen hadn't. 'What *did* she talk about then?'

'Work mostly.'

'Even when you were cosying up together?'

'Look, Miss Smith – not that I believe that *is* your real name ...'

'Well, you've got me there, Stephen. I don't know how you spotted it, but you're dead right.' I leant forward and lowered my voice confidentially. 'My parents did not christen me "Miss". Heaven knows why, but there you are. It's Grace. The Smith bit is kosher.'

Doubt flickered in his eyes. 'Really?'

'Brownie's honour, Stevie.'

'It's Stephen, if you don't mind. And you still haven't told me why you are looking for Kristen.'

'Snap.' I took a noisy suck of the last millimetre of my strawberry shake and reminded him we'd got as far as him meeting Kristen out of hours.

'I don't know where you got that impression ...'

'You were seen,' I said, embroidering Patrick's eavesdropping slightly. 'Saturday morning. Playing around with Krissy instead of a number nine iron.'

'I wasn't. Look, I don't know what you've been told, but it wasn't like that. I simply met her for a drink. To sort things out.'

'What things? And why couldn't you sort them out at work?'

'I was concerned she might make a scene. You know how people get the wrong idea – no smoke without fire.'

'And Kristen wanted to be the flame to your firelighter, did she?'

'She'd been coming on to me ever since she started work at Wexton's. It was quite subtle at first. She'd brush something off my jacket or adjust my tie when we were alone in the test area. Or lean against me when we were reading a print-out. It was nothing I could specifically object to. Not without seeming ... well ... rather prissy. Do you understand what I mean?'

'Absolutely. Welcome to the wonderful world of sexual harassment, Stephen.'

'On one occasion, we were working late ... she had a habit of wearing rather short skirts ... and ... well ... we'd gone up to my office and she sort of pushed her chair back and crossed her legs on the desk.'

'Did a Sharon Stone on you, did she?'

'No. No. I mean she did have panties on, but you could see everything. The cleaners walked in on us. It was extremely embarrassing. If it had been Joan, or even Amelia ... they could have misinterpreted the situation.'

'Could they?'

'Yes. They *could*. Look, I'm not denying I was flattered.

What man wouldn't be? Kristen is a very attractive young woman, and discovering that you've, well …'

'Still got what it takes to pull?'

'In so many words … yes. But I'm not stupid. If I started anything with someone who worked at Wexton's, how long do you think it would be before Joan found out?'

'What do you think she would have done if she *had* caught you out?'

'There was nothing to catch out.'

'Hypothetically. Would she have told your wife?'

'I don't know. Possibly. No. Joan has great faith in her own abilities. It's more likely she'd have bawled me out and got rid of Kristen.'

'This is Kristen who resigned suddenly and for no apparent reason, is it?'

He caught the drift of my scepticism. 'No. Absolutely not. I've told you. There was nothing going on and hence nothing for Joan to discover. I met Kristen that one time outside work and told her straight out that I wasn't interested. She either behaved appropriately in the office, or she started looking for another job.'

'How did she take it?'

'Philosophically. Told me there were plenty more fish, et cetera et cetera.'

'And after that, no more touchy-feely in the office?'

'No.'

'Were you surprised when she quit?'

He shrugged. 'People do.'

His glance swept around the bay and over waves with the blue-green sheen of peacock feathers. A group of divers had waded out from the beach and were bobbing in the swell; in their wetsuits they looked like a collection of seals in fluorescent face masks. 'I should prefer to live here rather than Seatoun,' he said abruptly.

'Wouldn't we all. Don't you have to be stinking rich before they let you in?'

'Are Kristen's parents wealthy? I assume that *was* her family you called on earlier?'

'So you should, Stephen. I yelled the name loud enough to be heard on the French coast.'

'Have they seen her?'

'No,' I said truthfully. 'Kristen's parents haven't seen her for some time. And I don't think you ever answered my original question. If you're not stuck on Kristen, how come you're prepared to follow me across the Channel just to see if I'll turn her up?'

'Because Kristen ... em ...' The words seemed to get stuck in his throat. He used the passage of a motor cruiser across the mouth of the bay to gain himself a few seconds. With its engine thrumming, it drove silver-white wings in front of its bow until eventually it disappeared behind the headland to the next bay.

'Because Kristen ... em ...' I prompted.

He dragged his eyes back from the ocean. 'Because,' he said through gritted teeth, 'the little bitch has ripped me off.'

My initial assumption, that Julie-Frances (a.k.a. Kristen) had had it away with the payroll or something was quickly squashed by Stephen.

'How the devil could she have done that? It's a cashless world, haven't you heard? Who the hell uses money these days?'

Well, Julie-Frances did for a start. But I saw Stephen's point; Wexton's, like most companies these days, used the Bank Automated Clearing System to pay salaries and invoices.

'The only money lying around is fifty pounds or so in the petty cash,' Stephen snapped. 'Do you seriously think I'd be wasting my time running after fifty damn quid?'

'So what are you chasing? What has Kristen got her sticky fingers on?'

Stephen flashed an anxious look around the cove. Apart from the students from the dive school, there were just a few walkers wandering aimlessly along the road that curved round the beach, and a noisy party saying loud goodbyes at the door of the Water's Edge Hotel after what sounded to have been a boozy lunch.

'I don't think we're being bugged, Stephen.'

'No. Right. Look, I really need to know who you're working for.'

'What makes you think I'm working for anyone? Maybe I'm looking for Kristen on my own account.'

'Are you?'

'No.' I weighed up the odds of Stephen telling me anything else unless I answered his question – and decided they weren't good. 'I'm a private detective. I was hired by an acquaintance of Kristen's who was worried she hadn't been in touch for a few weeks.'

'What acquaintance? Where?'

'That's confidential information.'

'I'll buy it. How much?'

'I don't work like that. You hire me, you get what you pay for. And in this case, the client wants complete confidentiality.'

'Why?'

'They're the shy type.'

'Listen.' He leant his forearms on the table and fixed me with the sort of heh-let's-put-our-cards-on-the-table-and-work-this-thing-out look that must have gone down a storm in the boardroom. 'We might have mutual interests. I mean, if we're looking for Kristen for similar reasons, it would make sense to pool our knowledge and work together.'

I pointed out I still had no idea of his reason for wanting to find her.

'I told you, she's stolen something from me. From Wexton's, to be exact.'

'Be even more exact. If it's not cash she's taken off with, what is it?'

'Information.'

'Valuable?'

'Reasonably so. But that's not really the problem. The thing is ... it relates to a government contract. If it were to turn up in the wrong place ... well, it could be very embarrassing.'

'Do you think that's the idea ... a dash of revenge for you telling her to keep her knickers up?'

'How the hell should I know? I just want the damn stuff back, before it gets into the wrong hands.'

'Foreign governments, that sort of thing?'

'What? No. It's not particularly sensitive. I mean, Sumata

is not military-orientated ... it's ... well ... how much do you know about computers?'

'I flunked Sonic the Hedgehog.'

'Right. Well, in very simple language, it's an intelligent node that controls the electronic functions within a building. It's not a particularly advanced idea. There are already commercial stations available that will do the same job, and frankly the government would probably have saved a fortune if they'd simply gone out and bought one off the shelf. But they don't work that way. They prefer to spend large sums of our taxes having machines designed to specifications that have been created by committees that would be hard pushed to put a plug on a toaster.'

I sensed we were mounting a hobby horse of Stephen's here, and unless I got off fast we'd be off over some Grand National grievance course.

'Did you go round to Kristen's flat?'

'What? No. Well, yes. Once. After I found the files were missing. But I couldn't get any answer. The bitch had already left.'

'What about before? Didn't you pick her up from the flat the day she left Wexton's?'

'Pick her up. No. Why the devil would I do that?'

A large, dark-coloured four-door car, Rachel had said. But she'd also said it was raining and the driver hadn't got out to help Kristen with her luggage.

'No reason. Just testing. So what do you reckon Kristen's plan is? I mean, if the files aren't that valuable ... what's her motive? Leave you looking like a berk when you can't deliver to the government?'

'I have delivered. Several weeks ago.' He shrugged. 'There were other file copies. Another set of computer disks.'

'So where's the panic?'

'I've told you. It could be an embarrassment for Wexton's. If she were to pass the files to a journalist ... You know how they can blow the most stupid stories up, create something from nothing ... the files have government stamps on them ...' Taking off his hat, he thrust a hand through his hair, leaving furrows in the dark strands. 'It's tough enough in this business nowadays without ending up on some unofficial black list because our security's a joke.'

'You're quite certain it was Kristen who took this stuff? I mean, someone else at Wexton's couldn't just have used her resignation as a blind to nick the files around the same time?'.

'No. It was her.'

'Why so certain?'

'The files were stored in my personal cabinet in my office. She left her company security badge in one of the drawers, OK?' Stephen snapped.

'Deliberately?'

'Probably. I'm sure she wouldn't have wanted me to miss the point. Listen ...' He took my hand. 'Your client ... if Kristen has stolen something from him ... or is it her ...?'

I removed the hand. 'I didn't look.'

I smiled. He glared. We were at stalemate again. And it was his move.

'I'll retain your services. To find Kristen. And my files. I assume you have no objection to working for two clients at the same time?'

'None at all. Double fees are always acceptable. But you might find calling the police cheaper.'

'No! I don't want the police involved. *At all*. Is that quite clear?'

'Crystal. Does anyone else at Wexton's know these files are missing?'

'No. I told you. They were in my cabinet. And I want to keep it that way. You're not to approach *anyone* else at Wexton's with this information.'

'What do the files look like exactly?'

'They're on a CD disk.'

'Like music discs?'

'Yes. Just like that.'

'Well, that should narrow it down. There's probably only a few million floating around out there.'

'Find Kristen and you'll find the damn files, I'm certain of that.'

I guess it was the moment I should have told him that Kristen had metamorphosed into Julie-Frances last summer. Particularly since he handed over a thousand-pound cheque as an advance without a murmur. But loyalty to Henry made me hold that little gem back. As my first customer, I figured Henry had the right to hear the bad news first. So instead I asked Stephen what he'd already done to locate Kristen.

Not much, was the answer. Apart from that abortive visit to her flat, he'd rung the Bayswater flop-house that was listed as her last address and got nowhere. And he'd rung Heathrow airport.

'Why there?'

'She said something about flying from there. A holiday.'

It was the first fresh piece of information I'd had for some time. I pressed him for more details.

'I don't know, do I? Just abroad. The Far East somewhere, I think. The airlines wouldn't tell me anything. They don't give out passenger information.'

His hair got the furrowing treatment from all ten fingers this time. I watched the way the ridges retained their shape. He must gel it. I wondered whether he dyed it as well.

'I just didn't know where to *start*.'

'Horses for courses, Stephen. I promise not to design computers and you leave the missing persons trace to me. How about her salary cheques? She had no bank account. She must have got someone to cash them. Maybe a guy called Bertram.'

'We arranged for her to encash them at the branch that handles Wexton's account. She originally asked to be paid in cash, but of course that was quite impossible. Bertram's is the company that originally had the Sumata contract. Before the government took it off them.'

'Took?'

'It was unusual. A cost-plus-type job. Very rare these days. The government pays all your proved costs, plus agreed overheads and profit. Bertram's ran it way over budget. Mainly because their chief designer was in the middle of some kind of breakdown and no one liked to mention it. The bloke was a genius but totally off his trolley at the end, frankly. Anyway, the government finally terminated their contract and passed it to Wexton's.'

'Would they have any reason to contact Kristen?'

'We had to check things occasionally. Old test programs mostly. It's normal practice.'

'Oh.' I'd been hoping to impress Bridgeman with my nifty footwork and incisive insights into the case. Instead of which I'd charged down a couple of blind alleys and kicked the wall.

Stephen glanced at his Rolex. 'The return flight's in an hour. I suggest we make a move.'

I was all for that. It meant he paid for my return taxi to the airport.

We parted company at Heathrow.

'How do I get in touch with you?' Stephen asked, feeding in coins to validate his car-park ticket. 'Should I come to your flat?'

'Definitely not. The company is in the book. Vetch's. Contact the office if you want me. Better still, wait for me to get in touch.'

'As you wish. I might see you on the motorway.'

He had to be kidding. There was no way my lovingly nurtured heap was going to keep up with a Mercedes. As it was, I got caught up in the rush-hour traffic on the M25; bottle-necked into a single lane through the roadworks on the southern section; fumed for an hour whilst the police cleared an accident; and drove the last section with one eye on the falling petrol level and the other on the rising temperature gauge.

By the time I reached the outskirts of Seatoun, I had a stiffening neck, an aching back and an approaching headache tippy-toeing across my eyebrows. Parking up by my flat, I approached the metal staircase down to the basement.

Zeb was perched on the third step, forearms resting on legs that were slightly too long for the tread. He leant back at the sound of my approach, tilted a pale face upwards and added a few well-chosen words guaranteed to get my headache off its toes and into a clog-dance.

'Grace,' he gabbled, 'something bloody awful's happened.'

Chapter 26

'You really are a total waste of a perfectly good skin, Zeb.'

After we'd done the what-happened-to-your-nose? routine and I'd established Zeb's visit was social rather than official, I invited him to shift his bottom from my staircase to my living room.

'I came round here for a bit of tea and sympathy. If I wanted to be insulted, I'd have gone to work.'

'CID still giving you a hard time?'

'I meant the crooks would ... oh yeah, very funny.'

'Don't sulk. You got the tea, didn't you?'

As a sort of stand-in sister in Annie's absence, I felt it was my duty to carry on with the Smith tradition of bullying, upbraiding and running the baby of the family's life for him.

I watched him slumped on my bed gloomily dunking a tea bag in a mug of hot water. He looked like the end of the world was, if not exactly nigh, certainly expected to make the long-range forecast within the next few days.

Which I guess, from Zeb's point of view, it was. Annie was on her way home.

He gave me an appealing look from beneath a floppy brown fringe. Appealing, that is, if you happened to be a labrador with strong maternal instincts. Since I didn't qualify on either count, I held back on the *there-theres* and passed over an ashtray for the sodden tea bag, and a bottle of milk.

'What are we going to do, Grace? I mean, she's going to go stark raving bonkers if she finds out we let squatters into her flat.'

'What's with this *we*, Zeb? This one is strictly down to you.'

'But you know them.'

'I know lots of people. They're not all crammed into Annie's flat. At least they weren't last time I looked. Unless you've been handing out keys wholesale this time ...?'

'I didn't hand ... Oh hell, Grace, can't you talk to them? Get them to leave? I mean, there's dozens of empty flats around, why can't they ...?'

'Break in somewhere else?'

'Well ... yeah ...' He tried the puppy look again. 'Be a mate, Grace. Help us out. You know how Annie's only just decorated. Think how upset she'll be if she gets home and finds a couple of tossers have wrecked the place.'

'I doubt if they'll do that. As a matter of fact, I rather got the impression it was Annie's interior decorating that was the major attraction. They didn't want one of those nasty damp places with the plaster peeling off the walls. Annie's suits them very nicely.'

'Well, it suits Annie very nicely too. And she's paying for it!'

'How true. Why not put this argument to them, instead of spluttering tea all over my laundry?'

I got up and moved the piles of washing I'd done the day of Kevin's unexpected visit last week. It was one of the major drawbacks to laundry; if you wash the damn stuff, you have to iron it. I supposed I'd have to get round to it soon – once I got fed up shifting it from surface to surface.

Zeb had apparently tried sweet reason on Figgy and Mickey already. 'But it's not easy when you're bawling through the letter-box. They wouldn't even open the door to me. I hung around a bit, thought I might be able to follow the bloke ...'

'And do what?'

'Well, you know ... squatters ... bet he's got a record ... don't happen to know his full name, do you? Or the woman's?'

'You mean you were hoping to nick one ... or both.'

'There's no need to sound so flaming self-righteous. I'm not talking about fitting anyone up. But if they break the law, I'm entitled to arrest them. In fact, it's what I'm paid to do.'

'OK, OK ... now who's getting self-righteous? And no ... I haven't a clue what they're really called. Why don't you ask them?'

'I did. Apparently Annie's playing hostess to Miss Naff-Off and Mr Get-Stuffed-Copper.'

'In that case, Zeb, I suggest you put in for some leave, starting tomorrow, and leave Annie to sort out her squatters.'

'I'm due in court Friday. I can't get leave.'

I grinned. 'You mean you've already asked?'

Reluctantly he nodded and gave a faint smile. 'I'm not like

this at work. I got commended once, you know? Talked down this bloke with a gun who was trying to hold up a shop.'

'Annie mentioned it. Water pistol, wasn't it?'

'Well, I didn't know that, did I?'

'No. No. OK. Put your feathers down. I'm not denying you've got bottle, Zeb.'

'Yeah.' He sighed heavily. 'But soon as it gets to one of my brothers or sisters throwing their weight around … especially Annie …'

'Well, let's face it, she's more to fling around than most.'

'I won't tell her you said that … if you'll just go talk to those two. *Please*, Grace.'

Maybe I had a dash of canine blood in me after all. This time the puppy eyes worked. I heard myself agreeing to have a quick chat with Figgy and Mickey.

'If you could do it first thing,' Zeb said eagerly as I shooed him out, 'I could get the flat cleaned up before Annie arrives. And then she need never know.'

'I don't do anything first thing, Zeb. The dawn and I have been strangers to each other for years … and I'd like to keep it that way. I'll ring you.'

As things turned out, I didn't get around to Figgy and Mickey until lunchtime. The combination of sitting around in the Jersey sun without a hat, followed by three hours of traffic jams and exhaust fumes, hit me after Zeb left.

Dragging off my jeans and top, I'd fallen into bed with the intention of having a quick snooze – and remained dead to the world until a couple of gulls and a cat started a noisy fight over a packet of dead chips outside my basement window in the middle of the following morning.

Now that the Bank Holiday was behind us, the weather had started to pick up again. Having walked into the town to bank Bridgeman's cheque, I'd come back along the prom with the intention of letting the sea breezes blow away any lingering headache before heading for Annie's; but turning back inland, I found fate had decided to rearrange my schedule.

'Henry! Yoah!'

It was odd the remembered responses we retain. It must have been years since Henry's eyes had sent any messages to his brain, yet the bottle-green lenses were still sweeping from left to right trying to locate the source of the shout.

It was nearly as daft as me waving frantically at him. At least the dog appreciated my efforts. I got a tail wave and a brief flick of a wet tongue.

'Hi, Beano. Morning, Henry. I was just on my way to see you,' I lied glibly.

'You've found Kristen?' he asked eagerly.

'In a manner of speaking. Do you fancy a cup of coffee?'

I steered Henry to an empty table in Pepi's whilst vaguely registering the fact that there was something odd about the place.

It took me a second to identify what was missing: noise.

Apart from a subdued murmur of voices from half a dozen customers, and a deep-bellied rumble from the hot-water urn, there wasn't a *doo-wap, yeah-yeah* or *shoo-bop* to be heard.

The situation was partly explained by the '*Out of Order*' notice on the juke box and partly by the appearance of Shane's wife, wriggling out from the back kitchen in one of the too-short, too-tight, multi coloured polyester sheath dresses she favoured.

She was barely half her husband's weight, and her strawberry-blonde beehive only tickled his chin when she balanced on her four-inch stilettos, but she knew exactly who was boss in that partnership. So did Shane. Which was why he was spending this morning digging out the fish pond she wanted in their back garden.

'He's a little treasure, that bloke. So what can I get for you and your mate, Smithie?'

'Two coffees, I guess.'

I'd sat Henry near the counter to give him plenty of opportunity to call across that he'd get these. He didn't.

'Can you stick them on account?'

'On account of what, darling? We ain't Harrods.' Scarlet nails unfolded like lily petals around an empty palm.

Reluctantly I counted out one pound and twenty pence.

'Ta. I'll bring them over. Does your dog want some water, love?'

'That would be most kind. Thank you, madam.'

I waited until she'd wriggled across with the two cups before bringing Henry up to date on my search for Kristen.

'Dead?' he repeated for the third time. '*Dead.*' Resting his elbows on the Formica, he dropped his head into his hands. The bowed shoulders trembled slightly. I wondered if his damaged eyes were capable of producing tears, or did the hurt just build up inside with no way of release?

To my relief, I didn't get to find out. Taking a deep breath, he straightened up and took a sip of coffee. The cup rattled as he attempted to replace it in the saucer. Putting my own fingers over his, I gently guided them in.

'I can manage,' he said sharply. 'I've had to.'

'Sorry.'

'No, it is I who should apologise. Didn't mean to ... still get ... wake up some mornings and forget ... think it's still dark ... even after all these years. Think I'd be used to it by now ...'

The appearance of Beano's water bowl brought us both a much-needed interruption. To give Henry time to pull himself together, I asked Shane's other half why the jukebox wasn't working.

'It's got an Out of Order notice on it.'

'I can see that. But why isn't it working?'

'Because it's got an Out of Order notice on it, of course.' With a wink of one much-mascara-ed set of lashes, she tottered back to the kitchen on thin tanned legs, the dress clinging to a bottom as flat as a chopping board.

'Are you quite certain?' Henry asked. 'About Kristen? Perhaps there is some kind of mistake? Duff info ... you know ...?'

'No mistake, Henry. Kristen Keats has been dead and scattered this past year. The girl you met was Julie-Frances Keble.'

I gave him a brief rundown on what I'd found out on Jersey.

'So now you're going to work for this Bridgeman chap instead of me? Offered you more money, did he? There's no honour anywhere these days.'

'Not instead. As well as, Henry. Assuming you still want

me to, that is? Now you know Kristen isn't the girl you thought she was?'

'Of course she is. She's still the same person who spoke to me on the promenade, isn't she? Still the same young woman who borrowed my *Little Dorrit* tapes. What does the name matter? She's still *my* Kristen ... whatever the name on her birth certificate might say.'

'So we're in business?'

'What about Bridgeman? Perhaps he won't wish to share your services.'

'He doesn't seem to object, and it would be bloody tough luck on him if he did. I've got a living to earn.'

'So you've told him about me?'

'Just that you exist. Don't worry, Henry, I kept the faith. Your identity is safe with me.'

His shoulders relaxed. 'Thank you so much, m'dear. It's just that ... the older one becomes, the more it seems to matter that one is the butt of other's laughter. I daresay it shouldn't ... but I suppose there are so many more things to ridicule as the old frame falls to pieces. It's hard to keep your dignity ...'

'Hey ...' I reached across and took one of his hands. 'There's nothing ridiculous in being concerned about a friend. The world's full of people no one gives a damn about. I think it's great you care about Kristen ... or Julie-Frances.'

'Kristen,' he said shakily. 'She'll always be Kristen to me.'

'Fair enough. Well, I've got to go and sort out a friend of my own ... Do you want me to see you back to the promenade?'

'Thank you, m'dear, but Beano and I have been navigating the town for many years. I believe I shall stay here and enjoy another cup of your friend's excellent coffee. If you'd call her over for me ...?'

'Sure.'

I got out of there before I had to fork out another sixty pence and headed for Annie's flat.

Figgy was out when I arrived.

So was I. Stranded on the landing talking through the damn letter-box.

'Look, come on, Mickey, I just wanted a chat. It was OK last time, wasn't it?'

'I guess. But Figgy says I mustn't. Not when he's out.'

I could see knees, thigh and a section of stomach. 'You're not showing much yet, are you?'

Ten fingers linked protectively over the bottom of her jumper. 'It's early yet. Last time I never ...'

'Wotcha, your Graciness.'

I glanced round as Figgy's grinning face appeared over the hall banisters and informed him I was sick of kneeling on this floor conducting a conversation with eight square inches of his girlfriend.

'So beat it.'

'You certainly know how to make a girl feel welcome, Figgy.'

'I know how to make a girl feel plenty of things, Gracie.'

'Including homeless.'

'Hey, this going to be another lecture on my anti-social habits? 'Cos if it is, I've had it all from that copper.'

'Can I come in? I've got something to tell you.'

Instead of answering, Figgy returned to the stairs and looked down.

'I haven't brought the heavy mob with me.'

'Just checking.' Inserting a key in the lock, he gave two shrill whistles through his front teeth and rat-a-tatted twice.

The safety chain was withdrawn and he opened the door and ushered me in with a low bow. 'Welcome to our humble abode, your Graciness.'

'Actually it's Annie's abode. Hi, Mickey ... how are you? Still chucking up?'

'A bit. But I'm fine really, ta.'

There was a slight glow to her face which hadn't been there before, and the rat's-tail hair-do was soft and gleaming, exuding the perfume of Annie's shampoo and conditioner. It mingled with other, more interesting smells, drifting from the kitchen.

'Been baking?'

'Sponge pudding. And I'm doing this Thai fish thing ... not out of a packet, I'm learning to do real cooking, Figgy.'

'Magic. But don't you go overdoing it, you hear.'

'Er, speaking of overdone ...?'

I have a very sensitive nose when it comes to food. I detected burning oil two seconds before the smoke alarm blared into action.

We all charged for the kitchen. Since Mickey was closest she got there first – and made a grab for the flaming pan.

'No!' Figgy shouldered her aside just as her fingers closed round the handle. Reaching past her, he flicked the cooker's power off.

I hastily ran the hand towel under the cold tap, wrung it out and flipped the wet cloth over the blaze. The flames died with a sizzling *shush*. With a howl, Mickey burst into tears.

'Heh, come on, kid, it's not that desperate.' Figgy hugged her fiercely.

'It is ... it ... I'm so useless. I can't do nothing by myself.' She locked her arms round his waist and buried her head deeper in the black T-shirt. 'You won't ever leave me, will you, Figgy?'

'Course I won't, babe. We're stuck together for life.'

So was dinner. I chipped at carbonised lumps of fish and vegetables that had welded themselves to the base of Annie's non-stick designer frying pan.

'It's all her f-f-fault,' Mickey hiccuped into the gradually spreading damp patch over Figgy's chest. 'If I hadn't been t-talking to her, I wouldn't have forgotten the pan was on.'

'Well, that's a bit rich.' I dumped the pan in the sink. 'I didn't ask you to move into my best mate's place and burn it down.'

'It ain't her fault. It's her hormones. Making you a bit forgetful, ain't they, babe?'

'Well, if you're planning a big family, I'd break into a flat near the fire station on your next move. Which incidentally is going to be pretty soon. That's what I popped round to tell you. She who pays the mortgage of this slightly singed des res is on her way home.'

Figgy shrugged. 'So?'

'So it's time to roll, Figgy. How long do you think it will take her to get you out of here?'

'She can try.'

'She'll do more than that. She'll succeed. Now, do you

really want Mickey in the middle of all that hassle? What if she lost the baby or something?'

I felt rotten as soon as the words were out of my mouth. Mickey gave a little wail, let go of Figgy and hugged both arms across her stomach.

'It's OK, babe. Nothing's going to happen. I promised, didn't I? Now you go have a lie-down. I'll clear up in here. Starting with her.'

He took a grip on my arm. I could have put him down easily, but I didn't want Mickey caught in the middle of a punch-up.

We circled each other in an awkward waltz, both trying to give the impression we were in control of the situation as we shuffled back into the hall.

'Let go, Figgy,' I murmured, 'or this baby is going to be an only child.' I moved a knee up.

He thrust me against the hall wallpaper and pushed his face near mine. 'Listen, don't you ever say that again. Don't you say nothing about her losing that kid. You understand me?'

'It's not me causing her all this hassle, Figgy. Why don't you take the Social up on their offer of a bed-and-breakfast place? It would be a start.'

'You seen the creeps they get in those places? Wrinkly weirdos wandering around with their trousers round their ankles; druggies shooting up in the loos; bloody kids and dogs whining and crapping all over the place.'

'So that excuses you bumming a free ride at Annie's expense?'

'You never taken something you wanted?'

He opened the front door with his left hand whilst propelling me towards it with his right. Behind us the unmistakable sound of someone throwing up into the sink drifted from the kitchen.

'Now look what you've done.'

'Me!' I twisted free and turned to face him. 'Listen, buster, perhaps if Mickey didn't wake up every morning wondering if she'll still be looking at the same ceiling come bedtime, she'd be having a less stressful time of it. Why don't you shape up; find a career that doesn't have a slightly lower number of job vacancies than being one of Santa's elves and stop thinking the rest of the world owes you a living. We all have to do jobs we don't like sometimes.'

Folding his arms, he lounged against the wall. Something that might have been a sneer twisted his lips. 'Yeah? Well, maybe some of us would rather stick to what we know we can do well. 'Stead of kidding ourselves we're some kind of hotshot detective when we're really just a sad little wannabe who couldn't find a lost kitty-cat.'

I took a deep breath, ready to return the serve with a real smash of an insult. It gave Figgy the chance he needed; darting forward, he thrust both palms against my chest and pushed. I was still trying to regain my balance on the hall landing when the door slammed in my face.

The brass letter-box flap flicked outwards. Two black lenses glittered behind it.

'Tell you something, Miss Wannabe-a-Detective? *I* know more about your cases than you do!'

'Meaning what?'

'Meaning I know something about that missing babe that you don't, your Graciness.'

CHAPTER 27

He blanked me after that. All the internal doors in the flat were slammed shut and the kitchen radio turned on full. There was no way I was yelling through that damn letter-box for the rest of the afternoon, so I went back to the office. It seemed an age since I'd seen the place and I wouldn't put it past Vetch the Letch to sell the building out from under us all if he got a better offer.

Plainly no lunatics with a real-estate fetish had passed by recently, since Janice was still thumping away on the processor as I sauntered into reception.

'Hi. Long time no see. Bet you wondered if I was still working here.'

'No. I do that when you're in.' She hit a key with a flourish and the screen flashed and blinked; icons expanded and receded in multicoloured patterns. 'You've had messages.'

'Be still, my beating heart. I suppose it's too much to hope that you've got any of them?'

Janice blew out an exasperated breath, picked up the waste-paper bin and scrabbled amongst heaps of rubbish.

'Here.' She slapped a yellow stick-it note, wet with coffee stains, into my palm.

'*Fond groot flot*,' I read. '*Murt see. Pogs will live giddon. Rung sunnest*. I didn't know you were fluent in Esperanto, Jan.'

She snatched the paper from my hands. 'Found great flat. Must see. Pigs will love garden. Ring soonest. It's from that estate agent bloke. He's called loads of times. Keeps asking me to go for a drink. Reckons he's got a sports motor. What's he like?'

'He's short. On everything, I'd say.'

'Oh. Best save him for a rainy day, then.'

'Good plan. If he shrinks any further you'll be able to wear him on your charm bracelet.'

Janice had dressed for convenience today – judging by what appeared to be lavatory chains around her neck and wrists and a couple of ballcocks dangling from her earlobes. Jangling loudly, she dived into the bin again. 'This lot's yours too.'

'Why did you sling them away?'

'It's my system. People take stuff off the desk but no one messes with the bin. Things stay where you put them.'

There were half a dozen other slips of paper. All saying the same thing: 'Zeb Smith rang. Have you done it yet?'

'Is that it?'

'Ruby – the reading wrinkly – came by. She left an envelope. It's on your desk. And Vetch wants to see you.'

'Why?'

'Didn't say. Vetch! She's in.'

The right-hand door swung open. In the days when the building had been a boarding house it had led to the communal lounge. Now it was the entrance to the office of our esteemed leader, landlord and sole (official) employee of Vetch International Inc.

I'd often suspected that Vetch moonlighted as a model for garden gnomes. He had the height (diminutive); the figure (rotund); and, most importantly, the ears (pointed).

'Sweet thing. Take a seat.'

With a beam of welcome, Vetch heaved himself back into the leather I'm-an-important-executive-style chair behind a desk the size of a snooker table. I had my usual flash image of him with a red pointy hat and a fishing rod and had to bite the side of my cheek.

'Gorgeous. Can it be that you are happy to see me?'

'Can you doubt it?'

'Frequently, sweet thing. Frequently. Particularly around the beginning of the month. Which, with an almost monotonous frequency, occurs after the end of the previous month – if you follow my reasoning.'

'You want the rent?'

'And the fee for the shared office facilities.'

'A receptionist who files messages in the waste paper and one lousy fax machine that doesn't work. Leastways, I never get any messages from it.'

'Possibly because no one ever writes to you. And let us not forget the warm glow that a brass plate and respectable premises raises in the bosom of our clients.'

'Does it?'

'Indubitably.'

'I'll take your word for it. None of my clients have shown any sign of glowing.'

'As I recall, the last didn't so much glow as burst into flames.'

It was a low blow. It wasn't my fault that my previous client had nearly got himself burnt to death. (Well, not entirely my fault).

'I'll give you half now, half later, OK?'

Vetch sighed. He took a deep breath, inflating his puffball of a face, and then gently blew it out. 'Delightful creature, do we have to play out this little charade every month? You have money. As I remember, you collected a considerable reward from a grateful parent for returning their precious offspring to the family bosom last month.'

'I got my car fixed.'

'Even allowing for the extortionate fees some mechanics see fit to charge, it is hard to believe that you paid three thousand pounds to have the faults relocated in that heap.'

'It's a classic.'

'It is indeed. A classic example of wishful thinking over mechanical knowledge. Now I hate to press you, but I do have another engagement ... so unless you wish to find your filing cabinets on the pavement tomorrow ...'

I gave him a cheque.

'Thank you. Now, that wasn't too painful, was it?'

'Not for you.'

'Try not to be bitter. Remember you are not just buying a room; you have purchased the benefit of my vast and varied experience. You have but to ask and my wisdom is at your disposal. Day or night. For instance, I can tell you that that motorbike death you are interested in was deemed to be an accident.'

'What ...?' I recalled that Janice had recently taken delivery of an envelope from Ruby. And I'd asked her to see if she could find any newspaper reports on Rob Wingett, Kristen/Julie-Frances' predecessor at Wexton's.

'You've been reading my flaming mail!'

'Not at all. I happened to run into dear Ruby in the foyer. Wingett was a diabetic, you know. With a somewhat unfortunate habit of neither eating correctly nor injecting himself on time. He appears to have been a traffic accident waiting to happen. The coroner delivered quite a lecture on the dangers of driving without the proper medication. He's a pompous little prick and there's nothing he likes better than the sound of his own tedious voice.'

'You're a fan, then.'

'I'm a brother-in-law.'

This was news. I filed it mentally, since contacts were all-important in this business. Maybe that was the point that Vetch was trying to make. For my rent money I was not only getting a room, but a hot-line to official channels.

'And what is your connection to the messily departed? Does the widow suspect foul play? Are the insurance company hanging on to their cash with a tenacity that would put you to shame?'

'Nothing like that. I was just curious as to how widely the death had been reported.'

I gave him a quick run-down on my connection with Wexton's – including the meeting with Bridgeman.

'Do you know, sweet thing,' Vetch murmured after I'd come to the end of my recital, 'I can't help thinking that naughty Mr Bridgeman is telling you a few porkies.'

'Oh?'

'Mmm …' Vetch wriggled forward on the shiny leather and linked his fingers on the desk. 'If this information is as low-key as your client claims it is, then it is hard to imagine he is going to spend his undoubtedly valuable time chasing around after you.'

'It's a government con …'

Vetch held up a palm. 'You explained. However, do you not read the papers? Surplus filing cabinets are sold off with the plans for high-security installations still in them. Secret papers are left in cars to be stolen by anyone with the inclination to put a brick through the window. The rubbish dumps of Britain are strewn with the personnel files of those charged with keeping our fine country ticking over. If the government chopped everyone off their bid lists who was a trifle careless with the filing, one can't help feeling their choices would be so severely limited it would almost amount to a case for the Monopolies Commission.'

'So why should Bridgeman claim to be trying to sort this out discreetly because he's worried about losing future contracts?'

'Possibly, gorgeous creature, because he did not wish to tell you the truth.' Sliding my cheque into his inside pocket, he wished me happy hunting.

Taking the hint, I stood up. 'Cheers, Vetch.'

'My pleasure, sweet thing.'

CHAPTER 28

Janice waved another yellow stick-it at me as I left Vetch's office.

'That copper's rung again. Annie's brother. Are you and him getting it together now?'

'Is that any of your business?'

'Annie won't like it.'

'Why shouldn't she?'

'So you *are*, then! Oh shit ...'

This last insult was flung at the phone, which had started to ring.

'Vetch'sjanicespeakinghowmaywehelpyou? Oh, it's you. We were just talking about you.' There was a fractional pause when the caller obviously asked who 'we' were. 'Smithie. Vetch has just been screwing the rent out of her again.'

'I don't pay in kind, Jan,' I said, grabbing the receiver.

'Don't suppose you get the chance. Even letches have standards.'

I'd assumed the call was from Zeb again, but it was Annie's mocking tones on the line.

'Hi. How's Leicester?'

'Where I left it on the M1, I should imagine. I'm in Exeter.'

'Zeb said you were heading home.'

'I was. But I saw this sign to the M5 and thought to hell with it – let's get the job wrapped up.'

'You sound cheesed off.'

'Luxury hotels aren't what they were. The bars are full of cute barmen who want to cry on my shoulder because their boyfriends don't want a deep and meaningful relationship. And the restaurants are full of dreary sales reps with witty chat-up lines such as *How do you like your eggs in the morning, beautiful?*'

'What d'you tell them?'

'Unfertilised. God, I can't wait to get home and crash out on my own couch. It'll be great.'

It would actually be rather overcrowded, but it didn't seem the moment to tell Annie that.

I passed the details of her new hotel to Janice – who took them down with a lip-pencil on her bare thigh.

'Any luck with Jersey?' Annie asked.

'Flew over for the day.'

'Swank.'

'True.'

'Did you manage to pin down this Kristen woman?'

'In a manner of speaking.'

'So what's cooking?'

'She was. Two thousand degrees centigrade on a low gas when last seen.'

'Hard luck, Sherlock. Did the client specify he wanted a live one?'

'It's a bit more complicated than that.'

'Got to go,' Annie said. 'I've a meeting fixed up. Tell me when you see me. I'll catch you next week if you're lucky.'

'You're not mentioning you and Zeb then?' Janice asked as I passed her the receiver.

'There's nothing to mention. Me and Zeb is business. And if he rings back again, can you tell him ... tell him I'm still working on it.'

'If I remember.'

With a clash of chains that could have given Marley's ghost an inferiority complex, she whizzed back to her processor.

I picked up the phone again and dialled Wexton's number. Now seemed as good a time as any to ask my client why he was messing me around.

Mr Bridgeman, I was informed, was working from home today.

Scrabbling around in my pockets and bag, I tried to find the sheet of paper with the house number. No luck. And for the life of me I couldn't dredge back the digits I'd dialled to reach Amelia. I tried the local directory and found the Bridgemans were ex-directory. I headed in that direction, confident in my natural ability to lie like hell when it came to inventing a suitable excuse to pass off the visit to any other members of the family who happened to be hanging around.

Pulling into the drive, I parked up between two small vans and a large covered truck and followed a roll of material that was being manoeuvred through the front door on two shoulders.

'Not here ... take it around the side of the house! For mercy's sake ... surely the excessive fees your company charges should encompass the provision of staff with the ability to understand simple one-syllable instructions.'

I caught a glimpse of Joan Reiss trapped on the stairway by the perambulating bolt of textile.

The front shoulder spoke: 'To the back we should it take, yes?'

'Yes. Isn't that what I've been saying?'

'Hokay.' He marched forward down the corridor.

'No ... no ... not that ... oh, all right, go on. You'll probably break more if you try to turn now. Ah, Grace, you're early. Thank heavens. There's rather more to do than I'd anticipated. Perhaps you could make a start on the upstairs bathrooms. And the small back bedroom. We'll have to use that as a guests' powder room.'

I'd forgotten all about the social event of the week: Amelia's fiftieth birthday party!

'Actually, I ...'

'You'd best rescue the cleaning materials whilst you can still get into the kitchen.'

A crash that sounded like an entire dinner service shattering roared down the passage from the back dining area.

'For heaven's sake ...' Joan shot off like an Exocet.

It seemed easiest to go with the flow. I wandered into the kitchen. A tart-faced female hanging prawns around the edge of a large glass tureen flicked me a casual glance.

'Bog patrol.' I waved a couple of cleaning sprays at her and cruised the house in search of Stephen Bridgeman.

There was no sign of him downstairs. Upstairs was unproductive too, until I knocked briefly on the final bedroom door and marched in.

Patrick thrust something under the bed and looked up with guilt written all over his face. It changed to a frown as he said: 'Oh. It's you. I thought Mummy had come back.' Flinging himself flat, he retrieved a glass-fronted picture. 'I'm wrapping her present.'

I took a quick look round. It was strangely impersonal for a kid's room. There were no posters on the walls, toys scattered around the floor or comics lurking in dusty corners. The only hint that Patrick might do more than sleep in here was the cluster of flashy-looking computer equipment crouched on the desk.

'Nice set-up. Can you use all this stuff?'

'No.'

With a corner of tongue poking through clenched lips, Patrick straightened the picture frame, lining up his present on the wrapping paper, then carefully sliced off the right amount.

'What's it for, then?'

'Daddy bought it for me. Boys are supposed to like that sort of thing, aren't they? But *I* don't.'

I crouched down beside him. 'What do you like?'

'Dogs.' He squirmed up on his knees and shuffled over to fetch a roll of tape. 'I wanted a dog. But Mummy said I wouldn't be here to look after him. If I lived with Gran, I bet *she'd* let me have a dog. I hate Mummy.'

'You've got her a present though.'

'Gran said I had to. I made it myself … see.' He turned it so that I could see properly.

It was a montage of photographs, with Amelia at the top of the frame. I picked out Bone and Patrick easily enough. There were several shots of a vaguely familiar young man. In the earlier ones he was short-haired, but later he'd sprouted hair, earrings and designer stubble. 'Who's this?'

'My brother Theo. He's not coming to the party.'

'He looks like your dad.'

'Does he?' Patrick bowed closer, touching his nose to the glass and misting a patch over Theo's face.

I looked at the fourth figure in the collection. Presumably Charlotte, the daughter Amelia had been visiting in California.

She was pictured smiling prettily with two little fair-haired girls in one shot, and again with the same kids, plus an older man with the sculptured hairstyle favoured by American politicians, in another.

But the centrepiece was a large studio shot of Charlotte's foursome, flanked by three crop-haired late-teens whose combined shoulder width must have justified the use of a wide-angled lens. The middle one in particular seemed to have forgotten to remove the padding from an American football jersey before climbing into a chequered suit and baring the finest set of teeth that an orthodontist could supply. Perhaps the poor girl was still growing into her looks.

'Who's this lot?'

'They're Charlotte's other family ...' Patrick stabbed the sculptured hairstyle. 'From when *he* used to be married to another lady. Before Charlotte seduced him, Gran said.'

'Not to you she didn't, I'll bet.'

'No. She was talking to Daddy,' he agreed, unabashed.

Sliding his fingertip over the glass, leaving a smeared trail, he came to rest on a Polaroid snap of a red-faced infant. 'And that's Charlotte's new baby. I'm his uncle. He's called Eugene Bridgeman McClusky the Fourth.'

'Let's hope he's not dyslexic.'

'Pardon?'

'Never mind. Want a hand?' He was getting well and truly tangled up with tape, paper and carpet fluff by now. With me hanging on to the escaping corners, he finally managed to bundle up a messy heap swathed in sticky bands, with stick-on rosettes and a message label.

The frown crinkled his large brown eyes again. 'What shall I write on it, do you think? She said we weren't to tell anyone about this being her fiftieth birthday. But if I don't say Happy Birthday she won't know what it's for, will she?'

I assured him Happy Birthday would be fine just so long as he didn't say which birthday it was. 'I think the party's a bit of a giveaway anyway, Patrick.'

'Yes.' Tongue protruding again, he formed careful round strokes. 'Mummy didn't want a party, but Gran made her have it.'

'I heard. Where is your mum, Patrick? And your dad?'

'They've gone to London. Mummy said she hadn't got anything to wear for her party. Which is a lie. Because she's got loads of clothes. More than anybody. Absolutely *millions and millions* ...'

'Yeah, right ... Has Bone gone with them?'

'No.'

'Is she around?'

'Don't know. Gran, where's Bone?'

I turned. Joan Reiss was coming along the top corridor with two vases of flowers in her hands. 'I have no idea, Patrick. And I do wish you'd use her proper name. Eleanora is so much prettier than Bone.'

'She's not pretty. She's a sister. Look, I've finished. Grace helped me.'

'That's very nice, dear. I'm sure Mummy will be pleased. Shall I ask one of the workmen to carry the vacuum cleaner upstairs, Grace, or can you manage?'

There was nothing subtle about Joan Reiss. She handed me the vases with instructions to put them in the back bedroom once I'd polished it.

'I'll bring you some others for the bathrooms as soon I can get to the flowerbeds to cut them.'

'Looking forward to it already …' I muttered.

The chaos downstairs had taken on an organised pattern. The workmen I'd followed in were erecting a small open-sided pavilion at the bottom of the garden. Others were dotting tables over the upper section of the lawns and placing squat Japanese lanterns amongst the flowerbeds.

The french windows in the dining room had been wedged open to allow the caterers to lug boxes and crates in through the back *en route* for the kitchen. The dining table itself had been joined by several others. The prawn-arranger from the kitchen was carefully placing bowls of water containing floating flowers and candles at precise points along the snowy-white tablecloths.

I collected my hoover and lugged it upstairs again. After twenty minutes of noisy vacuuming, spraying and sploshing, I locked myself in the Bridgemans' *en suite* bathroom and read a copy of *Hello!* that was lying on the bath side until I heard Amelia's voice coming up the stairs.

'And we got the most *fabulous* dress for you. You'll love it.'

Leaping up, I dumped pine disinfectant down the loo and unlocked the door.

'Hi! Just finished.'

I waggled sprays and cloths at the trio on the landing. Amelia was burrowing under layers of tissue paper. She shook out a dress. 'Isn't that just perfect?'

The shadow over Bone's face darkened. 'God. It's *gross*. I wouldn't be seen *dead* in it.'

It was an ankle-length creation in white and blue that would have been at home in a Jane Austen movie. On another girl it would probably have looked quite good. But Bone was no more a floaty voile and ribbon person than I was.

'Don't be so ungrateful. It's cost Daddy an absolute fortune.'

'Big deal.'

'*Please*. Wear it for me. It is my birthday.'

'I thought we weren't mentioning the big Five-O.'

'Don't spoil your mother's day, please, chicken.'

'Oh, all *right* ...' Snatching the dress, Bone stomped off.

Stretching on tiptoe, Amelia smacked a lipsticky kiss on her husband's cheek. 'Thank you, sweetie. You are wonderful with them. I suppose it's because they just adore their daddy.'

Stephen looked vaguely embarrassed by this endorsement. 'I'll ... er ... grab a shower in the other bathroom.'

'Fine.' Amelia wriggled away into the main bedroom, calling back over her shoulder for me to bring the rest of her goodies.

'Stephen has bought me *the* most divine dress ... Would you like to see?'

I was aware of Stephen's puzzlement. He wasn't entirely sure I was there to see him. With a none-too-subtle eyebrow wriggle he indicated we should talk downstairs.

'I'd love to see the dress, Mrs Bridgeman. I'll just take my cleaning stuff back down.'

'Oh, leave it in the hall. Here ...' She jiggled the dress box eagerly, her face alight, like a small kid at Christmas. 'There! What do you think?'

It was full-length cream silk, low at the neck and slit at the sides. Very stylish but not exactly garden-party attire.

'It's very ... em ...'

'Isn't it just ...' Amelia agreed. 'But you know what they say about having it and flaunting it.' Flicking the dress on to a hanger, she hung it behind the door and started peeling off the suit she'd been wearing, casually dropping clothes on to the carpet.

Stephen was still hovering in an indecisive limbo. Amelia dismissed him with another kiss and an instruction to dress in the spare bathroom as well. 'If you don't mind, sweetie? Oh –

and I'll need my diamonds from the safe. The drop ear-rings and the necklace. You are a darling ...'

He was thrust back on the landing.

'I'll get tidied up, shall I, Mrs Bridgeman?'

'Call me Amelia. Ghastly name, isn't it? Sounds like someone's maiden aunt ... but everyone hates their names, don't they? How did you get called Grace ...?'

Whilst she chattered, Amelia had been peeling off. With no apparent embarrassment, she dropped her bra and knickers on the carpet and strode over to the dressing table stark naked. 'I'm going to make this my signature scent this evening ... Stephen bought me the entire collection, moisturisers, soaps, you know. He's such a generous sweetie. What do you think?'

She unstopped a fluted glass bottle and thrust it under my nose.

I couldn't resist it. 'Fabulous ...'

I'll say one thing for Amelia; she could take a joke against herself.

With a giggle, she resealed the bottle and asked if I could open the rest. 'Only I've just had my nails manicured.'

Twisting a towel around her hair, she ran a bath, added a long string of glutinous oil from the ranks of Ali Baba-shaped bottles lined up along the bath surround, and sank into a pit of steam, froth and scented air.

'Mmm ... blissssssss ...'

The noise from downstairs was slackening, indicating that the catering arrangements were in place and the guests weren't yet. It was as good a time as any for a quiet word with Stephen ... particularly if the word was 'liar'.

CHAPTER 29

Except I couldn't find him. The other bathrooms were empty and the only response I got from the bedrooms was 'Get lost' shouted from behind Bone's door.

The study doors were locked. I wandered on. The full buffet table looked terrific. Wall-to-wall designer food flanked by rows of champagne bottles. Joan and the prawn-arranger hurried in from the terrace as I helped myself.

'Oh, good … This is Grace. They're short of waitresses. I said you'd be happy to help out. I'll pay you the cleaning rate, if that's acceptable?'

'Mmm …' I nodded vigorously, teeth clamped over a couple of vol-au-vents and a slice of peppered ham.

'Good. Splendid. I must go and change.'

She left. The prawn-arranger fixed me with a nasty stare and informed me that the first rule of working for her company was you didn't eat the food.

I swallowed hard. 'That bad, eh? Don't worry, they won't notice once they've knocked back a few bottles of the sparkly.'

Stephen and I finally crossed paths in the front hall.

'We need to talk, Steve … at least I get to talk, and then you get to answer …'

'I don't think I care for your tone, Grace.'

'I don't care for your story. I've been checking it out, and it sucks.'

'Not here. Come on.'

He urged me down the cellar steps. I tried again at the bottom.

'Kristen …'

'Hang on …' Taking my arm, he pulled me around and under the stairway until we were facing the security-coded door I'd noticed before.

The door responded to his tapping out the numbered sequence with a gentle sigh and a hiss of released locks. It swung back to reveal a short, narrow room lined with wine racks.

'Neat …'

'Thank you. I designed it myself. It keeps the bottles at optimum temperature.'

'They valuable then?'

'Extremely so in some cases. It's a hobby of mine. Now, you were saying you had some doubts about the veracity of my story?'

I laid it on thick, making Vetch sound like some kind of world authority on government contracts. 'There's no way you're going to be permanently embarrassed by a few stray files, so what's the real agenda here, Stephen?'

He looked at me coolly. Reaching over, he twisted a dusty bottle a fraction of a turn. 'Do you know, Grace, I don't believe I care to be called a liar by someone I'm paying. Is there any reason I should take you seriously?'

'Just the one. Kristen Keats has been dead for over a year.'

I spelt out the situation and had the pleasure of seeing the smug self-assurance draining away.

'Oh my God,' he said when I'd brought him up to date. 'I knew I should never have trusted the little bitch. What the hell am I going to do?'

'Tell me the truth for a start. What did Kristen – or rather Julie-Frances – really nick?'

'Information. I've told you.'

'But …?'

The but was simple – if you happened to have a degree in (very) advanced electronics. I didn't. With difficulty I managed to grasp that Stephen had invented the equivalent of the holy grail when it came to nodes.

'Imagine,' he explained, his face shining with enthusiasm, 'coming home to your flat. The lights come on automatically as you move from room to room. The temperature is ideally suited to your personal preferences because the computer has learnt to understand what you require. The video has recorded that historical documentary you wanted to see even though you didn't programme it to do so. It's learnt your habits, you see. The supermarket has delivered an order you didn't place, because your refrigerator has detected what's running out and has automatically dialled the market's computer. Your electricity and gas meter readings have been sent to a remote terminal and the bill automatically paid from your bank account. How does that sound?'

'Like I could be seriously broke in a week.'

'It's the future, Grace.'

'It sounds more like something out of *Star Trek*.'

'No. It's not. The technology has been available for some time. There are already some buildings where it has been incorporated.'

'So what's so special about your baby?'

'The beauty of my design is that it can be produced at a tenth of the normal cost and yet works at ten times the speed. The key is to have the node installed *as the building is constructed*. That way everything else has to be compatible with my Sumata. Once you're in – you're in. And everyone else has to work a hundred times as hard to dislodge you.'

'I'll take your word for it. So why the secrecy? I mean, wouldn't you have more chance of selling this little gem if you *told* someone about it?'

'I did. I sold it to … well, never mind who … a foreign manufacturer had agreed to produce it …'

'And you get …?'

'Cash up front, plus a fixed percentage of sales.'

'So far I can't see the problem.'

'The problem, Ms Smith, is that all my work is based on research and design funded by the government. Not to mention Bertram's.'

'Bertram's?'

'The company who had the contract originally.'

'I know who they are. What have they got to do with this?'

He gave me a look I'd last seen when I'd failed to master shoelace-tying after my mother's fourth demonstration.

'They did the base designs … in fact, they did rather more than that. Their designer was brilliant. He must have known what he had. He'd gone far beyond the original specification. I couldn't believe it when I started unravelling his notes.'

'Is this the bloke who had a breakdown?'

'Yes. That was a piece of luck for me. As he became more unbalanced, he seems to have grown more and more secretive. I'm sure no one at Bertram's had any idea what he was working on towards the end. They'd obviously just bundled everything up and sent it to Wexton's once the contract was transferred. It took us weeks just to catalogue everything.'

'And then you realised you'd hit a goldmine and started ripping off the government?'

'I wouldn't put it like that. At first it was just an experiment almost … to see if Bertram's designer really had come up with what I suspected. It was still very rough … I had to put in a lot of my own thoughts …' He moved restlessly along the racks, twisting bottles and leaving fingerprints in the dusty coatings. 'It was exciting. I started off in design, you know ... I wasn't sure I still had it ... and then when I saw everything coming together ... after years of negotiating payment terms and delivery dates and fawning over idiots who don't care about quality providing they can shave half a per cent off the price ...'

'Didn't the rest of the staff think it a bit odd? A managing director getting his hands dirty?'

'We were pushed at the time. Several contracts had hit snags complicated enough to tie up the other design staff. They saw it as the MD leaping in to do a bit of fire-fighting.' Stephen had come to a rest against the narrow section of brick wall between the racks. He was examining the seal on an oddly shaped bottle. 'This came from Waterloo.'

'Got a good off-licence up there, have they?'

'I was speaking of the battle, Ms Smith.'

'I was being facetious, Mr Bridgeman. You were telling me about building this Sumata with your own fair hands.'

'Hardly. The work is theoretical. It's done on the computer.'

'And Kristen – or rather Julie-Frances – cracked your little scam?'

'It was *not* a scam ... it was an important piece of research ...'

'Which you had no right to sell?'

'Yes I did! The intellectual property rights in all our designs are retained by Wexton's. That's standard commercial practice.'

This prevarication – not to mention all the big words – was really beginning to get up my nose.

'Look – you made it. You own it. You sold it. End of story. Where's the big deal?'

Stephen thrust a hand through his hair in a gesture of exasperation. 'I've just told you, haven't I? Think of it as a car. Bertram's produced the sub-frame – at the government's expense. Wexton's added the engine, the wheels and the upholstery – ditto at the government's expense. And then I put in the stereo system, the sun roof and central locking system out of my own pocket.'

I finally got it. 'So if you want to sell the car, you've got to pay the government some kind of fee for their bit?'

'A royalty payment – yes. But even that isn't the worst of it. I could have lived with that. It's the time factor. Do you know why most inventions succeed? Because they were first. Because they hustled, got in people's faces, grabbed the market by the throat. So when people went to buy they automatically thought of that product name; not because it was any better, but because it was the name they knew and what the hell, everyone else had it, so it must be good – right?'

'Absolutely.' I knew zilch about marketing, but I knew not to interrupt a fanatic in mid-spout. People have been blown up for less.

'If I'd have taken this to the government, do you know what they'd have done? They'd have passed it to a committee. Who'd have spawned a sub-committee. Who would have begat a quango. Jesus ...' He paced a few steps between the racks. 'You've no idea what it's like dealing with these people. They've got no interest in actually *selling* anything. Their only motivation is to preserve their own little empires. So they call meetings; and issue minutes; and refer the matter for "expert" opinion. Expert – that's a joke. Most of them think a chip is something you coat with salt and vinegar. And in the mean time a competitor, someone in a country not blessed with a civil service whose sole role in life is to add sandbags to the trade barriers ...'

He was well gone. Sticking two fingers in the corners of my mouth, I let rip with a whistle that rattled my tonsils. At least it had the desired result. He shut up.

'OK,' I panted. 'I get the message. So when did Kristen, or rather Julie-Frances, get it?'

'Soon after she arrived. I was running something through one of the computers. She started chatting, looking at what I was doing. Do you want to hear something laughable? The reason I employed Kristen was because her CV was barely adequate. The contracts we were working on didn't require any special skills. Just someone to read off results and log them accurately. A super-drone effectively. No initiative, no special spark up here ...' He tapped his cranium. 'Just someone to churn the bread-and-butter stuff out ... I didn't bother to hide what was on the screen because I didn't think there was a snowball's chance in hell she'd understand it.'

'Not a smart move, Stephen.'

'You're telling me. She even managed to get into my private computer files when I wasn't in the office. She came to the house just before Christmas and told me she knew what I'd been doing and how much did I think her discretion was worth?'

'What did *she* think it was worth?'

'A lot more than I was prepared to pay.'

I was suddenly glad I was the one at the door end of the wine cellar. Stephen must have read the question in my eyes.

'No. I did not shut her mouth for good. In the end we came to a mutual agreement. She took twenty per cent of the front payment, plus five per cent of my share of each royalty. And a fat fee from the manufacturer for supervising the testing for the first few months' production.'

'The manufacturer being located ...'

'There's really no need for you to know that, is there? Let's just say it was out East and far enough away to give us both jet lag.'

'You were going out there too?'

'The deal was I'd stay for a couple of days; get things signed up and so on. And then I'd fly back and Kristen would stay on. She said she fancied living abroad for a while. More opportunities.'

'But you didn't go?'

'I couldn't. The damn customer changed the date for the final shake-down on Sumata at the last minute. The original Sumata node, I mean, the one the government were getting. They brought the meeting forward to the first. A full complement, quality, security, technical, all decided to descend on us.'

'Why? Did they smell a rat?'

'I doubt it. They smelt a freebie day out by the seaside at our expense. But unfortunately Joan was there when the call came in and she told them I was free. I hadn't put the Far East trip in my office diary for obvious reasons. And I couldn't afford to take the chance of rattling the government lot by suddenly asking to move the meeting date back. Since that business with the Abercrombie contract they've been super-sensitive to the possibility of missing something so bloody obvious that even they could be sacked for incompetence if they overlooked it. For much the same reason, I decided to remove every trace from Wexton's of "my" Sumata ...'

'The turbo-charged version ...'

'If you like ... Anyway, I placed everything on the CD ... and then destroyed all other copies. It was probably unneces-sary, but I was so close ... When you were a child, did you ever look forward to a treat so much that you became totally convinced that something dreadful would occur to make it not happen?'

'Hurricanes at picnics and raging toothache at birthday parties.'

'That kind of thing, yes. In my case, I was this close to being rich ...' He pinched an infinitesimal fragment of air between thumb and forefinger.

'You're not exactly on Income Support, are you, Stephen? Detached house, swimming pool, double garage, his-an'-hers luxury cars, kids at private schools, wife in designer frocks. I should be so poor!'

'Wealth is relative.'

'Not in my case it's not. I haven't a rich auntie to my name. And believe me, I've been looking for years.'

'My money isn't inherited, Grace. Whatever I've got, I work damn hard for. And frankly I'm fed up with it. I'm sick of having to go into that factory every day. Of having to put in hours evenings and weekends sorting out this week's mess, so we can move on to a fresh crisis next week. I'm fed up to the back teeth with unreliable suppliers, non-paying custom-ers and whingeing staff. I don't want to spend another ten or fifteen years chasing orders and worrying myself sick about cash flow, overdrafts ... Do you remember that cruiser that sailed past the bay in Jersey? That's what I want.'

'So sell some of this posh plonk and get yourself a boat.'

'Not the craft. The lifestyle. The luxury of being able to spend days doing as I choose. Of not being tied to a desk. I don't want to work for my existence any more, Grace. I want to sit back and let the money flow into my bank account.'

'Preferably one that isn't in contact with our wonderful tax office?'

'Yes. It would be a foreign account. But the government have only themselves to blame ... if they choose to adopt an antiquated attitude to modern business tech ...'

'Yeah, OK, I got the message. Did Mrs Reiss know about this scheme?'

'Joan? You must be joking. My mother-in-law has what might quaintly be described as strong moral fibre.'

'What about Amelia?'

'No. She wouldn't have understood anyway. She has a talent for spending money but very little grasp of how it's actually made. *I am, therefore I shop* is my wife's motto.'

'Or possibly the other way round. So you and Kristen ... or rather Julie-Frances ... had a jaunt out East fixed up. When was this, incidentally?'

'Beginning of May. That was the earliest the customer could be ready at their end. We'd originally planned to go on the Friday, the first; Amelia would have been *en route* to Los Angeles, Joan was having Patrick, and Bone was off staying with some pal in London for the weekend. The idea was I'd spend Saturday and Sunday out there, call in sick Monday and hopefully be back at my desk Tuesday.'

'What if anyone rang the house?'

Stephen shrugged. 'Answerphone. I can pick up messages anywhere. And then the damn meeting at Wexton's got switched. Which meant that I not only had to be in for Friday, but I had to be there the following Monday too.'

'How come?'

'We always have a post-shake-down meeting in-house the next working day. If I'd tried to get out of it, Joan would have started asking questions. I tried to put the Eastern lot off, but then they started getting paranoid; they seemed to imagine we were holding back because we'd had another bid for the design. In the end Kris ... I mean Julie ... look, let's just call her Kristen, OK?'

'OK.'

'Kristen was to go out alone, with the designs. I'd follow as soon as I could set it up here. I bought her a new personal CD player and some music discs. She'd have carried the file out amongst those.'

'Why? I mean, can't you just send all that kind of stuff down the telephone lines these days?'

'You can. But you never know who's going to intercept it. I daresay I could have encrypted it, but quite honestly I wasn't inclined to risk it. The deal was Kristen would hand over the disk once she saw them send an electronic transfer to my bank.'

'Very trusting of you.'

'Stupid, you mean. Yes, I can see that. But I was *so* close ... And where was her incentive to rip me off? She was on to a good deal and she knew it. If she tried to go it alone, she'd have had to find another buyer, and that's not as easy as you might imagine.'

'How did you find your buyer?'

'There's a chap ... I'd met him at conferences over the years ... he's always on the look-out for a way to cut himself a good percentage. He put me in touch with the Eastern company.'

'Isn't it possible Kristen ...?'

Stephen shook his head emphatically. 'No. He wouldn't deal with someone he didn't know. He's not that stupid.'

'You just can't tell a Board of Trade investigator from a real human being these days, eh?'

'Something like that,' Stephen agreed. 'Could she have gone back to this friend you mentioned? The one who was concerned about not being in touch?'

'If she had, he'd hardly be employing me to find her.'

'So it *is* a he. A boyfriend?'

'A friend,' I said flatly, annoyed with myself for being tripped up so easily. But at least I hadn't blown Henry's identity completely. 'Can we open one of these? I'm gagging.' I pulled out the nearest bottle at random.

Stephen snatched it back and slid it carefully into its cubbyhole. 'Not the Margaux, for heaven's sake. It's sixty years old.' Kneeling, he selected a bottle from the bottom of the stack. 'Here. This has been rather disappointing, I suppose we may as well open it.'

He had all the wine waiter trappings in a small drawer

built into the racks. I had to wait whilst he sliced, extracted and sniffed cork, before tipping a mouthful into a small silver ashtray. 'There aren't any glasses. You'll have to make do with the tasting dish.'

'I'll take a swig out of the bottle.'

'It isn't Coke. Nobody *swigs* out of my bottles.'

He gave me several more ashtrays of red as we talked. It was trickier than it looked. Half dribbled down my chin and ended up on my blouse.

'So,' I said, nudging a few droplets back up my chin with my middle finger, 'you waved goodbye to Kristen – and your files – Thursday afternoon. Did she contact you at all after that? From the airport, for instance?'

'No …' He took a mouthful of the wine himself. 'I mean, I last saw Kristen on Friday morning, not Thursday.'

'Oh?'

'She had to get out of her flat that day. The Thursday she left Wexton's, I mean. She was going to spend the night at a hotel. But her flight wasn't until late afternoon … and, well … I felt safer having those designs under my eye for as long as possible, and since Amelia was staying up in town anyway … she had an early check-in for her LA flight; well, Kristen spent Thursday night here.'

'So it *was* you who picked her up from the Beamish Court flat that evening?'

'Yes.'

'For a cosy little evening chez Bridgeman?'

'There's no need for the pathetic attempt at innuendo. I spent the evening preparing for the meeting with the government contingent, and she spent it watching videos. Then we went to bed – separately.'

'And in the morning?'

'For me – quick shower, quick breakfast, and out of here. Kristen was still in bed. I told her how to set the alarm system, and said goodbye for now.'

'Weren't you worried about someone walking in on her?'

'Who? The cleaner had already walked out on us.'

'I was thinking of your mother-in-law. Doesn't she have a key?'

'Yes. But no reason to call. Are you fantasising about Joan

cooking chicken casseroles for the neglected husband? Don't. Believe me, she never comes near the place unless Amelia and the children are here.'

'How was Kristen getting to the airport?'

'She had a cab booked for two thirty. The driver said he came but couldn't get any answer from the house.'

'You checked?'

'Well of course I did. I'm not totally without sense, Ms Smith.'

Just mostly by the sound of it. Still, it wasn't my place to tell my customer he was green enough to qualify as Wimbledon turf. Well, not until his advance cheque had cleared anyway. So I asked him if the alarm was set when he got home Friday.

'Yes. It was.'

'When exactly did you start to suspect your master plan was going down the plughole?'

'I don't know … I suppose … she should have telephoned on Saturday, but the system isn't too good in some parts of the country. And besides, there's the jet lag; it can hit you like a brick wall …'

'Brick walls only move in motor insurance claims in my experience, Stephen. So, come late Saturday, panic's setting in. Did *you* try to contact *her*?'

'Naturally. She wasn't at the hotel. They said she had never checked in. I thought perhaps she'd changed her mind; gone to another hotel.'

'You mean by this point you'd started clutching at straws. When did you start lunging at the whole haystack?'

'Late Sunday. The manufacturers contacted me. They couldn't understand why Kristen hadn't been in touch. I told them there had been problems this end … they weren't best pleased.'

'And then you went round to Kristen's flat? What on earth made you think she'd go back there?'

'I didn't. I'd just tried everywhere else. I drove up to Heathrow Sunday night. They wouldn't tell me anything. Not even whether she'd caught the flight or not. And I tried that place in Bayswater. Her old address. They were worse than useless. I even rang some chap who'd given her a reference; all I got was an answerphone message about pixie pottery. After that I didn't know what to do … except wait for the design to surface …'

'And then what … leap in and say "Excuse me, but I stole that first"?'

'I don't know. I hadn't thought that far ahead. I just wanted the files back. I *must* have them back. It would take a year at least to duplicate the work on them … even assuming I could do it. And that's about ten months too long. Nothing stands still in this business. In a couple of months someone else will have produced their own Sumata and that's it …'

'They'll be the ones cruising around Jersey while you slog over a hot desk.'

'Yes.' He grasped the top of my arms suddenly, lifting me up slightly and closer to him. 'I *need* those files, Grace. The Eastern lot will still deal, I'm sure of it. If you can locate them in the next few weeks, I'll make it worth your while. What do you say?'

'Put me down or I'll knee you.'

'What? Oh, yes, sorry.'

He let go and finger-combed his hair in that familiar gesture.

I pulled my blouse off my skin, and discovered wine splodges liberally splattered down the front. 'Damn.' I licked a hankie and dabbed. 'We'd best be getting back. It's gone very quiet up there.'

'This section is fairly soundproof.' As evidence, Stephen opened the rubber-sealed door and ushered me out. A low buzz of noise flowed around us.

Another question occurred to me. 'Do you know someone called Figgy?'

'I should think it is highly unlikely. Who is she?'

'He. He's a street entertainer in Seatoun. Does an act on roller-blades. Mornings in the square; afternoons on the prom; six o'clock and ten thirty outside the amusement park.'

'I'm rarely in any of those places at those times. Why do you ask?'

'He seemed to think he knew something about Kristen's dropping off the planet. But I shouldn't get overexcited. It's more likely he was trying to wind me up.'

The hall was deserted as we emerged from the cellar, but Patrick charged down the stairs.

'Mummy says she doesn't want the diamonds. She wants the gold necklace and the ear-rings you bought her in Dubai. And she wants Grace to bring them up.'

'Oh, damn, I forgot the jewellery. Hang on here a minute, Grace.'

I'd intended to skip as soon as I'd spoken to Stephen, but interestingly spicy, sizzling-type smells were drifting across the passageway. And then there were all those rows and rows of champagne. It seemed a pity to leave before I'd investigated the possibility of leftovers. Besides, I was curious to see how the posh people partied.

Stepping into the downstairs cloakroom, I soaked the towel in cold water and dabbed at the wine stains again. They turned a paler pink and spread copiously. Unbuttoning the blouse, I flapped, trying to dry the material.

The door was opened suddenly. I fumbled to conceal my modesty – not to mention the depressingly flat chest – before I realised it was Bone.

'Hi. Have you found him yet?'

'We're talking Tom Skerries here, are we?'

'Natch. Who else?' She bolted the door, closed the toilet seat, perched on it and offered a packet of cigarettes. I shook my head.

Flicking the disposable lighter, Bone blew a stream of smoke and wriggled into a more comfortable position. She'd changed from the jeans she'd been wearing earlier. But instead of the Jane Austen creation, she was now in a plain black round-necked dress with short sleeves and a skirt that barely covered her butt.

'I think you're going to have to face facts, Bone. Tom isn't going to make Claudia's hoedown. Can't you find someone else to take you?'

'Of course I can. Dozens of blokes. But I want ...'

'Tom. Yeah. Right. But I think it's time to stand up to Claudia and Livia and the rest of your mates and give it to them straight.'

'Who are you to tell me what to do? And if you haven't found Tom, what are you doing here?'

'What makes you think I haven't been invited to the party?'

'Well you wouldn't be. You're not the sort of person Mummy and Gran know.'

I looked down at her, leaning back against the cistern, blowing clouds of blue smoke through glossed lips. Her expression was neither superior nor embarrassed. It was just the way things were. People like the Bridgemans didn't know people like me on a social level. So much for a classless society.

'I'm with the caterers. Undercover. Surveillance.'

'Really?' She looked torn between doubt and nosiness. 'Who are you watching? Maybe I could help.'

'I'll get back to you on that.'

'Can I have my money back?'

'You what?'

'My money. I gave it to you to find Tom. And you haven't. So I want it back.'

'It doesn't work like that. I'll have to calculate how many hours I've spent on this investigation. Plus expenses, of course. Then we settle up.'

'Oh?' She frowned slightly. 'I don't think that's fair.'

'Tough, kid. That's business.'

CHAPTER 30

'Look,' I said stepping over Bone's black patent boots to reach the door, 'why don't you start running an eye over the substitutes and I'll stay on the case. This is a funny business ... just when you're about to give up, something cracks wide open. You never know, I might have nailed Tom down by the end of the week.

It was a prophetic guess; although I didn't know it at the time.

'Yeah, sure. Right. And I might be engaged to Brad Pitt by midnight.'

'Well then he'll be able to take you to Claudia's party

instead, won't he?' I said cheerfully, unbolting the door and returning to the hall.

Stephen was twitching impatiently by the stairs.

'Here, take these.' He pushed two black velvet drawstring bags into my hand. 'You'd better hurry. Amelia will be wondering what the delay is.'

Amelia actually gave no sign of noticing there had been a delay. In fact she looked set to provide the biggest one of the evening. She was still in the sunken bath, twiddling the gold seahorse taps with polished toes.

'Hi, Grace. Are you any good at opening champagne bottles? The way those corks come out just scares me to death ... wheee ...' She waved a wet foot in an arc, dripping suds over the surround. 'There's one on the dressing table ... would you be a sweetie ...?'

We watched an Australian soap on a television built into the vanity unit, sipping champagne from tooth-mugs whilst Amelia frothed up her bath bubbles occasionally and I lounged on the white pile carpet. The rich certainly knew how to party.

'Oh well,' Amelia sighed as the closing signature tune filled the room. 'I suppose I'd better start getting ready. Pass me a towel, could you?'

There was a slightly damp bath-sheet and a couple of hand-towels tangled up with a jogging suit in a corner. Bandaging the sheet at breast level, Amelia dabbed her arms dry with one of the others and sat on the floor to buff drops from the legs.

'Pretty perfect, isn't it?' she said, raising the left one and rotating her ankle.

There's nothing like being your own number-one fan. 'Not bad,' I agreed. 'Do you work out?'

Amelia laughed. 'Not the leg. But thanks anyway. I was talking about the tan. I had it applied this morning. There's a scrumptious little place behind South Molton Street that can make you look like a zillion dollars.'

The sound of car doors slamming and the odd 'hello' was drifting up from below. I suggested I'd better be getting back. 'Mrs Reiss has taken me on as casual help for the evening.'

'Then casually help me. Please. I need someone to rub

cream on my back. Mother will lecture about accepting the inevitabilities of age; Bone will probably carve her initials in my skin, the mood she's in. And if I ask Stephen ... well ... we could get distracted, if you know what I mean.' She gave me an oblique smile, half teasing, half coy, whilst hugging the towel a fraction tighter to outline her body with more definition. 'It's still as good as the first year we met.'

'You're lucky.'

'Oh, I know. I mean, when I look at some of my old girlfriends ... on their third or fourth divorce ... How about you? ... Anyone special?'

'No.' Images of Kevin Drysdale smiling at me over that candlelit table nudged treacherously in my mind. 'Yes. I mean, there *is* someone special. But we're not together. There are complications.'

'A wife?' Amelia asked, tipping a pool of cream into her palm and sweeping it up her arm with smooth strokes.

'Yes. Not that that's the problem. The relationship's more or less over. It's ...' I must have been missing Annie's ear more than I'd realised. I heard myself telling Amelia I'd blown the boyfriend out by giving him a ultimatum. 'No more quickies. A relationship or nothing, I said.'

'And he chose nothing?'

The legs were getting the cream treatment now. I admitted to the back of Amelia's bent neck that I didn't actually know what he'd chosen. 'Half-term, you know. He has to keep up a happy families act.'

It sounded pretty pathetic as I said it. Almost as bad as being suckered by the old my-wife-doesn't-understand-me routine.

'He has children?'

'Don't they all.'

'All the best ones, I suppose. I mean, once you get past a certain age, if no one else has got there first, you start wondering what's wrong with them, don't you? Not that I was ever in that situation. I just *knew* ... the first time I saw Stephen ... he was the one. It was the same for him. He couldn't get enough of me; still can't. Here ... do my back, there's a sweetie.'

The bottle fumbled between us, slippery with cream. A stream of white oily gunge splattered on to my jeans.

Amelia gasped. 'Oh God, I'm so sorry ...'

'It's OK. They're used to it.'

Hot water and a soaked towel succeeded in spreading the mess over most of my stomach and down my knees.

'Did it stain?' Amelia asked. She'd abandoned creaming in favour of heated hair rollers. 'There's a fabulous shop in town, it recycles clothes, so even quite poor people can afford designer labels. I take all my out-of-date outfits there. They had Versace jeans for fifty pounds last time I was in. I'll give you the address.'

I had my own little second-hand shop actually; where they did second-hand chain-store jeans at two quid a pair and dug a well with the profits. But I thanked her anyway and watched fascinated as she started to lay out rows of brushes along the dressing table. Michelangelo could have painted the Sistine Chapel with less.

'Well, I guess ...' I tried to leave again.

Amelia waved me down. 'Don't go. I'll need you to check my blending is OK. I can't go to my own party with hard edges, can I?'

The make-up was dabbed, powdered and blended on the backs of her hands until she'd achieved the effect she wanted, and then applied to the face.

The face-lift scars disappeared. The eyes seemed to grow larger, long-lashed and shaded to a subtle smokiness. The cheek bones sprang into sharper relief. Lips became fuller, outlined in one colour, filled in another, glossed in a third. Perfume rose from pulse points in ten-pounds-a-time sniffs. The rollers came out and the hair was twisted and pinned into a casual fall.

'Now the clothes ... those first ...' She pointed to a pink box.

I burrowed under tissue paper as soft as marshmallow and drew out a pair of tiny lace-trimmed satin briefs. The shop receipt fluttered out with them. They worked out at about five pounds per square centimetre, by my calculations.

There was no room for a bra. I fastened her into the cream silk dress and provided a balance whilst she stepped into golden sandals. 'Now – the final touch.' She tipped the contents of the velvet bags out, inserted gold drop earrings into her lobes and clasped a heavy necklace around her throat. 'Stephen's birthday present last year. There. Finished. How do I look?'

She looked incredible; a doll modelled in cream and gold – and conceived no more than twenty-five years ago.

'Unbelievable,' I said truthfully.

Her face lit up with real joy. 'It is good, isn't it? The best ever. I knew whatever I had to do, it would all be worth it in the end.'

Consciously or unconsciously, one manicured nail traced the outline of the now invisible scars behind her ear.

I checked my watch and found I'd been up here for two hours. 'Don't you think we should be going down?'

'Sure.' With an excited giggle, Amelia grabbed my arm and squeezed us together. 'Just let me take a proper look.'

She twisted the key in a wardrobe door. It swung open revealing a full-length mirror on the inside. Our joint reflections stared back at us.

Amelia looked like a million pounds. I looked like you couldn't have got back a ten-pence deposit on me.

The bathroom steam had drawn the grease into my hair, making it obvious the roots needed retouching – all two inches or so of them. My nose was sitting in the centre of a pale-purple and yellow island of bruising in an otherwise anaemically pale skin. The wine-stained blouse was still erratically patterned in pink splodges as well as being unevenly buttoned so that I looked lopsided. And the jeans were now two-tone: dry denim to the knees and water and oil stains from there on upwards. I was either going to be taken for the resident bag-lady or the latest in couture slick.

'Come on, let's party ...' Amelia dragged me towards the hall. 'Hang on tight, I don't want to arrive head over heels showing all my you-know-what.'

She dug in harder to my arm and took the stair banister with the other hand. We made a slow entrance to the back dining room. There were a few people helping themselves to food and drinks from the tables, but most of the guests were out on the lawns. They were seriously swish. By the looks of it Joan had gone over to the most expensive country club in the district and banged the dinner gong.

'Come on,' Amelia murmured.

We made out way out on to the terrace, still arm in arm. Dusk made itself felt sooner on this patio area, which was in the deeper house shadow. Some of the Japanese lanterns on the flagstones and amongst the terracotta planters had been lit and were sending out a soft glow that was attracting the early summer insects.

Amelia moved to the edge of the balustrade and stood quite still. I'd have said she was totally in control, if she hadn't been gripping my hand with a squeeze that had cut off the feeling in my fingers.

A couple of people nearest the terrace noticed her. One raised a Rolexed wrist in greeting. She didn't appear to see them. Her gaze remained fixed out over the lawns and flowerbeds, apparently entranced by the trad jazz band in striped blazers and straw boaters who were blowing up a storm in the pavilion at the far end of the gardens.

Gradually the gentle roar of conversation started to fade as more and more groups noticed Amelia, stopped talking and turned to stare. The band got the message at last, and responded in the most spectacular style. With a crash of cymbals they marked a second of total silence.

Then the applause started; spontaneous tiny pockets of pattering that spread out, joined together and turned into a glorious chorus of slapping skin. With a gentle sigh from parted lips, Amelia released me, drew herself up and walked the few steps to the terrace stairs, nodding and smiling to each group.

It was a brilliant entrance.

I just hoped it was spectacular enough to ensure no one had noticed me. Because amongst Amelia's new fan club, I'd noticed Kevin Drysdale's familiar figure. And even if I wasn't sure what footing our relationship was currently on, I had my conceit. After the black-plastic-bag ensemble last time, I preferred not to be seen looking like a damp bag of chips today.

Stephen had walked forward to meet his wife at the foot of the steps. Possessive pride was written large all over his normally serious face. She laid one hand on his arm and allowed herself to be led around the gardens. It was very much a grand progress.

'Can you believe this party? It's so *naff*.'

'Hi, Bone,' I said without turning my head.

She drooped herself over the balustrade next to me and watched the procession. Amelia seemed to be acting as a magnet, drawing the rest of the guests behind her like streams of iron filings.

'Champagne buffet and jazz bands ... and a barbie! It's well prehistoric. Claudia's parents had a Thai party last month. The guests had to wear Thai clothes and they had genuine Thai musicians and dancers. Her father even flew in a chef from Bangkok to supervise the food.'

'Why don't you stop trying to keep up with Claudia and just do what *you* want to do?'

I knew the answer before I asked the question. Because at fourteen you want to be one of the pack. Come to think of it, it's a pretty good place to be when you're pushing twenty-nine. Unless the pack turns on you. But enough of my former career – Amelia's acolytes were heading back towards the balustrade. And Kevin was with them.

'You sound like Gran,' Bone said, kicking the stonework. 'Why don't you get out of my face and get yourself a life?'

'Is that what you tell your gran?'

'No.' Unexpectedly she grinned and the attractive kid under the sulk appeared. 'I wouldn't dare. See ya.'

She whirled round and disappeared through the french windows. It seemed like a good move. Kevin was getting nearer by the second.

The catering supervisor tried to direct me behind 'salads and quiches'.

'Sorry ... emergency ... loo ...' I trilled, heading for the hall. I glanced back. Amelia was trailing the flock up on to the terrace.

'It's in the garage ... you must all come and see it ... it's just so fabulous ... it's one of the joys of being married to a man who just adores giving me presents ...'

They were coming through. I darted into the library and locked the door. Feet tramped past. They'd already had enough drink to make any entertainment acceptable; even if it was only standing around making purring sounds over Amelia's new white Merc.

There was a telephone extension in here; it seemed a pity to waste the opportunity. I dialled the local CID office on the off-chance Zeb might be working the late turn. He was.

'Where have you been?' he demanded. 'I've been ringing and ringing your office. Annie could be here any minute. She isn't, is she?'

'No. I've good news and bad news. First – Annie's changed her mind. You've got a reprieve for a couple of days while she trawls the West Country for dodgy dealers.'

'Yes!!' I could feel, if not see, Zeb punching air on the other end of the line.

'Also ... have you ever noticed Annie's frying pan? The swishy job; all stainless steel and ceramic bits? Well, you'd better go and buy a new one. And see if you can find anything to clean scorch marks off kitchen surfaces.'

'What! Ohmigod, I'll kill them.'

'Well, it's boosting the clear-up figures, I guess. Commit the crime, then solve it. But if you end up in the dock, Annie might just get to hear. Best to get rid quietly if you can, wouldn't you say?'

'I guess ...'

'Glad you think so ... Listen, Zeb, Annie mentioned you've a sister who works for an airline, that right?'

'Tally. One of the twins. What about her?'

'Just that I need a bit of info. It would probably sound better coming from you.'

'Me? Why should I want ...' Zeb was a bit naive, but he wasn't slow. He got the message: Squatters + Request For Information = Blackmail.

'You wouldn't!'

'I would.' I gave him a second to decide which was the worst scenario, then said: 'Got a pen handy? I need to know if a Kristen Keats or Julie-Frances Keble flew out anywhere over the weekend of first May. Probably a Far Eastern destination but I can't be certain. Will Tally be able to check Gatwick and Stansted airports too?'

'How the hell would I know? Who says I'm going to ask

her anyway? You wouldn't really drop me in it with Annie. Would you?'

He was just far enough this side of unsure for me to be certain he'd ask. Whether this Tally would deliver was another matter. As a last thought, I asked him to get Bridgeman checked out for that weekend as well. After all, I only had Stephen's word for the sequence of events – and clients had been known to lie. In fact, most of mine seem to make a speciality of it.

'I really should hate you,' Zeb moaned.

'Well, you'll have to get in line. There's better men than you out there waiting to hate me. Phone me at home or leave a message at the office. Must go, or the chilled champagne and smoked salmon will be gone.'

A cautious recce of the hall confirmed that most of the guests were still out the front. I whipped back the other way, intending to get myself some supper and find a quiet bush at the end of the garden that I could eat it under. I was frustrated by the sight of Joan Reiss on the terrace talking to Larry Payne.

It wasn't so odd they should know each other, I guess. They had a lot in common – money. However, it made things a bit tricky, since I'd told Payne I was a private detective. Joan, on the other hand, thought I was the world's sloppiest part-time cleaner. And Stephen would presumably prefer her to go on thinking that ...

I started to retreat again and got cut off by the catering supervisor.

'Do you have *any* intention of working this evening?' she hissed between clenched teeth.

'Sure thing.' I darted behind a table. The move put a long curtain between myself and the duo on the terrace, although I could still hear Payne's bullish tones.

'Reversed drainage, see, that was your problem, Joanie. See those flagstones ...' A heavy shoe stamped out two hard thumps on the paving stones. 'Set wrong ... you get the wrong canter and it doesn't matter how many pipes and drains you mess around with ...'

'Yes ... well I'm sure Amelia was very grateful to you for

sorting things out so promptly … Have you tried the lobster? I believe it's particularly …'

'These amateur johnnies don't know that … or they don't give a shit … make it look pretty and grab the cash fast, that's their motto …'

'Actually, I believe Stephen stopped the cheque until the work was redone … Perhaps you might care to try the barbecue …?'

'There's no substitute for experience … get yourself a professional … saves a bloody fortune in the long run …'

'Yes. I'm sure you're right, Larry. If you'll just excuse me for a moment …'

'Have you seen those stonework joints? Master mason couldn't have done better … here, take a look …'

They headed along the terrace to the far corner, Larry with the enthusiasm of a bull scenting a herd of cows on the pull, and Joan with the resignation of the perfect hostess whose arm is being held in a vice-grip.

I slipped back to the front. Amelia's audience were collected in front of the garage making oohing noises over her car. It gave me the chance to get across to mine and hook out the sunglasses from the parcel shelf. On the way back, I helped myself to a long black lacy scarf hanging in the cloakroom. With both ends crossed under my chin and flicked down my back, and the spectacles pushed into place, I could have passed for Audrey Hepburn – in very dim lighting. At any event I hoped I looked sufficiently unlike Grace Smith to get past Larry Payne.

Selecting a plate of nibbling tit-bits at random and grabbing a glass, I darted through the french windows and plunged into the densest clump of rhododendrons.

I wasn't alone.

CHAPTER 31

Somebody had left a wheelchair in here. Its elderly occupant had been dozing peacefully until I crashed through. Now his scraggy neck jerked and lifted a round face the colour of polished beechwood. Blue eyes with the slight opaqueness of early cataracts twinkled as they peered doubtfully at me. 'Do I know you?'

'No.'

'Well, that's a relief. I can't abide it when I forget.'

'I'm Grace Smith.' I sat myself cross-legged on the leaf mould by his feet and offered the plate. 'Fancy a nibble.'

We grazed in companionable silence until he nodded off again over a goat's-cheese brioche. Beyond the bushes I caught glimpses of feet and snatches of conversation.

'... nobody goes to San Marino any more. It's far too crowded.'

'... I see Minnie Drysdale has decided the grass isn't greener after all. Of course, I always thought she was mad to leave him. He's been desperate to get her back, you know.'

'... you need balsamic vinegar. I specifically told her that. Would you believe the wretched girl actually *drenched* it in that ghastly brown stuff they serve in fish and chip shops. My God, where do they find these au pairs ...'

'... Uncle Alfie? Where are you, Uncle Alfie?'

My dinner companion jerked awake again. I guessed he answered to Uncle Alfie. Scrambling up, I wheeled him forward on to the lawn, not caring whether Kevin-flaming-Drysdale saw me or not. So he and Minnie had parted by mutual consent, had they – the lying toad.

Joan Reiss hurried over. 'Uncle Alfie, there you are. I was becoming quite concerned.'

It was odd hearing a woman of her age calling someone 'Uncle'.

'This young woman has been taking very fine care of me. We're going to listen to the band now.'

It was the first I'd heard of it, but I was game if he was.

'I don't think he should have any of the barbecued meats, Grace. It's too late for his digestion. And make sure you wrap up, Uncle Alfie. It's getting cooler now. And I think alcohol would be unwise ...'

I rolled Uncle Alfie gently away down the sloping lawns until Joan was out of earshot.

Unexpectedly he chuckled. 'She's a grand bossy girl, isn't

she? Her father said she came out of her mother's womb telling the midwife what to do.'

Recognition suddenly clicked into place. Uncle Alfie must be Alfred Carnegie, the co-founder of Wexton's Engineering.

He seemed pleased that I knew. 'Not that I had much to do with the engineering. I had my own business: I was an accountant. Still am, I suppose. What is it my great-nephew says? Old accountants dinna fade away, they just fail to balance eventually.' He gave another chuckle and slapped the sides of his wheelchair.

The nap and walk seemed to have revived him. He started tapping along with the saints who were currently marching in.

'He was a fine cheeky devil, Wexton,' he said out of the blue. 'Employed me to do the books for his new company. And then asked me to put in one hundred pounds in return for a ten per cent stake because he couldna afford to pay me!'

'What did you do?'

'Jacked him up to fifteen per cent and took the deal. Best thing I ever did. They've played me fair over the years; verra fair. She was a Wren, y'know, young Joanie. Her sister Blanche too. Used to come home on leave at weekends. We all knew that Reiss chap didna have a chance soon as she set her cap at him. He was engaged to another lassie, y'know. She soon saw her off. Know what I do sometimes?'

'What?'

'I tell her I've left ma shares to that son-in-law of hers. I havena, of course. But my, it's a treat watching her face and thinking mebbe there'll come a time when she canna have her own way over the company. Do you not think I might have a steak?'

'Mrs Reiss said ...'

'Bugger Mrs Reiss. I'm not having a female I've known since she was a wee girlie with scarred knees telling me what to eat.'

'Fair enough.' I wheeled him into line at the barbecue.

I peeked over the nearest shoulder. There wasn't a charred beefburger or sausage in sight. The chef nursed fillet steaks, lobster tails and salmon to mouth-melting perfection before flipping them on to china plates. You even got silver cutlery and linen napkins to go.

The shoulder must have sensed me peeking. It turned, swishing a curtain of black hair against my nose.

'Hello,' Marina Payne said. 'Fancy seeing you here. Is this social or work?'

'Bit of both ...' Apart from Uncle Alfie, no one else I knew was in earshot. 'Listen, I'd be grateful if you'd not mention the day job.'

'If you like ... but you could be the hit of the party, you know. Private investigator sounds much more interesting than solicitor, dentist or ...'

'Builder?'

'Especially builder. People leap flowerbeds at my approach because they think I'm going to try and sell them a kitchen extension.'

She waved to someone on the lawns. I glanced back and saw Amelia was flitting from group to group. In the softly lit dusk she looked almost unreal – a fairy creature from *A Midsummer Night's Dream*.

'Never think we were best mates at St Aggie's, would you?' Marina said.

'No.'

'Thanks. You could have lied and said I didn't look quite ready for the knacker's yard yet.'

'I didn't mean it like that. I just thought ... you'd have had a less bubble-headed best mate, frankly.'

'Sometimes your mates choose you.'

She paused to turn away and point out a couple of lobster tails to the server. Once again I had the nagging sensation of knowing her from somewhere other than Swayling's building yard, and then she'd turned back and it was gone.

'Did you manage to catch up with Tom Skerries?' she asked.

'No. I caught up with everyone else – his wife, his kids, his sister-in-law, his drinking mates – but Tom remains a myth.'

'You're not mything much ...' Marina smiled. 'As a matter of fact, I might have something. I meant to call you ...'

She was interrupted by a shout from the terrace. 'Listen ... Listen, everyone ...'

The band took their cue and delivered another rolling crash of cymbals.

'Hi … everybody listen …' Amelia clapped her hands. 'I'm going to open my presents now.'

We all got the message. This was a participatory event. We duly headed back to the terrace. Amelia giggled and gurgled until her audience had collected. There was a pile of wrapped parcels on one of the terrace tables.

'OK. Now you've all seen that *glorious* car my lovely husband bought me …' She blew a kiss at Stephen, who was perched with one buttock on the terrace rail. 'And this is another little *surprise* gift …'

She drew the curling golden string of a tiny box and started to unwrap it. I didn't pay much attention. Kevin was in the crowd a few paces ahead of Uncle Alfie's wheelchair. Judging by the way she was hanging on his arm, the female with him must be Mrs Kevin Drysdale.

I could only see the back view. Which was OK, I guess – if you happen to *like* size twelves with small butts, perfect legs, flawless olive skin and a long tumble of gleaming black hair.

A smattering of applause brought my attention back to Amelia again. She was proudly displaying a pair of diamond ear studs.

'Now, what shall I open next …?' With one finger to her lips, she tiptoed her other hand over the parcels.

'Mine …' Patrick pushed forward. 'Open mine, Mummy.'

'Yours? All right … which one is it?'

Gathering the wrapping disaster to his chest, Patrick offered it to her.

Raising her eyebrows in conspiratorial excitement to her audience, his mother wrestled with the sticky tape. 'Darling, whatever have you got in here? It feels ever so *exciting* …'

'I made it.'

'*Made it* … well, that makes it a zillion times better, doesn't it? Oh, it's a *picture* …' Amelia rustled off the paper.

'It's all of us … see. There's you, Mummy. And all of us … me and Bone and Theo and Charlotte.'

'And all the grandchildren, of course,' Bone said, turning the frame slightly to give everyone a better view.

Amelia's face changed as the light died from it.

There – caught in technicolour – was Amelia above the picture of those three hulking American teenagers. OK, they were only step-grandchildren, but the illusion was destroyed. She was no longer the beautiful ageless fairy princess; she was just a middle-aged mum of four with the cash to buy expensive make-up and clothes.

I caught the mocking expression flitting across Bone's eyes and understood. It had been her idea, not Patrick's.

Her brother was beaming proudly. Despite his earlier claim to hate his mother, she was still his mum and he wanted her to be pleased.

Amelia looked at him. Then at Bone.

'You bitch.' She drew back her arm and hit Bone across the face so hard that the girl was flung back on to the flagstones.

Stephen broke the paralysis that froze us all for a moment. Stooping, he tried to help his daughter up.

'Get off. Let me go ...' Kicking and scrabbling free of his grip, Bone sprang down the steps of the terrace and raced away around the side of the house.

'What's the matter? Mummy?' Patrick looked bewildered. He tried to catch at his mother's skirt.

Amelia whisked it free. 'Stay away from me. How could you ... it's all your fault. It's everyone's fault ... I told you I didn't want a party ... I hate you all ...'

'Amelia ... stop it this instant!'

Stephen's attempts to restrain her were rewarded by a stinging slap across the face. We all watched fascinated as the imprint of her fingers developed on his skin.

With a sob, Amelia hitched up the designer frock and ran back indoors. Stephen muttered what might have been an apology and followed her inside.

Patrick had had enough of the grown-up world. Instead of the congratulations and kisses he'd expected for his efforts, he'd unleashed an unfathomable hatred. He promptly burst into hiccuping sobs and threw himself at his grandmother, wrapping his arms tightly round her waist.

'It's all right, Patrick, Mummy's not feeling very well ... Come and help me inside for a moment.' She guided him gently with an arm around his shoulders in through the french windows.

The rest of us let out our breath with a massive collective *WOOOOO*.

It was a decisive moment. Did we all make our excuses and go home now that our party hosts had plainly gone off the whole idea? Or did we figure it was a pity to waste all the time and money that Joan Reiss had poured into this posh bash?

What do you think?

The band let rip with a swinging selection of rock-and-roll. It gave me a brief moment of nostalgia for the fry-ups at Shane's greasy spoon.

'Let's get those steaks, Uncle Alfie.'

We loaded up at the barbecue, and rescued a couple of glasses of orange juice from a passing waitress. I'd intended to intercept Marina Payne and find out what she'd been planning to tell me about the elusive Tom Skerries, but I couldn't see any signs of her plain pink suit on the lawn.

We circulated. It was an odd experience. I discovered I was invisible. Uncle Alfie, happily eating off his lap, got the odd tight smile and nod, but I was treated like an extension to the wheelchair. After a while it dawned on me that they thought I was some sort of paid nursing attendant.

I took the steak plates back into the house, collected two desserts and took Uncle Alfie on a tour of the grounds, still trying to track down Marina.

The old boy seemed quite happy to bob along wherever I chose. Sounds of laughter and splashing drew us into the barn.

Half a dozen guests were skinny-dipping, sending waves of chlorinated water over the discarded piles of clothes scattered over the tiles. I stayed long enough to check none of them was Marina.

'By heavens, did you see the bust on yon blonde?' Uncle Alfie cackled as we wove back between the rhododendrons.

'Shame on you. You'll go blind.'

'I am anyway. Might as well enjoy it.'

He chuckled away to himself and then suddenly his head fell forward. Alarmed, I checked his pulse and breathing. He was fast asleep again.

I pressed on, rounded a large bush – and came face to face with Kevin and his wife.

'Hello, Grace. I thought it was you. Minnie, this is Grace Smith. She's a friend of Dad's. You remember, the one who sorted out the Marilyn Monroe business for him.'

A friend of Dad's. So that was his story, was it?

Minnie widened her huge brown eyes. 'I'm very pleased to meet you, Grace.'

'Same here,' I lied. 'If you don't mind, I'd be grateful if you'd not mention my job. I'm sort of undercover tonight.'

I tipped my glasses to the bottom of my nose as I spoke in order to give Kevin the full benefit of my you-two-timing-liar glare.

'Did you have an accident?' Minnie asked, staring at my multicoloured face.

'No. I did it on purpose. Excuse me, I'm working ...' I barged past them, catching Kevin's toes with the wheels and silently wishing acute PMT on Minnie.

Marina was still nowhere to be found. I tried the front of the house. The drive and verges were now clogged with parked cars, making it difficult to manoeuvre Uncle Alfie. I was bending down, unsnagging him from a bumper, when Stephen Bridgeman stalked out of the front door and headed down the drive.

A couple of seconds later Bone followed. She'd pulled a short denim jacket over her dress and was hunched into it, collar up and hands thrust into the pockets.

I straightened up as she came opposite us. 'That was a rotten thing to do.'

She didn't bother to pretend she'd no idea what I was talking about. 'How was I to know she'd take it like that? I mean, it was just a flaming joke, for heaven's sake. What's the big deal about being fifty?'

'Then why set Patrick up? You could at least have had the guts to take the blame yourself.'

She kicked the gravel. Tiny stones splattered against the chair wheels. 'He's OK. Gran's with him. He's already got a labrador puppy out of it. He ought to be grateful to me. At least he doesn't have to put up with *her* trying to put him in dresses made for six-year-olds and pretending, like, you can't possibly be old enough to have *started* yet. Stupid bitch …'

The nearest car got pebbledashed by another shower of stones as Bone lashed out – and then she was flouncing away towards the gates.

'Why didn't you ask Marina Payne if she knew where Tom Skerries was?' I shouted after her. 'If she's such a big mate of your mum's?'

Bone came to a quick stop, swung round and clipped back. 'Because she *is* a big mate of my mother's, of course,' she said in a voice pitched just loud enough for me to hear. 'Not that she'd worry, but if she told Daddy …'

'That his fourteen-year-old daughter was dating a married bloke with three kids,' I finished for her.

'I'm not dating him. Not any more. I just need to get him to Claudia's dance. And anyway, I did ask Mrs Payne. I rung up the building yard loads of times, pretending I was different people, but she always said they didn't know Tom. Which was a rotten lie. But they were probably fiddling on his tax or something. Tom said they all did it. That's why it was OK for him to take their customers.'

'More fool him. Is Marina around?'

'She was upstairs talking to Mummy through the door. The stupid cow's locked herself in the bedroom. She says she's never coming out again. We should be so lucky. I'm off.'

She swung away and clumped towards the gate. Night had finally fallen, and with no lighting in the front apart from the beams of a car that was trying to manoeuvre off the verge, her dark outfit was soon lost in the gloom.

'Spunky little thing, ain't she?'

'Hello, Uncle Alfie, I thought you'd dropped off again.'

'Just conserving my strength. What are we doing amongst all these cars?'

'I was looking for someone. Hang on …' I heaved him round and headed for the front door.

'Doesn't look much like her mother, does she, yon spunky bit. Got a touch of old Jack Wexton in there somewhere, though. Happens like that. Looks skip a generation. Joanie's girl now, she favours her Auntie Blanche, Joanie's little sister, may the puir soul rest in peace.'

'Dead, is she?'

'These many years. Puir girl died on her honeymoon.' Those milky eyes tipped back and stared into mine as I tilted the chair to get it up the front step. 'I gave her away, you know. Asked me to since her father was dead. Proudest moment of my life walking down the aisle with little Blanche on my arm. Seeing her like that ... in white lace and satin ... there wasna a man in that church, married or not, who wouldn't have changed places with young Henry that morning.'

'Henry?'

'Her man. She married a chap called Henry Summerstone.'

CHAPTER 32

Henry informed me he wasn't denying the connection. Which was magnanimous of him, considering it was a matter of public record.

'You didn't exactly volunteer the information either, did you? I mean, didn't you think that the fact your missing jogger worked for your sister-in-law's company was just the tiniest bit relevant?'

'No.'

I threw my best *oh yeah* sneer. It was totally wasted. Even if Henry hadn't been blind, the room was pitch dark anyway, with the only light filtering in from a forty-watt bulb in the hall.

It was late. It had taken me a while to shake off Uncle Alfie after he'd dropped his little bombshell. With Amelia having a mega-sulk in her bedroom and no sign of Joan, I hadn't liked to abandon him in case he trundled off into the rhododendrons again and got forgotten until the next weeding session.

I'd tried wheeling him to the edge of a chattering group and leaving him there, but when I glanced back from the terrace, they'd all edged away, leaving him stuck in the middle of the lawn like a rather bizarre garden ornament.

Trotting back, I'd trundled him to the edge of another lot clustered around one of the tables and left again.

It was like dropping a blob of detergent into greasy water. As one they broke apart, reclumped and spread out over the garden.

In the end it had taken me nearly an hour to find someone the old boy knew, and by that time there was no sign of Marina Payne anywhere so I'd headed out for Henry's and a spot of self-righteous tantrums. And found myself falling over the furniture in a pitch-black dining room.

Henry had pointed out that he had no way of knowing when the bulbs blew until someone came to the house and told him.

'Have you got a spare? It could be dangerous moving around in the dark,' I'd asked after flicking the switch fruitlessly.

'For whom, m'dear? I have been moving in the dark for over forty years and I can honestly say that Beano has never complained about the lack of facilities in the billet. Where are you, boy?'

The dog had responded to a couple of sharp clicks of his master's fingers. I'd heard his tail beating enthusiastically against the furniture as he moved nearer. There's something unnerving about having a wet nose thrust into your crotch when you can barely see the rest of its owner.

'Do you mind, Beano? I'm not that sort of bitch.'

'Allow me.' Henry's hand had dropped to my knee and was following the route upwards. I forstalled him by finding the business end of Beano's muzzle and shoving him away. Henry commanded him to lie down.

With a sigh, Beano panted away until just his amber eyes were staring unwinkingly from a corner.

'You're very late, m'dear. Are you here in response to my message?'

'What message?'

'I left one on that answering contraption at your office. I was wondering if you had any news for me. I take it you do?'

'It's more a request. For information. And I'm sorry about the time, but I had trouble getting away. I've been to a garden party. In fact, I'm surprised we didn't bump into each other there. Doesn't Joan Reiss invite you to her knees-ups? After all, she is your sister-in-law.'

I didn't detect any reaction in the stiffly seated figure, but Beano's antennae were more finely tuned to his master's vibes; he'd whined at a pitch that made my teeth itch.

After a short pause, Henry had admitted the relationship. And then calmly added he didn't see it made the slightest difference to our business.

'Of course it makes a flaming difference!'

'In what way? May I offer a nightcap, incidentally? Tea or coffee? A snifter?'

'No. Thanks,' I added grudgingly. When I'm on to a good self-righteous rant I just hate to be interrupted. 'If it's not such a big deal that you're related to the directors of Wexton's Engineering, how come you didn't mention it when I told you that was where Kristen, or rather Julie-Frances, worked?'

'I found it irrelevant. Who told you about me? Not Joan, I should imagine.'

'No. It was a man called Alfie Carnegie. He's ...'

'I remember Alfred. I can see him now, escorting Blanche down the aisle. Isn't it strange the things that stick in one's mind ... perhaps because it was one of the last days I saw. I'd been watching the vicar, staring at him so hard my neck was stiff with the effort ... he had a port-wine birthmark shaped like Malta on his left cheek ... then the music changed and I turned my head – and there was Blanche, with the sun coming in through the rose window and lighting up her hair like the palest golden silk. I got a pain, an actual physical pain in the centre of my chest just looking at her ... smiling ... gliding towards me. I couldn't believe that she was really mine, that this ... enchanted creature had actually agreed to be *my* wife.'

My eyes had become more accustomed to the lack of lighting and I could see the fingers of his right hand clasping and twisting the sweater over his heart; now they relaxed and his shoulders slumped. 'I'm sorry ... you must forgive an old man, but you see, in my head I still look like the young chap at the altar that morning ... and Blanche, my beautiful Blanche, she'll always be as she was on that day to me.'

Awkwardly I moved over to sit beside him and took a hand. 'No. It's me who should apologise. It's just ... you can see it looks bloody odd. You pay me to find someone, I discover she's working for a company you're related to in a manner of speaking ... and you don't bother to mention the fact.'

'Because there is no relationship, m'dear. That ended on the day Blanche died. Indeed, it would never have started if Joan had had her wish. She was still trying to run Blanche's life, as she had done ever since Blanche was small. Joan had a very forceful personality and, if I may say so – and who else could – a blind faith in her own invincibility.'

'She still has.'

'I think it was the first time Blanche had ever stood up to her. Perhaps if she hadn't, she might still be alive ... in the end I suppose you could say Joan was proved right when she said I would ruin her sister's life. She blames me, of course. I was driving the car.'

'On your honeymoon, Uncle Alfie said.'

'Scotland. It was getting dark, raining ... we were coming down into a glen ... hit a patch of mud ... I couldn't hold it ... we went over the edge. Blanche was killed outright, her neck broke. And I ...' He touched the spectacles.

'I'm sorry.'

'No you're not, m'dear. It was a very long time ago. And no doubt you can't imagine that an old man like me could ever have felt love or passion. I was in hospital in Edinburgh for months; they operated six or seven times. At first they thought one eye might be saved, but in the end an infection set in so it had to go. Joan and Derek came to see me in the hospital. I had no family of my own and I remember I was quite touched at the time that they should have made that long journey on my behalf ... given their earlier antipathy ...'

'Derek didn't like you either?'

'Derek did pretty much what his wife wanted ... and what she wanted in this instance was for me to sell my share in Wexton's to Derek. Blanche and I had made wills in each other's favour so everything her father had left her came to me.'

I did a bit of quick mental arithmetic. If Uncle Alfie owned fifteen per cent of the company, then assuming Joan and Blanche had been left equal shares, Henry must have been sitting on forty-two and a half per cent at that time.

'You agreed?'

'It seemed sensible. I needed money for medical care ...'

'Didn't they have the National Health back then?'

Henry snorted. 'I'm not quite that ancient, m'dear. Of course they did. But there were other expenses – convalescence, home nursing, someone to sort out the cooking and cleaning ... As Joan so kindly pointed out, these things mount up, and with a substantial sum in the bank, earning interest ... anyway, the upshot of it was I sold ... bloody stupid move, I saw that later ... matter of fact, I tried to take them to court later. I was full of drugs, painkillers and the like, didn't know what I was signing away ...'

'What happened?'

'Nothing. Lawyers didn't give it odds ... said expenses could bankrupt me ... all right for the Reisses of course ... they had plenty of money to put up a fight. Anyhow ... upshot ... nothing, no case, no restitution, no damn money. Are you surprised I don't wish to boast any sort of connection with Joan Reiss or her family?'

'I guess not.'

'May I ask if this is getting us any closer to finding Kristen?'

'Julie-Frances.'

'The name scarcely matters. It is her current location that is of importance. Do you have it?'

'No.' I had to admit that the last definite location I had for Kristen/Julie-Frances was the Bridgeman house.

Quickly I filled Henry in on her movements up until the morning Stephen had said goodbye to her and gone off to his meeting at Wexton's.

I'd had a bit of a tussle with my conscience on whether I should tell Henry about Stephen's scheme to rip off the Sumata designs, but in the end I figured he'd been my first client so he had a right to anything I found out about Kristen's motives for disappearing.

'She may have just decided to go in for a bit of private enterprise. Grab the designs and sell them elsewhere. I'm getting the airlines checked out to see if I can get a handle on her ...'

'She was a thief ... a lying little cheat. My God, is there no honour left in this world?'

'We don't know that. She might just have ...'

'Have what?' Henry snapped. 'Been smitten by a light on the road to Slough and decided to confess all? I think Bridgeman might have had a visit from the Fraud Squad by now if that was the case, don't you, m'dear?'

The bitterness in his voice surprised me. She'd really got to him. How long would it be before he trusted anyone else enough to let them penetrate the loneliness, I wondered? A heck of a time, I suspected.

'So what happens now? Will this airline tracing faddle work?'

'It might.' I'd half expected him to tell me to can the whole investigation.

'Then you can keep me informed. I wish to know as soon as you locate her. I shall have words to say to that young lady. She has proved to be a great disappointment.'

Boy, that was going to have Julie-Frances quaking in her pink suede mini-skirt, I thought ruefully, pointing the car back towards the promenade.

I'd approached his house along St John's Road via the inland route and I could have got home the same way, but after an evening of rich rollicking I suddenly felt a yen for a bit of common old nightlife.

And you didn't get much commoner than downtown Seatoun. The reverberation of the games machines and thundering beat of the music were tingling through the base of my feet on the car pedals. There were more kids around than normal; probably due to half-term. They tended to come down for the evening; party until their money ran out; then crash out on the beach if the rain held off, or clutter up the shelters and station waiting room if it chucked it down. The police usually reckoned to round up at least half a dozen cars nicked from London the day before on Bank holidays, summer weekends and school holidays.

Down on the front, the steadily strobing blue pulse of the emergency vehicle parked up round the corner beyond the cinema stood out amongst the strings of multi-coloured fairy lights and pewter moonlight reflecting off the sea.

Coming up on it, I assumed it was a police van collecting up a contingent of those who'd decided to round off the evening by slinging a rubbish bin through the plate-glass windows or starting a fight with some other thickos who hadn't shown them 'nuff respect.

It looked like I'd missed the arrest, since the light was pulsing on and off on the top of the ambulance dispatched to collect up the non-walking wounded.

A huddle of spectators were watching the free show, eyes fixed on the attendants bending over something on the pavement, whilst their mouths opened automatically to accept another chip.

I'd have driven straight past if my eye hadn't caught a glimpse of yellow. Pulling over beyond the ambulance, I sprinted back. They'd just got the casualty strapped into the stretcher and were preparing to lift.

'What happened? How bad is it?'

The paramedic nearest me glanced over her shoulder. 'Do you know him?'

'Yes,' I said, looking down at the bruised and dirt-covered face held immobile by a neck brace, 'I know him. He answers to Figgy.'

CHAPTER 33

'Oh no yer don't, sticky fingers!'

I resented that 'sticky fingers'. I'd have resented broken fingers even more. Which was what I'd have ended up with if my reflexes had been a fraction slower. As it was, I managed to snatch them back a millisecond before the size twelves crashed to the pavement.

So much for doing my good deed for the day. Selfish indifference is definitely a healthier attitude to life. I'd got my nose smashed in protecting Rachel in the Downs social club the other night, and now I'd only just missed a broken hand trying to rescue Annie's radio cassette player.

I'd spotted it half lying under a rubbish bin about twenty yards beyond the spot where Figgy had ended up. It was well stuck. I'd just managed to gently ease it free without adding any more scratches to the case when that foot crashed down.

I leapt, rolled and straightened up in one movement before he could get a grip on me. 'Hi, Terry. That was a close one. Still, no harm done.'

As proof I extended my middle digit and waggled it under his nose.

Rosco scowled. As usual he was wearing the peaked cap a fraction closer to his eyebrows than required by regulations. He thinks it makes him look macho. The patrol car was pulled off the road behind the ambulance and I could see his partner moving amongst the spectators with her notebook.

'Pity you missed, really. I could have done with the compensation money. Did they not cover unnecessary force on your training programme, Terry? Oh I forgot, they must have done. You've been commended for it several times, haven't you? Or did they say cautioned?'

'At least I wasn't chucked out for taking bungs from pond-life.'

'That one's nearly as old as the *Titanic* look-out's *I think there could be a little bit of ice ahead, Captain.*'

'True, though, weren't it? And bigger than everyone thought.'

'Not a phrase that Mrs Rosco uses much, I would imagine. Are you planning to stand here trading insults all night ... or should you be doing something about that hit-and-run.'

'Who says it was a hit-and-run?'

'Practically everybody before you turned up. You know how the sight of a police uniform brings on an instant plague of don't-want-to-get-involved-itis.'

'Right. I'll soon sort them out.' Terry squared his shoulders preparatory to a spot of witness intimidation. 'But first I'll have that, thanks very much.'

He grabbed the radio before I could stop him.

'Oi, give that back, it belongs to a friend.'

'The victim's a mate of yours, that what you're saying?'

'Not exactly. The radio's on loan from a mutual acquaint-ance of us both.'

'Fine. Tell this mutual acquaintance to come claim it from the station.'

'No need. Give it to DC Smith.'

'Zebedee? What's he got to do with it?'

'He's also mutually acquainted with the owner. I'll give him a ring later. See it got home safely.'

Terry got the hint and told me he didn't nick from ambulance cases. We were just squaring up for another slanging match when he leant forward and took a deep breath. 'You been drinking?' His eyes sought and found my car parked just ahead. 'And driving?'

'I'm not over the limit,' I said with more confidence than I felt. After the champagne in the bathroom, I'd tried to stick to soft drinks ... more or less ... and I'd eaten a lot of food, I reassured myself. Plus there was the delay whilst I settled Uncle Alfie ...

'I'll have to ask you to take a breath test, madam,' Terry said, his official tone rather spoilt by the anticipatory leer all over his handsome (if you like that sort of thing) face.

We were interrupted by his partner. She was a tall, leggy brunette with looks that could melt cheese and a voice that could have turned the milk sour in the first place.

Terry preened a fraction harder. 'What we got then, Gina?'

'Naff-all really. Got a witness reckons she *might* have seen something. Sez a big car, dark blue or black, just smashed into the bloke. Never swerved or nothing.'

'Joyriders?'

'Dunno, she never saw the driver. Mind, she's so spaced out I ain't dead certain she saw the flaming car at all. 'Ello, Grace.'

'Hiya, Gina. Still riding with medallion man?'

'Yeah. Looks like it. What happened to your face?'

'I got belted.'

'Looks good on her, don't it, Gina?'

Telling Terry to stow it with a casualness that said she issued the same suggestion a dozen times a shift, Gina said: 'Medics reckon you know the bloke, Grace. That right? Only he ain't got no identification on him.'

'He answers to Figgy. He's a street entertainer.'

'Address?'

I opened my mouth ... and swallowed what I was about to say. Annie knew plenty of people in the force and I didn't want her unintentional sub-letting of her flat to get back to her via the canteen grapevine.

'Not sure. A squat, I think. Tell you what, I know his girlfriend. I could have a scout round, see if I can find her.'

'We don't need your help, Smithie ...'

'Yes we do, Ter. The hospital's going to need a proper name and medical history, ain't they? He could be a bleeder or something.'

'No. I'm sure Terry would have recognised a relative, wouldn't you, Terry?'

Any comeback from Terry was cut short by a more urgent tone from the ambulance's siren as it prepared to leave.

'I'm going to ride up the 'ospital wiv him, Ter.'

Gina ran back and Terry stepped into the road to hold the traffic as the ambulance sped away. I did a bit of speeding away myself before he remembered the breath test.

Mickey had plainly been waiting up. She called from behind the door almost as soon as I'd rung the bell.

'Figgy, is that you?'

'It's me, Mickey. Grace Smith.'

'What do you want? You can't come in.'

'Can you open the door, Mickey ... Figgy's had an accident.'

The safety chain rattled in its slider. She opened the door wide enough for me to see she was dressed in striped pyjamas (hers presumably) and a cream towelling robe (definitely Annie's). Her complexion was several shades paler than the robe.

'What kind of accident?'

'He's been knocked down. They've taken him to hospital.'

I read all the emotions flitting over her face: fright, wrong, disbelief.

'Look, it's not a trick. Ring the accident department, the ambulance should have arrived by now. There's a telephone directory in the bottom of the bookcase.'

She let me in. 'Is he hurt bad? He's not going to die, is he?

She held her hands flat over her stomach. 'Who else would take care of us?'

'I don't know how badly he's hurt. But they'll need details. Name, date of birth, medical history if you know it.'

'I don't know ... I'm not sure ... he had chicken pox once, does that count ...?'

'Shouldn't think so. Stick some clothes on and I'll run you up the hospital.'

She moved like she was on automatic pilot. I wanted to scream at her to hurry up, but after she'd had three tries at fastening her trousers and couldn't get the button aligned with the hole, I ended up taking over and helping her into sweatshirt and trainers.

'Come on.' I put an arm round her shoulders and urged her towards the door. 'I'm parked across the road.'

She sat staring bolt ahead through the short journey, her hands gripping the shelf on top of the dash so tightly I could see every individual vein standing out like some diagram in a medical textbook.

The accident and emergency department was the usual mixture of grumblers, drunks and the patiently resigned. I marched Mickey to the toughened glass cubicle marked 'Reception'.

'Say you're his fiancée,' I murmured, pushing her forward. 'It makes it easier if they can put down some sort of relationship. I'll go and see if I can find out how he's doing.'

The examination cubicles were all curtained across, but Gina was killing time outside the far one.

'How's he doing?'

'Not so hot. Busted a leg and some ribs, they reckon. And 'e's had a bang on his 'ead. That's the one they're getting revved up about.'

'I brought his girlfriend in. She's up at reception.'

'Oh, great.'

The curtain swished open long enough for us to glimpse Figgy in a cot bed. Lumps of torn and bloody clothing were dropping to the floor as a nurse wielded a large pair of scissors, whilst a doctor was scribbling on a clipboard. The sister in charge was adamant there was no chance of talking to him until tomorrow – late tomorrow.

'I've got his fiancée here … and she's pregnant,' I explained.

'Oh. I see.' The sister's brisk expression softened. 'Shall I have a word?'

Gina had turned away to relay the progress report on her radio; now she swung back and announced she was off. 'No sense 'anging around. Be someone up to talk to 'im tomorrow. See ya.'

There aren't that many ways of saying 'your man's got several broken bones, possible internal bleeding and maybe a cracked skull'. The sister did her best and was helped by the fact that Mickey seemed to be on another planet part of the time, but even she got the message eventually: Figgy was in serious trouble and the next few hours were crucial.

'Can I see him?'

'They'll have taken him to x-ray by now. Best to let them get on as fast as possible. I'll come tell you as soon as there's any news. Will your friend be staying with you?'

I couldn't see I had much choice. I fetched a couple of teas from the vending machine and we settled into the plastic chairs amongst the two-year-old magazines and endlessly droning television set that no one was watching.

'Do you think he'll die?'

The correct answer was 'Definitely not' followed by a lot of reassuring noises.

'I don't know. But they're good here. If anything can be done … you know?'

'Yeah. I know.'

She sipped the hot tea. I watched the curtain of sun-bleached mouse hair revealing and concealing her face as she dipped to each mouthful.

'How long you and Figgy been together?'

'About two years, maybe a bit less.'

'What about your family?'

'Haven't got any – just Figgy.'

She lapsed into a blank-eyed stare. I took her hand and we sat like that for a while, watching the ambulance crews coming and going and the waiting room gradually empty.

'He's not really bad, yer know,' Mickey said finally. 'He

knows he shouldn't have broken into your friend's flat like that. He only did it because of ...'

She rubbed a hand across her stomach again, like Aladdin reassuring himself the genie was still in the lamp.

'I was going to have one last year. We were squatting in this block of flats then. In Shepherd's Bush. Loads of people were. It was sort of official. The council knew we were there and everything. Figgy got all this paint and paper and stuff and done ours up ... for the baby, he said. He got a cot and a pram and all this kid's stuff, expensive brands too. He was so proud he was going to be a dad, you know?'

She turned big grey eyes on me and I nodded encouragingly. 'So what happened? Did you miscarry?'

'One of the blokes in the other flats was dealing drugs. He got raided ... and he figured someone had grassed on him.'

'And Figgy was splashing cash around on baby gear ...'

She nodded, swallowing tea that had gone stone-cold by now. 'He'd been getting the material cheap at car-boot sales ... he's good at doing things up ... but they didn't believe me. They broke in when he was out, you see ... one of them punched me in the stomach ...'

I gave her a hug. She leant against me.

'Did the police get them?'

'Figgy wouldn't let me make a statement. Said they'd get bail and come after me again. We moved to another squat ... miles away ... but I hated it, I kept thinking they'd find us, so ...'

'You found yourselves a very desirable beach hut.'

'It was only supposed to be for a few days. We really did mean to get a proper place, but the bed and breakfast the Social offered was so awful ... and ... your friend's flat is lovely ... She's so lucky ...' Her voice caught.

'Another tea,' I suggested, grabbing the empty cup and bolting. Empathy isn't my strongest talent.

We went through six more cups whilst we waited, interspersed with frequent trips to the loo. The night sounds of the hospital became quieter and stiller. The waiting room emptied as the casualties from chucking-out time at the pubs and clubs were cleared. Ambulances came and went occasionally, but even they had slackened off. Figgy had picked a quiet night to get knocked down, which was probably lucky for him.

After her hesitant justification for Figgy squatting in Annie's flat, Mickey had become monosyllabic, answering questions with a listless yes or no until she'd finally lapsed into a weary trance, staring blindly at a magazine that stayed open on the same page for nearly two hours.

I used the time to wrestle with my conscience. That description of the car that had hit Figgy fitted Stephen Bridgeman's motor. I kept getting other picture bytes: me describing Figgy to Stephen in the cellar – and telling him he might know something about Kristen's disappearance; Stephen stalking out of the house while I was ducked down trying to untangle Uncle Alfie's wheelchair, that car revving and manoeuvring at the far end of the drive whilst I was talking to Bone.

I pointed out to my conscience that it had been a couple of hours later that Figgy had been hit.

Sure, my conscience agreed. *But, like, he's not going to pile up on the pavement outside the amusement park, is he? Under all those bright lights with plenty of witnesses? Some of whom might be sober enough to take down the car number. Much smarter to park up near and take Figgy out as he goes round that dark corner where all the shops are shuttered and there's no reason for anyone to hang around. I mean, let's not forget you were kind enough to tell him the performance times.*

'Thanks for mentioning it,' I muttered.

'What?' Mickey jerked out of her trance.

'Nothing. I was just thinking aloud.'

'Oh.' She went back to the tattered article on Ten Things to do with Sour Bread Dough.

So, my conscience needled, *maybe you should just mosey on over to that payphone and suggest to our finest in blue they might like to check out Bridgeman's car for forensic evidence. Before he puts it through a car wash.*

I tried justifying myself. 'Look, Bridgeman hired me to find Kristen – who admittedly has now turned into Julie-Frances – but he still wants me to track down the lady and his missing files.'

Could be a double bluff. The guy works out you're looking for Kristen, so he decides to employ you. That way he gets to find out how much you know. Maybe he knows damn well what happened to Kristen. Maybe he made it happen.

'Why should he?'

Insurance policy. If things did turn nasty over this node thingy of his, he could always claim she stole the designs. Or perhaps the lady just got too greedy.

'Bollocks.'

Do you mind. I'm not a conscience who's used to such language.

'Well, it doesn't make sense. I could always testify that he'd told me he and Kristen were in it together.'

Assuming you take care when crossing the road from now on.

'Two accidents might be difficult to hide.'

Perhaps he'll just pay you off. A nice fat bonus. What would you say to five thousand to forget what he told you about his set-up with Kristen? Well?

'Don't rush me. It's a tough call.'

The doctor came down ten minutes later. Mickey sat bolt upright, her fingers forming a tourniquet around my wrist, her wide eyes fixed on the approaching figure as if she could draw the news from his skin. At least it saved him asking which of us was Figgy's fiancée. He took the chair opposite her.

'He's OK. His head injury isn't as bad as we feared; there's no bleeding into the skull that we can see. There was some internal bleeding from the ribs but we've sorted that out. And we've pinned his right leg. There's a fracture ...' he sliced across his own shin, 'and another higher up which is cleaner ... we've left that to heal naturally for now.'

'Will he still be able to skate?'

This was plainly not the question the doc was expecting. 'I ... er ... let's wait and see what the physios can do.'

'Can I see him?'

'For a moment. He won't be properly with us until lunchtime, I suspect. I should get home and get some sleep, young lady. By the looks of you you could do with it.'

I hung around outside in the corridor while they took Mickey into the ward and let her kiss her well-out-of-it fiancé.

She returned clutching the yellow roller-blades to her chest. A wheel was missing from one and the other was shattered around the ankle area. 'They said to bring his things in tomorrow.'

'Fine.' I yawned. 'I'll drop you home.'

She gave me a shy, grateful smile. 'Thanks. And thanks ever so much for stopping with me. I couldn't have stayed here alone. You've been dead brilliant.'

Since she was in a grateful mood, I grabbed the opportunity on the way home to ask her if she knew what Figgy had been talking about when I called the other day.

'When he threw me out he hinted he might know more about one of my cases than I do. A missing woman. The one I asked you about that first day. A friend of the old blind man with the dog?'

Mickey shook her head, still clutching the roller-blades to her chest as we bounced over sleeping policemen. 'No. He never said nothing about her to me. How would he know anyhow?'

'I wish I knew,' I admitted, sliding into a parking space outside Annie's flat. 'You going to be OK on your own?'

'Oh yes, I'm fine now.'

She got out of the car and promptly threw up in the gutter.

Scrambling out my side, I detached her from the passenger door she was using for support and helped her inside. Clinging together, we climbed the internal stairs to the first floor.

The tom-toms gave us the first hint that all was not well. They were propped in the hall by Annie's door.

'How did ...?' Mickey looked puzzled. She took in the plastic sacks and wire supermarket baskets lined up further along the carpet. 'Oh noo ...' She burst into tears yet again.

I leant on the bell until the safety chain went on and the door opened a fraction.

Zeb blinked through tousled hair. 'Oh, hi, Grace. Won't it keep? I've only just got to bed. You've no idea how many of these so-called "twenty-four-hour" locksmiths aren't. Still, here I am. Lawfully in possession of my sister's flat. With a new lock in place.' He slapped it gleefully.

Mickey's sobs turned into a keening sound as the combined effects of shock, relief and tiredness hit her at once.

'For heaven's sake, Zeb, her bloke could have been killed tonight.'

'Er, yeah ... I heard. Sorry. How is he?'

'He'll live, apparently.'

'Great. Well, all's well ... and all those other clichés ... Night.'

Mickey flung herself at the closing door. 'Wait. What am I going to do? It's my flat.'

'Not unless you've got a proper rental agreement, it isn't. You'd best find somewhere else to squat. Now I must get some sleep ... I'm in the witness box tomorrow. Night, Grace ... and thanks for tipping me off.'

'You what?'

'The radio. Terry Rosco dropped it in. Gave me the gen on the bloke being carted off to hospital. I owe you.' He dropped me a large wink and shut the door.

Mickey got her second wind and demonstrated it by whacking me straight in the middle of the healing bruises.

CHAPTER 34

I put her up anyway. It was that or leave her in a shelter on the front.

With the fold-up bed extended, my guest room looked even more like a condemned cell. And I discovered something else about myself; I didn't like having a house guest.

By the time we'd crashed for a few hours, rolled out of bed and telephoned the ward to confirm Figgy was doing fine but still asleep; had a bath ... and telephoned to confirm that Figgy was *still* doing fine and *still* asleep; breakfasted on stale-ish toast and Marmite ... and telephoned the ward to et cetera, et cetera ... I knew I was going to have to find Mickey alternative accommodation.

It was nothing personal; I just felt like my space had been invaded. And she was playing havoc with my telephone bill.

I slung the dirty dishes in the sink whilst she was on the phone for the hundredth time and grabbed my keys. By the time she hung up I was ready to chivvy her outside and into the car.

'But if Figgy wakes up and I'm not there ...'

'Two minutes,' I promised, swinging right and heading for the sea front. I just hoped Rachel wasn't out.

She wasn't. And, as anticipated, she fell on Mickey with zeal – and yoghurt cake.

'Just a nibble, darlin',' she insisted, slicing out a half-pound wedge. 'You got to keep yourself healthy, for the little one. You look a smidge peaky to me. You been eating properly? I know what you girls are ... diet, diet, diet ... you're not careful you'll get that nervous-rexy.'

'She's been living in a squat,' I said, without going into details.

'No!' Rachel's eyebrows shot up into the walnut-whip wig. 'Darlin', this is not good ... you don't want no nasty damp slum for a new baby ...'

'And now what with her boyfriend laid low in hospital ...'

'But he'll be out soon ... they said so ...' Mickey's eyes flew to the carriage clock ticking away amongst Rachel's china ladies.

I headed off the request for a lift to the hospital by asking Rachel if she could introduce Mickey to the new mum across the hall. And in an apparent burst of inspiration suggested she could show her over the vacant flat upstairs. 'It's not been let yet, has it?'

'I don't think so. That estate agent, he comes round the other day. Asked me how we'd feel about having pigs in the back garden. Pigs, I ask you! What sort of klutz keeps pigs in a flat? But for you, darlin', it is perfect.' She patted Mickey's arm. 'Nice little bedroom for a nursery. And any time you want a baby-sitter, you only got to ask.'

'But we can't afford it. They'll want a deposit, and rent in advance. And references ...'

'Pooh ... these things can be sorted out. The owner's a friend. I'll write, tell him you're good people.'

'Figgy won't accept charity.'

'Charity. What is charitable about a loan? The banks, they make them all the time ...'

I'd found a new nest for my cuckoo chick. It was time to leave. I recalled a sudden urgent appointment at the office.

'But the hospital ... you said you'd give me a lift.'

'Don't worry, darlin', I got a car. And maybe we got time for a little baking before we go. Sometimes that hospital food is not so good ...'

'But he'll need his things ... clothes and toothbrush ... it's all at Grace's.'

I promised to meet them at the ward with the plastic sacks – thereby ensuring Mickey had no excuse to come back to the flat.

Since I'd said I was going back to the office, I figured I might as well check in. It meant driving past the police station. The conscience which had been snoozing since last night woke up ... stretched ... and kicked.

Go on ... get in there and tell them the hit-and-run could have been Bridgeman.

'It's too late. He'll have washed the car by now. It was a stupid theory anyway. It was probably just some bunch of drunks in a stolan motor ... Besides, Bridgeman's cheque won't have cleared yet ... and if I don't eat, you don't either.'

I wound the window down and inhaled the sharp aroma of ozone caught in the freshening breeze scudding across the billows. A few drops of wetness – rain or air-blown spray – touched my cheek, and I could see the empty deckchairs whipping and cracking on the sands, indicating a strengthening easterly wind.

It looked like the weather was about to take another somersault. Wednesday's brief bright spell was on the way out. It was lucky for Joan Reiss that it had happened that way round. A howling gale would have been the final disaster in her already memorable garden party.

But then I doubted Joan ever left anything to chance. She struck me as the sort of woman who'd order up sunshine ... the sort of woman who'd dare a raindrop to fall on her carefully planned celebration ... the sort of woman who was currently sitting in the hall of Vetch (International) Inc ...

'This lady wants to see you,' Janice announced needlessly.

I could have guessed that. It was something about the steely glint in the eyes as she rose from her chair and said quietly: 'May I have a word, Miss Smith? In private.'

'My office is upstairs.'

She preceded me up. Once we were out of Janice's hearing I asked how she'd found me.

'It was hardly difficult. Larry Payne asked me what a private investigator was doing snooping around the party. Up until then I wasn't aware that one was; although I had realised it was unlikely that you earned your living as a cleaner. This is the only agency listed in the local yellow pages. Had you not been employed here, I should have tried further afield.'

Her gaze swept the office. It was the only thing that had recently.

'I'm glad to see your dismal efforts aren't confined to paid cleaning.'

'No. I'm just a natural-born slob. And you never did pay me, Mrs Reiss.'

'Then I think we may consider ourselves equal in that department.' She moved a chair opposite the desk and settled herself with an expression that indicated she wouldn't be shifting from that position until she got some answers.

It was a grey-checked trouser suit this morning; all brisk chicness and don't-mess-with-me.

'Now, I should like to know why you are investigating my family.'

I did a quick mental assessment of my options. Telling her to push off wouldn't work. She'd just go on probing and niggling until she found a way into the case. On the other hand, if I told her about the missing files, I'd be dropping Stephen right in it. Henry's original commission seemed my best bet.

'I'm not investigating your family, Mrs Reiss ... I was hired to find a past employee of Wexton's. A woman called Kristen Keats.'

'The test engineer? But she left ... some weeks ago.'

'I know. Trouble is ... she hasn't been seen since that Friday morning.'

A slight frown flitted across Joan's lightly made-up face. 'Hasn't been seen by whom? Who hired you? Her family?'

'A friend of hers was worried. He expected her to be in touch, and when she didn't show ... well, he got a bad feeling about things.'

'I see. Well, whilst I can see that that might, just conceivably, justify you snooping around the company, I still fail to understand what you were doing at my daughter's house.'

Yep, that was a tough one. And I'd have liked some notice so I could have worked on a really creative lie. As it was, I had to fall back on a partial truth.

'I'd heard gossip ... about Mr Bridgeman and Kristen ... hints that there might be something going on. But,' I added hurriedly, 'there seems to be nothing in it.'

'Of course there is nothing in it. Stephen would hardly be foolhardy enough to have an affair under my nose.'

'That's more or less what he said.'

'You've spoken to him?'

'Yes. He was very helpful ... Looks like I'll have to start searching elsewhere.'

'That seems to me to be an excellent idea. Because if you attempt to return to the house again, I shall certainly call the police.'

I was tempted to point out that it wasn't her house, but instead I told her to give my love to Uncle Alfie.

The frostiness thawed slightly. 'Yes, I suppose I should thank you for looking after him.'

'It was a pleasure. He's a nice old boy.'

'Yes. He is. And one of the few people left now who remembers my father.'

'And your sister. He seemed very fond of her.'

'Blanche, yes, everybody loved Blanche.' Her gaze slipped back into the past for a moment and then I saw her give herself a mental shake. 'I'm sorry I didn't have the opportunity to spend more time with Uncle Alfie.'

'I think he appreciated you had your hands full. Did any of the family make it back to the party after the ... er ... problem?'

'No.' She hitched her bag over her shoulder and stood up.

'I've never understood Amelia's obsession with growing old. There is nothing she can do to alter the fact.'

'But a hell of a lot of cosmetic companies would go bankrupt if we didn't keep trying.'

I actually got a small smile from her. Since we were being chummy again, I asked her if Patrick was OK.

'Yes. Thank you. It was a cruel trick of Eleanora's, but I think she's realised that now. Despite appearances, it's because she loves her mother and wants her attention, rather than the opposite. Well, I'll say goodbye, Miss Smith. I don't imagine we'll meet again. I wish you luck in your search and I hope you find Miss Keats safe and well.'

Nobody would ever find Kristen Keats again in this world, but there was no point in confusing matters by bringing in Julie-Frances' name change.

'Thanks.' I opened the door for her. Janice was just coming out of Annie's office.

'Is your phone off the hook? Some woman keeps trying to call you.'

I glanced back at the desk. The receiver was hanging slightly to one side. 'Yes. It is. I don't suppose by any unlikely chance you broke the habit of a lifetime and asked for her name? Or her number?'

'Told her to ring back. And there's no need to be sarky. I take plenty of your stupid messages. Here y'are.' She slapped a stick-it on my blouse. 'That Summerstone bloke left a message on the answerphone. Wants to know if you've found Kristen yet.'

Joan had reached the head of the stairs. I saw her spine go rigid and the knuckles on the hand holding the banister whiten to gleaming ivory.

'Cheers, Jan. Remind me to get you a ticket to the Bermuda Triangle for Christmas.'

'I think,' Joan said, 'we should return to your office, Grace.'

I was no longer Miss Smith. It was gloves-off time. I let her back inside but told her I couldn't possibly discuss clients.

'But I have no doubt Henry Summerstone has discussed *me* with you. And I can imagine the sort of unfeeling monster

I've been portrayed as. So we'll skip over that aspect and you can tell me why Henry wishes to find this young woman.'

'No, I don't think I can … Joan.'

The glare went into thermo-nuclear mode. Joanie was used to getting her own way. She swallowed her ire with very obvious difficulty.

'Look, Grace, I'm not trying to cause trouble for you, but in my experience anything that involves Henry Summerstone invariably ends in grief. The man has – and indeed always has had – only one interest in life … himself.'

'That's a bit strong, isn't it? Coming from someone who ripped off a blinded man lying in a hospital bed?'

'I see. Well, you've obviously had the Summerstone edited highlights of this matter. Are you interested in hearing my side of the story?'

'Sure. Why not? Would you like a coffee?'

She accepted, but I could see she had second thoughts when she saw the state of the mugs.

'No milk, sorry.'

'Black is perfectly acceptable, thank you. Now … Henry.' She sipped and frowned. 'Henry was a very handsome, and very charming, young man. He was also greedy, in debt and lazy. My sister fell in love at first sight and wouldn't be dissuaded from the marriage.'

'Do you think *he* loved *her*?'

Joan considered. 'I think he may have convinced himself he did. But had Blanche's money disappeared before the wedding, I'm quite certain Henry would have found some excuse to call the whole thing off. Frankly, I've always thought that, in reality, the whole attraction was more lust than love. He was keen on sex. With Blanche and anyone else who was available. Blanche simply happened to have the misfortune to be the one with the cash.'

'It doesn't excuse you and your husband ripping him off after the accident, does it?'

'We did not cheat him. The price we offered for Blanche's share of the company was fair. And Henry was more than eager to accept it at the time. He had no interest in running Wexton's. As it was, he got a generous capital settlement and an agreed proportion of Wexton's profit for his lifetime.' She caught the flash of surprise in my eyes and smiled grimly. 'I presume he didn't mention that part of the contract?'

'No. At least, I never asked. I'd just assumed it was a one-off payment.'

'Well, now you know better, Grace. Henry spent a great many years squandering Blanche's inheritance on good living and what used to be referred to as bad women. He has also caused us a fair amount of embarrassment over the years, protesting about discrepancies in his share of the profits. Derek and I took out several injunctions to prevent him causing further nuisance at the factory. After that his efforts became more ... inventive, shall we say. Now since I've been forthcoming with you, perhaps you'd be good enough to tell me why he wishes to find Kristen Keats.'

I couldn't do that. She wasn't paying me, Henry was. And I couldn't afford to make moral judgements about my clients. If I did, I'd starve. The best I could do was assure her that Henry's interest was not connected to Wexton's.

'I see.' Her tone implied she saw a lot more than I'd intended. She stood up to leave once more. 'Well, goodbye again, Grace. Should you have occasion to speak to Henry, please give him my very worst wishes. I'll see myself out.'

I made sure she had before returning to the office. There was the envelope I'd completely forgotten about, tucked under the phone.

Ripping it open, I found a bill for six hours' work and a note from Ruby, plus a photocopy of a news report on Rob Wingett's death.

'*Checked all the dailies,*' Ruby had written. '*This is all I can find. Glad to have the cash by Friday if you can manage it. Cheers.*'

I unfolded the single sheet of paper and scanned it before closing my eyes and – with an effort – putting myself back in the library at the Bridgemans' house. Concentrating hard, I made myself 'see' the phone – and this time I managed to 'see' the number on it too.

Patrick answered.

'Hi, is Bone there?'

'Yes.'

'Can I speak to her?'

'I *suppose* so.'

The silence went on for so long I was beginning to wish I'd broken into Annie's office and used her phone. I was about to ring off when Bone picked up.

'Hi, it's Grace Smith.'

'What do you want? Have you found Tom yet?'

'No. Are you engaged to Brad Pitt yet?'

'Ha bloody ha. What do you want?'

'Have a good time last night ... after you left home?'

'It was OK. Bloke I hitched a lift with wanted to go to the pub.'

'Bloody hell, Bone, you don't half ask for trouble.'

'Butt out. I can take care of myself. So if you just phoned to have a go at me ...'

'No. Listen, remember when you and your friends were talking in Pepi's café? About going round your uncle's place to watch a video? I phoned to ask if your uncle's name is Henry Summerstone.'

'Yes. Why, do you know him?'

Not as well as I'd thought, by the looks of it. 'He'd be a great-uncle then, really?'

'Suppose so. Didn't even know he existed until a couple of years ago. He and Gran had some kind of mega-fight once. She doesn't like me going up there, but I like him. He's cool. Doesn't lecture me like *some* people.'

'OK. I get the message. Be in touch.' I hung up before she could ask why I was interested in her uncle.

I wanted another word with Henry, but I had a few things to do first.

Rooting around the filing cabinets, I unearthed a pocket tape recorder before returning to the flat, loading Mickey and Figgy's bags into the car boot and heading up to the public library. I'd intended to make a couple of quick calls and then get round to the hospital, but the librarian couldn't supply what I was looking for.

I tried the Winstanton branch, but that was shut. Eventually I ended up driving around four branches, and by the time I returned to the hospital it was early evening. Mickey fixed me with reproachful eyes.

'Sorry. Urgent enquiries.' I heaved the bags on to the bed. 'How you feeling, Figgy?'

'I'm doing all right ... according to the docs.'

Propped up against the white pillows in a pale-blue hospital gown and all that black hair framing a face drained of colour, I have to say he didn't look too brilliant. However, the accident did seem to have had one interesting side effect. He'd lost the 'sarf Lundin' accent and acquired a Home Counties public-school one instead.

'Have the police been to see you?'

'Hour ago. I wasn't much help. I didn't see anything. Just felt a jolt and next thing I know I'm waking up in here.'

'You didn't see the car? Or driver?'

'Nope.' He gave me a wan smile and took a firmer grip on Mickey's hand, rubbing his thumb reassuringly over her fingers. 'Thanks for looking after this one for me.'

Looking at him like that, a little knot of excitement unfurled in my stomach. I'd finally made a connection that had been eluding me for the past week. Backing up, I took a look at the folder of case notes at the foot of the bed.

'Look, your Graciness, there's something I have to tell you. About your case ... that missing woman you were looking for ...'

'Save it, Figgy. I have to make a call ...'

CHAPTER 35

'Thanks for ringing.'

'That's OK. I'm great at organising other people's lives. It's only my own I have difficulty with.'

'Well, it's easier when you're standing back from the problem.'

Marina Payne flicked the heavy swath of black hair from her shoulders and applied a lighter to her filter tip. Once again I got that *déjà vu* feeling of having met her somewhere before. Only this time I knew why.

I'd known as soon as I'd seen the name on Figgy's charts: Fergal Iain Glenn Payne.

I'd decided to go back to the flat and telephone Marina on the hitting-two-birds-with-one-stone time-and-motion theory.

However, my other bird had gone to ground. I knew I'd put the Keats file somewhere safe, but by the time I remembered where, retrieved what I wanted, and driven back to the hospital, the big reunion scene had been played out. Marina was one side of the bed looking moist-eyed; Mickey was the other looking apprehensive – and Rachel was cruising the ward with an enormous smile and enough food to withstand a nuclear winter.

Figgy demanded to know who the hell had asked me to interfere. 'Maybe I didn't want my mum to know I was in here.'

'Sure you did, Figgy. Do you know how many miles of coastline there are in the British Isles?'

'No.'

Neither did I, actually. But I figured it ran into thousands. 'But when Mickey wants to come to the seaside, you end up in the next town to your mum. And six times a day you're out on the street making out like a six-foot blackbird on wheels. Unobtrusive or what?'

Marina asked: 'Do you want me to leave, Fergal?'

'No. You might as well stay now you're here.'

'Fine. I'll wallow in the warmth of your welcome in a second, my love. I'm just going to slip outside for a smoke and a quick word with Grace. Don't run off now.'

With a sardonic grin, she'd tapped his broken leg and led the way out to the car-park, which was the nearest place she could light up. Letting go a lungful of smoke, she offered the packet.

'Given up, thanks.'

'So have I. A dozen times.' She thrust it back into her jacket pocket. 'He looks so much older. It's stupid, but whenever I pictured him, it was always as the boy who ran away. And now he's going to be a father himself.'

'I'd have said something sooner. Only today's the first time I've ever seen him without his shades. He's the dead spit of you. I hope you don't mind my wishing Rachel on them as a surrogate granny?'

With a snort of amusement, Marina blew out a quavering smoke ring. 'Do I strike you as the sort to knit baby clothes and go gooey-eyed over a chocolate-smeared kisser? Kisser – listen to me. I used to use proper English once. Comes from marrying my bit of rough.'

The description was used with a tender amusement that told me it wasn't something she regretted. And it gave me the opening I needed. I took out the letter I'd removed from my Keats file.

It was the letter Julie-Frances had written her friend whilst she was on remand. I'd folded it so that the sender's and recipient's names were out of sight.

I gave Marina a brief rundown on my search for the missing 'Kristen' and then held out the sheet, pointing to the paragraph that began: '*If Bill had had any sense he'd have got out and given the silly little twerp an ache to go with his name.*

'I did wonder – ache … Payne?'

Marina scanned the rest of the letter, and laughed. 'Yes, that certainly sounds like my man. I remember Bill Carr. We sold him a second-hand earth-mover … he couldn't pay.'

'Sounds like Larry got pretty steamed up about it. Staking out Dover docks and all that …'

'He wasn't looking for Carr. It was around the time Fergal ran off.'

'Nevertheless … I couldn't help noticing they'd had some building work done at Wexton's recently. Was that you?'

'Renovation. What about it?'

'Well, I just thought … if your husband recognised Carr's ex-girlfriend … and he was still sore about being ripped off …'

Marina shrieked with laughter. 'You think Larry put her in the foundations. For God's sake, this is Seatoun, not downtown Chicago. The insurance paid off the cost of the earth-mover when Carr went bankrupt.'

'But it must have hit your husband's pride … being ripped off like that. I hear he's not a man to take a boot in the mouth lying down.'

'Well, unless he's being attacked by a kick-boxer, that's the position he's most likely to be in, isn't it? Look ...' She crushed her cigarette into the tarmac and took my arm, moving me along with her. 'Have you ever heard the story of the crack shot?'

'I think that one got past me.'

'He used to fire into chalk circles. All his shots were smack in the centre of the target. And it didn't matter how big the circle was ... two feet or two inches ... he got a bull's-eye. One day they asked him how he did it. So he showed them. He fired at the wall first ... *then* he drew the circle round the hole afterwards.'

'You trying to tell me your husband waits for a piece of nastiness to happen, then claims the credit?'

'Not always. But quite often. Especially nowadays. I'll not deny he was a bit of a wild lad when he was younger; that was probably the attraction – made him seem so much more desirable than the rest of the pack. But these days it's more in the mind and the threat than the actual doing.'

'He sent someone round to sort out Tom Skerries when he found out about him poaching customers and nicking your stock.'

'True. But I don't think their orders included doing a Paul Daniels on him. He was supposed to get a fright – not disappear. Although he seems to have managed the latter trick quite efficiently on his own.'

I wasn't entirely convinced her husband was the toothless tiger she'd like me to believe. But there wasn't much I could do about it now. And talking about Skerries reminded me she'd claimed to have some information on him last night.

'I looked for you at the party again, but you'd done your own disappearing trick.'

'Trying to persuade Amelia to forget that stupid picture and come down. I don't know why I bothered really. She always was capable of some pretty spectacular sulks when she set her mind to it. When I got I tired of talking to a locked door I helped myself to a couple of bottles of champagne and got Larry to drive me home. We had a private party in our own garden. Which reminds me ... I'd better get this flat sorted out for the happy couple before they discharge Fergal.

There's nothing like an adult child in the next room to inhibit all that swinging from the chandeliers.'

'Skerries,' I reminded her.

'Oh yes ... Tom. I had a weird fax from the Munich police the other day.'

It was about the last thing I'd expected.

'They – the police – had just had to deal with an abandoned van. It had lost its number plates ... vandalised, I guess ... but it was left-hand drive and they found a half-used pallet of tiles in the back, with an advice note addressed to us. They wondered if it was one of ours. I think they wanted to sting us with the bill for towing away. I denied all knowledge, naturally. But it sounded to me like Tom's van.'

'How the hell did it get to Germany?'

'Ferry. Shuttle. Autobahns. Take your pick. Anyway, I must get back and give Larry the good news.'

'Will he take Figgy – I mean Fergal – into the business, d'you reckon?'

'He may not want to be taken. There's still the skating.'

'He's broken his leg.'

'It'll mend.'

'Might leave a permanent weakness. In fact, I'd almost bet on it.'

'Why?' Marina's motherly instincts were finally placed on red alert. 'Have the doctors said something?'

'No. But he couldn't land a job with *Starlight Express*. And he came home, didn't he?'

She got the point immediately. 'And now we've all got a face-saving reason for the end of his bid to skate. That's sad.'

'But handy.'

'Very. Because, believe it or not, he's actually quite a talented builder.'

'I have to go myself. Give the happy couple my best.'

I'd got as far as the hospital gates when I spotted Mickey in my rear-view mirror. Either she'd popped out to do a quick aerobic work-out in the car-park, or she was trying to attract my attention. I circled around.

'We thought you were coming back,' she gasped, leaning down to my open window. 'Figgy wants to see you. He said it was important.'

We had to scour the parking lot and bins to find a discarded ticket that hadn't expired yet. Marina had left by the time I got back to the ward and Rachel had popped upstairs to see her friend Ada in Women's Medical.

'You've got ten minutes, Figgy,' I told him. 'After that it's a thirty-quid fine for the car-park ... and you pay it.'

'It will only take a couple of seconds.'

'Nice accent. Did the bang on the head scramble the vocal cords?'

Figgy grinned. He really was a dead ringer for his mum. 'Got ter speak like the natives, ain't yer?' he mocked, returning to his 'sarf Lundin' dialect. 'Otherwise they reckon you to be a plum. Didn' wanna get duffed up, did I?'

'Not when you can come home and do it.'

'Yes. Well, at least that wasn't personal.'

'Wasn't it?'

'How do you mean?'

'Are you quite certain the driver wasn't out to get you?'

'Course they weren't. It was just another spacehead with stolen wheels. They boast about it in the arcades. Compare notes on who's managed to steal the motor with the most poke. Who'd want to run me over? Apart from my dad ... and Mum assures me he was home, so he's got an alibi. Now can you shut up and let me say what I've got to say.'

'Fire away.'

'First off ... thanks for looking out for Mickey.'

'You're welcome.'

'Secondly, I'm sorry about taking your fat mate's flat ...'

'You're definitely not welcome ... past or present ... and lay off the "fat".'

'Cholesterolly challenged, then. Anyhow, I had to get Mickey in somewhere decent ... she couldn't have stood that hut much longer. But I'll pay your mate some rent, soon as I get sorted out.'

'No! Absolutely not. Don't speak, phone or write Annie. Make like you've never set foot in that building ... understand?'

'Whatever you say, your Graciousness.'

'Great. Now if you've finished grovelling ...'

'I haven't. Park yourself again. This is the important bit

coming up ... important for you anyway. You know the first time we met, when you were asking about the blind wrinkly with the dog, and the babe girlfriend. Well, I lied when I said I'd seen her coming out of that block of flats. I've never seen her.'

He gave a convulsive swallow, and told me the whole story.

CHAPTER 36

I drove back to Henry's house too fast.

I knew I was going too fast when I saw the blue lights in my rear mirror and the flashing headlamps two inches from my bumper.

In theory Terry should have stayed with the car whilst his partner did the patter. But Rosco wasn't going to let an opportunity like this get away.

He kept it formal; not a flicker that he'd recognised my registration number and that it was on an unofficial black-list run by those officers who thought I'd got off lightly when I'd been allowed to resign from the force rather than face a disciplinary hearing.

'Do you know what speed you were doing along the front?'

'No. I never look at the speedometer. Don't you know?'

Terry flexed his shoulders and tossed the keys he'd already taken from my ignition. 'Will you step out of the car, please, madam.'

We'd already collected a small audience prepared for the early-evening entertainment. A circle of jaws chomped steadily on burgers, chips and chicken dippers as they enjoyed my virtuoso performance on the breathalyser and Rosco's award-winning tyre-prodding and tax-checking routine.

We'd just about gone through the entire performance when a Porsche drew into the kerb behind us and the estate agent I least wanted to see sprang out.

'Hi. Pigs!'

It wasn't the brightest thing to say to a couple of coppers.

Especially this particular couple. You could see the sinews bulging and knotting in Terry's neck as he descended on Jason.

The spectators were with Jason, urging him on with whistles and catcalls. It took the poor bloke a while to realise what he'd done. Long enough for me to spot Janice in his front passenger seat.

I wandered over and leant inside. 'Thought you weren't going out with him?'

'He said he'd let an apartment to a record producer. I thought it was worth a shot.' She wrinkled her nose at the threesome now having a row over my car. 'He's a real little shit, isn't he?'

'We didn't really get that well acquainted ... but speaking of shits, you remember the day Henry Summerstone first turned up at the offices?'

'What about it?'

'How come I got him? Why didn't you pass him over to Vetch ... or one of the others?'

She told me. It wasn't too flattering.

Jason's tantrum was now in full spate. 'Of course I'm old enough to drive. Listen, you moron, my father knows the Chief Constable ...'

'Finished with me, Terry?' I asked.

He barely glanced at me as he flicked my keys back and told me to watch my speed in future.

Jason was a trier, I'll give him that. Even as they were thrusting him in the back of the patrol car, he resisted long enough to shout, 'I've found a flat. Pigs welcome. No problemo.'

'No porkers,' I yelled back, restarting my ignition. 'Gone to the great sty in the sky. Cheers, Jason.'

I managed to find a public phone that was working and tracked down Nola at the social club. She filled me in on the background behind her earlier remark that security at Wexton's had been tightened up a couple of years ago after a break-in, before I headed back along St John's Road.

Henry answered the door with Beano in his usual tail-wagging mode tagging along behind. I didn't waste time on social chit-chat.

'Coming through, Henry.' Barging past, I headed straight for the lounge.

Henry followed me in. The green glasses were twisting this way and that trying to locate me. 'Grace? What are you doing?'

'Checking out your tape collection, Henry.' I was on my knees by the cabinet, shuffling plastic cases. 'Assuming this system is alphabetical, I guess *Little Dorrit* will be between *Hard Times* and *Martin Chuzzlewit*.'

'I wasn't aware that you read braille?'

'Public libraries are wonderful institutions. You'd be amazed what you can pick up. In my case ... a braille dictionary. Bear with me, I don't suppose I can do this stuff at anything like your speed.'

He stood listening to me fingering my way down the shelf for a while longer, then said abruptly: 'Second row, sixth tape.'

'Thanks.' I slammed shut *Decline and Fall of the Roman Empire*. When the library hadn't been able to come up with a braille dictionary I'd just taken out the heaviest book I could see ... after all, Henry couldn't.

Taking a seat, I waited for him to do the same.

He sat opposite me, pulling the dog closer and trapping him between his knees as he stroked the silky head.

'I'm sorry, m'dear. I should have told you the truth ... but one of the hardest things to take at my age is ridicule. To know that people are laughing ... not even behind your back, but to your face ... and you can't see them. I was afraid if I admitted to the real situation, you'd be disgusted. So I invented that story about Kristen taking the tapes. I couldn't admit to knowing too much about her appearance, or indeed her address ... I thought it would look strange.'

'Whereas the real situation is ...?'

'We had a brief relationship.' He held up a hand to check a laugh I hadn't uttered. 'I know how unlikely that sounds. And believe me, I was as surprised as you undoubtedly are ... After so many years, to experience such intense joy again ... it was beautiful, and very precious to me. Then she left ... with no word. I wasn't sure what to do. Perhaps it hadn't meant anything at all to her. Perhaps it was just a laugh ... a joke on her part. Or maybe she'd thought that a clean break was kindest ... I had no way of knowing. In the end I came up with that missing tapes story. It seemed a face-saving way of making contact with her, with no embarrassment on either side. If something *had* happened to her, I might have been in a position to assist. And if she'd simply decided she didn't want anything more to do with me ... at least I should have peace of mind. Now that we know about her past ... well, perhaps the disappearance wasn't as out of character as I'd thought. I wish she'd confided in me, I might have been able to help.'

'Bollocks, Henry.'

I dug into my file and extracted a sheet of paper. 'This is a photocopy of the report on Rob Wingett's accident.'

'Who?'

'Give it a rest, Henry. OK, as reported by the local *Herald*: *A motor-cycle accident last Friday resulted in the death of the driver. Rob Wingett, (thirty-six), lived locally and had been employed as a test engineer at Wexton's Engineering in Seatoun for the past ten years. A police spokesman said no other vehicles were involved.*

'That's it. The only press report of that accident. Yet according to Kristen's file at Wexton's she applied for that job after reading about Rob's death. Now I know times are tough, but it's hard to swallow her sitting in London scanning every local rag in the country in the hope that someone will have dropped dead in a job she fancies. You put her up to it.'

'Why me? It could have been anyone. Stephen Bridgeman, for example. That story about her stealing files always sounded a little bizarre to me. Perhaps there was a previous relationship.'

'No relationship. But even if there had been ... Stephen didn't pay Figgy to set me on the right track.'

'Who?'

'The roller-skating squatter you paid to take me to Kristen's flat.'

Figgy had confessed from the hospital bed: 'The blind man

... I spoke to him a few times ... early mornings, when we were in the hut. Mickey never knew ... she always slept in later than me. Anyway, a couple days before you came along, he told me someone would be round asking questions about a woman. Told me what she looked like ... and then he gave me fifty pounds to describe her to whoever turned up and point out that flat to them.' Leaning back, he'd closed his eyes and smiled weakly. 'Sorry, your Graciness, but a guy's gotta do what a guy's gotta do.'

Henry asked why he'd bother with such an elaborate charade. 'Why not just tell you myself and instruct you to find her?'

'Yeah, I wondered about that myself. And then I found out why you'd employed *me* in particular.'

'He asked me who worked cheapest,' Janice had said off-handedly.

'Cheapest, in this case, Henry, meaning *not-so-hot*.'

'In *most* cases, m'dear. Do you have a point?'

'You wanted someone who'd be bright enough to track down Kristen for you ... but preferably not smart enough to work out it was you sent her into Wexton's in the first place. After all, you ended up in the dock last time you tried a similar trick.'

Nola had explained, over a barrage of American baseball commentary from the club television, that someone had broken into Wexton's a couple of years ago and been caught escaping with assorted accounts files. He'd been given a two-year suspended sentence. And so had the bloke who'd paid him to do it. She couldn't remember the names.

'It was you, wasn't it, Henry? Where'd you get the burglar from? The One-Stop-Drug-Shop next door? You're still on that suspended sentence. If it had come out you'd tried a similar trick again, you could have found yourself inside serving the rest of your time. This way you get to keep your distance and plead ignorance if it comes out you're the one who hired me. I can even swear you didn't realise Kristen was working at Wexton's, can't I? The way I imagine it is, you picked her up in a bar or club somewhere. She's out on parole, living in a dump, short of cash. And she's not adverse to a little amateur prostitution if she needs a bit of spending cash.'

'What makes you think I pick up young women in bars?'

I moved across to sit next to him. Whipping out my pocket tape recorder, I switched it on.

I can't click my fingers. But the two finger clicks I'd persuaded the helpful librarian to record rang out. Beano whined, twisted free of his master's grip, padded across to me and thrust his nose into my crotch.

'Neat trick, Henry. How long did it take you to teach him that one?'

'I'm sorry, m'dear. Don't quite follow.'

'Oh, come on.' I rewound and clicked again. Beano nuzzled with more enthusiasm. 'Aren't you going to rescue me from your dog's embarrassing attentions? And have a quick feel whilst you're in there? One of Bone's friends reckoned you were a groper. The shy one, of course. The one who wouldn't make too much fuss. You wouldn't have tried it on with the others, would you? They'd have given you a quick knee-castration job. And you needed Bone to get all the hot gossip from Wexton's.'

'So I enjoy contact with the opposite sex. The loss of one physical sense doesn't eliminate the need for others, you know.'

'OK, so you ... or Beano ... make contact with Kristen. Was she Julie-Frances Keble or Kristen Keats by then?'

'Julie,' he said grudgingly. 'I never knew her real surname, believe it or not, until you told me in that café the other day. And I did not pick her up in some sleazy club as you fondly imagine. I met her on a park bench. She was extremely unhappy. She'd found a technical clerking job that was way below her capabilities but a criminal record rather limited her options.'

'She told you about that?'

'People tell you all sorts of things if you're blind. You'd be surprised. Apparently there had been some talk about her completing her degree, but she – in the bizarre parlance of today – "couldn't get her head round it". She spoke about getting out ... wanted to live abroad. Make a fresh start. She was complaining about the number of countries not prepared

293

to let someone with a drug conviction in. I made some joke about her getting a fake passport and she said she wouldn't have to, she knew where she could lay hands on a real one. Then she told me about her friend Kristen.'

'And you suggested a little industrial espionage.'

'Wexton's were holding out on me. They're supposed to pay me a fixed share of the profits. Yet the amount has been decreasing for years. Hard times, they said. Reduced share of the market. Everyone taking a cut. Poppycock, sheer bloody poppycock. Young Bone was full of it last summer: Bridgeman was going to buy her a show-jumper; take the family on some expensive jaunt abroad; move to a bigger house. The only person taking a cut in that little set-up was me.'

He was nearly spluttering with rage. I guess, from his point of view, it could have looked like that. After all, he didn't have the privilege of knowing Bridgeman's plans to rip off his own designs. However, I would have thought an accountant would have set him straight on the legitimate profits.

'I tried that. Waste of time. They pulled the wool over his eyes. Charged me a fortune to tell me I wasn't being robbed, when I knew damn well I was. I can't live on the pittance Joan and Bridgeman see fit to dole out to me ... and I won't.'

'So you hired Julie to become Kristen Keats.'

'In a manner of speaking. When she told me about this Kristen and her engineering background, I realised she could be my chance. She was still hesitant about using her friend's documents. She had images of ending up in a foreign jail. After two years in a British one, it wasn't an enticing prospect. So I suggested a dress rehearsal. Live as Kristen for a few months, see if she could pull it off.'

'And do a little spying on the side.'

'Why not? She was merely collecting information that I was entitled to. And with the promise of substantial commission from whatever additional profits I should obtain as a result of her activities.'

'And did she? Collect it, I mean.'

'She said she thought she was on to something. Some anomaly at the company. Naturally she had to move slowly, in order not to alert them to her suspicions. That's why I'm concerned about her disappearance. I never went to her home, nor she mine. It would have ruined everything if someone from Wexton's had spotted us. I am ...' he touched his glasses, 'a somewhat distinctive figure. Hence the early-morning meetings on the promenade. Just a chance encounter, no more than a few words exchanged if anyone should happen to be watching. When she failed to show up I knew something was badly wrong. In the end I risked contacting Wexton's ... anonymously, of course. They said she'd left. Well, I didn't believe that for a start. And then when the estate agent said the flat had been re-let ...'

Terrific ... I'd spent most of this investigation duplicating Henry's moves. Oh, the joys of having a paranoid pensioner for a client.

'I'm an old man, m'dear. And blind. It would be easy to devise a plausible accident if anyone should wish to dispose of me. I arranged for you to receive sufficient clues to identify Kristen quickly, but I couldn't risk you letting on to Joan or Bridgeman that I was connected to her. You see, I believe Kristen found out something significant. She had no plans to leave Seatoun. They made her disappear. It would be simple enough to fake her notice; that secretary of Bridgeman's has been lusting after him for years, according to Bone. She wouldn't have objected to fiddling the paperwork on Kristen's personnel file. And they could have sent back her flat keys themselves.'

It wasn't a bad theory if, like old Henry, you didn't know about her joining up with Stephen Bridgeman's bit of private enterprise.

I do admire a girl who can seize her opportunities. She'd strung Henry and his 'substantial bonus' along as a fall-back if nothing came of Stephen's scheme, and in the mean time, she'd put the squeeze on Bridgeman.

It must be catching. Henry tried to put the squeeze on my leg as he asked me if I intended to go on searching for Kristen/Julie now I knew the truth?

'Of course I do, Henry. After all, that's what I've been paid for. Besides, I hate to abandon a case midway.'

'I'm very grateful, m'dear. And don't worry, I shall see you don't lose by this.'

He squeezed again. I intertwined my fingers with his. Very

firmly I applied sufficient pressure to make him gasp with pain and try to release my grip. I kept it tight as I said firmly: 'If you ever try to touch me up again, Henry, I'll knock whatever teeth you still have left so far down your throat they'll collide with your bunions.' I let go and stood up. 'I'll see myself out.'

I took a detour up to the Downs Estate to bring Tom Skerries' nearest, if not exactly dearest, up to date on his progress.

They'd set up a barbecue on the patch of concrete outside the social club under a hand-printed notice announcing 'Beer 'n' Barbie Tonite'. Someone had run an extension lead out of the front door and the hard core of regulars were grouped round a portable TV watching cricket whilst they drank.

Nola was balancing the scooter against one hip and licking the mustard from a hot dog. She took the news about Tom's van with total indifference. 'Told yer, didn't I? Useless bugger's pushed off.'

'But why Germany?'

Nola didn't know. And she plainly didn't care either. 'He was always on about going abroad ... well, Germany's abroad, innit?'

'Last time I looked it certainly was. Nola ...'

'Yeah?'

'Kristen.'

'What about her? You found her yet?'

'Not exactly. Is there any chance Tom could have known her?'

'Tom? No. Don't think so. Mind, he'd like to have done. All that flashing leg in a mini-skirt. Just his style. Why'd you want to know?'

'They both seem to have left the area at the same time. And Larry Payne's company did some work up at Wexton's. I thought they might have got together.'

And of course there was the woman hiding her face in Tom's van the morning they'd both disappeared. But there was no reason to tell Nola that. As it was, she was openly derisive of the idea that Kristen might have had anything to do with her brother-in-law.

'She's got a degree, ain't she? Oi, Donna ...' Two fingers

inserted in her mouth and a lungful of air produced a shrill whistle and a spray of partly chewed sausage. 'Sod it.'

She was still mopping down her T-shirt when her sister appeared from the club, carrying the baby and flanked by her two little boys.

Pierce and Liam beamed on spotting me.

'Forget it, kids, I'm broke.'

'She reckons Tom's gone to Germany,' Nola announced. 'Not got any mates there, 'as he?'

'Dunno.' Donna jiggled the baby on her hip and reinserted a dummy. 'Might have. They got sea in Germany?'

'Gallons of the stuff; is that relevant?'

'Maybe he's gone to sort out his bar. Never thought he said Germany, though. Thought he fancied Majorca or Greece.'

Nola slapped on her scooter helmet and advised her sister to get real. 'Only bar that waster's ever gonna own is cut-price toilet soap. Where's he going to get enough cash together to buy a business? Just as well, too. I know how it would have been. He'd have been flexing his pecs at every sex-starved bimbo in the place while you did all the work. You're better off without him, Donna ... you can do better. I gotta get up Wexton's.' She twisted the ignition on, kicked up the rests and roared off.

Donna smiled doubtfully at me and diffidently asked if I wanted to come in.

'No ... thanks. I'd best be getting back.'

To what exactly? I asked myself. Nothing, to be truthful. But I didn't fancy an evening with Donna Skerries. In company she was OK, but on her own that veneer of baby sick and dull acceptance that anything the world slung at her was fine by her could really get on my nerves.

It just goes to show how important it is to pick the right bloke, I told myself, motoring back to the flat. Better none at all than the wrong one. Well, that was my excuse anyway for spending an evening curled up with a warm tandoori and a fuzzy television.

I'd just levered the cardboard covers off the tinfoil containers and readjusted the horizontal control with a couple of hefty slaps when the telephone rang.

'Yes?'

'I thought I was never going to raise you. Is it too late to save my brother's life?'

My initial thought was that one of the local loony-tunes had dialled at random. Followed by the even more worrying thought – one of them *hadn't* dialled at random. Then the light dawned.

'Miss Tally Smith, I presume?'

'You presume right. I hear I have to give you this flight information or you're going to throw Zeb to the she-wolf. I've been trying to reach you at your office all day.'

'Sorry. I've been out. I didn't think you'd get back so soon. Are passenger details that easy to get hold of?'

'If you've got a computer analyst with the hots for you on tap.'

'Terrific. Hang on ...' I dragged a pencil out of the muddle on the table and spread the takeaway bag flat. 'Shoot ...'

'No chance. I want the story on Zeb first.'

'Are we talking all major airports here?'

'And most regional ones; there's just a couple of private ones he couldn't access in the time.'

I made her promise not to tell Annie and gave her the rundown on the squatters.

She exploded with laughter at the other end. 'What a prat! OK, your two female passengers ... there's no record of either a Kristen Keats or a Julie-Frances Keble travelling over the designated period ... viz. Friday May the first to Monday May the fourth. There was a reservation in the name of Kristen Keats on the Friday flight to Manila, but she was a no-show. Dag ... my bloke ... came up with three other Keats, but two are male and the other was airline staff. So I guess she's not the one you're interested in. There were no Kebles at all.'

'Fine, thanks.' I scribbled 'zilch' on my bag. It wasn't definitive, of course. She could just as easily have got on a ferry or hopped on the Eurostar – assuming she'd left the country at all.

'Now as far as Bridgeman goes – that's more common than you'd think ... twelve travelled over that period. An initial would have helped.'

'S for Stephen. Didn't Zeb tell you?'

'No. I just got the surname. He was babbling a bit at the time; it's your own fault for intimidating him so effectively.'

'OK … give me the list.'

'Can't. I got fed up waiting to catch you, so I put the printout in the post a couple of hours ago. I remembered the details about the women, but as for the rest … you'll have to wait until the postman shows. And please … you absolutely didn't get any of this from me …

'I can't even recall your name. Incidentally, is Tally short for something?'

'Tallahassee.'

'Hard luck.'

'It's better than my twin. At least I don't have to put up with endless innuendoes about hot cats and tin roofs.'

'Tennessee, right?'

'Yaw'll betta believe it, honeychild.'

CHAPTER 37

Figgy was giving a show that Nureyev would have been hard pushed to top. Spinning, wheeling, leaping and pirouetting, he flew over the pavements outside the amusement park. The neon lights reflected like a multicoloured petrol sheen in his shades.

The crowd were laughing and applauding; all except me. I could see the car. Huge and dark, with headlights like malevolent eyes, it was bearing down on Figgy. I wanted to scream at him to get out of the way, but all I could do was applaud and shout: 'Fabulous, darling.'

I heard his bones shattering and splintering as he hit the pavement. Blood gushed from his mouth and ears. His glasses fell off and he looked directly at me – once. Then the lights went out.

The same scenario played itself out, again and again. It was like being trapped in a snuff video that had got stuck in a permanent loop. I woke up drenched in sweat, my mouth too dry to swallow and the taste of salty tears I hadn't known I'd cried drying on my cheeks.

I made black tea, then sat cross-legged on my bed sipping and deciding on my next move.

Not that I really needed to think about it; deep down I knew I was going to investigate Stephen Bridgeman's movements after he left the party on the night of Figgy's accident.

If Figgy had been nearly killed because I'd told Bridgeman he knew something about Kristen's disappearance, then I had two options. One: I go to the police and tell them everything that had happened to date. Or two: I dig around myself – and either clear Bridgeman or land him right in it.

If I chose option one, there was a ninety-nine per cent certainty Bridgeman would demand his money back. Option two reduced the odds to fifty per cent (if I found out he *was* guilty).

I tidied the flat first; and then brought the Kristen Keats file up to date; bashing out notes on my ancient portable and typing up an account for Stephen.

A quick bath, hairwash and a liberal dose of slap over the bruises and I was ready to face the world. I grabbed the file, intending to take it to the office. It promptly collapsed, showering papers over the floor.

'Sod it.' I junked the lot together, looked round for a carrier to put them in, couldn't find one and ended up just thrusting the account in my pocket. The rest could wait.

I dropped into the office to change into my best suit; it's a grey-striped four-piece: jacket and waistcoat plus trousers for cold days, short skirt for hot. With my plain black court shoes and dark glasses in position, I looked pretty stylish in my opinion.

More to the point, I looked nothing like Shona, scourge of the tax office. Even if I was working for their boss now, I still preferred to avoid difficult questions from Bridgeman's staff if possible. There was always the chance one of them might have a civic conscience and report my little performance to the tax inspectors.

'You going to a funeral or a job interview?' Janice asked when I sauntered downstairs and helped myself to some of the 'shared office facilities' (viz. an envelope for Bridgeman's account).

'Neither. This is what the sophisticated young business-woman is wearing this year. As opposed to a recycled three-piece from World of Leather.'

Janice flexed and stretched in the black leather catsuit. 'I'm breaking it in for the weekend.'

'I hope you're not going out with Jason in that get-up. He's not old enough for anything kinky.'

'No chance. I blew him out after they arrested him. They sent this dishy officer back to drive his car and he's taking me to a club in London tomorrow. His mate works security there, reckons he can get us in the VIP lounge. All the big stars use it. I'll be able to network. What you got fixed up for the weekend?'

There was no way I was admitting I was the sort of sad person who hit the supermarket on Saturday evenings to buy a single-portion microwave meal and a can of lager and spent Sundays wishing that Monday would arrive sooner rather than later. 'Party, party ... you know how it goes. They're a wild lot. Could wake up in Samarkand come Monday.'

'Where's that?'

'Er ... China, I think. Somewhere out East anyway.'

'Like your pigs come from?'

'Sort of. But they've gone to that big sty in the sky now.'

'You said. Last night. Accident, was it? Our dogs are always getting run over.'

Had she twigged that those damn porkers were a joke and decided to play along, or was she really as dumb as she appeared?

'Times are hard, Jan. Did you know a peasant family could live on a whole pig all winter?'

'You didn't!'

'Chops, bacon, sausages ... Don't worry, they've gone to a good home.' I slapped my stomach and grinned.

'You rotten murderess. Here. There's a letter come for you.' She spun the envelope out, letting it whirl across the hall like a maple seed.

I picked it up from the mat as I went out. It was the computer printout from Tally, listing the Keats/Keble flight position she'd outlined on the phone last night and the dozen or so Bridgemans she couldn't remember.

I took a quick scan as I wriggled into the car. They were listed alphabetically rather than in date order. A. Bridgeman (Mrs) was right up there at the top with her Los Angeles flight on Friday, but after that came a C.B. Bridgeman who'd caught the Glasgow/Heathrow shuttle on Sunday, followed by C.M. who'd boarded a flight at Gatwick bound for Amsterdam on Saturday.

S. Bridgeman leapt straight off the green-striped page and hit me in the eyes; leaving me excitedly skimming over the information that it was the flight Julie-Frances had been booked to take: Heathrow/Manila, 1 May. Then my mind caught up and brought the 'N/S' at the end of the line to the bouncing eyeballs' attention. No show. He simply hadn't got round to cancelling his seat.

The receptionist at Wexton's was terribly sorry but I couldn't see Mr Bridgeman because he wasn't *in*. 'He's not expected at all, I'm afraid. Do you have an appointment?'

'No. I just popped in on the off-chance to leave this.'

I waved the account envelope. She extended a hand.

'Sorry. I need to deliver it personally. Is he at home?'

'Oh, I couldn't supply his *personal* address, I'm afraid.'

'No need. I was there the other night, Amelia's birthday bash.' I event-dropped shamelessly just to let her know she wasn't dealing with just *anybody*. 'I'll catch him later. Thanks.'

It was the first time I'd seen the factory in full working mode. Wandering back to my motor, I caught glimpses of production workers in the sort of capped and gowned outfits I usually associated with the deli counter at the supermarket. They were hunched forward over those benches I'd seen the other day, little frowns of concentration on their faces as they fitted components on boards like a load of meaningless jigsaws.

I was suddenly very glad I was self-employed; even if it meant I was often self-*un*employed. Small grey clouds were billowing in across the North Sea as I turned the car and headed for the Bridgeman house. Way out on the horizon a herd of white horses were being chased by the strengthening wind. Occasionally one crashed into a floating buoy, sending a burst of spray up and over the bobbing bell cage. It wasn't exotic; it wasn't even pretty; but it beat being locked in some factory for nine or ten hours a day, five days a week.

I parked beyond the gates to Bridgeman's house rather than driving up to the door. I had some idea that I might be able to slip in unnoticed and take a look at the blue Merc before I tackled Stephen.

The garage doors were going to be the biggest problem. Not only were they electronically controlled but they were visible from most rooms in the front of the house. My best hope was that the cars had been left outside on the drive.

They hadn't, but as a consolation prize the garage was wide open and both Mercedes were inside.

There were no convenient smashed headlights or dented paintwork on the blue one. Not that I'd really expected there to be. If there had, no doubt the car would have been safely deposited in a body workshop somewhere out of the district by now.

There was a shelf above my head with the usual assortment of junk that always seems to end up in garages – including a flashlight.

I played the beam over the tyres. Something glinted within the treads. Gently probing and teasing, I extracted a sliver of yellow plastic. It had been held by a speck of mud within the incised pattern, and the fact that the tyres were nearly brand new and unworn was probably what had prevented it from being crushed further.

There weren't any other fragments of roller-blade that could be seen with the naked eye, but no doubt forensic could find a few – if they tried. It wasn't definitive – he could always claim he'd picked it up in the road – but every little helped.

The house was still quiet. I hadn't decided on my approach to Stephen, but given that I now had some hard evidence that he'd tried to kill Figgy and could have been behind Julie-Frances-Kristen's disappearance, back-up seemed a good idea. Normally I'd have filled Annie in on the situation, but in her absence it would have to be Vetch the Letch. I'd have to find a phone and let him know where I was before I tackled Bridgeman.

'Hi, Grace!'

I jumped and spun round. Amelia had come round the side of the house and was waving as she jogged down the drive.

'Sorry, were you ringing? I was in the pool house. I was going to have a sauna, it's just fabulous for cleaning out the pores. Is this one of your days? I'm so dippy when it comes to remembering rotas and things. Didn't Mummy give you a key?'

She stopped a foot away from me; a happy bundle of good spirits, white teeth and tossed blonde curls. It was as if the toe-curling tantrum of the birthday night had never happened.

'Do you want to get started right away or have you got time for a coffee?'

Plainly Mummy hadn't told her she'd sacked the home help.

'Coffee would be great. Thanks.'

'Terrific.' She flashed that expensive dentistry and giggled, linking arms as she guided me down the side path. 'Let's have it on the terrace. Shan't be a mo.'

She abandoned me on the patio and tripped back through the french windows with a wriggle of that enviably small butt.

The remains of the other night had already been cleared away by the caterers, but the garden still had a slightly bedraggled and trodden-down air.

If Stephen turned up now I'd have to find some way of getting him alone, but at least I had the consolation of knowing he was unlikely to strangle me whilst Amelia was skipping around the place. Even she might manage to come out from under the self-obsession and hair long enough to notice hubby burying a body under the patio.

Patio? I looked down at the neatly jointed stones beneath my feet. They appeared new. In fact, you could see where a fresh section had been re-let into the stone balustrade.

I used the phone in the study to call Swayling's. Thankfully

Marina Payne answered. Cutting through the niceties, I asked her straight out when her husband had worked on the Bridgemans' patio.

'Just after the last Bank holiday. Why?'

'I'll explain when I see you. Do you know what was wrong with it?'

'The surface was relaid badly. Larry put a new lot down. He had a wonderful time. It's not often he gets to play mud pies himself these days.'

'Thanks. Love to Figgy and Mickey. Bye.'

Amelia hadn't reappeared yet. I settled myself into a chair and crossed my ankles on the coping. Those nice new tiles under my seat had gone down a few days after Julie-Frances/ Kristen had last been seen being given a lift from her flat to this house.

Oddly enough, Marina's assurances that her 'bit of rough' didn't play dirty any more must have made a greater impression than I'd realised. I didn't for a second suspect Larry of helping with the burial. But what if the body was already several feet down? There was no reason for him to dig; he'd have packed the soil down, wouldn't he, to make a firm base?

Amelia wiggled back holding a tray containing two long glass tumblers containing dark-red liquid. 'Sorry this is taking so long. I brought this new coffee brewing thingy back from the States and it doesn't seem to work. I thought we'd finish up the wine whilst we waited for the silly thing to heat up. You don't mind the wrong glasses, do you? It's the really good stuff ... at least Stephen says it is ... To tell you the truth, I can't tell the difference myself. But I don't like to confess ... he's so proud of his collection. Well, cheers ...'

She touched her glass to the rim of mine and sipped, using the top of her forefinger to wipe away the wetness from under her bottom lip. We were back with the frosted look today, together with the jeans and silk top. But the silver Navaho jewellery had been replaced by gold bangles and huge hooped earrings.

'Great party,' I said. 'Pity you missed most of it.'

'Oh, that.' She drew up her legs, crossing bare feet on the

chair. 'Mummy's furious with me, of course. Never mind that I didn't want the party in the first place. Do you think you ever reach an age where parents think you're old enough to make your own decisions?'

'I doubt it. Especially if you're not admitting to reaching it.'

I took a swig of the wine. It tasted off to me. But perhaps that was what expensive plonk was supposed to taste like. If you've been hanging around for a hundred years or so, I guess you're entitled to be a bit ripe.

'I hate getting old,' Amelia said abruptly. 'I thought I wouldn't. At least, I mean ... I thought it wouldn't show.' She examined a lightly tanned arm, twisting it to let the sun play over the skin. 'Everything seemed to be OK for a long time. Then it all started going wrong: horrid brown age spots and lines and things. It's not fair the way it happens just at the time when you can't have babies any more. If you're not pretty and you can't give him children, why shouldn't a man go looking elsewhere?'

'Same reason you're supposed to stick to the forsaking-all-others lark when he gets a beer belly and looses all his hair, I guess.'

I was interested to see that Bone's contemptuous analysis of her mother's maternal instincts wasn't based on pure bitchiness. There had plainly been some truth behind her assertion that Amelia had had children to keep Stephen firmly chained to the marital home. It was a risky strategy, I'd have thought; but no doubt after thirty-odd years, Amelia knew her own man best.

'It doesn't work like that, though, does it?' she pouted. 'We girls are brought up to stand by our man. But men ... well, nature wants them to put it about, doesn't it? Scatter a bit of seed around ... keep the human race going. That's how Charlotte got her man.'

'Char ... oh, the California girl.'

'Stepmother of those three ghastly lumps of overweight flesh. She went out to LA as a mother's help ... and helped herself to the husband. I blame his first wife. The silly cow should have taken one look at Char and put her straight back on the plane. I'd never have let a package of raging sex hormones into my spare bedroom. No way. Have you met Stephen's secretary – Ms Suzie Ayres?'

'At the office.'

'I chose her. She's just so perfect. In love with Stephen but without a ghost of a chance of ever attracting him. She keeps all the other hot little bitches well away.' She took a large gulp of wine, sending nearly half the contents of the glass down in one smooth movement. 'I don't blame the girls ... I wouldn't want to be married to a man who was totally unfanciable. But that doesn't mean I'd let him go ... ever.'

'Fine. Is he working in the study today? Only I noticed the car as I came in and I wouldn't want to disturb him ...'

'He's not here. He's taken Patrick up to see some dinosaur exhibition in London. They went on the train. It's a big treat for Patrick; trains, I mean. We never use them normally, they just seem full of the strangest people.' Draining her glass, she toasted me with the empty tumbler. 'Cheers.'

I sent down another few inches of my own drink. Once this posh plonk got past the taste buds, it wasn't too bad at all. I was beginning to experience a not unpleasant sensation that the top of my head was floating a few centimetres above the rest of my brain.

'They're staying with Patrick's godparents for a couple of days. So I'm afraid the skirt was a waste of time, sweetie.'

'Skirt?' I looked down at the grey material and back at Amelia, surprising a slight smirk beneath the half-closed lids. Then the delayed message negotiated the alcohol-bathed nerve paths to my brain. She thought I'd come up here to flash my thighs at her hubby.

'Listen, Mrs Bridgeman ... I'm not after your husband, honest ... I've got enough problems with ...' With someone else's husband, if I was being strictly accurate here. 'With my own love life,' I finished lamely.

'Oh, it's OK. I realise you two may have had a quick tumble, but I'm just letting you know it's hands-off time now.'

'A tumble ... Look, I don't know who told you that ...'

'I saw you. On party night. Coming out of the wine cellar.

307

The least you could have done was button up the blouse properly.'

Fragments of memory came back: the damp towels in her bathroom; the tangled sweatsuit I'd had to retrieve from the carpet; the bottle of champagne.

'You came downstairs ...'

'I wondered why Stephen was taking so long with my jewellery. I just slipped down to find out. And there you were, and nicely rumpled after a bunk-up with my husband.'

And, I remembered, I'd told her I was involved with a married man with kids, who was having to play happy families with his wife over the half-term.

Amelia laughed and stretched, arching her back and extending her arms to full length above her head. 'I think he saw he'd got the best deal at home by the time you made your next entrance, don't you?'

Of course he would have ... If there *had* been a contest, Amelia would have won it by a mile ... especially after she'd kept me in that steam-filled bathroom, dropped an oil slick of moisturiser all over me and clamped me firmly to her two-thousand-quid dress and six-thousand-dollar face-lift as she swept out on that terrace. And to think I thought she was being chummy!

'Look, Mrs Bridgeman, Amelia, I wasn't doing anything with your husband except being debriefed ... Oh hell ... I mean ...'

'Oh, it doesn't matter now ... forget it ... I'll go and see how the coffee's doing. Ciao for a sec.'

I wanted to charge after her and put her straight, but it didn't seem worth the effort somehow. Pushing my chair back, I tried to recross my ankles on the balustrade again. This time they wouldn't meet.

'Oh, to hell with it ...' I dragged the invoice I'd intended to give to Stephen from my pocket. Maybe I'd just leave it with Amelia. She'd probably steam it open as soon as I'd gone ... but that wasn't my problem, was it? I was sick of the lot of them. Come to think of it, I couldn't be bothered with anything much at present. Crossing my arms on the table, I pillowed my head on them.

A bird sang noisily in my ear. The twittering trills were

getting on my nerves. Wearily I picked up a tiny pebble from the patio, looked round for the blasted feathered pest and flicked the stone.

It went in completely the wrong direction and pinged against the french windows.

'Darn ...' I flexed my shoulders and shook my head, trying to clear it. The wine had gone straight to my empty stomach, decided it didn't like the view and made for my head instead. I needed something to concentrate on.

Taking the folded list of flight details from my other pocket, I made myself read each word slowly and carefully.

I got to the end of the first line. Part of my mind told me there was something wrong. The other part refused to have anything to do with the idea. It just wanted to go to sleep and it wished its other side would kindly belt up, switch off and give it a break.

'It doesn't work ... isn't that a bummer? I'll have to send it back to LA, I guess ...' Amelia dumped a contraption of chrome and smoked glass on the table with a thump. The reverberations went straight through the metal table and rattled my teeth.

I got a grip on them by clamping my jaw tight. Taking a few deep breaths, I forced my tongue to form the words: 'Amelia ... the night before you flew to California ... the thirtieth ... you stayed over at the Heathrow Sheridan, right?'

'Sure. I always do if I've got an early flight.' She peered at the coffee machine's plug, waggling it in front of her nose.

'But according to this printout, your flight left at 23.04 that day.'

'Oh, that was the second one, sweetie. I had to cancel the first. Would you believe, I got all the way to the airport and discovered I'd forgotten my passport. I told you I was a real bubblehead.'

'What did you do? About the passport?'

'Do? Well, I came home to get it, of course.'

'On the Friday.'

'Well, natch, as Bone would say.'

'Was anyone here?'

'That girl was. The dark-haired one ... I think she used to

309

work at Wexton's. She was in the bath ... *my bath*, I mean. She'd even used my oils and bubbles.'

'What did you do?'

'Do?' She flicked back the frothy curls and widened those big blue eyes in surprise. 'Well, I killed her, of course.'

CHAPTER 38

It was a joke, right? You don't just come straight out and announce you're a murderer. Not unless you're a total psycho. And Amelia might be an airhead but I didn't think she was clinically insane.

Just to check, I asked if she was crazy. At least that was what I meant to say. It came out as: 'Yoooo ... craze ... craz ... mad?'

My jaw seemed to be unaccountably slack. The tongue wouldn't go where I wanted it to; it was flapping around behind my teeth like an unanchored guy-rope. I let it lie down. It seemed like a good idea; so I decided to join it.

Amelia was still chattering. She was more irritating than that damn blackbird.

'It was finding her in our bathroom that was just so unbelievable. I designed those rooms. All the carpets and fittings, everything. It was our private place; mine and Stephen's. How could he do that to me?'

'Ummmm ...' My head felt much better now I was holding on to it.

'Do you know what got me mad? Her feet. Can you believe that? She was slumped right down in the bubbles with a foot up on the edge. Most people have ugly feet, have you noticed? It's one of the first things I look at on the beach.'

'Mmmmmm ...' I decided I'd be much comfier if I just pillowed down on my arms.

Amelia was still rambling. 'You can't fix feet. You can have most bits tucked or smoothed or nipped, but you're stuck with feet. Feet get old with you. They get bunions and corns and arthritic knobs. And she was young, with silky flesh, with

310

no lumps or brown spots or skin tags. I just grabbed one of the jars of bath oil and hit her. She didn't see me. She didn't even know I was there. Her eyes were closed and I suppose the headphones stopped her hearing. Then I got hold of her feet and I pulled them. She went right down under the water. She didn't kick or struggle or anything ... just whoooosh ...'

Her hand swooped over the table top like a submarine diving. It passed my nose and rose again out of sight. I tried to turn my head and follow its trajectory but couldn't make it. My eyelids were tired so I closed them again.

'It's much easier to kill someone than I'd imagined. I supposed I'd always thought it would be terrifically physical, you know? I didn't even realise she was dead for well ... ages, it felt like.'

A hangover had never had this effect on me before. With difficulty I made my mouth form the words: 'Dope, what is it?'

'Dope? Oh, you mean those fabulous capsules. I got them in California too. Those American doctors are fantastic. You can get pretty much whatever you want. They had these incredible sleeping tablets, I just had to bring some back. Sleep is so important, you know. Stops black circles under the eyes.'

Sleeping tablets were a relief. I'd been half afraid she'd slipped something more lethal into the wine.

'The bottle said two, but I emptied six into your glass.'

So I'd had a triple dose mixed with alcohol, and all on an empty stomach. A lot of it was probably in my blood stream already, but I forced two fingers down my throat and heaved up a mouthful on the terrace.

I'd hoped the vomiting action might wake me up a fraction, but it didn't seem to have much effect as I levered myself to my feet. I was braced, ready for Amelia's attempt to wrestle me back to my seat. But she didn't even try.

I caught fractional glimpses of her shadow on the lawn as I wove my way down the stone steps and across the grass. I think I had a vague idea it was better to stay in the fresh air rather than go back through the french windows. I intended to go round the side of the house, back down the front drive and out on to the main road where with any luck a passing motorist would pick me up.

Only the house wasn't where I'd left it. If only the damn lawn would keep still it would have helped. But it kept rocking like an unstabilised ship in a force-ten gale. One minute the barn side of the garden was way up above my head and the next it had plunged down and the opposite row of rhododendron bushes was waving around in the sky.

Finally I took the sensible option and lay down again. The grass and damp earth felt deliciously cool against my cheek.

I figured I must have gone to heaven. Which was odd considering my track record. Perhaps they'd lowered the entrance requirements. But how else could I have ended up in a room with wall-to-wall booze?

From my current position – flat on the floor – I let my eyes wander upwards over those ranks of bottle bottoms peeking from the racks. Did I have to pick one or was this my own private little store for eternity?

I sat up. At least I tried to, but there was something wrong with my legs. Levering myself on to my elbows, I discovered the problem. Several yards of heavy, rusting chain had been wrapped round my legs from knee to ankle and secured with a massive padlock at the back of my heels.

I tried twisting and using the hasp of the lock against the links to see if I could lever them apart. It was no use. The rust was only surface deep; underneath, the chain was solid, the metal strong enough to restrain an ox. Maybe that was what it had originally been intended for; I'd seen similar ones in local farm museums.

On bottom and elbows I wriggled the length of the room. She'd dumped me in her husband's wine cellar. From my memory of the house layout, that meant I was under the kitchen.

With a bit of pushing and wriggling up the far wall, I got to the door handle. It was a lever style – recessed into the heavy metal – and it refused to budge despite leaning my entire weight on it.

My best hope seemed to be the small cupboard where Stephen kept his wine buff's paraphernalia.

There were several sets of tools in the cupboard; stored in leather boxes lined with green or red velvet, each implement sitting in a hole tailored to fit its unique shape. Some of the cases even had Stephen's initials embossed in gold leaf. It looked like this was the present for the man who had everything. Including – unfortunately – a homicidal wife.

I considered the factor of inherited genetic tendencies as I negotiated my way around that lock. The female line in this family seemed to have the possessive instincts of pit bulls. Once they got a hold on their men, they never let go. I considered the evidence for this phenomenon: there was Bone with her emphatic '*I want*' when it came to Tom Skerries; California Charlotte who'd seen off the mother of those lardish lumps to grab her man; Joan Reiss who'd marched another girl's fiancé down the aisle; and finally Amelia, who'd gone through four pregnancies to produce children she didn't want in order to keep Stephen committed to her. And who was now menopausal and saw any younger woman as a potential threat.

It wasn't a pleasant thought for a female under thirty who was currently trapped in Amelia's basement with a lock she couldn't – *damn* – *well* – *pick*!

Exasperated, I used the floor as a grinding stone to try to file down a foil cutter. The blade was too wide and I couldn't get a turn on it once I'd inserted it into the keyhole.

My head was throbbing and my mouth was so dry the tongue was sticking to the roof. I desperately needed a drink but I couldn't risk the wine; it would just dehydrate me further. My fingers were cramping with the effort of pressing and holding those tiny instruments. As a break, I bumped and dragged along the narrow space between the racks just to check whether there was any non-alcoholic drink stored down here.

There wasn't. I began to know how Midas must have felt when everything he tried to swallow turned to gold.

Occasionally the metal probe skidded and jabbed a finger. I discovered that sucking the wound helped to get the saliva flowing. Maybe Amelia had left my hands free in the hope I'd get totally pie-eyed and she could pass my death off as alcoholic poisoning.

My watch said it was nearly six. I'd arrived about midday, so I guessed I'd been unconscious for approximately five and a half hours. My bladder was bursting. I desperately needed a pee.

The crack of the opening door lock caught me by surprise. I didn't have time to thrust my assorted lock-picks back into the cupboard.

'Oh, you've ruined Stephen's tools. He'll be so upset, he's just the most perfectionist pest when it comes to this cellar.'

The jeans and slip top had gone; replaced by a knee-length T-shirt with a picture of Snoopy on the front. She had a tousled, fresh-woken look about her which was further enforced by a large yawn and arm stretch which allowed me to observe she wasn't a natural blonde. 'Morning.'

'Morning?' I readjusted my internal clock. It wasn't Friday evening; it was nearly six on Saturday. I'd been out for almost eighteen hours. No wonder my bladder was in trouble.

'Look,' I said firmly, 'if I don't get to a loo in the next couple of seconds then Stephen's going to have a lot of clearing-up to do in here. I presume he's equally fussy about piddle all over his precious cellar?'

'Oh no, don't. It will smell. Wait ... hang on just a moment ...'

I'd been hoping she'd unchain me. I'd been wriggling my feet as I worked to keep the circulation going and I figured my best shot would be to use one of the bottles as a cosh as soon as she'd unlocked the padlock, and then try to get to the door. If I could get it slammed and shut her in, I'd be able to make the cellar steps, even if it meant crawling up them.

Instead she darted out and came back a moment later with a bucket.

'You've got to be kidding. How am I supposed to sit on that?'

'I don't know. You'll have to manage. I'll wait outside.'

I was strongly tempted to leak all over the floor just to ruin her day. But pride made me wedge the pail in between one of the racks and the cupboard and then do the same to my bottom.

When Amelia returned, she was carrying a hockey stick. 'If you get right back against the wall, I'll empty it.' She raised the stick over one shoulder and advanced cautiously as I squirmed away. My home-made lock-picks were removed along with the bucket.

The chain weighed a ton. It was like doing a work-out with weights – and I hadn't done too many of those recently. The strain was already making me pant. Coupled with the after-effects of the alcohol and drugs, I started to have difficulty breathing.

I spat with what little spittle I had left, ignoring Amelia's pained moue. 'I need something to drink. And eat.'

'Oh, sure. Silly me, I wasn't thinking. Hang on there.'

I had a choice?

She was gone fifteen minutes or so this time. Returning with the emptied bucket – which now exuded a smell of disinfectant – and a carrier bag.

I'd slipped a wine bottle out of the racks and put it down by the cupboard, where it was in easy reach, whilst she was gone. If persuasion failed, I was aiming to sling it at her head and hope I scored a knock-out.

The reappearance of that bucket didn't fill me with hope. She was plainly planning to keep me here for … how long?

'I don't know,' Amelia admitted when I put the question. 'I just don't *know*. I can't think. It all just went round and round my head last night and I didn't get a wink of sleep.'

'You should have taken a sleeping tablet.'

She missed the sarcasm and agreed it might have been best. 'But I didn't think to save any. I slipped them all in your drink. Maybe Charlotte can send some over from the States. Do you think that would be allowed? Or would Customs get really dreary about that sort of thing?'

I didn't know and frankly I didn't care. 'Look, I'm gagging here. Did you bring anything to drink?'

'Oh, sure. Silly me, I'm just chattering on here and you've not had your breakfast. Here.'

She flipped the carrier by its handles along the floor. There were a couple of small bottles of mineral water inside, plus some cereal bars and an apple.

Amelia stayed at the entrance with the door partially open behind her whilst I gulped down a whole bottle of liquid.

'Thanks.' Wiping off my mouth with the back of my hand, I leant back, tried to look relaxed and asked her what now.

'I told you ... I don't know. I didn't have time to plan what to do with you. I mean, I knew I had to do *something* when I saw you looking at the car. There weren't any marks or blood on it. I remembered to check for those. But you found something didn't you? I saw you.'

'It was you, not Stephen, who hit Figgy?'

If she was still on the cellar steps when the two of us emerged looking like we'd had a quick tumble in the wine store, it stood to reason she must have overheard me telling Stephen about Figgy's supposed knowledge of Kristen's disappearance.

'Why should Stephen want to run that boy over?' Amelia thrust her hair off her face and gave a cute frown.

'No reason at all now. I'd just assumed ... it was his car. And I saw him leave the party early. When you were having a sulk in your bedroom.'

'Oh, that. Well, I had to find a reason to get out of that wretched party after what I heard you say to Stephen about the skater. I just climbed out of the bedroom window and down the creeper while Marina was being beastly to me through the door. Stephen went for a walk. He usually does when he's really wound up.'

I'd been unwrapping one of the bars. Now I looked up sharply. 'You engineered that row with Patrick to get away.' The image of the poor kid's devastated face re-formed in my memory.

'No I didn't. I was going to pretend to have a migraine until I saw that terrible picture. It was a really bitchy thing to do, making it look like I was old enough to be a grandmother to those gross children. Bone can be the limit at times. It's because her father spoils her. Well, he spoils all of them. I knew, the first time I saw him take Charlotte in his arms, that I'd found a way to keep him. That's why I can't go to prison. Do you see? He'd be here, with the children, and before you know it some other hot little bitch would have moved in.'

'Mrs Bridgeman, Amelia, your husband isn't having an affair with me ... and he wasn't having one with Kristen, whose real name; incidentally, was Julie-Frances.'

'He was going away with her. There were two air tickets in her bag.'

'It was a business trip. And he'd already decided not to go. He was ripping off some designs Wexton's had done for a customer. They were selling them abroad. She blackmailed him into taking her on as a partner.'

'Honestly? Blackmailed?' Amelia's face lit up. 'Well, that's just wonderful news. I knew she wasn't his type really.'

'And neither am I. So how about untying me?'

'You know I can't do that.'

'What are you going to do with me?' I wasn't sure I wanted to hear the answer.

'I don't know … I wish you'd stop going on at me about that. You're giving me the most dreadful headache.'

Tough. I suggested again she might like to let me go. 'Figgy's on the mend and it doesn't sound to me like you meant to kill Kristen, or rather Julie-Frances.'

'Oh, I didn't. At least I don't think I did.' She wrinkled her forehead and put her forefinger to her mouth. 'It's hard to remember exactly how you were feeling about something after the moment's gone, isn't it? I just know I was full of this explosive rage … and I wanted to hit her, and smash her face in … and push her under that water and …' The frosted talons opened and closed, squeezing thin air.

'I get the picture. But you didn't intend her to die?'

'Didn't I?' She relaxed again. 'No. I suppose not. I told you … it was such a shock when I found out how *easily* people die. I pulled her head up out of the water by the hair. I hate the feel of wet hair … it's so slimy.'

I eased my fingers towards the wine bottle.

'I did think about giving her mouth-to-mouth resuscitation … See,' she widened her eyes pleadingly, 'I'm not completely heartless. I was going to try and help her. But I couldn't. She was all wet and slippery and I couldn't get her out of the bath. She kept sliding back. In the end I let the bathwater out and then I could see her all over … it wasn't just her feet that were beautiful … and I thought about Stephen … and what he'd been doing to that body and …'

'… and you thought *sod it, let her stay dead.*'

'Yes. I did.' Her mouth hardened. 'I wrapped some towels

317

round her in the end and pulled her out. And then I couldn't think what to do with her. It's not like all those ridiculous films and television programmes. You can't bury a body under the patio, can you? I mean, all that levering stones up and cementing them down. It would take forever.'

'Course it would.' I laughed weakly. Under the patio. Stupid idea. What idiot would come up with that one?

'There just isn't *anywhere* around here to hide a body, you know.'

It wasn't something I'd ever considered before, but I guess she was right. We had no moorland or wide-open grasslands. It was all farmers' fields within sight of roads. Even the accessible coastland was built up with bungalows, beach promenades and shallow tidal flats that would sweep any embarrassing cadavers straight up amongst the pedalos at the first incoming tide. North Bay had a few cliffs and rocky drops, but they were overlooked by small parking bays at what the council fondly imagined were photographic viewpoints. It might have been feasible in the dark with a high tide running, but in broad daylight getting rid of your inconvenient corpse could rapidly turn into a spectator sport.

'I did think about the garden, perhaps. But he said it would be a really cretinous thing to do,' Amelia said.

'Who did?'

Amelia gave me that stupid-little-me look again. 'Oh, sorry, didn't I say? The man turned up to mend the patio. On that morning of all things. I honestly don't know which of us was more amazed. There I am, dragging this *stark*-naked body over the dining-room floor, and I turn round and there he is. Standing on the patio watching me through the french windows.' She gave another one of those girlish giggles. 'I'll never forget his face.'

'I thought Larry Payne fixed the patio the following week.'

'Oh, I expect he did. It was in a dreadful state. All wonky and water pooling everywhere. Stephen was really cross with me for using a cowboy. But he was very hunky ... and funny. He really thought he was God's gift ... he even tried it on with me.'

The light broke in a ten-thousand-watt burst of illumination. 'Tom Skerries. You hired Bone's boyfriend.'

'Bone's ... Heavens, don't tell me she's reached the bit-of-rough stage already. She said he'd done some work up at the school. She had one of his leaflets, so I gave him a ring. It looked all right at first ... the patio, I mean ... then it started sinking after the first deluge and Stephen stopped our cheque. He made me phone and tell Tom to come back and make good.'

'And he went and turned up right in the middle of your mur ... accidental killing. You can't get the help these days, can you?'

'Actually ... he was very helpful. I don't know what I'd have done without him. It was him that stopped me leaving her here. Otherwise I'd probably have done something really stupid like digging a hole amongst the bushes. As if the gardener wouldn't have noticed a six-foot trench.'

'You discussed that, did you?'

'Of course. Over coffee.'

'Coffee?'

'Well, OK, so we both had a little brandy in it as well. But don't give me a bad time about drinking and driving, OK? We'd both had a shock, we needed something.'

I was having trouble getting my head round this scenario. What had they done with the body during this drinks party?

'I left her behind the sofa. In case anyone else wandered round the back and looked in, you know?'

'And this didn't bother Tom at all?'

'Oh no. We sat in the kitchen.'

'Of course you did. Stupid of me.'

This was beginning to sound surreal. Perhaps I hadn't come round from the effects of the drugs yet?

'I explained about her and Stephen, and Tom was incredibly sweet ... he said he quite understood and he'd give me a hand to clear up the mess if I liked. Well, that's when we discussed where to put the body. Tom said it would be best to take her a long way away from Seatoun. He said that would confuse the police if she was found. And of course I said I couldn't because I had to catch a flight to LA today. I had an appointment ...'

'Your face-lift?'

'Cosmetic restructuring.'

'Whatever. I take it Tom offered to do the corpse run?'

'Yes. He was such a sweetie. We put her in the back of his van with all her luggage and clothes.'

'Was there a CD disc amongst them, by any chance?'

'Several. She had one of those personal CD players on in the bath. Didn't I tell you that? I just bundled up everything I didn't recognise in the bedroom and bathroom. I mean, I was in an incredible rush, wasn't I? I *had* to catch that flight because the surgeon I'd booked with ... well, he's just the best ever according to Charlotte ... he's done all the film stars ... and if you miss your slot ...'

'Yeah, OK. I get the picture. You couldn't have a little thing like a dead body come between you and a stretch-and-stitch job.'

'There's no need to sneer. You'll get old one day.'

Was that a promise? I could only hope so. I asked her what happened after she and Tom had loaded up his van.

'We went to the post office.'

'You mailed her somewhere?'

'Of course not. As if we'd be that stupid. Tom's tax disc had run out and I thought it would be just the most incredible bad luck if he got pulled over and the police looked in the back. So I insisted he went and bought a new one before we left. And of course he didn't want to leave the van parked with a body in the back; he said it would be an effing rotten break if somebody stole it. And I wasn't going to leave her here in case Stephen came back. I certainly didn't want her messing up *my* car. In the end, I left my car outside the supermarket car-park and sat in the van while he went into the post office. That's where the skater was performing in the square ...'

'Did you think he'd recognised you?'

'No. Why should he? I didn't know him.'

'Fergal Payne. Marina's son?'

'Fergal!' The wide-eyed frightened-fawn look returned. 'It can't be. He had dark glasses and long hair and ... oh heavens, she'll be so *mad* with me if she finds out. But I *had* to ... don't you see ... he was jumping near the back windows of the van, and I know we'd covered the body, but I thought ...'

'He never saw a thing. What Figgy knew was unconnected to anyone in this house.'

'Oh dear. What a mess. Are you sure he's going to be all right?'

'Fine. Reconciled with parents. Engaged to lovely girl. Daddyhood on the horizon. Don't worry about him. I doubt they'll even press charges. So how about letting me out of here and we'll think of some way to fix the other mess.'

Amelia shook her head, flicking the blonde tumble over her face. She licked her lips, picking away strands of hair that had stuck to her mouth. 'You know I can't. I've told you about the killing. And hiding the body.'

'But I can't prove anything, can I?'

'Can't you?' She thrust the mane off her face; hope sparkled in her eyes.

I pressed home the idea. 'Think about it. No body. No evidence of a crime. Even Tom Skerries seems to have evaporated into thin air.'

'He's gone abroad. At least that's what he said he wanted the money for. To put into a bar his friend had started somewhere.'

Well, that explained Skerries' motivation. And there's me thinking he was just an old-fashioned knight in shining armour riding to the rescue in a transit van.

'How much did you give him?'

'He asked for ten thousand pounds. Well, of course that was just ridiculous. I don't have that sort of money.'

'You could have fooled me.'

'It's *true*. I have assets, of course. Unit trusts, PEPs, investment funds, that sort of thing. But who keeps that sort of money in a current account?'

'So what did you do?'

'I just racked my brains. I mean, I couldn't even offer him some of my jewellery because Stephen had gone and changed the safe combination again. He's always doing that and I really wish he *wouldn't*. All I had on me was a thousand pounds and maybe another two thousand I could get out on my cash cards. In the end I had this wonderful brainwave. I sold my car.'

'Just like that?'

'No! It was incredibly difficult. Even though I had all the papers, they wouldn't give me cash. They kept offering crossed bank cheques and Tom said that was no good, he didn't have an account. In the end we found this really obnoxious little man in a junk yard in London who offered me eight thousand. Which was just outrageous because it was worth at least three times that.'

'He probably thought it was nicked.'

'Really?' She gave a gurgle of pleasure. 'How fantastic.'

'Where was Tom during this tour of used-car dealers?'

'Well, following me in the van, of course.'

'With the body in the back?'

'Yes.'

How come fictional murders aren't like this, I wondered? Where are all those meticulously planned, cleverly plotted deaths like in Agatha Christie and P.D. James novels? These two would have been more at home in a Quentin Tarantino movie. Talk about disorganised.

'Well, I was getting quite frantic by then. In the end Tom said, all right, he'd take eight, plus some money that girl had in her bag. So we settled up and I got a taxi to Heathrow. He did offer to drive me, but it seemed best that he got started on getting rid of the you-know-what. He was going to take it somewhere up north and drop the luggage and bits of pieces off on the way. Then he was going to go over to the continent to … what was it he called it … suss out his friend's bar.'

'Didn't it occur to you that you were taking a big risk? He could have turned up on the doorstep any time and asked for a top-up on the eight grand to keep his mouth shut?'

'I thought of that!' She came a few steps further into the room. I shifted my grip on the wine. 'I'd got him to pick up the bath-oil bottle … the one I'd hit her with … to get finger prints, and then, when he was in the post office, I'd put it in my shoulder bag. I showed him it just as I was getting the taxi. And I said if he ever told, I'd say I'd come home and found *him* with the body and he'd just terrorised me into helping him.'

'And you've still got that bottle, have you?'

'Oh no. I put it in a rubbish bin at the airport. Well, it would just have been a nuisance on the flight. And providing he thinks I have it, it doesn't matter, does it? Do you know, he was quite hurt that I didn't trust him. It was really rather sweet.'

There wasn't much else to say. I slung the wine bottle. The base clipped the rack as it left my hand and deflected to the right slightly. It sailed past her head and smashed against the door, spraying damson-coloured splodges over her nightshirt, in her hair and down her legs.

'Oh God ... oh hell ... you *bitch*!' Stepping back incautiously, she landed on a sliver of broken glass. It didn't improve her temper. 'You ungrateful *cow*!'

'Ungrateful! What have I got to be grateful about?'

'I left the light on for you, didn't I? So you wouldn't wake up and find it all creepy and dark. And I didn't tie your hands or gag you or anything.'

'You have, however, trussed me up and bolted me in the cellar.'

'Yes ... well ... I *had* to do that. I have to *think*. And you can damn well stay shut up in here whilst I do it!'

She banged the door shut and turned the locks.

There wasn't much doubt in my mind as to what she'd eventually decide. It wasn't going to be as easy as an impersonal hit-and-run cocooned in a metal cage travelling at sixty miles an hour. Nor was she going to be able to hide behind a burst of incandescent rage that would conveniently dull the guilt receptors until it was all over. This time, when she killed, she was going to have to do it in cold blood.

Mine.

CHAPTER 39

I rationed the remaining bottle of water. If Amelia stayed mad about my abortive escape attempt and didn't bring down any more supplies, it might have to last me until Sunday night.

By then she was going to have to make up her mind – one way or the other. School started again Monday, which meant

Patrick and his dad would be returning home and I'd have to be gone.

Since she hadn't mentioned Bone at all, I assumed she wasn't around. Perhaps she'd already gone back to St Aggie's after the half-term.

Movement was tricky. It meant leaning weight on the links, and the pressure was causing bruising and scraped skin all over my legs. I kept going anyway, in order to stop the muscles and circulation seizing up on me. I wished now I'd put the suit trousers on; at least they'd have provided some padding.

Amelia had overlooked one of the wine tools. It had tumbled under the racks; I bent and straightened it as best I could and continued to jiggle at that blessed lock. Because the amount of bend in my legs was restricted and the padlock was fastened behind the ankles, it meant hitching over from the waist and working with my arms at full stretch.

Before long every muscle in my back, shoulders and fingers was aching and screaming out to be left in peace. Unfortunately, if I didn't get the damn lock open, they were going to get their wish. In my heart, I knew it was hopeless anyway. There was no way I could pick a lock with a twisted scrap of metal unless the lock happened to be defective.

I was frightened, because the more I thought about it, the more I realised how isolated my life was. Who was going to notice I was missing? I didn't live with anyone; I was nobody's 'significant other'; I never phoned home; I had no landlord to worry about unpaid rent.

My work routine could best be described as fluid; I came and went as I pleased. How long would it take before it occurred to Vetch or Janice that they hadn't seen me recently?

And if it did, would they bother to do anything about it? I'd told Jan I was hitting the party scene this weekend. In fact I'd implied I could be waking up in China with a stonking great hangover come Monday. It wasn't the sort of thing a normal person would take seriously; but with Jan – who knows?

The person most likely to miss me was Annie – who was away in the West Country and not due back until the middle of next week.

I had visions of ending up like one of those cases in the papers: pensioners boarded up in empty flats for years; dusty bags of bone and rotting clothes that fell apart when someone finally broke in to disconnect the gas supply.

Only in my case, I'd be disintegrating in some landfill site or reservoir, I reckoned.

And in a few months' time someone – Shane, perhaps – would remark: 'Anyone seen Smithie recently? Must be ... what ... ten, twelve weeks since she scrounged a fry-up off me.'

I tried to be positive. I'd left the Kristen Keats file on the table in my flat. When someone eventually got around to breaking in to find me, that would surely point them in the right direction. At least my murderess wouldn't go undetected.

My psyche pointed out that if this was my idea of positive, it would hate to run into my negative viewpoint in a dark alley.

I tried another track. Amelia had left the light on despite my assault; which showed she wasn't all bad. And perhaps when she sat down upstairs and thought about killing someone ... *really* thought about it ... she'd decide it just wasn't on this time.

There were other options. She could make a run for it. Close off those unit trusts and whatever and move abroad. Change her name. Get a new life.

No, I didn't buy it either. Why bother? Getting rid of me was the easiest option.

How would she do it? A gun would be fastest and safest for her; but I hadn't seen a gun cupboard anywhere in this house. The proverbial blunt instrument or sharp knife seemed likeliest.

'Course, she'd need time to get things tidied up,' I informed that stubborn padlock through gritted teeth. 'So she couldn't wait until the last minute.'

I wished I'd asked her to be a bit more specific about Stephen and Patrick's return time. Were they coming back early or late Sunday?

My fingers were too numb to hold the probe again. I nibbled on one of the cereal bars and gave myself a quick talking-to. There was no way some blonde middle-aged bimbette was finishing me off. When she came back, I'd smash the hell out of her and escape. It was simple.

Lying flat on my back, I practised raising my legs and thumping them out more or less where I judged Amelia's stomach would be. After a couple of tries I was exhausted. The sheer weight of the chain made it a virtual non-starter.

Breathing deeply, I waited for my thundering heart to return to normal rhythm. I was listening to the blood rushing through my ears, and the sounds of activity outside took a while to filter in.

I listened. There it was again. Something falling. And then something else. Different weights and different heights. I had to guess someone was searching amongst the cellar junk. It could have been Amelia, of course. Maybe she was trying to remember where she'd last seen the axe.

There was only one way to find out. Taking a deep breath, I yelled for help.

The door opened a few seconds later. Struggling into a sitting position, I found myself facing Bone.

'What are *you* doing here?'

'An aerobic workout. Get me undone here, eh? Then we'll talk.'

'How?' She stepped delicately over the wet floor and peered at the chains. 'Where's the key?'

'You tell me. Your mother's probably got it.'

'Mummy? What's she got to do with it?'

'Well, what do you think I'm doing down here? Some kind of weird bondage ritual with the cellar rats? Look, just find the key, will you. Is your mother upstairs?'

Bone shrugged. She was back in the micro Lycra skirt and top today, with over-the-knee leather boots. 'No one's around. I let myself in.'

She twisted the padlock and tried to disengage the bar – I gave an involuntary kick as the pain from my chafed and blistered skin shot up my leg.

'Sorry.' Bone sat back on the heels of her boots. 'But I don't understand. I mean … why?'

'Find the key first. Or something to file through these links if you can't. Has your dad got a toolbox?'

'That's a pretty sexist remark, isn't it? Why shouldn't I have a toolbox? Or Gran.'

'Fine … whoever's toolbox … I'm not proud. Just get me something to cut with, OK?'

'Yes, all right. Hang on.'

She left the door open. I lay back savouring the moment. A view of the cellar; a nibble of my breakfast apple; imminent freedom. Paradise.

I selected a couple of bottles that looked as if they'd be seriously expensive and put them carefully to one side. Stephen owed me a bonus after last night.

'Here. Will this do?'

It was a rasp, not much bigger than a nail file, but I wasn't in a position to be fussy. I started on a reachable link. They were thinner than the padlock and I figured it would take me less time to saw through one.

'Listen, while I'm doing this, can you call the police?'

'What for?'

'For! Bloody hell, Bone, your crackpot mother has just drugged me and locked me in the cellar all night. Isn't that enough?'

'Yes, but … *why?*'

It seemed kinder not to tell her the whole story, so I temporised with: 'She thought your dad and I were an item. But we're not – honest. Now go make that call … please.'

'Mummy really did this? Because she thought you and Dad had had it off? Wow!' She sat cross-legged beside me. 'Do you think they'll send her to prison?'

'I don't know. Maybe.'

I saw the flicker of doubt pass over Bone's face and recalled something her gran had said about the girl playing up because she loved her mother. I'd taken that as fond-granny-speak at the time. I should have realised Joan knew her granddaughter better than I did.

'Probably not,' I said quickly. 'Especially if I keep my mouth shut.'

'Would you?'

'I'm easily bribeable,' I said truthfully. And if the situation really had been a simple case of misplaced jealousy, I might have let them buy me off. But there was no way I was keeping quiet about Julie-Frances' murder. Or Figgy's hit-and-run, if it came to that. So the best plan was to get out of here before Amelia reappeared.

We heard the footsteps above at the same time. Instinctively we'd both glanced at the wine-store ceiling, as if we could see right through it. I was still craning upwards when Bone snatched the rasp from me.

'What the ...' I lunged and grabbed her wrist.

She was half standing. Grabbing the wine rack for support, she brought her left boot down on my arm, broke free and backed out of my reach.

'I'm sorry, but I have to talk to Mummy first.' Her chest rose and fell under the Lycra. Shallow, frightened breaths. The streetwise chick was dissolving before my eyes into the not-yet-adult girl who still needed her mum.

'Bone? I thought you were staying with your grandmother.'

Amelia had come down the cellar steps during our fight and was now standing in the doorway, dangling a set of car keys.

I'd forgotten about the motor. It must have been sitting outside on the verge where I'd left it all night. 'Those are mine.'

'What? Oh yes, I found your car. I've parked it around the back. Isn't it a perfect *heap*? Why don't you get it fixed?'

'I just did.'

'Really? Goodness.'

'Mummy, did you really beat her up because she and Daddy were at it?'

'I explained to Bone that this was all a misunderstanding,' I said warningly. 'About you thinking I was having an affair with your husband.'

It gave her a chance to go along with the story and pull back from the next step. After all, there was a witness now. Surely she had to back off.

Amelia reached over and adjusted one of Bone's shoulder straps that had slipped sideways. It was the first intimate gesture I'd ever seen her make to either of her children. 'I'm in the most awful mess, darling. I really don't know what to do next.'

'What kind of mess?'

'Come upstairs. I'll tell you.'

'Hang on. What about me?'

'You'll just have to stay here. I'm sorry, but you do see I can't let you go, don't you?'

'No, I bloody well ...' I choked back the rest of the angry shout as Amelia started to pull Bone out of the cellar and close the door. Desperately I yelled at the narrowing gap: 'At least ring your grandmother. Tell her what's happening here, Bone.'

I'll admit I cried a bit. I was bruised, exhausted and scared. And after the brief rush of adrenaline generated by the hope of escape, I hit reality with an even harder thump this time round.

It didn't seem possible that I could die like this. I started to make all sorts of bargains with God. If he let me out I'd remember to send cards for Mother's Day in future. I'd stop being mad at my dad for believing those lies about me taking bribes when I was in the force. I'd put an effort into making friends and finding unmarried lovers. I'd place myself in the centre of a warm, loving circle who'd panic if I was twenty minutes late back from the supermarket.

I sipped the water and took small portions of the cereal bar every half an hour. By mid-afternoon they were both exhausted. I had to use the bucket again. The disinfectant couldn't quite mask the scent of urine.

Moving my legs became harder and harder, and it was tempting to just lie down and forget it. Give up and go with the inevitable. I let my eyes close.

I woke up half propped against the cupboard; the metal cooling my cheek and the angle giving me a crook in my neck. Dry-mouthed again, I checked my little kingdom to see if anything had happened whilst I'd been out of it.

It hadn't, of course. My prison was unchanged. I needed something to do to keep myself awake.

Amelia must have taken my bag, but I still had the invoice and Tally's airline printout. I could tear them up and leave messages hidden amongst the bottles. Stephen would find them eventually. Perhaps Joan used the place as well. I had no pen, but I could prick my fingers ... they'd even be able to do a DNA match on the blood later to prove I'd written them.

Eagerly I thrust my hand into my jacket pocket. It was empty. They were all empty. Amelia had taken the papers whilst I was out cold.

I ran though every swear word I knew at the top of my voice, then took up the improvised lock-pick and scratched at the inside of the cupboard door. In wavy letters I put my name, the current date and added: '*Amelia B. killed me*'.

This wasn't such a great plan either, I decided. It sounded like I was accepting the inevitable. Bending full stretch again and ignoring the protesting agony of straining back muscles, I jammed the lock-pick in the padlock and turned.

The locking bar clicked open.

I couldn't believe it. I froze for a moment, leaning back against the cupboard and staring at that gap. All I needed to do was push a link off and I was free.

The padlock came away easily but I made the mistake of trying to brace my legs against the chain and release it that way. It parted a few millimetres. Just enough to let me know how numb and cramped my limbs had become.

The door handle clicked, sending me diving forward in a frantic effort to untwist the links.

I was slow, my fingers dropping the heavy chain.

I'd expected Amelia. But it was Bone who burst through and dived on me, using her arms to pinion my legs down again.

'Mummy! Hurry.'

I grabbed her hair and yanked her head back, chopping up under her nose with my other hand. She bit me – hard.

Amelia had flung herself down on the floor and was struggling to get the padlock back in place. It clicked closed a darn sight easier than it had opened.

With a final frustrated kick, which failed to land, I gave up and squirmed up into a sitting position again.

'So what now?' I panted.

I'd asked Amelia, but it was Bone who answered. 'We've a plan.'

'Bully for you. If it doesn't involve getting these chains off and showing me the front door, I don't want to hear about it.'

I looked her over. The Lycra outfit had been replaced by

the jeans and checked shirt I'd seen before. The make-up-less face looked young – and determined.

'You have to hear about it. See, we've decided it has to be a car crash. You'll have an accident when you're drunk. You drink a lot anyway, so no one will think it's off the wall or anything.'

I had a horrid feeling she could be right about that, but I pointed out that forensic science had got pretty sophisticated. 'The police can spot a phoney crash these days. Soon as they see these chain-shaped bruises they're going to smell a whole colony of rats.'

'I've thought of that. The car will catch fire. There's a petrol can in your boot that's already rotten. We've made it a bit worse ... so the fuel dribbles all over the boot. We thought if you went over the cliffs at North Bay, where the road's really winding, it would look best. Someone hits the crash barriers on that stretch at least once a week. If we loosen one a bit and you go right through you'll roll the last bit to the edge.'

Her voice was calm, as if she was discussing the arrangements for my first bungee jump. This was her big chance. Her mother needed her. And if she could pull this off, Amelia would be forever in her debt. The way she saw it, all the love and approval she craved from her mother would be there for the asking from now on. Had I really expected anything else? She was fourteen and selfish as hell.

'I scored these down the arcade.' Bone unscrewed a twist of paper. Two pale-green tablets lay in the creases. 'It's E.'

'Well, that's really thoughtful of you, Bone. The idea is that I still get murdered, but I get to feel good about it, is that it?'

'Sort of. I thought ... it might make it a bit easier on you.'

'No. You thought it might make it a bit easier on *you*, kid. Well, I've bad news. I'm allergic to the stuff. Took it once; ended up in intensive care. It's on my medical records. There's no way I'd be daft enough to pop Ecstasy. You might as well write "fix" all over my forehead.'

It was a lie, but I was gambling on her swallowing it. I needed to stay as much in control as possible.

Bone retwisted the paper and returned it to her pocket. 'I

suppose we'll have to just do it then. It's dark enough now. Go get the things, Mummy.'

Amelia trotted out obediently. As Bone had bloomed, she'd diminished. For the first time she looked her age.

I had one last try with Bone. Did she realise, I asked, that she was about to commit cold-blooded murder?

'Natch. I'm not a total thicko. But ... see ... she's my mother.' Her round face with its slight dusting of summer freckles just beginning to show pleaded for my understanding. 'You'd do it for your mum, I'll bet.'

Would I? I don't know. Perhaps she was right. Different moralities suddenly apply when it's someone of your own, don't they? I assumed Amelia must have confessed to killing Julie-Frances and told Bone she'd be jailed for life if they didn't shut me up for good. It was no different, I guess, than a mother protecting a son she knows in her heart of hearts is a serial rapist.

Amelia came back with several large black plastic rubbish sacks, pushed them inside each other and concertinaed them up until she was grasping the wide neck.

I fended her off with both arms.

'If you don't let us,' Bone said, 'I'll knock you out with something really heavy.'

They'd have managed it eventually. It seemed sensible to co-operate. At least that way I stayed conscious and I'd get out of this cellar.

I dropped my arms. They flipped the sacks over my head, pulling them down to hip level. The first breath I took sucked warm plastic into my nose and mouth. I was suffocating. I started to panic. Had that been the idea all along? Perhaps the car-crash scenario had been a ruse to get me to go along with my own asphyxiation.

The tape was lashed round, binding my arms to my sides. I thrashed about, twisting my head from side to side. It made things worse. The moist plastic set like a second skin over my face.

A hand groped over my nose. I bucked, expecting it to push down. Instead it started tearing at the suffocating bandage until my nose and mouth were free.

Relieved, I relaxed. The chains were removed and replaced by another thick band of tape around my ankles.

They'd left the plastic over my eyes, so I had no warning of what was coming next until a finger and thumb pinched my nose closed. Instinctively I opened my mouth. A glass bottle was thrust in and vodka poured down my throat. I choked a lot back but enough went down to explode into a burning ball in my stomach.

I was still coughing and gasping for breath when hands grabbed in my armpits. Another set of arms wrapped around my legs.

'OK? One … two … three … lift.'

I rose a few inches off the floor. Amelia was at my head. She was having difficulty retaining her grip because of the plastic. My bottom kept bouncing and scuffing along the cellar. Each step of the staircase was negotiated in a series of bum-numbing heaves and thumps, with Bone pushing from the feet end.

I guessed that we turned towards the back after that. I knew I was right when we descended the patio steps and I was dumped on the grass, and Bone's voice asked where the keys were.

'I left them in the dash, darling – why?'

'We need them to unlock the boot.'

I sensed them both moving. Their voices came from several yards away. For some reason they seemed to imagine the plastic shroud had cut off my hearing as well as my sight.

'Mummy – it will be OK, won't it? I mean, you're sure you can stop the car in time?'

'Of course I can, darling.' Amelia's tone became softer and gentler. I could almost see her slipping a comforting – and uncharacteristic – arm around Bone's shoulders. 'I've told you, we'll just frighten the hot little bitch and teach her to keep her hands off your father in future. You don't want Daddy to leave us, do you?'

'Well, no … but …'

'Trust me, Bone. We'll set the car rolling towards the edge and I'll drag the handbrake on at the last minute. And if she tries to report us to the police, we'll both swear we were home all night.'

It was a rotten plan. The scrub grass grew lush up there at this time of the year. Once the car started moving the wheels would slide on the slippery surface and applying the hand-brake would just lock them whilst the vehicle's own weight kept it moving until we skidded over the edge. Not that I believed Amelia had any intention of braking before I launched into space. But at least it explained why Bone was going along with my murder. She wasn't trying to protect her mum from the consequences of Julie-Frances' death – she probably didn't even know about it. Instead Amelia had conned her into believing this was all a nasty little charade to stop me luring Daddy – and Daddy's cheque-book – from the family home.

Once I'd gone over that cliff, no doubt Amelia would be tearfully claiming that flaky little her had messed up again and they'd both better keep their mouths shut in case they ended up on a murder charge.

I felt the vibration of returning feet against the cheek that was resting on the grass. 'Bone,' I gabbled, 'she's lying. Your mum killed Kristen Keats and she's going to kill me too. She's not going to put the hand bra …'

Lousy guess. My listener thrust a scrap of material into my mouth. It tasted of Amelia's scent. Bone returned a second later. By the time I'd spat the gag out I was bundled into the boot and the small amount of light that had been filtering in from the nose hole in my plastic shroud was cut off.

The enclosed space already smelt strongly of petrol. I wriggled around, feeling lumps under myself. I kept all sorts of junk in here. But as far as I could tell, none of it had sharp edges. I squirmed in a circle, searching for bent metal along the boot lid. Several times I caught the petrol can. Each collision was marked by a sloshing sound and a stronger aroma of fuel. Eventually I located a fragment of jagged metal jutting from the locking mechanism.

I snagged the plastic and tore more from my face. I couldn't see anything much, but it made me feel better.

With no vision to speak of and most of a bottle of vodka being absorbed into my blood stream, I was swimming in and out of reality. I think I must have passed out briefly, because

334

the roar of the engine vibrating through my body took me by surprise. I jumped, rolled and lost the metal fragment.

I tried to twist back to it. The movement was jolting me up and down; each obstruction in the road sending me slamming up into the boot lid. It felt like we were doing at least seventy along the back road.

Nausea overwhelmed me. Orange and red lights were dancing before my eyes, swirling around like wreaths of smoke. The petrol fumes were choking me and adding to the hallucinatory effects of the alcohol.

I was riding on a cushion of clouds now. The motion continued to throw me against the metal, but somehow it didn't seem important.

My ears were full of wailing, which rose in ever-increasing decibels. It ricocheted inside the warm fuggy prison. I was bouncing a lot more: bounce up; bounce down; bounce up. Someone was giggling about it. I think it was me.

Then suddenly I was flying. Bang! I hit the lid with three times as much force as before. And then everything was still.

Perhaps I'd died already. I hoped not. I didn't want to spend eternity in a petrol-filled boot. If this was hell, it was a real rip-off.

The flood of light and fresh air took me by surprise.

'What the fu ...?'

Fleshy fingers dug into my face and tore the plastic off my head. I peered blearily upwards and smiled.

I knew what had happened. Amelia had been speeding in my car with its distinctive paint job and much-memorised registration number. It was a chance for an arrest that at least one cop wouldn't have passed up for a lottery win.

Levering myself to the edge of the boot, I beamed at the bemused face beneath the copper's hat. 'Hi, Terry!'

With a satisfying whoosh, I threw up all over Rosco's highly polished shoes.

Epilogue

Would you believe they couldn't charge Amelia with murder?

No body; no evidence of a crime; no motive. It was her word against mine that she'd confessed to killing Kristen (a.k.a. Julie-Frances).

They got her for false imprisonment and assault on me, of course. And the hit-and-run on Figgy is under consideration by the Crown Prosecution Service. But since they were first offences she was given bail. (Bone was granted it automatically on account of his age.)

So whilst I was lying in a hospital bed recovering from an overdose of alcohol and assorted serious bruising and pulled muscles, the Bridgeman family were back home enjoying the good life of swimming pool, sauna and sunbeds.

It seems Amelia kept her head when they tried to question her and stuck to her story about flipping when she thought I was having an affair with Stephen. All she'd intended to do was teach me a lesson by scaring me a bit and then dumping me somewhere. And no – of course she hadn't said anything about crashing my car and burning me to death. As for killing this Kristen Keats person – no way! The woman was simply a former employee of Wexton's who'd given in her notice and left the company some weeks ago. She could be anywhere.

She was actually in a flooded quarry in Wales. Her body surfaced about four weeks later, during a routine search for a lost kid who'd wandered away from home. There was no sign of her luggage down there, so presumably Tom Skerries had kept his word and dumped it at various locations along the route.

He finally surfaced too, in a manner of speaking. In Turkey, working in his mate's bar which he'd just bought into as an equal partner. When he was tackled about his sudden influx of ready cash, he denied ever having heard of, let alone met, this Kristen Keats bird.

He admitted that yes, sure, Amelia Bridgeman had given him the money. Sold her motor to raise the readies, in fact. See the thing was, he and her had been having a bit of a ding-dong – well, you know what these bored housewives are like, always throwing themselves at him. And then she'd gone and panicked when she thought her husband might be on to them. Begged him to get lost for a bit, she had. Even given him the money to go see his mate Omar.

He'd driven over far as Germany, hadn't he, until the poxy van packed up on him, then he'd hitched a lift on a truck. Advantages of travelling light, see, just grabbed his stuff and hit the road. He knew he should have let the family know, but he wasn't one for writing. And his Donna had forgiven him. Matter of fact, she and the kids were flying out next week to take a look at their new flat.

She did too. First-class. It was no good my pointing out that Donna Skerries didn't have that sort of money – unless someone had found Skerries before the police and paid out an extra little sweetener to make sure he came up with the above story.

Forensic evidence was a non-starter as well. The German police had scrapped the van Tom had dumped in Munich – any remnants of Kristen/Julie-Frances still adhering to it were now crushed into a metal cube somewhere in a landfill site. And there wasn't one single fingerprint from Julie-Frances in the whole of the Bridgeman house when they dusted it. Plainly the Bridgemans had finally managed to employ a cleaner with more commitment to the job than me.

For a couple of months it looked as if Amelia, with the help of an overpaid barrister, might get away with a suspended sentence and a few hundred hours' community service. And then the Skerries clan returned to the UK to pack up for good.

Zeb's boss – DCI Jackson – got a search warrant, ostensibly to look for the building materials Larry Payne claimed Skerries had been helping himself to. And you'll never believe it – Tom still had a traveller's cheque made out in the name of Kristen Keats in his possession.

That proved a bit tricky to explain, when he'd sworn he'd

never heard of her. In the end he admitted everything. With that corroboration, they searched the Bridgeman house with microscopic thoroughness this time and came up with a minute patch of blood that had seeped between the sunken bath surround and the fitted carpet. It was a DNA match to Julie-Frances.

They charged Amelia with murder but eventually dropped the case against Bone when I insisted on making a statement saying she'd been coerced by her mum into helping with my disposal.

She came to see me at the office; all sulk and attitude. 'We wouldn't really have done it. Aced you, I mean. I told you Mummy was a few tracks short of the full CD when it came to Daddy. You should have kept your paws off.'

'Believe me, Bone, I kept my paws and indeed every other part of my anatomy well away from your dad. But then you know that, don't you? Face facts, kid, your mum is more than a few tracks short. She killed Kristen, remember?'

Bone shrugged, thrust back her chair, crossed her boots on my desk and took out a packet of cigarettes. 'They haven't proved it yet, have they? Got a light?'

'No. How's Patrick?'

'OK. He's going to day school next term. Gran's fixed it.'

'Good.'

'Yeah. It'll stop the pest whining, I guess.'

We stared at each other across the desk. 'So how about you?' I asked. 'You OK?'

'Me? Sure. Why shouldn't I be?' She returned the unsmoked cigarette to her bag and stood up. 'Anyhow, just thought I'd call and say so long.'

'And thanks for getting me off the hook with the police, Grace?'

'No. Why should I? You got to hang on to all my money even though you never found Tom for me, didn't you? I figure that makes us even. So long then.' She sashayed out without a backward glance.

I figured that was that. Going downstairs later, I found out she'd left a plastic carrier with Jan for me. It contained a bottle of her dad's obscenely priced ancient plonk.

But all the above was in the future. Whilst I was lying in my hospital ward, contemplating life, the universe and what to tick on the daily menus, I had a satisfactory flood of visitors.

Zeb headed the deluge. 'I feel really rotten about this,' he announced, fixing those large puppy-dog eyes on me.

'That makes two of us.' I eased myself up on the pillows. 'But don't get bent out of shape about it. I'll live.'

'Yes. I know. I talked to your doc; he says you'll be out in a couple of days. I didn't mean that. The thing is ... I'm off to Derby on a course tomorrow, so I was wondering ... since you're in no state to work ...' He handed me a bundle of notes. 'Could you nip out and buy that frying pan before Annie gets back?'

Marina and Mickey turned up with wedding plans, flowers and a large box of Belgian chocolates. I had to turn down the kind offer to be a bridesmaid.

'Just imagine how I'd look in the wedding pictures, Mickey,' I advised, peeling down the blanket to give her the bruises in fuller technicolour glory.

'Oh, but it's not for weeks yet. And anyway they're my pictures – and you've been dead brilliant about everything. I wouldn't mind what you looked like.'

'Then you're a nicer person than me, Mickey. But I'll still pass, thanks for the offer. How's Figgy?'

'On the mend,' Marina said. 'He and his father are already arguing twenty-five hours a day, so situation nearly normal.'

'Speaking of *nearly* normal ...?'

Marina caught my drift: 'I've seen her. She swears she didn't know it was Fergal.'

'I believe her.'

'So do I, as it happens. But that's not the point. I've told her we're through as friends. Mind you, I've been saying that since we were eleven, so who knows ... Amelia has always had a way of getting what she wants in the end. One way or the other. And what she's always wanted – chiefly – is Stephen Bridgeman. I wonder if he'll stick by her.'

'I think so. I doubt if Stephen's one to let a little thing like murder come between husband and wife.'

I said as much to him when he had the cheek to turn up at the next visiting session.

'I'm flattered you think so highly of my loyalty, Miss Smith.'

'I don't. I have a very low opinion of your morals. And you know what they say – about like attracting like.'

His expression acquired a veneer of frost as he asked what I meant by that.

'Oh, you know all right, Stephen. In your own ways, you and Amelia are as greedy and dishonest as each other. The only consolation is, you won't be getting rich in a hurry. Any news on – what's it called – Sumata? Is the Far East still on board?'

'No.' He stood. 'I believe they've found another designer. In the Philippines. As I told you ... things move rapidly in this business. I'm pleased to see you're not badly hurt. I'll wish you goodbye.'

'So long, Stephen. By the way, don't even think of asking for a refund. I'll be hanging on to the advance.'

Rachel turned up next. I was buried under enough food to keep the entire hospital going if it came under siege any time in the next few weeks.

'Just a few snacks, darlin',' she cried, bobbing over to seize my face, plonk a kiss on each cheek and whack me in the eye with a slipping wig. 'I must go. Ada ... poor soul ... last hours ... I'll bake more soon.'

Henry didn't visit. I managed to get to the phone and bring him up to date on the situation.

'So these designs of Stephen's have gone,' he said shortly.

'Yes.'

'And even if they turn up now, they're virtually worthless, since someone else has got their nose ahead in the race?'

'That's about the size of it, Henry. Oh, and in case you missed my saying it the first time round, your good friend Kristen was murdered.'

'Then you've brought me precisely nothing for my money? Frankly, Grace, I'm very disappointed in you.'

'Frankly, m'dear, I don't give a damn.'

(Several weeks later he actually had the nerve to ask for a refund since I hadn't located Kristen for him. I refused. He threatened me with the press – private investigator rips off blind pensioner sort of thing. I'd have toughed it out but

Vetch the Letch reckoned it would look bad for the company's image and put the screws on, so I ended up having to give Henry back half his cash. The last I heard he was still living in St Johns Road and slandering Wexton's to anyone who was daft enough to listen.)

I'd limped back to my hospital bed to find Terry Rosco stuffing himself with the Belgian chocs whilst his two offspring were opening every tin and box left by Rachel and sampling the contents.

'Nice of you to drop by Ter. And bring the family as well.'

'Been to see their mum up in maternity.' He ruffled another layer of chocolates. 'There's no hard centres in here.'

'Tough! Another Rosco about to be inflicted on the world, is it?'

'Had them.' He smirked and thrust out his chest. 'Twins. Dead spit of me, they reckon.'

'Never mind, Terry. They might grow out of it. Are you leaving soon, I hope?'

'What? Oh yeah. Just popped in to tell you we've got your motor up the station.'

· 'Thanks … it was nice of you to take the trouble.'

For a brief moment I thought I might have been misjudging the self-satisfied creep.

'Yeah … they're thinking of doing you for driving an unroadworthy vehicle. They were wondering where you bought the MOT certificate. See ya.'

He flipped the chocolate box back on the bed. The genetic mutations he claimed as his sons and heirs did the same with Rachel's offerings. They strutted out of the ward like three pit bulls on steroids.

All that aggression had made me weary. After I'd bounced the thick layer of crumbs off my bed, I lay down and closed my eyes. When I opened them again, it was dusk outside and Annie was sitting by the bed.

'Hi, Sherlock,' she murmured. 'How are you feeling?'

'Bloody awful. What are you doing here?'

'Auditioning for a job as neuro-brain surgeon. What do you think I'm doing here?'

'No. I meant what are you doing *here*. Why aren't you in cream tea and pasty land?'

'Finished early. I drove back this afternoon.'

'Who told you I was here? Zeb?'

'Jackson. Zeb's off on a course. I dumped my stuff at the flat and came straight over.'

'I'm flattered.'

'Don't be. I couldn't believe anyone could actually be daft enough to get herself beaten up on two consecutive jobs. What happened this time?'

I brought her up to date whilst she searched amongst Rachel's cakes to find one that didn't have teethmarks from the junior Roscos.

'I'm useless,' I informed her miserably.

'I know,' she said, biting into an apple and cinnamon crunchie.

'I only caught Amelia through a pure fluke.'

'I thought she caught you.'

'Don't split hairs. The point is ... I got it all wrong ... I went up to the house because I thought Stephen had done Kristen in ... and hired me as a particularly clever double bluff.'

'Listen, kid, no one wanting to be particularly clever would hire you.'

'Cheers, Annie.' I flopped back against the pillows and watched her sort out another munchie. 'You're looking fatter.'

'Don't get bitchy just because you screwed up.'

'Change of subject. How much?'

'Eight pounds.' She stretched legs encased in black jeans. 'Four on each thigh.'

In a last fit of loyalty to Zeb, I advised her to stay off the fried food for a while.

'I intend to. I'll have to get back on an exercise programme. Fancy some more early-morning jogging, get you back in shape?'

'No point. I'm giving up the job.'

'Oh yeah?'

I opened one eye. 'Absolutely. I'm useless at it. I didn't get one thing right on this lot. I shall find sensible employment. Shop assistant. Bank clerk. Window-dresser.'

'Don't be ridiculous. Ask yourself a simple question: did you make any money out of this farce?'

'Thanks for the choice of description. But yes, since you ask, I suppose I did OK. There's Henry's money. Plus Stephen's retainer. And Bone's cash too. I was going to refund some of that, but I figure she owes me ... so I guess for a couple of weeks' work ...'

I rallied. Life wasn't just about money, I informed Annie.

'For God's sake, tell the doctors to tone down whatever you're on. It's causing a total personality change. And don't even think about changing your job. It's a stupid idea.'

'You really think so?' I smiled at my absolute best mate.

'Definitely,' my absolute best mate said firmly. 'You'd be crap at anything else. So you may as well stick to being crap at what you know best. By the way, is it still all off with you and Kevin Drysdale?'

'Even more so. He's gone back to his wife.'

'That lot can't be for you then.'

She nodded to the ward door. Kevin was heading in our direction with an armful of blooms swathed in cellophane and pink ribbons.

'Hi, sexy. These are from me ... and Dad.'

'Low trick, Kevin.'

'Sorry?'

'I like your dad. You know I wouldn't chuck his flowers into the sluice.'

'I'll leave you two to it.' Annie helped herself to a fudge brownie and stood up. 'Give me a ring if you need a lift home. Bye, Kevin.'

Kevin hooked the chair closer and sat down near enough to brush his fingers over my forearm. The fine hairs prickled and stood up.

'How are you feeling?'

'How do I look?'

'Bruised. Belligerent. Confused.'

'Yep. That's me all right.'

'Have I done something to offend you, Grace?'

'Apart from lying through your teeth, you mean?'

'When did I do that?'

'You told me you and Minnie had split up by mutual consent.'

'Did I? When?'

That threw me. Now he asked, I couldn't actually recall the exact moment. Had that one just been wishful thinking on my part?

'Listen, Minnie decided she wanted to call time on the marriage. She said she felt we were in a rut, drifting along in a relationship because we were too lazy to do anything about it. She didn't want to wake up in thirty years' time and wonder what might have been.'

'And what did you say?'

'Something flip. Like she'd been reading too many women's magazines or something. But she left anyway. And I was as mad as hell for a few weeks. I mean, nobody likes being dumped, do they? And then I began to get used to being "I" rather than "we"; I started to enjoy myself. Which was ironic really.'

'Because Minnie wasn't?'

'Yes. Life on her own wasn't what she'd expected.'

'So she's back.'

'She's back.'

'And that makes you happy?'

'It makes the boys happy.'

'Don't hide behind your kids, Kevin. That's really naff.'

He smiled and thrust his hand through his hair in a gesture I now recognised was mainly embarrassment. 'Sorry. You're right, of course. I like being a family again. I didn't know how much I'd missed them. But I like you too, Grace ...' He took an envelope from his pocket. It had the logo of a local travel agent on the corner. 'Two tickets to Venice. I bought them the day after our date at the Italian restaurant.'

'Take Minnie.'

'She doesn't like Venice.'

'Take your dad.'

'He wouldn't leave the donkeys.'

'Get a refund.'

We both stared at each other over the extended envelope. It was a free weekend with a bloke to die for. Only a couple of days ago I'd been stuck in that cellar regretting a lost opportunity. And what the hell – Minnie had set him loose.

What right did she have to expect to rein him in when it suited her?

I took the other edge of the envelope. And folded it back into his hand.

'Sorry, Kevin. I just can't see me as the other woman. Give me a bell if you and Minnie ever decide to call it a day for good. And thank your dad for the flowers.'

My last visitor turned up as I was packing to leave. He waved an identity card under my nose. It didn't leave me any the wiser. What on earth did the RSPCA want with me? I didn't even own so much as a goldfish.

The inspector enlightened me. They'd received a complaint which they felt obliged to follow up.

'What complaint?'

He consulted his notebook and gave a small, tight smile. 'It concerns the illegal slaughter of two Vietnamese pot-bellied pigs, Miss Smith.'